Ghost *of the* Southern Cross

BY NELLIE P. STROWBRIDGE

Maiden from the Sea

Catherine Snow

The Newfoundland Tongue

The Gift of Christmas

Far From Home

Ghost of the Southern Cross

inspired by true events

Nellie P. Strowbridge

FLANKER PRESS LIMITED
ST. JOHN'S

Library and Archives Canada Cataloguing in Publication

Strowbridge, Nellie P., 1947-, author
Ghost of the Southern Cross / Nellie P. Strowbridge.

Issued in print and electronic formats.
ISBN 978-1-77117-324-7 (pbk.).--ISBN 978-1-77117-325-4 (epub).--
ISBN 978-1-77117-326-1 (kindle).--ISBN 978-1-77117-327-8 (pdf)

I. Title.

PS8587.T7297G46 2014 C813'.54 C2013-908419-3
C2013-908420-7

PRINTED IN CANADA

MIX
Paper from responsible sources
FSC® C016245

This paper has been certified to meet the environmental and social standards of the Forest Stewardship Council® (FSC®) and comes from responsibly managed forests, and verified recycled sources.

Cover Design by Graham Blair Edited by Paul Butler and Annamarie Beckel

FLANKER PRESS LTD.
PO BOX 2522, STATION C
ST. JOHN'S, NL
CANADA

TELEPHONE: (709) 739-4477 FAX: (709) 739-4420 TOLL-FREE: 1-866-739-4420
WWW.FLANKERPRESS.COM

9 8 7 6 5 4 3 2 1

We acknowledge the financial support of the Government of Canada through the Canada Book Fund (CBF) and the Government of Newfoundland and Labrador, Department of Tourism, Culture and Recreation for our publishing activities. We acknowledge the support of the Canada Council for the Arts, which last year invested $157 million to bring the arts to Canadians throughout the country. *Nous remercions le Conseil des arts du Canada de son soutien. L'an dernier, le Conseil a investi 157 millions de dollars pour mettre de l'art dans la vie des Canadiennes et des Canadiens de tout le pays.*

Dedicated to the memory of Great-Uncle James Maley and other sealers of the SS *Southern Cross* who lost their lives in the 1914 sealing disaster. Also dedicated to the victims and survivors of the SS *Newfoundland*.

Remembering Jacob Taylor Kennedy and Elizabeth Emma Maley Kennedy, my grandparents, and Maggie Taylor, a pseudonym for James Maley's sweetheart, all of whom found their way into this novel, a novel inspired by true events and the love of two women for their men who loved the sea.

From eternity, in the beginning
He created me, and for eternity
I shall not cease to exist.

Sirach 24:9

As long as we have memories, yesterday remains.
As long as we have hope, tomorrow awaits.
As long as we have love, today is beautiful.

Author unknown

part one

Prologue

FOXTRAP IS A TRINITY OF LAND, SKY, AND SEA FRAMED IN ONE LOOK. You cannot see the land without the sky and sea, and you cannot see the sea without the land and sky. There is a jumble of dwellings down lanes and in turns: saltbox houses and cottages, all painted bright colours, beside barns, sheds, and stores, some ochre red, others weathered grey.

Many people take farming seriously and keep a kitchen garden in front of their house and a larger garden at the back. Sometimes they grow enough vegetables to stay them through the winter. Sometimes not. Since the sea is close to their doorstep, some farmers keep a punt or flat tied to a stagehead hung out over the water, legs deep in rocks holding them in place. Residents use their boats to fish for a winter supply, and later to cut wood on Kelly's Island. Sometimes they use them to go for a jaunt to Bell Island, a short distance across the water. Full-time farmers, whose fathers before them staked acres of land, often harvest a bountiful crop, enough to sell to residents of the meandering southern shore outlined by sandy and rocky beaches.

People along the shore hold steady against inclemency, asking for mercy, praying for westerly winds when northeasterlies sweep across the land and roar over houses, howling down chimneys, scattering wispy dark smoke. Houses shudder but hold strong, keeping the families inside safe and warm.

Sounds echo through the land and across the water from Monday morning to Saturday evening. Early Sunday mornings, after residents have spent six days of toil and turmoil on the sea or on the land, silence is a sound in itself, a calmness that can be heard fizzing in one's ears. The morning holds its breath as sails of clouds drift across the sky and the sea ripples away from the land and returns to nibble the beaches. The morning breaks open and people stir and heed the call of church bells pealing across the land. Church is a place God-loving people go regardless of their circumstances, the place other people go because of their circumstances. It is the place most people have gone many times because of tragedy. Graveyards tell the story of loss. A loss will come for which the church will offer solace, the graveyard none.

1

MAGGIE TAYLOR WAS in the habit of watching Matthew, her father, take his boat out on the water, it squaring away before the wind, its gaff topsail full as he sailed across to Kelly's Island to cut wood or to bring home a load of fish to sell to farmers who had no time to fish. She hoped he'd find a pirate's treasure, on the island named after a pirate, and they'd be rich. Then her father could stay home and jig fish off the stagehead all day long. Some days she ran through woodbine, stirring its honeysuckle flowers, their perfume spraying the air as she hurried in bare feet over the gravelled path to the beach. Other days she lay in long grass out by Windsong Lane and daydreamed of pirate Kelly's gold hidden on the small stretch of Kelly's Island. If there was a scud of cloud in an uneasy sky and rumbles through the great throat of the sea she didn't notice. Nothing was going to keep her father from coming home.

One Monday in July 1897, dark clouds baffled above Foxtrap Beach where Maggie played. The nine-year-old, though slight, looked tall as she stood against the sky on a wall of smooth stones: sea treasures pushed up from the deep. She had spent much of the afternoon on the beach waiting for a glimpse of her father's small, black boat on the horizon. Most days he was home by suppertime. She had often waited for him as he steered the boat against the glass eye of a noon sun, and other times under the furrowed brow of evening, amidst the traffic of other boats, birds, and pothead whales. Sometimes she ran back and forth across the beach, tossing a small stone into the air and catching it on the back of her hand. She dropped the stone and picked up a leafed string of knotweed and put its tiny, white flower to her nose. "I'd bring Mam the flower if she was good to me."

In her pocket was a sand dollar, the flowery outline of the seashell traced by her fingers over and over as she gazed past the head of Kelly's Island, her green eyes fervent with longing and dread. It would happen sometimes that her father had to put in to a small inlet for shelter from a sudden storm or rogue sea. Other times when it was past dark and there was no sign of his boat, she would give in to the pull of her stepmother's voice and hurry up the path, stopping to look back. She would giggle with delight when she spied a speck of light from the lantern swinging on the boat's bow. The boat would sail near enough for her to see her father, and her arm would swing into the air. When it was close enough for him to hear her, she would call, "Pappa." Her father's rosy face would open in a generous smile; he would lift his arm straight up and wave. She would dance along the shore, hitching up her dress, and run into the waves, her laugh resounding across the cove.

Her father was home! She was safe from Myrtle, her stepmother. Together they would go up to supper smiling.

Now, time and again, she glanced at the sky as if fearing the light would fade and darkness would cover the world. Other children had gone home and she was left alone on the beach. Night settled over her like a black cloud obscuring her view of the ocean and the land. Still, she stayed, ignoring a grating voice like a line with a fish hook pulling on her ear. Her stepmother would be waiting, angrier than ever that Maggie's father had not come home with wood for her fire and a cod for supper. Finally Maggie gritted her teeth, turned and started up the path to the house, her feet like two heavy stones.

Two days passed and her father had not come home.

Elizabeth Maley, another child who sometimes played on the beach, hurried over to Maggie, who was standing alone, the tail of her dress shivering though the air was warm. She caught hold of her hand and squeezed it tight. "Your pappa will come home. You'll see." Then, as if sadness in the other little girl's eyes was too much, she ran off to her own house. Maggie stayed, swishing her toe in the frilly seaweed that trailed through water.

* * * * *

Mary Jane and William Maley lived in a peaked two-storey house up from the ocean and had a clear view of children playing on the beach. Caroline Maley, their sister-in-law, who had dropped in from next door for a visit, leaned on the window leaf and shook her head. She tutted above the sound of Mary Jane's knitting needles clicking in and out of a half-knitted sweater. "I don't know what to make of that poor streely child," she said. "Never a needle put to the rips in her clothes or a loose button tightened."

Mary Jane rested the knitting on her knees and looked up at her sister-in-law. "Someone should take that child away from the stepmother who cares not a bit about her. There she is, then, with the tail of her dress between her teeth, and not a show of interest in anything on land while she dawdles in the water."

Rebecca, Mary Jane's daughter, chided, "Now, Mamma, you and Aunt Caroline got better things to do than cast your eyes about the place like a man with a jigger seeing what he can haul in."

Mary Jane ignored her daughter and went on. "The father likely got blown into some cove, and no one there was eager to pass the news, least of all him if he's been taken with a younger woman." She murmured, "Out with the old, in with the new."

Rebecca shook her head. "But the child, he—"

"Since when did a child keep a man in his place?" Caroline asked.

Rebecca knew her aunt was thinking of how her neighbour's husband had gone in his boat to the fishing grounds, how neither his hair nor hide was found, and she mourning herself all to pieces, sick in bed for days. Weeks later someone spotted him in a St. John's public house with a young woman on his arm, and they laughing to kill themselves. *Too handsome for Ida Snow to keep* was whispered around the place. However, Rebecca knew that Maggie's father was so struck on his little girl he would not abandon her.

Sometimes Maggie came to the house with Elizabeth, Rebecca's half-sister. Mary Jane smiled thinking of a spring day when the timid little girl had sidled into the house past William, who'd let out a grunt as she passed.

"Have some cream on your bread, rich cream from the cow's aftermilk," Mary Jane had offered.

Maggie shook her head. "It's Lent, sure."

"No odds, me child, if it is, but it's not," Mary Jane said. "The Holy Season is long gone. No one told you, I s'pose." She spread a generous helping over the bread. "Here! What goes into your body won't hurt your soul. Enjoy what you can get."

Maggie swallowed in anticipation. "For your sake I'll take some, but don't tell Mam else I'll have a knock in the side of the head. She thinks it's still Lent."

Unaware of the eyes on her from different windows in the place, Maggie dropped the tail of her dress and ran along the beach, her small, bare feet pressing their shape into the sand. The tide rose and water gurgled its way into her small footprints, pulled sand again and again until the footprints were gone. She kept running until she reached a pebbly part of the beach where her father's stage stood. Wind, sweeping off the water, caught her dress and flapped it like a ship's sail. She stood silent and straight, staring out to sea. Her father had always come home. Her small, white teeth pressed into her lower lip until they drew blood. Still, she stayed, alone and shivering until the sun dipped behind the hill. Its orange afterglow spread across the sky promising a good sunny day, one sure to bring her father home tomorrow. She sidled over to a huge rock known as a logan stone. It lay lodged on its edge and balanced by nature. Maggie had heard her father say that it was like the island of Newfoundland, itself caught on a ledge. Unlike the island, a wisp of wind could dislodge the logan stone, but a man couldn't move it. It was her place to lean when she grew tired of waiting.

Finally, she slid down to a large, flat rock and sat on it, pulling her legs up under her dress. Then she folded into herself, her arms around her knees, her head resting there. She stayed motionless as if fastened like a barnacle. Her eyes had watered from the strain of looking out over the choppy waters. Now they were closed.

"How long is your boat, Pappa?" she had asked him one day as he pushed strings of oakum into its seams with a flat blade and hammer. He finished what he was doing and went to get a mop and bucket to tar his new punt. He lifted his sleeve to wipe a sweaty forehead, and answered, "Long enough for two lops but not long enough for three."

She had screwed up her face. "Uh?"

He explained, "She's long enough to climb two waves. She dips her nose into the third lop, and spray goes right over her bow." He grinned and added, "I can handle her."

Boats belonging to other children's fathers had appeared on the shifting dark waters and had been collared and anchored long ago.

Now Maggie opened her eyes and whispered, "Your boat must bring you home. You have to save me from *her*."

She straightened up, pulled her plait to the side of her mouth, and bit on it like a cat playing with its tail. She looked up at the little house, its windows darkening in the fading light, then turned back to the beach. Salty water teased the land with its playful roll, licking dull stones. Flecks of gold, silver, and sunrise pink emerged, showing stones fit for a queen's necklace. She saw the flash of the evening light on a seagull's wing as it soared above the ocean, and the silhouette of a boat in the distance, and she felt a rush of excitement. *Could it be Pappa with a load of fish?*

The boat continued on across the bay away from Foxtrap.

Still, she waited. *You have to come!*

"What is the child doing now?" Mary Jane asked.

"She's still waiting for her father's punt," Rebecca said, squinting. "No one has told her."

Mary Jane tried to be optimistic. "Without a body, no one knows anything. No news can mean good news. The heart of the child is wrapped around her father. She'll lose her mind, her blood turn. . . ." Her voice trailed.

"She needs to know," Caroline said.

Elizabeth, coming down the stairs, heard the grown-ups talking. She felt afraid for her friend. "Know what?" she asked.

"Nothing," Mary Jane said. "Have your drink of milk and be off to bed."

Once Elizabeth went upstairs, Mary Jane put down her knitting and let out a sigh. "Hope can hold only so long."

Caroline went home while Mary Jane and Rebecca kept watching.

Mary Jane sputtered, "No one knows what goes on in that house now that there's no sign of the father."

* * * * *

Maggie's thoughts bobbed up and down like a corked bottle in water, going to the woman in the house on the hill, and then to her father out on the water. She tried to pull her mind away from her stepmother, who any moment might call her away from the beach, from the constant rush of water in and out anchoring her to a comforting place.

Finally, as the evening closed in, Myrtle's angry voice reached down. Fear like a wild animal cornered Maggie. Her arms fell to her side, hands tight, knuckles white. She began to run, dropped back for a quick glance at the sea, and then quickened her step as if pulled toward the house by the insistent voice. Her suntanned face turned for one moment toward the faces at the window of Mary Jane's house.

Rebecca stood behind her mother taking in the sight of the child. Fine curls at her broad forehead escaped from light hair pulled back in a plait. Her skin was like fine clay, her nose small and upturned just enough to be appreciated.

"Not enough flesh on that child to bait a hook," Mary Jane said.

Maggie stepped into the porch and braced herself against the wall as Myrtle, her face tight and hard, her eyes small and cold, gave her a clout on the side of her head. She scolded her. "Here we is, then, with the clothes all washed and dried and you comes home with your skirt tail sodden with water and seaweed." She shook her head. "When will it be all done, the toil and the weariness of it?"

"When we're dead." Maggie didn't mean to say it. Sometimes something in her mind just popped out of her mouth. She winced even before her stepmother's rough hand hit her cheek. As if that was not enough, she pinched her neck, her sharp nails cutting the skin. Maggie's eyes stung with hot tears as she ran past her stepmother and climbed the ladder to the attic room, a tiny space with a triangular window that framed the sea. She looked out, though she couldn't see anything through her tears. Her father was gentle and attentive to her. She had overheard her stepmother accuse him of spoiling her.

"She's me own flesh and blood," Matthew had answered.

When he wasn't around and Myrtle threatened to knock her head off, she imagined it rolling down her chest, her eyes shaking out of their sockets. When her stepmother said she'd skin her alive, she imagined the pain of it and she cried, afraid her stepmother would get angry enough to do just that, leaving her looking raw and bloodied like a skinned seal that sealers often brought home from a hunt.

Day after day she watched for her father to come home, scanning the ocean, her eyes squinting against the sun's bright light. She idled away the time gathering stones until her hands and dress pockets were full. Then she sat emptying her pockets into her lap. She had picked up a pure white rock, a lacy patterned one, and a grey rock looking as if it had been dribbled on by white paint. Now she laid aside the rocks and picked up a dark stone with a thick, white ring. It was as smooth as an egg and shaped like one. Her father had told her a story about cruel boys who had gone to all the birds' nests they could find. They had gathered the eggs and carried them to the beach where they mixed them with smooth stones to fool the birds. He said that eggs taken from the nest grew cold and hard and the mother bird rejected them. Now she imagined that inside each oval stone she had gathered was a little bird who never had a chance to fly; if she held the stones tight, they would warm and soften and the baby bird inside would peck its way out and fly away—something she'd like to do.

On Maggie's ninth day waiting for her father, the stones and other treasures in her dress pockets felt too heavy a burden, and she spilled them on the beach. Instead, her clenched fists filled the pockets. Inside one fist she held a god rock: an all-white stone her father said was lucky. She tightened her hand over it, her nails digging into her palm. She sighed and started a slow gait up the path to the house that hadn't seemed like a home since her mother died.

That night she dreamed that a piece of driftwood, something fastened to it, was rolling against the beach. As she got closer, she saw a grey hand and the familiar brown speckled guernsey and stocking cap her mother had knit for her father. She squeezed her eyes tight as screeching gulls swarmed over the body. Sobs gurgled in her throat. Then she screamed, her throat burning with her cries. Rough hands whirled her around, smothering her in her stepmother's rough brin bag apron.

She woke in the dark with her arms wrapped around herself, her bedclothes kicked on the floor. Her eyes widened. *It wasn't real! I had what Pappa calls the darnies!*

The next day Maggie walked from one large round rock to another, her arms outstretched as if she were balancing on a tightrope. Then she dropped to a large shelf, her tiny bum settling, her knees holding her elbows while her feet absently played with a cobbled bed of stones. She imagined that her father had been taken by pirates. God would strike them dead with a thunderbolt and her father would sail the pirates' black ship, heavy with treasure, home and they would live happily ever after.

She looked past the stagehead and a low rock wall separating her from another, more sandy beach. Names floated on the air as children called to each other: Elizabeth, Emily, Olivia, Laura, Jamie, Noah, Zachary. . . . When the tide was out and until it began rolling in over the landwash they ran from beach to beach, sand sticking to their bare feet and legs like caplin spawn.

Water surged and puffs of foam strayed along the shore. Elizabeth lifted foam on her hand. "Ocean clouds!" she called. "I've got ocean clouds."

The children ran into the ocean dipping their hands into the foam. They called, "Me, too!"

All except Maggie, who stared out to sea—alone.

Mary Jane frowned as she watched Maggie from her upstairs window. She turned with a smile toward Elizabeth and the other children running and leaping into the air, leaving footprints that the tides would wash away as if they never were. It would be years before the children would be part of the same sad story, one Mary Jane could not even imagine. No one could.

2

Two years before, Maggie's attention had been drawn to the bawling cow inside her father's barn. She had tiptoed close to the open door and had seen the cow struggle to born her calf. Her father had pushed the barn door shut. Later, she heard him tell her mother that after the cow gave birth she wouldn't get up. He had put his hands over her nostrils, forcing her to struggle for breath and get to her feet, so she could be cleaned of the afterbirth. The healthy calf nuzzled her mother's teat and then latched on. A few days later the cow sickened and died. Maggie's father explained that the calf took all the mother's strength.

Maggie watched her mother's stomach grow, and one day when she found her mother asleep in the rocking chair and saw movement under her apron, she felt a knot of fear. Then one evening she followed her mother's cry. She pushed open the bedroom door to see her mother's white knees spread wide, a pool of blood on white sheets, her face upturned in anguish to the midwife. Holding in a scream, Maggie fled to her bedroom. The next morning her father stood in the doorway, his voice leaden with the words, "Your mother passed away."

The air around her pressed in as if to smother her. "Passed away? Where?"

"She's gone to heaven," her father said, his face crumbling.

Maggie ran into her parents' bedroom. Her father was wrong. Her mother was asleep. She tried to shake her arm, but it was stiff and hard. "Wake up, Mamma!"

"She can't," her father said, his face dark and sad.

Maggie pressed her lips against her mother's cheek. She knew then that her mother had gone away and left a body that was cold and deaf and dumb. Her eyes once bright enough to light up a day, now closed, her smile like sunshine gone. Beside her lay a small, white-faced creature. She stared at the wrinkled face. *A leprechaun or a fairy, not my sister like Pappa told me.* She touched its skin, as hard as candle wax, and pulled her mother's blanket over the baby's still face, knowing it would never mewl and latch on to her mother's breast. Her face hardened. "You killed my mamma."

She dropped to the floor and curled in a ball on the hard surface and dug her head into the braided mat, where she stayed for a long time. She knew that no matter how many times she shook her mother she would not move and wake up, and if she put her hand over her mouth like her father had done with the cow she would not get up. Sobbing, she climbed the stairs to an attic room and lay on the bed. This small room had always felt warm around her like a coat. Now it felt empty and cold.

She heard the hoarse pull of her father's saw and then the sound of hammering. After a while she could see through the small window that her father and a neighbour were carrying a pine box toward the house. She listened with dread to the heavy scuff of the men's feet on the landing before they entered the porch. The box would take her mother away. She drifted from the sound of voices as women came to wash and lay out her mother.

"Don't be thinking anything bad," the midwife said to Maggie's father sitting by the coffin in the back room, his head resting on the edge. She patted him on the shoulder. "Fishermen are lost at sea. Women are lost to childbirth. It's the way of nature. People leave the earth for a better place, but they never leave our hearts."

Maggie's Aunt Liddie from Middle Bight urged her to say goodbye to her mother. She reluctantly drew near, past the baby beside her, and reached to kiss her mother's cold face.

Not even her father's arm around her shoulder could soften the blow of her mother's coffin being lowered into a hole in the ground, shovels of earth clobbering it.

"Mamma!" Maggie screeched. She threw her body across the mound of earth.

Soon the displaced earth settled over her mother and the land grew grass and then it was as if her mother wasn't there.

"In heaven," Aunt Liddie said.

"In here," Maggie said, holding her hand over her heart as she stood above her mother's grave months later. Sights and sounds skirted her mind about the day her mother left her. She wouldn't let them in. She couldn't rise above the feeling that the terrible thing that had taken her mother would be back.

Liddie's voice seemed far away. "I'd take care of you but for the brood of children filling me house. Maybe another relative will do her duty. Your father can't get his work done and mind you as well."

Maggie sat half on and half off a chair, her legs dangling, one arm wrapped around a back rung, her hand tightened in a fist. She wasn't leaving her home.

"Maybe your father will find you a stepmother," her aunt said.

Maggie's green eyes darkened. "A stepmother! A mother to step on me."

Myrtle hadn't stepped on her, but she was not like Maggie's mother, who had smoothed her hair, cupped her cheek, and pulled her so close she could hear her heart beating.

Now Maggie's father had disappeared and Myrtle made her leave her own bedroom for the room in the attic. She lay on the bed sobbing. The only two people who had ever loved her had left her.

One day, after Maggie came up from the beach thirsty and hungry, she slipped her finger into a pan of milk cooling in the porch and lifted an island of cream from its milky waters. She had it almost up to her tongue when there was a chop across her back, her stepmother's voice sharp as a knife: "You little thief!"

She was at the mercy of a woman who liked men, not children. Myrtle already had men visitors. One gave Maggie a greasy grin and patted her bum, sending shivers up and down her spine.

"You'll not be staying here now that your father's gone," her stepmother said in a cold, hard voice. "You'll need a relative with the means to feed you. Henry Batten in Bareneed is willin' to take you. You'll live with a fine man whose wife is partial to children. Bareneed is fastened to *Portagrave*, the longest finger on a hand of communities. Your people, the Taylors, are Church of Englanders from there, so it's as if you'll be goin' home. The Battens'll be happy to raise you. They have a grown son gone away to Canada."

"This is my house," she answered, her eyes bright and round with fear.

"It was yours when your father lived. Now it's mine and you belongs elsewhere."

Maggie thought of the little nooks in the house, her hiding place for her collection: a dried, small, orange shellfish her father called a fish doctor; tiny pieces of glass and porcelain she'd found on the beach among tiny stones she had gathered.

As if reading her mind, the woman said, "You'll take your duds and other scraps of things you've minded."

Maggie straightened against her fear and looked at Myrtle, unflinching. "I'll stay until Pappa comes home."

Her stepmother's eyes showed narrow, icy blue glints. "His boat come ashore up the bay. It was found nibbling at the beach. Like a hungry horse, it was. Someone already claimed it."

"How do you know it was his boat?"

"Never you mind." She gave her a push. "Now up to your room. There'll be someone to take you off me hands in a day or so."

The next day a boat drew near to her father's stage. Maggie stood still, imagining it was her father coming home to be with her, not a stranger coming to take her away.

3

Elizabeth Maley, Maggie's best friend, stood on the stagehead. Her eyes, usually bright and wide, now squeezed out tears. "I wish you didn't have to leave," she said.

Maggie hadn't heard her come down the path. She was too busy gazing out to sea, still hopeful of seeing her father.

Elizabeth had seen Myrtle grab Maggie by her hair and knock her down. She had heard her squealing like the pigs in Abe Porter's slaughterhouse. Elizabeth's tongue had clapped in anger. Her mother had never hit her, and her older half-sisters and half-brother ignored her most times. She wished that Maggie were her sister.

Once, last year, while she was sitting on the outdoor steps playing with her doll, she'd seen Myrtle out by her door shaking Maggie. Elizabeth had pulled a round stone from her gimp pocket and had thrown it for all she was worth right into the woman's fat bosom. She whispered under her breath, "I hope I've knocked off a nipple and let the air out of her big udder."

"What! You brazen little hussy," the woman called. She ran after Elizabeth, but Elizabeth was too quick for her. She skittered down the path and out over her father's stagehead and down the rails.

"Climb down here," Elizabeth called, "and I'll pull your legs off." She began to sing,

"I see England, I see France
I see the legs of raggedy pants."

Myrtle had backed away in a huff muttering about the dirty-mouthed little girl William Maley had bred.

Maggie stared in admiration. Someone had stood up for her. She made sure her stepmother had gone back up into the house. Then she ran toward Elizabeth.

Maggie hooked her finger into Elizabeth's, as if they were breaking a wishbone. They said in unison, "Friends always." Maggie slipped a piece of worn glass from her pocket and put it into Elizabeth's yellow gimp pocket.

Elizabeth took a smooth, variegated stone from her pocket, licked it to bring out its colours, and spat away the salty taste. She gave it to Maggie, who loved stones as much as Elizabeth did. Elizabeth saw stones as a living part of the earth, imagined them as children of the large round rock her mother had warmed every winter night by the fire and put in her bed.

Maggie felt akin to Elizabeth for other reasons. One day she had seen Elizabeth running along the path. An uncomfortable look crossed her face. The elastic in her underwear must have let go because her fleece bloomers were falling down around her feet. She looked around to see two big boys, Mark and Jud, looking at her. They began to snigger and Mark chanted,

"Lizzie's bloomers fell on down
An orange pumpkin on the ground
She picked it up a dirty brown."

Jud laughed and banged the other boy on the back. "Mark yourself down to be a poet."

Elizabeth stooped and stepped out of her bloomers. She pushed them under her arm just as Mark pulled on her pigtail. She swung around, her eyes flashing. "Do that ag'in and I'll knock you off your block."

He grabbed her plait a second time and held on. Dirt flew against Elizabeth's legs as she turned and slapped his face.

Mark let go of her hair and rubbed his cheek. He ran to the top of the hill, stooped, and turned holding a rock. He flung it, taking her in the back. She lurched forward, then got her balance as the boys' voices in unison followed her:

"Fat braid, baby brain, you're no good
Chop your arse for firewood."

They were the same boys who took baby robins from their nests and cut them to pieces, and bobbed the tails of stray cats or bashed in their brains.

Mark called to Maggie, "Your father's gone. He'll never come home."

He turned back and the boys took off laughing. Maggie stood biting her lips and thinking, *What does he know!*

She watched Elizabeth, unfazed by the boys, walk on the wall of stones by the side of the beach, her bloomers still under her arm. Water, white and churning, sent its cold spray dashing against her legs. Elizabeth didn't squeal and jump back as Maggie and other children might have done.

Now, after Elizabeth had gone home, Maggie stood by the stone wall and stared at the dark body of water stretching farther than she had ever travelled.

Big! her father had called the ocean, spreading his arms.

Clouds, like fists, squeezed out rain, dropped it like pellets to pockmark the sea. Maggie's small, flat stone flew from her outstretched hand, making a silent, twirling motion as it tiptoed across the dark ocean and disappeared. Wind swept in as cold as her stepmother's look, the night descending like a dark veil over her face.

4

Myrtle had a kinder look than usual as she bundled Maggie's clothes in a quilt Maggie's mother had made, kinder still as she said, "Go on to the boat. Your uncle will be up to carry your belongings."

Maggie didn't look back as she made her way down to the stagehead where her uncle waited.

Henry was a large man, his face sizable under a flat cap with a lip that shaded his eyes. He hoisted the cap off his bald head, looked at her, and nodded. "We'll get along if you'll heed the missus."

Maggie looked up at him and blinked against the bright sunlight. Her lips trembled. If she answered him she'd be sure to cry. He gave her bonnet a pat and reached to lift her. He held her in his arms, beach treasures rattling in her pockets, as he climbed down the rails to the boat. He went back up to the house to take Maggie's belongings. He hurried back down and stowed them in the boat's cuddy.

Until now Maggie had travelled only along the shore in Foxtrap.

Bareneed, where her father's relatives lived, was miles and miles away. She tried to remember everything her father had told her. He said the earth was round, not flat. She had asked anxiously, "If the earth is round like a ball, will we fall off if we go too far over the hill?" He had hugged her close. "No fears of that. The earth is larger than you can imagine."

She had liked her father's stories. He'd look out over the beach and begin: "There once was a little girl who lived in a little house with her mamma and pappa above the beach. They were all sitting at the table having a cup of tea and fardy—Irish bread to you, little one—on a set of green dishes the mamma loved. The sea hove in and grabbed the legs of the house and dragged everything out to sea. The plate the little girl was holding sailed through the open window and was dashed on rocks below. A lit candle on the window leaf toppled into the sea with a tiss. The whole family was taken out to sea to be seen no more. Pieces of green glass now worn smooth is what the sea left to remind us what the sea can do to anyone who gets too close to it."

"Is that your story or the truth?" she had asked, wanting it to be a story.

"It is what you believe it to be," he had answered, cradling her against his shoulder. Now she opened her hand and smiled at the piece of green glass on her palm, like the piece she had given Elizabeth.

Elizabeth had brought Maggie a white angora tam when she knew she was leaving. Maggie lifted it to wave goodbye to Elizabeth and her brother, Jamie, who stood a distance from the stagehead. Then she held it against her heart, soft and warm like a kitten.

"You like her—you do," Elizabeth teased her brother as the boat sailed away.

Jamie wouldn't tell Elizabeth what had happened days ago. Maggie had come up the path twirling a buttercup between her fingers.

"Do you like butter?" she had asked him.

"Uh!"

She had pushed the buttercup under his chin. "Yup, you do. Its yellow shadow is bright on your skin."

"You could have just asked me," he had said, giving her a shy smile.

"And why would I do that?" She had let out a tinkling laugh.

Now he gave his sister a scornful look. "She's a girl. I don't want to play with girls unless they're tomboys like you."

"Wave, Jamie," Elizabeth said. She lifted her brother's arm and his hand flew into the air.

At that moment, something passed from Jamie to Maggie, something unexplainable. She felt the pull of his dark, grey eyes.

Maggie settled into her uncle's rocking boat, grabbing the gunnels to steady herself. As the boat moved out into the ocean, she turned to the sound of a voice calling goodbye. Elizabeth was running from rock to rock, her arms waving like wings. Hurrying along the beach were other children lifting their hands and waving. She made out the faces of Emily, Laura, Olivia, and Zachary. Soon they became tiny specks. She'd likely never see any of them again. Tears streamed down her face. She stuck her thumb in her mouth, something she hadn't done for a long time.

Elizabeth kept a constant look at the boat until it became a tiny spot on the vast ocean. It disappeared from sight and she followed Jamie as he turned and ran up the path.

She sat on the porch landing holding Betsy, her doll. "I've lost my best friend," she told Betsy, who didn't look at all sympathetic. She dropped the doll and ran inside.

She sniffled to her mother, "Maggie's gone away, gone to Bareneed."

"Proper thing! Thanks be to God!" Mary Jane exclaimed. "I've often wondered what was to become of the child." Mary Jane had thought Maggie to be far away in thought even while she and Elizabeth played cobbyhouse with pieces of pottery and shale. She had sometimes given her a slice of lassy loaf and a cuddle, and Maggie had responded with a bright smile before darting away. Maybe she would finally have a safe place in Bareneed. The outport was a short distance from Hibb's Cove, the place where Edward Kennedy, Mary Jane's first husband, had once lived.

Mary Jane glanced through the window. In the distance, away from the noises of people and wild and domestic creatures, ships seemed to move across the ocean in peaceful silence as if on a mysterious voyage. Taking people away from the earth itself, it seemed. Maggie was like a sapling pulled out of the ground, its roots shivering. Hopefully she would be transplanted in a good place. Mary Jane turned back to kneading a pan of dough.

Elizabeth pinched a piece of the dough. Jamie was right behind her for his share. The two children ran outside chewing dough like taffy before swallowing it.

William smiled from the doorway of his shed at the sound of small footsteps. He watched the two children with amusement. "Any more than one pinch of dough and your bellies will blow up like a cow's udder," he told them.

They looked at him, both lifting a finger at the same time. Elizabeth said, "We had one pinch, Pappa. That's all."

5

Maggie's head felt as heavy as a rock. She turned to look toward the ocean opening up, held, it seemed, by the curved arms of the sky.

"Do you have any money?" her uncle asked.

"No." Then her face brightened. She loosened the string on a bag she carried. "In here I have a sand dollar."

"A seashell is worth nothing," he said.

"It's worth something to me," she answered. "I gave it to me mamma before she took sick."

Her uncle looked at her. "Never mind," he assured her. "We have plenty of food and shelter, everything a little girl needs." Then he turned away.

Her lips trembled. *A little girl needs a mamma and pappa.*

They sailed into Bareneed, where little boats bobbed on gentle waters like nesting birds. The sun was strong and warm like a generous smile, though it was October. In a valley, away from cleft hills, lay meadows sheltered from easterly winds that often swept the highlands. Peaked houses, built on uneven land, shaded in bright colours, gave the place a tumbled look. Half-grown boys hung around the beach firing off homemade guns. They let out a whoop each time a crow or a gull fell out of the sky.

Henry shook his head. "One less crow is always good. It's fair shocking the racket a crow can make. It got eyes like Satan and a bawl so loud you'd think it was being pinched to death."

Afraid that a stray shot might hit someone he told the boys, "Scurry on home."

They darted away with their guns tucked under their arms. Two small boys jumped into a flat hauled up on the beach while two older boys tried to dislodge it. It scraped over small stones and gravel as they pushed it into the water. The older boys jumped aboard and one of them grabbed the oar, pushed it through the score, and started to scull out into the bay. The other boys tipped their hands in the cold water and let it fly into the face of the boy sculling the boat, their laughter like a flat rock skipping water.

Brazen like boys at home, Maggie thought.

Maggie's uncle shook his head. "I don't know what to make of them young fellars. They's up from Hibb's Cove, sure they is. Young Jacob Kennedy, the one sculling, is the only sensible one among 'em. But never mind."

Henry nodded toward a small house beside a narrow lane. "We'll go up and you can meet your Aunt Louise."

Louise was standing in the doorway rubbing her hands down a white apron.

"I wouldn't have come," Maggie said, "but I didn't want to hurt your feelings, you being family and all." She gave her aunt a strained look.

Louise lifted a hand to her hair, which was parted in the middle and pulled straight back from the sides and coiled at her poll. She straightened a pin and smiled at Maggie, her brown eyes warm.

"Dear child," she said, "it's not about feelings. Your uncle asked for you out of duty, and you'll make yourself useful with all the goings-on in this place. It's not to the queen's palace you've come, but we're comfortable most of the year. The easterlies bring the wild winds with their chill, but it's probably no worse than what you've suffered." Her look took in Maggie's ragged dress and the yellowing bruises on her legs. "We could shorten your name to Mag."

"No," Maggie answered firmly. "I need the full name my mother intended."

Her aunt shook her head. "It's hard to keep a full name when everyone's in such a hurry to get out their words. They shorten words wherever they can. In this place there's no trees to break the strength of strong winds; gusts sometimes takes words out of our mouths."

Maggie buttoned her lips. The wind wasn't going to get her words.

She followed her aunt inside and went to a settle, where she huddled with her thumb in her mouth. Her aunt took the bag she'd laid beside her and went upstairs.

"Your thumb don't want to be in your mouth," Henry told her. "Sure, 'tis dark in there and wet and your teeth looks like headstones. Your tongue'll pin your poor thumb to the roof of your mouth until it's frightened ter death."

Maggie's eyes widened.

"Now then," he added, his voice ominous. He bent down until his tobacco breath swirled around her like steam from a swamp, "If you keep sucking your thumb it'll break off and go down into your belly. If you want it back, you'll have to yuck it up." He raised an eyebrow. "Then there's the matter of gettin' it back on your hand."

Maggie let her hand drop and her mouth open. She stared at him in horror.

"See," he said, nodding toward her hand. "Your poor thumb looks white and shrivelled. It's already started to let go of your hand."

"I only do it when I'm scared," she whispered. "I won't do it anymore." She hid her thumb in the palm of her hand, her fingers folding over it.

He smiled and stood up. "That's a good girl."

When Henry went outside she reached into her pocket and found the smooth, round stone Elizabeth had given her. She closed her hand around it.

Her aunt came back down and set food on the table. She glanced at her husband. "There's no flesh on that child." She turned to Maggie and asked, "Don't you have a mind for food?"

Maggie tried to keep her body steady but it held a tremor. She hoped her aunt wouldn't notice the shiver in her dress as she answered, "It's my nature, Aunt Louise."

"Nature or not, there's no need to be as thin as a whipping post. Come and eat, then."

Maggie slipped into a chair at the small wooden table, her fists in her lap. Her stomach had always felt too tight to let food in while she was sitting at the table facing her stepmother.

Her aunt and uncle dug into their meal of lobscouse while Maggie looked down at her empty plate.

Louise looked up. "Take hold. Spoon yourself a plate of food from the bowl. There'll be no tending on yer."

Maggie reached then to take a scarce amount, afraid of a slap on her fingers.

Henry, taking in her timid reach, grabbed the spoon and filled her plate. "There you is, then. A full stomach encourages mind and body."

After they had eaten, her aunt slid a small stool toward her. "Get on this and wash the dishes. Scrape every fingernail full for the pigs. Don't lose a whit."

She did as she was told and then she was hurried along upstairs to a room with a small bed under a window framing the sea. She slept better than she had expected and without one dream that she could remember. After breakfast she helped wash the dishes and tidy the pantry. Then she sat on the kitchen floor, her slim, bare feet under the warmth of the sun shining like a golden shaft through the large window. Dust motes danced in the sunlight like tiny fairies. Heat from the fire in the hearth brought a tincture of red to her cheeks. After a while she got up and wandered outside, her aunt's voice following her, warning, "Not too near the water, mind you, and not too far up on the hill."

In the valley she felt she was breathing in the earth's breath, but on top of Bareneed Hills she took the breath of the sea into her lungs, its strong, salty scent assailing her nostrils. Bareneed Hills was rightly named, a place that poked its bare knuckles up into the sky, taking on wind and rain, summer's warmth, and winter's chill. She looked down to Port de Grave, not *Portagrave* as her stepmother called it. Houses and other buildings nestled beside hills in from winding roads; others stood on grey cliffs. Boats rocked in the bay.

Maggie could see the remnants of a stone building that her uncle later explained was a jail where both the guilty and innocent had been housed a long time ago.

Maggie often woke to the thump of paddles against thole-pins as boats sluiced through water and then the scraping of a boat against the beach as it was pulled up over sand and beach stones and she would think, *Pappa is home.* Then she would curl around herself and cry, remembering that she was far from home and her father would never again lift her for a cuddle against his arm.

"The sea," he had told her, "is always travelling, coming to shore, running back out and coming back in. Sometimes it prowls the shoreline like a cat with a bird in its mouth coming to lay its victim at our doorstep. Sometimes it's the body of a fish or a fisherman."

She looked through the window and followed the sea to its curved line against the grey sky, followed its sprites swimming one after the other, white foam carried on dark water. Even if her father's boat had been taken by the sea, she could imagine her father swimming toward her alive.

One morning she left the house and climbed the stairs of her uncle's shed. Through the window she saw a long jut of land dipped, like a finger, in icy water. The window framed it like a picture, a lonely picture, its point deserted.

Her uncle came up behind her. "That's Salmon Cove," he said. "The place looks uninviting on a rainy day or when it's shadowed in snow. On sunny days with snow sparkling under a bright sun it looks like a quiet, welcoming spot, though it's not," he added tersely.

"Why not, Uncle?" she asked.

"You be the curious one, for sure. But it's all better left to rest. Those stories never get told right. Go on, now, off to help your aunt."

Maggie had little trouble falling asleep each night after helping her aunt with the day's work and having a little play outdoors. She had her own candle to light her way upstairs, with a warning from her aunt to spare it or be without. She snuffed it as soon as she was in bed, not wanting to have to climb the stairs in the dark. She liked the little bed built tight against the slanted ceiling in the roof and the little window that sometimes framed the moon.

She often slipped out of bed and stared through the window at a full moon hanging low, melting into a silver path across the ocean. She imagined scooping up handfuls of silver water. She spoke to her father as if he could hear her. "You and I can see the moon at the same time no matter where we is. Only Mamma's gone for good."

She turned from the window, then back as something caught her eye. A light was wavering across the water, straight across to where a red rock jutted out from the land. A mysterious light, not originating from land or from a boat. She must ask her uncle about it.

She was soon asleep and dreaming that she lived in a family of brothers and sisters. She felt the heat from her sisters' bodies as the little ones curled around her like soft pillows keeping her feet warm. Sometimes her hand strayed outside the quilt and she woke in the darkness to find she was alone. She pulled her hand back under the covers to warm it under her ribs.

She tried not to think about her stepmother sending her away. "Try to mind her, Maggie," her father had said. "I married her too quick, not knowing she's lemon and pepper, hard to take, her tongue like a cat-o'-nine-tails."

She had looked at him puzzled. She knew that cats could have nine lives, but she'd never seen a cat with nine tails. It was hard to understand adults. Now she knew what a cat-o'-nine-tails was. Uncle had one hanging in his shed. "A souvenir of worse days," he told her. "A good many men got a lick from that one." He leaned closer. "More than a lick. The dark spots are blood. But it wasn't as bad as getting hanged."

Her aunt, coming out to the shed to fill a jar with molasses from a stowed keg, told him, "Don't be gettin' the child's innocent mind on things too hard for her to understand."

"'Tis her learnin' about life," he said. "It's only right for her to know that a woman from around here was convicted and hanged after her husband disappeared."

Her aunt filled her molasses jar and went back up to the house.

"Who's the woman sitting at the window next door?" Maggie asked.

Her uncle crinkled his brow and lifted his cap off his head. He squinted his eyes. "That's Bridget. It was her mother who was hanged."

"I've never met anyone whose mother was hanged," Maggie whispered. "But my father disappeared, too. I'd like to go see her."

"It's best if you didn't. It's not too often she shows her face out around the place since she come back from bein' away. She can't take the talk and all."

"I'd like a look at her, then."

"She looks the same as anyone else, though she carries heavy memories. I'm sure she wouldn't turn down havin' her name in your prayers."

* * * * *

Maggie was sitting on a rock wall swinging her legs and looking out to sea when she caught a glimpse of a tall woman crossing the lane on her way to the outhouse, her grey hair plaited and looped.

"Hello," the woman said in a soft, pleasant voice. "You're the little girl come to stay with your uncle."

"I know about your story," Maggie said.

"Every life has a story," Bridget answered with a frail smile.

Maggie shrugged. "Mine's not very interesting."

"It will be," Bridget promised. "You want to go home, don't you? Everyone likes to go home to where they belong." Her look went beyond Maggie to Salmon Cove. "I went away once."

"Was it for very long?" Maggie asked.

Her answer was brisk. "Long enough. This is where I belong."

Maggie's lips formed a pout, her eyes stormy. "It's not where I belong."

"Then go home."

"I will, some day."

That evening she stood by the rail on her uncle's bridge and watched high tide pull a sheet of water over the foot of the beach. She looked toward the sea, to the dance of sun sparkles, and gritted her teeth. *I should be home in Foxtrap.* She wondered then if her father had come back and if the children still played on the beach and if there would ever come a time when she could sit on the beach with them, especially Elizabeth. She stayed until night blackened the place. Then she drew in the sharp, salty air and sighed before turning her back on the sea.

The nights turned cold and her aunt offered her a heated rock wrapped in muslin. She placed it under her bedclothes at the foot of her bed. It lay there shaped like a giant beachy bird's egg she and her friends had discovered when she lived in Foxtrap.

She'd go back home sometime. She would. Just like Bridget did.

part two

6

WILLIAM MALEY HAD built his pine house on the level. Thirteen steps led to an upstairs. A second set of narrow steps led to two small rooms built in the peak of the roof. The house had a long porch and, off the kitchen, a sitting room. The porch walls were covered with sheeting paper. Three model boats leaned against squished wallpaper in the sitting room. Their wooden sails, painted white, were shaped as if stirred by a gentle wind. The house was bordered by wild roses, lilies, honeysuckle, crabapple trees, and berry bushes. William lived alone, a thirty-three-year-old bachelor, a farmer and fisherman of little sustenance that anyone could tell. He liked the warm, damp scent of his farmland and the cool and reviving breath of the lively sea.

Beside his house, in a weathered barn, he kept a grey horse to help with his farmland and, down by the stagehead, his small punt was collared with his father's Irish killick. William never strayed far on the sea, only far enough to gather fish for winter. Just up from the beach in the triangular pond named Paddy's Pond—after Patrick, William and Joe's grandfather—William set cone-shaped eel baskets. When he caught a barrel of eels, some of them two feet long and big on the round, he would go wild with glee, anticipating the journey on his horse-drawn wagon to St. John's to sell them to the upperdees who paid in cash. Sometimes he saved an eel for himself. He kept a frying pan on the stove with an inch of grease in it from rendered fatback, which he called ladder and skirt. Most times he cooked in the pan, ate out of it, and left it on the stove for another time.

There were times when William believed he would always be a bachelor. He had never seen a woman he wanted, though he lay in bed aching to be a part of some woman's life and have children running in the lane. Time was long when a man had only himself. Lately, though, he'd been thinking about a woman he'd caught sight of in Long Pond. He'd gone there to help a man whose well went dry. William was a water diviner, a dowser, or a water witch—whatever anyone wanted to call him. He took no money. It was a gift he gave freely. The man needing help was the next-door neighbour of Mary Jane Kennedy, a widow with three children. William had caught Mary Jane watching him as he took a forked alder about three-quarters of an inch thick at the base and about a foot long. He held the prongs of the fork, palms facing up and the base pointed away from his body. Children followed him as he walked carefully, one foot in front of the other as he held the Y-shaped dowsing rod in his search for a spring of water. When he found it, a force pulled the stick down.

The neighbour was grateful to William for locating a place for him to dig a new well. With a nod to Mary Jane standing on her doorstep, he said to William, "Now there's a fine form of a woman for you, a bachelor man." To Mary Jane, he said, "Have this man and you'll always have buckets of water." Mary Jane had blushed and hurried inside.

After his visit, William asked Caroline, who had once lived in Long Pond, about the widow.

"The poor woman," Caroline said with a sly look, "is left with three small children. She'd likely make for a good sister-in-law."

Mary Jane woke morning after morning while it was still dark with one question: *How can I raise three fatherless children alone?* Edward John stirred beside her. He'd been sleeping in his mother's bed since the drowning. If the child hadn't been sleeping beside her she would have lit the lamp, let its light and warmth lift her spirit. Instead she turned to the warmth of her child's soft body, drew it into her embrace, and fell asleep. The strident sounds of cock-a-doodle-doo awakened her to daylight and a renewed surge of uncertainty. She remembered her Grandfather Bussey's words to her when she was a child as he sat on a log by his sawhorse. "It's a long road, Mary Jane, a long road gettin' from where you is to where I is. A lot of things can happen. A lot of things do happen. You probably don't understand what I mean," he said, cupping his large, veined hand over her small, soft one.

Whatever road her grandfather had been on, she was on now: the road of hard knocks, its landslides capable of burying her and her children. Tidal waves of fear washed over her. Edward's two brothers had moved to Long Pond not long after he did. They had helped him build his house and he had helped them build theirs. Now that their brother was gone, they hinted that Edward's house belonged to them. They seemed unmindful of his children needing a home.

"There's a lonely bachelor down in Foxtrap," her sister said. "You've seen him goin' along the road selling his vegetables, his old horse trottin' along in no hurry, and him calling from his perch above the wagon, 'Git 'e up!' He's clean over himself if not his place. His fingernails are pared, his face washed, and his good pants kept creased under his pillow in case of a funeral, the only time he thinks of the church. That's the news from Caroline Maley."

"I remember him," she said, to her sister's surprise. "He's the dowser from Foxtrap."

William Maley knocked on Mary Jane's door one day. She opened it to see a short man with a jolly, ruddy face and a head of light hair fine and thin.

He told her, "I'm not rich in dollars, just a house with a barn, shed, and an outhouse, a stable and a few end shelters. I own a few acres in on Dun Hill's road." He passed her a sprig of boy's love. He later told his brother Joe with a shrug, "What other kind of offering could I bring?"

She bent to the minty scent of the plant, murmuring that she needed time to think.

"I'll be back in a few days to see if you're willin' to take me on," he told her.

She nodded and closed the door. One day, after she had spent a few nights walking the floor in trepidation, she saw, in the distance, William coming along the road with his horse and wagon.

The bachelor had also spent a few nights wondering what he was letting himself in for. Finally, he hitched his wagon to his grey horse, cracked his reins, and was off down the road, the empty wagon swinging back and forth over potholes.

He slowed the horse as he got close. It plodded up the narrow lane and over its rise. To hide his nervousness William began singing under his breath,

"King William was King George's son and all the royal races won
On his head he wore a star and in his mouth was a big cigar
Come choose to the east, come choose to the west
Come choose the one you love the best . . ."

He reined in his horse and unlatched the gate leading down the path to Mary Jane's house.

"Down on the carpet you must kneel
While the grass grows round your feet
Salute your bride and kiss her sweet
Rise again upon your feet."

He stopped suddenly as Mary Jane opened the door and looked out at him.

She knew what she would bring to her new home. Her father had imported and planted an apple tree in front of their house. The sweet, white apples had five points. She would bring a basket of last fall's apples from the cellar, a sapling from the large tree, and a handkerchief holding seeds to be planted by William's house.

She went back inside and came back out wearing a grey coat. She had pulled over it a long, coloured shawl—her wedding shawl. It came down past the tops of her boots. Her three children trailed her; her arms were so full she couldn't hold their hands. She had left all of Edward's belongings, taking only what belonged to her and the children: clothes, samplers, and bed linens she had sewn herself. "I've found a man who says he'll let me share what's his," she had told Edward's brothers. They had responded with a satisfied nod as they stood in the middle of the kitchen ready to take the house.

William stowed the family's belongings and settled the children in the wagon. Then he helped Mary Jane climb up to the seat beside him. They came to Church Road and the wagon snaked its way around the turn of the gravelled path beside the graveyard, its headstones leaning in whiskers of brown grass. They went on down a knob and William's house came in sight. William stopped the horse and jumped down. He lifted the plank holding the gates and swung them wide. He led his horse close to the house and hitched it to a post. Then he opened the door to his small porch and Mary Jane followed him inside. The children hesitated and then chased their mother.

William's look flickered over the children. He looked back at Mary Jane. "The children are yours and mine now," he said with a smile. "I've taken you and gotten fully-made youngsters in the bargain."

Mary Jane's eyes were bright as she nodded.

Rebecca gave him a vexed look, her clenched hands at her side. Fannie held her rag doll to her chest, and Edward John a toy soldier, as they edged in to sit on the seat standing against the wall along the table. The seat William had made especially for them smelled of new wood. They sat quietly, their faces solemn. William looked at them, not knowing what to expect from a stranger and her children. "There's some leftover porridge. I mostly make a batch for meself. That can last for a few days."

Mary Jane smiled. Porridge for supper—breakfast food for a family, supper food for a bachelor. A generous pitcher of milk stood on the table, cruds of cream floating in it.

"Look at that," said Joe looking through his window. "William went and got himself a little widda woman. She's older than William and likely dry dough by now."

Johnny, Joe and William's brother, was sitting by the stove on a low stool. He lifted his head contemplatively as if to see with his mind. Johnny was delicate, his skin as white as a cup, his eyes sunny blue. He had been crippled and blind since he was thirteen. "Is she pretty or no?" he asked.

"She'll do, from what I can see of her," Joe said.

"Let's get on over and stand for the weddin'," Caroline said, rushing to tidy herself. "The minister will be on his way."

Caroline and Joe stood as witnesses while the children watched. That night, after Mary Jane's new in-laws and the minister left, the children were washed and tucked into bed. William went, too. He lay in crisp cotton sheets holding the scent of wildflowers as a sea breeze drifted through the window. Life was good. When Mary Jane finished her work she came to bed, and when William reached for her, life was even better.

Early the next morning, Mary Jane turned away from William and slid out of bed. The sky lay low and heavy over the sea, and then clouds tore abroad like pieces of tow and the sun burst out like a bright light. Wind bent trails of smoke from chimneys of houses down the road, scattering them in the air. Mary Jane looked out over the land, the rich soil holding the seeds of life, treasures for an autumn harvest. Robins and blue jays flitted through supple green leaves. Today she didn't have to worry about how to feed her family. The world from this small place seemed perfect.

Mary Jane changed William's house, if not his ways. She threw out his stained pillows filled with dried seaweed and sewed new ones made from blue-striped, white cotton and stuffed them with feathers. She stitched pillowcases and rubbed soap along the seams to keep bugs and dust out. She re-cased his mattress.

While William was outside chopping wood the aroma of cloves, brown sugar, and cinnamon filled the house and wafted out through an open window. Mary Jane had removed the core from some of the apples she had brought with her and stuffed them with raisins. As the pot of apples boiled on William's small stove, their skins grew tender and split. Mary Jane lifted the ladle holding an apple and juice and filled a dish, topping the apple with cow's cream.

William, coming into the house to Mary Jane and stewed apples, knew he was going to like being married.

The Saturday night following their mother's marriage, the children had their baths in a long, wooden tub, its seams caulked the way William waterproofed a boat. They went to bed and settled in sleep.

William lay napping on the daybed while Mary Jane stripped and stepped into the tub, stretching the length. She let her body float and roll. Then she rubbed Castle Suds, a fine quality of hard soap, over her skin.

Before marrying Edward she had asked her mother, "What will I do when Edward reaches for me?"

"Squeeze your eyes tight," she had replied, adding with a self-conscious laugh, "Just your eyes."

The Bible said that Adam knew his wife. She hadn't known Edward, had never seen him without his clothes. He had come to her furtively, gone haphazardly to take his pleasure. It was done always at night, always quiet, before and after the children came. Never once did he know that she felt her body rise in need. As he lay beside her, spent, she felt full and longing for release until her body subsided, its hunger pushed aside by sleep or a crying child. Her longings were kept at bay during the day by routine chores.

Now, after her bath, she heated water on the stove and filled the tub for William, lathering the water into bubbles. She laid out his fresh suit of underwear, woke him, and then shyly asked him to step into the tub. She washed his back, rubbed it, kissed him, and laughed at his embarrassment. She was done with holding back.

That night she kept him wanting more.

"I didn't know women were like this," William said, facing her in the warm light of the kerosene lamp on their nightstand.

She smiled at his words.

"Rest comes easy when there's a rack of woman to cuddle into," William murmured as he pulled Mary Jane against his lean belly. They drifted into sleep.

William sat at the small wooden table looking pleased, as if he was ready to break out in a song or let some mischief off his tongue. The kettle was sighing on the stove and Mary Jane was lifting bowls of porridge from the iron pot, heat flushing her face, her cheeks like ripening apples. She brought the bowls of steaming porridge to the table, topped by stewed apples left over from supper the night before. Rebecca looked up at her mother and across at the strange man. She took a spoonful of brown sugar and dropped it into her bowl, then a dab of butter. It melted, spreading across the porridge like lava. Sugar glistened in a pool of milk rimming the bowl. Rebecca was going to have as much food as she wanted now that her mother was no longer a widow. Her mother didn't even look to caution her. The other children rushed to do the same. Their new stepfather could feed them. Until now he'd had only his own mouth to fill.

"Now," said William. The children stared at him, Edward John's spoon in midair.

"I'll let you in on an auld Irish Grace." He pointed to himself. "Grace be here, and Grace be there." He pointed to the children. His hand swung to circle the table. "And Grace be everywhere." He lifted his empty spoon and said rapidly, "Now let's all take up our forks and eat as fast as we are able."

"Spoons," said Edward John, "not forks."

"I sit corrected," he said, stirring globs of brown sugar through his porridge. "I can see we have spoons. Forks are nowhere in sight."

Mary Jane shook her head, a hint of a smile reaching her wide blue eyes. At that moment she was glad she had married William. Humour was a good way to start a day. It freed the spirit from care, if only for a time.

"I'm a queer stick to have as your father," William said. "But we'll find enough food from the ground and the sea to keep your bellies from growling at me."

Mary Jane hadn't meant to let out a sigh. The lump of fear that had been lodged inside her since Edward's death came loose and let go. The children saw her reach her small, reddened hand to cover William's heavy one. They too felt the tight feeling, held inside them since their father's death, let go. Rebecca wanted to get up from her chair and hug him, but she couldn't get past the truth. He wasn't her father. William was her stepfather. She'd heard bad things about stepfathers. If he wanted to be a real father, he'd have to get his own children.

When Fannie wouldn't eat onions he tapped her on the nose, squinting in her face. "If you wants to grow hairs on your chin you have to eat onions."

She giggled. "I'm a girl. I only want to grow hair on my head."

He squinched his eyes and leaned toward her. "A girl, so you is."

Mary Jane gave William a quick glance. She had made a good choice. Whenever William paid attention to the children her heart warmed and opened toward him more kindly than ever. *The way to a woman's heart is through her children. A woman can love a man who is kind to her children.*

Sometimes, if the children were restless and cross, William, not used to their noise filling his once quiet place, glared at them and muttered, "You'll all be put in the orphanage asylum."

They huddled together as he swung the door back and went out, hurrying to get away to his own space in the shed.

Mary Jane smiled, knowing his bark was worse than his bite.

The next spring she pressed the plain faces of marigolds, the expressive faces of pansies, and the sweet petals of roses between two boards to leave for a few months. They would dry as light as butterfly wings for a collage to be displayed on the wall. She took a small blue vase she had brought with her and filled it with a posy of everlasting flowers for William's shabby table.

When William and Mary Jane's first child was on the way, Mary Jane opened her handkerchief holding the seeds she'd brought with her and planted them in the garden beside the house and alongside her apple sapling and William's crabapple trees. She smiled. Who would think that brown seeds pushed into the dark earth would rise into a green tree that would sprout white apples, its sweet flesh as white as a full moon?

"I thought me brother had no nature," Joe told Mary Jane after Elizabeth was born. When Jamie was born he said the same thing.

William had stared in wonder when Mary Jane gave birth to Elizabeth and again when Jamie was born. "I had a hand in their makin'. Fancy that," he told Mary Jane.

She smiled. "Children are the fruit of our lives."

He gave her a rascally grin. "Just be thankful they're not vegetables."

The young children took Mary Jane's mind off Rebecca, who had left home to marry Matthew Greenslade. Edward John and Fannie didn't take to their younger half-brother and half-sister. They often taunted her.

"We're our mother's first children," Fannie said. "You don't belong to us."

Elizabeth gave her a defiant look. "Me and Jamie's our pappa's only children, so there. You don't belong to our father." She stuck out her tongue and ran across the field.

Elizabeth often sat on her father's knee, the rockers on the chair creaking on the pine floor, while fire crackled in the small kitchen stove and sunlight beamed in through the window. "You almost didn't get born," her father said. "I was a bachelor. A deep-dyed one, some would say. If it hadn't been for the widda, Mary Jane, I wouldn't've had a woman and the joy of me own two youngsters."

Sometimes he wheeled Elizabeth and Jamie in his wheelbarrow around the yard shouting and laughing until night fell.

"Why does the moon grow so big when it's comin' over the hills?" Elizabeth asked her father.

He always had quick answers. "The sky's so big the moon looks small. The hills's so small the moon looks big."

Elizabeth played behind the large wooden chair her father sat in when her mother had the rocker. She ran her finger up her father's legs when he was asleep, startling him awake to utter, "Ump, ump. There must be a mouse about."

Jamie toddled toward him raising his arms and throwing his head back in glee.

William's house was no longer an abode for a bachelor. It now held the heart of a family.

7

One summer day Mary Jane lifted her head from where she stood leaning in over the washtub scrubbing William's overalls over the roped glass board. There were shouts of delight from children playing on the beach whenever they discovered a piece of coloured glass among sea urchins and starfish. She straightened her back, lifting a hand with drifts of soapy water, and pushed back a loose strand of hair.

"Children are collectors," Mary Jane said. "Their work is as important to them as ours is to us."

"Until they come looking for somethin' to eat," William grumbled.

"They never for a moment think of growing up and becoming us," Mary Jane replied. "To them we work too hard and have nothing to look forward to. Some of them won't grow up, or if they do they won't live a long life." She was thinking of Rebecca, who had grown up and married Matthew Greenslade, only to die a year later in childbirth. Mary Jane had hidden her sorrow deep inside her while she cared for her other children. She couldn't unburden herself to William. He would never understand the loss of a child.

She turned, startled at the sound of a scream, then caught her breath in relief at seeing Elizabeth and Jamie chasing each other on the beach. Elizabeth had been mopish after her friend Maggie Taylor was sent away to Bareneed. Distance and time had eased the loss. She had settled down with other friends: Olivia, Emily, and Laura.

Gina, Olivia's younger half-sister, usually joined the children on the beach. Today it was her turn to fill the water barrel. She had hurried along swinging her hoop and buckets on the way to the well under the hill. On bright days sunlight showed her face leaning in, her image fluctuating as she dropped the empty bucket down, settling whole as she drew the bucket of water back up. She always filled her buckets to the brim to lessen her trips. This time, as her young arms strained to lift the bucket over the lip of the well, it tipped and water splashed over the ground. She leaned to lower her second bucket into the well and slipped on wet grass. She had been warned that a water sprite was in the ocean waiting to take small children, never that there was one in the well waiting to cover her mouth with a cold, wet hand.

Down she went, head over heels, gulping moist air as her fingers spread out, her hands reaching to grasp the slimy, slippery rocks with wood lice clinging to them. Her fingers slipped past them and her head went under water, cold, stinging, and stunning, breaking around her head.

Johanna, Gina's mother, hadn't paid attention to the scream. "What's taking that girl so long with the water?" she muttered as she wiped her hands on her apron. "Gone off, she is, then, and I kept idle waitin'. I've a mind to whip her behind." She hurried outside and down toward the well.

The squall of cries coming from the direction of the well stopped everyone within earshot. The mother making her children's beds, the woman with her hands in a pan of dough, the children on the beach, and a fisherman mending nets on a grassy knob near the beach all heard the cries of anguish and rushed to Johanna pointing down the well.

Only the fisherman had the presence of mind to pull Johanna away and look down to see Gina curled under water, her eyes in a blank stare.

"Sweet, modest, and such a dear smile." That was said at the wake.

"It's such a pity she can't hear you," Johanna said, her eyes puffed and red.

Elizabeth couldn't talk to Olivia about what had happened. At night she lay on the floor by the stove's chimney hole and listened to her mother and Aunt Caroline below. They were loose in their talk when the children were gone to bed. Asleep, they thought. They were saying something about Gina's father, who was Olivia's stepfather, something that made no sense. Her mother and aunt were having what Reverend Petten might call unrestrained gossip, a sin in God's ear. She tried to forget what she'd heard and hadn't understood.

Elizabeth dreamed about Gina, dreamed she was looking down into the well where the little girl had fallen. She saw the reflection of her own shocked face distorted by the water the child was kicking to find a footing. "Catch hold of the bucket and I'll haul you up," she called. Then everything went quiet. Someone touched Elizabeth's back. She turned to see Maggie. "You can't save Gina," she said. "God is taking care of her forevermore."

She woke thinking of her friend gone away. One day she would see Maggie Taylor again. She was sure of it.

Elizabeth didn't want to look at Gina in her coffin, but her father urged her on. "It'll teach you to have an eye. Death lurks in the strangest places, not always on the sea."

She crept forward and gazed on the marble face, its domed lids forever hiding big blue eyes, the colour of marsh irises. The mouth was frozen in an expression Elizabeth had never seen. She let out a gasp and drew back. The gritty scent of death, dark and dense, drew the air out of her nostrils and she felt herself falling. Her father caught her as she fainted.

The next morning, Elizabeth and Jamie turned their spoons over and over in their bowls of porridge as if they had lost their appetite. Mary Jane watched them, sorry for children to be pressed hard by the death of another child.

"If I die, don't put me out in the ground for worms to get me body," Elizabeth said, her lips trembling.

"No, we'll pickle you and keep you in a pork barrel," her father joked. Then he looked at the other children. "That goes for you, too."

Mary Jane hastened to tell the children, "Your father is being his foolish self."

William took a slurp from his cup of tea and set it back down in its saucer. He gave the children a serious look. "Now you've seen that life is not forever. You got to do everything you can to keep it as long as you can." He gazed out over the ocean. "Neither the sea nor the land is ever satisfied."

"I know that," Mary Jane said, her face solemn. "Neither the sea nor the earth gets enough."

After Gina's drowning, the children on the beach became more aware that if calm water in a well can kill, then ocean waves are to be feared even more. They didn't want to end up like Gina, cold as a beach rock in winter and buried in a grave forever.

The waft of fresh bread drew the children up from the beach to Mary Jane's house. They pressed in against the table eyeing steaming loaves of bread. Mary Jane carefully cut into the crust of one loaf and slipped the sharp knife in a slow, gentle thrust through the soft belly. The children, their eyes still etched in sorrow, wet their lips and held out their hands, the scent of salt water on them. Mary Jane spread molasses over each slice. It ran over the hot bread, and the children caught it with their tongues before it could spill over the edges.

"Aunt Mary Jane, you makes the best slice of lassy loaf," Olivia said, licking the sweet dark traces of molasses from her lips. "Maggie and Gina used to think that, too."

Mary Jane smiled. *That girl is as sweet as molasses and soft as butter on a warm day.* She had watched Jabe, Olivia's stepfather, at the funeral, silent and apart. *There's something about him . . . something unpleasant . . . something worse.*

After the girls left her house, skipping and hopping back down to the beach, Mary Jane murmured to William, "They're all part of this place, part of each other, and the same story through near and distant relatives. Some day each of them will go apart from each other."

William nodded. "Like Maggie. The poor mite."

"Yes," said Mary Jane, her look distant. "They'll all come back into the story, all except Gina."

Laura, Olivia's younger cousin, scuffed along the path down to the beach in Gina's shoes, a rag in each toe so they would fit. Elizabeth was emptying sand from her shoe when Laura sat down beside her. She reached out and took Elizabeth's hand.

Elizabeth smiled when she asked, "Do you think Gina minds me havin' her shoes?"

Elizabeth shook her head. "For sure she don't. In heaven she'll have new ones."

Laura let out a sigh of relief. Her thin face relaxed, but her big blue eyes kept their strained, empty look. It would be a long time before anyone would learn part of her story—never all of it.

Jamie loved the sea, the way it was always changing, alive with seething emotions that drew his eyes to its many faces, its sun-dappled look one day and its icy dark stare the next. Spring brought ice pans covering the face of the bay. Jamie had learned how to spring away from a wavering thin ice cake to the safety of a large, steadier one.

Joe watched his nephew's daring behaviour and called as Jamie jumped ashore and ran up the lane, "You're at it ag'in, you young rascal, jumping ice pans."

"Don't be doin' it. It's dangerous," Caroline added as she stood on the door stoop.

"I'm practising for a berth on a sealer."

"'Tis a long time before you get on a ship. You're but an alder shoot, and it's hardship enough on the sealing ships," Joe called.

Jamie shrugged. "I don't mind. Me cousins will get me a berth some day."

Joe shook his head. "It won't be your father, fer sure. He knows the danger, and your Uncle Johnny knows it for sure. Johnny's got a game leg because of the sea. He can't walk as far as the smoke from the chimney."

Jamie shrugged. "That's far on a windy day when the wind's in its favour."

"I s'pose it is, then." A sad look crossed his face. "Johnny can't walk no matter how much wind is behind him."

"How did Johnny get that way?" Mary Jane asked William one night as they lay in bed. William stirred beside her and turned his back, not wanting her to know his part in it. "Johnny don't want anyone to speak about that terrible time," he said, his voice wobbly.

Mary Jane reached her hand to the small of his back. A tremor went through it. She understood. When people talk about a tragedy they want to forget, it becomes part of a new day, a day that needs to make its own memories. Her memory of Edward's death and her sorrow over her daughter's passing surfaced. She tossed and turned, trying to push away thoughts she couldn't dislodge. Finally she drifted into sleep and woke the next morning to the sounds of the children calling to each other. She promised herself she wouldn't think about things she couldn't change.

Jamie had watched his father trap eels in Paddy's Pond. He lifted a twig basket from the cool shade of the pond's lily pads and overhanging greenery, joyful as he felt the weight of the basket, and eyed an eel stretching languidly. William told Jamie, "The eel slithers through warm water, always exploring. Then one day it sees a contraption made from rope and twigs. Its tongue reaches out and its body follows. It slides inside and curls as if asleep, not knowin' that its weight has pulled the opening shut. It's caught. There's all kinds of traps in the world for all creatures." He looked toward the bay.

William turned back, opened the trap, and grabbed the undulating eel. He banged it against a rock, killing it. Then he rolled it in the sand so it wouldn't be too slippery to skin.

Jamie tried to keep his father's pace as he hurried up from the pond to the shed. He squeezed his eyes shut as William lifted the eel up by the tail, cut the skin around the body, and pulled it over the head. The fins went with it. Jamie followed his father to the house and inside the kitchen, where William sliced the eel in two parts. He placed the pieces in the pot and covered them with cold water mixed with milk, salt, pepper, and a teaspoon of vinegar. While the pot boiled he sang,

"Summer is a prosperous time,
Full of food on which to dine,
Paddy's eels, the finest kind."

Jamie showed more interest in fashioning wooden boats from raw wood than in catching eels. Like his father, he had a natural hand for carving models for boats. He had nailed several half-models to the porch wall. When Jamie was small William had taught him how to shape and plane them smooth. Some day Jamie hoped to fashion a boat after his models, a boat with cod pounds. He planned on catching so much fish the pound hatches would barely hold down each load.

* * * * *

"The beach is livid with caplin," William called one late June morning as he sat repairing a cast net with needle and twine.

"Alive," Mary Jane answered back.

"No, livid," William insisted. "If you were trampled over, you'd be livid, too."

Elizabeth ran toward the beach, her eyes wide with excitement. She watched her father's arm lift and the balls of his seine catch sunlight as the casting net swung out over a black cloud. William dropped the load of flickering fish on the beach and Mary Jane slipped a bucket under the swarm of silver-belly caplin, and then another: two buckets of caplin to salt for the winter. William drew in another net full of fish to fertilize Mary Jane's kitchen garden.

Elizabeth, her bare legs spattered with spawn clinging to her legs like wet cornmeal, reached to grab a caplin swimming ashore. She slipped and fell face down in the shallow water. She stood up, spitting out salt water and spawn. Her mother grabbed her hand and took her up the path beside Paddy's Pond, where she drew a bucket of fresh water and threw it over her.

Elizabeth's dark hair matted on her head as water streamed down, her blue dress clinging to sun-browned legs.

William glanced their way as he passed them with a pan of caplin to be fried for supper. "Ah, you've been baptized, me maid," he called, never thinking that one day the word would take on new meaning for Elizabeth.

Elizabeth sat at the table and unzipped the fried caplin, parting its sides and flicking the wispy backbone into a dish. She remembered how Maggie had loved to wade into the water and squeal as she tried to hold a writhing caplin in her hand. She wondered how she was doing and when she'd be back.

8

Jamie got braver in jumping spring ice as the years went by. He and his cousin Noah played games of hop and rock, dipping the pans, their blue shadows riffling as the pans flopped water under their feet. When Jamie lost his balance and fell in, Noah helped him back up onto a pan. He lay there shivering and spitting out briny water. They were done for the day.

"Get on in here, you stun mortals," Mary Jane called as they hurried up the path. "You'll drown yourselves for fun, and who'll pay in grief and misery? Not you! You'll be dead. It'll be those left behind. That's who!"

William scowled as the boys dried themselves by the fire. "I tell you now, lads. Don't be goin' on the ice. There's cracked and broken pans everywhere, and snow fluffed over a pan like a shadow, making the pan look bigger. You step on the snow and you'll disappear. You won't even find the bottom of the ocean for your bed."

Noah shrugged. "All the young fellars jumped pans in your day, the same as now."

"You're right, for sure," William said. "Even the young maids had a turn. Becky, our older sister, tried to follow Joe and me one mornin'. She took a careful step on one ice pan to straddle the bigger one we were on. We jumped up and down making our end of the pan flop under water. We laughed at her screams but cried when she lost her balance. We managed to pull her out from under the ice. It was a close call. Mam scolded us: 'I'd kill you all if you went on the ice and got drowned or lost.' She burst out laughing at her silly words. Then she began to cry."

William always gave Jamie a dark look when he asked him about Johnny.

Now Elizabeth turned from the pan of dishes she was washing and asked, "What made Uncle Johnny blind and cripple?"

William looked weary, his voice strained. "It was a bad winter and when it was dyin' everyone was stretching food, makin' do. Cellars and pantries were nigh bare. People spared the soft carrots, wrinkled turnips, and hairy, white, grainted fingers of parsnips. Salted fish and eels were all eaten. Once the vegetables were gone, doughboys with molasses or jam was a standard meal. Then jam and molasses got scarce and the flour barrel was showin' its bottom. On times a hen dropped a surprise—an egg for breakfast, just to save itself from being dinner.

"Far in the distant offshore, a light shadow could be seen. Ice was comin', hopefully bearin' the gift of seals. The smell of fresh meat was only a memory for many households. Now there was a chance of rich meat to nourish bodies weakened during the long winter months.

"All along the shore people kept watch for a seal easy to capture. Every day Pappa and Uncle Edward squinted against the strong light of the sun on ice hopin' to catch a glimpse of a dark spot out on the floes. Mam told me about the morning of the misadventure, how she was turnin' over her bedroom mattress and fluffin' it when a feather escaped and winged through the air toward the window. She turned and caught sight of a dark spot far out among rafters of ice. The ice had been driven by the wind into layers pinnin' each other tight as far as the eye could see."

William lit his pipe, took a draw, and went on. "Mam must have thought about the seal flippers she'd be tastin' if that seal was in her pantry. She knew that Pappa would have been off with his blunderbuss if he and Joe and meself hadn't gone to cut wood."

William pulled in a heavy breath. "One time after me and Joe brought home a seal, I punched Johnny in the shoulder and taunted him: 'Not man enough, you're not, to bring home a seal. You're a boy, sure.'

"Johnny turned away. He wasn't one wantin' to go far on the ice. He didn't have the sea legs for it, and here I was ragging him. He was thirteen when he noticed the seal Mam had seen." William swallowed hard, as if he was choking up. Then he continued. "It wasn't only for our family. There were neighbours who were sparin' and sharin' their bit of flour and jam, tryin' to hold on to their seed potatoes. Johnny had heard Mam murmur that people's blood was thin this time of year. There were many hungry people and few sightings of seals."

William stopped abruptly, as if he couldn't go on. He looked at Elizabeth. "If you want to know what happened you'll have to ask Johnny."

"I will," she said, determined to get the story. She pulled off her apron, grabbed a shawl from a hook on the kitchen door, and ran over to see her uncle.

"I want to know everything about the time you went on the ice to hunt a seal when you were a boy," she said.

Her uncle lifted his head toward her voice. "You do, now, do you?" he said, his voice distant. His blindness was a constant reminder of that time, the terrible moment when he believed he was lost on a drifting ice pan. He turned away from Elizabeth's expectant look and toward the warmth of the stove and huddled, his shoulders trembling as the memory of that time rushed at him, one he had no intention of talking about to anyone.

* * * * *

That morning Johnny had been struck by the beauty of ice pans sparkling like diamonds in a calm sea under a bright sky. Ice had rimed rocks along the shoreline and had raftered against the legs of his father's grey stagehead. A patchwork of pans spread as far as the eye could see, and on one pan in the distance he was sure he could make out a large seal. He'd surprise everyone by bringing home a seal that would make fat morsels for the pot. He got dressed and raced down the stairs. He ran to the shed and grabbed his father's gaff and knife. He figured he could hurry over the packed ice before the pans loosened. He stumbled along the rough terrain sweating with the exertion. He could hear the surging and the cracking and flopping as small pans shifted from shouldering others.

His gaze had been so intent, keeping the seal in view, afraid it would slip into the sea, that he hadn't paid enough attention to ice loosening. Ice pans were widening, blue-hued fingers reaching under bay water. Taking a deep breath, he jumped from one pan to another, ice crunching under his boots, his lips splashed with salt water.

He imagined his father's voice: *Jump leaning forward so you'll fall flat on the pan. A misstep could put you under water. Ice doesn't make for a comforting grip.*

The pans widened and were too far apart for him to jump from one to another. He was on an ice pan like a cloud drifting on an incredibly soft blue sky. He gasped in wonder, forgetting his peril for a moment. He steered the pan with his gaff toward his target, getting close enough to lift the gaff and find the weak spot on the seal's head. Just as he went for his mark the old hood seal reared up and snapped at the gaff, knocking it away from him. He jerked back from the savage jaws. The pan rocked and he flounced into the bone-chilling sea. His mother's voice, with her nightly reminder, rang as clear as a bell: *Kneel and say your prayers before you gets in bed and you'll find strength for the day.*

He said his prayers, begging for strength as shock waves bit into his skin, knifing every bone in his body. His arms and legs grew numb as he willed himself back up on the flopping ice pan. He curled around himself, quaking with cold and the fear he'd drift into the wide mouth of the sea and be lost. He remembered feeling a hot sting in his legs before he lost consciousness. The rest of his story came from a man on Bell Island, a seven-mile distance from Foxtrap.

Caleb Taylor was always on the lookout for a seal. He'd get up and scan the ice, though he couldn't see far on account of weak eyes. He said, "I think there's a seal out there this mornin', Maud, me maid." He hurried into his warm clothes and reached for his gun leaning against the wall in the back porch, always ready should he need it. Anyone else knew well enough not to touch it.

Maud told people how she would never forget the sight of her husband hurrying down the path to the beach and the excitement she felt as he aimed. She watched as his finger bent around the trigger and he fired. She heard a scream and she couldn't remember later if it had been hers or Caleb's. She ran outside and down to the beach. "What have you done?" she asked in a strangled voice.

He dropped the gun and fell to his knees, his hands over his face. "I think I shot someone."

"A boy, Caleb. You shot a boy. I saw him rise up his arms after you fired. Your sight's not the best."

Caleb was already hurrying toward his punt. He quickly pushed it out through sloppy ice pans and jumped aboard. Johnny had been shot and knocked into the water. Caleb recognized him as a Maley boy. He dragged him into his boat and sculled back to his house where Maud waited. She skinned Johnny of his wet clothes, dried him, and dressed his wounded legs. Then she wrapped him like a papoose in warm blankets and held him while she lifted a cup of tea laced with brandy to his blue lips.

It was a nettlesome night for the community of Foxtrap. Everyone looked into the dark night wondering where the young boy was. Martha went into the room Johnny shared with William and said the prayers Johnny would have said before getting into bed. She added a prayer for Johnny's safe return. From under his bedcovers William added a weak amen.

Caleb brought Johnny home to Martha and James a day later. He was full of regrets, saying over and over how sorry he was for mistaking the lad for a seal. "The young fellar's not the best," he said, his eyes watering. "He was near gone when I got him."

Both legs were swollen where the shot had broken the skin and gone into tissue and muscle. Martha gathered him to her, her hand going to his forehead. "Sure his fever is high and he's shaking terribly."

Johnny heard his mother's voice one morning. He stirred in the bed. "Mam, it's been a long night. Why isn't it day yet?"

She couldn't answer.

"Mam!"

She swallowed hard. "It *is* daytime, Johnny."

He reached a small white hand up to his eyes.

"We'll wait, Johnny," she said in a soothing voice. "You've had a bad sickness."

He was not only blind from a fever. He was crippled, his legs useless from the shot. He couldn't even hobble with a stick.

"He'll be someone's care all the rest of his born days," Martha said sadly.

Not once did she berate William for tormenting his brother. She always said that a person's conscience is his accuser.

When Martha died and Joe married Caroline Taylor, a caring woman, Johnny was taken to the new house they built across the path from the family orchard. Caroline took good care of Johnny, keeping him neat as a pin. He huddled beside the Niagara stove on a little stool, as if the chill that had entered his veins like ice pellets while he was on the ice pan was still there. The stove kept him warm on the coldest day, his legs in long stockings Caroline had knitted for him.

"Bogey-warped is what he is," Joe said. "I'd make him a chair with wheels if he'd come outside."

One day, after Jamie came home from seeing Johnny, William smacked him on the back and told him. "Johnny is a bachelor who got no use out of his God-given gift. Don't let that happen to you. I almost did."

"For sure I won't," Jamie answered, a determined look in his eyes.

part three

9

MAGGIE TAYLOR LIVED her life somewhat easy in a household uncluttered by other children. She quieted her longings to go home by filling her days wandering over the hills and along the beach when she wasn't helping her aunt with chores. Now and again she was caught by one of her aunt's bad moods. One morning she was stirring the porridge. Her mind wandered and she stopped for a moment. She hadn't noticed her aunt's vexed look. "Maggie!" The voice was harsh. "I didn't give you room and board for holding the family to hunger."

Maggie dropped the spoon and it slipped beneath the gummy porridge in the pot. She wished more than ever that she could be home with her father.

"Come on, me maid," her uncle said. "Your lip is out far enough for someone to sit on."

She smiled at her uncle and forgave her aunt, knowing it wasn't her daily nature to scold.

One morning her aunt came up to the garden where Maggie was picking dandelion leaves for the pot. She looked up and her aunt said, "My news won't get any better by not tellin' it today. Your Aunt Liddie in Middle Bight alongside Foxtrap wants you."

Maggie's heart lurched. "She didn't want me before."

"She wants you now, then. She's been sick since her latest child. Her older girls have gone and gotten themselves married."

Maggie frowned. "So that's it."

"I'm sendin' you to tend on her only because she's got half a dozen youngsters she can't care for now that she's in bed with a milk leg. She was in a bad way with hardly a chance of living. She's improved some, but with her husband needin' to be plantin' the ground and gettin' his punt and trawls ready for fishing, help is needed. You won't have time for everything. She's not fussy. Sling a wet face cloth over the youngsters' faces once in a while and make a batch of bread each day. She'll thank you for it."

Maggie imagined a milk leg as blotchy white, full like a cow's udder. "How will she get rid of the milk in her leg?" she asked.

"Bedrest," Louise answered. "Milk leg is an infection in a vein that Liddie will recover from with rest and patience."

She patted Maggie's hand. "You'll be closer to home."

Her face brightened. "I will." Then her eyes clouded. Her father wouldn't be there.

Nights later, she dreamed about her stepmother. A rough hand took hers, squeezed it tight enough to hurt. "Go on, now," her stepmother said. "Get your feet into the tub. Stop shivering like someone in the fits. Cold water is good for you. . . . So you want that last piece of bread, do you? Well, you haven't earned it, climbin' around the beach all day."

One bright summer morning a skiff sailed into Bareneed. Its owner, William Kennedy from Hibb's Cove, tied up at the wharf and hurried up the path to Henry Batten's house. When he left Maggie was with him, waving goodbye. She lifted her sleeve to wipe copious tears. Her aunt and uncle had been good to her in their own way. She wondered if anyone would be as good to her again.

After they left the boat tied to Foxtrap wharf, William, his round, whiskered face breaking into a smile, told Maggie he was off to visit some relatives before he filled his boat with firewood. "There's already someone on his way to take you to your destination," he assured her.

She wasn't waiting long before the driver of a horse and wagon drew up beside her. The stranger lifted his hat, showing a dark-looking face. Dark like someone from the Labrador, her aunt would say. Maggie felt her heart jump when he called, "If you're Maggie Taylor, I'm here to take you to your Aunt Liddie's."

She climbed into the wagon, her lips tight. They bumped over rutted paths with deep potholes as they made their way to her new home, not so far from where she had her first years. Now Foxtrap looked damp and unfriendly, a strange place humped above the sea as if recoiling from its fierce nature. She wanted to hurry away but the wheels of the wagon were grinding on, pebbles flying under the wooden wheels.

When she jumped down from the wagon beside the path leading to her aunt's house she whined, "I don't want to be here."

The driver shook his head. "Hurry on inside, me maid." He clicked his tongue and the horse started to trot away.

She looked around at houses settled against hills and nestled in valleys, a place full of people she once lived near, now strangers, their lives as closed to her as their doors.

The porch door to Liddie's house was flung open, but it wasn't to welcome her. Children burst outside shouting and laughing, caught in a game of lalleck. Aubrey, the children's father, was behind them. He gave Maggie a grateful look when he spied her.

"Come with me," he said.

She followed him into the house and through a hall to a room where a woman lay in bed, a baby beside her.

"My, my," Liddie exclaimed, "the look of you! You're almost fully grown and the face and eyes of Aubrey's sister, who was your mother. She won't be dead as long as you're alive."

"Me mother! You remember her?"

"Indeed I do. We hung around together when we were young. She was a bit older, but that was nothing."

When no one was looking, Maggie went to the mirror in the parlour and looked into it, pretending it was her mother she was looking at. She let the heels of her hands slip under her small chin, her fingers sliding up to cup her face as if it were her mother's. *Sure, you made me very heart, the heart that will always carry you in it. Now all I have to do is look in the mirror to see you.* For the first time since her mother died, she thought of her with a smile.

Liddie was a rough woman with a strong jaw and piercing grey eyes and a tongue not easily bridled. "Pour the children their porridge, not too thick. Allow a share for each. Their stomachs will take more than they need on the say of their eyes. Dress the youngest and rub a washrag over her muns. The older children can dress and wash themselves. The outdoors is where they'll go for the day until their growling bellies brings 'em home."

After Maggie had seen to the children she rushed back to do her aunt's bidding. She placed a dressing on her aunt's leg according to her instructions. She changed the baby, powdered his behind with cornstarch, and dressed him.

Liddie nodded her approval. "You're better than any nursemaid I've heard tell of," she said.

Now and then, as years passed, Maggie thought of Elizabeth and Jamie and the other children, now grown. *They wouldn't know me. We're strangers.* She was surprised one day when Aubrey said, "Your stepmother is gone off with a man twice her age, his boat larger than your father's was. I can't see anything else but that the place is yours."

"Mine! Me own place!" she exclaimed. "I'll be wantin' to go there as soon as Aunt Liddie's on her feet."

"Which will be soon," Liddie said, "though I'll still need help with the children off and on."

Maggie could scarcely swallow the lump in her throat as she hitched a ride on a horse and buggy going that way. She traced her steps to her father's house, feeling a sense of loss and dread. It was a cold house now. It had been a cold house after her father disappeared. A large oval rock lay on the floor by the stove. Her father had heated it for her on cold nights. After he disappeared, it stayed cold. It was too heavy for her to lift to the stove and her stepmother hadn't bothered. She touched familiar things: a rocking horse, a toy boat, and in the cupboard her mother's special cup-and-saucer set. She remembered her mother's worn hands cuffing the cup, her tea a golden brown pond, her soft sighs of satisfaction as she tipped the cup to her lips.

Maggie climbed the stairs to the attic. A bumblebee droned against the dusty window. She wiped the tiny pane, giving her a clear view of the beach, the names of the children who had played there tumbling through her mind. She, and the children she had known, had grown beyond frolicking on the beach. She wondered where they were. She wanted to see Elizabeth but she felt awkward. What would two young women, distanced from their childhood and its interests, have to talk about? She found herself walking on by the homes of the children she had known, on back to Liddie's house.

She had taken her mother's Bible and her cup and saucer. Now she poured a cup of tea just as her mother used to do when she felt unsettled. She lifted the cup to her lips, the image of her face wobbling in its rich sienna depths. Its hot breath swirled up to meet hers. She looked down to the bottom curving around a yellow rose that seemed to float and drift up in a sweet fragrance that reminded her of her mother. Each sip flowed in a whisper over the black and gold filigreed rim. She drank, leaving the yellow rose bone dry.

For the next year she drank from the cup every day. When Bea, one of her cousins, knocked it on the floor and broke it, the look on the little girl's face stopped Maggie from getting angry.

The memory of her mother holding the cup could never fade.

10

Maggie had known that sooner or later she'd bump into Elizabeth Maley, and maybe Olivia and others who had played on the beach. But it was Jamie she saw first. It was the first time she'd laid eyes on him all grown up. He passed her going into Eli Butler's shop. His smoky grey eyes met hers and his strong, firm mouth opened into an easy smile as he stepped back. "You've got the look of the people around here, though I can't place you," he said.

"Jamie?"

"Maggie?"

They laughed in unison and when Maggie pushed open the door he was behind her.

"Now then, aren't you the tall one! I heard you were about, come back from your Uncle Henry's all grown up. Elizabeth wondered on times whether she should go see you. But it was so long ago. . . ."

"A very long time ago," she said. She felt the dread from that time and knew why she had kept her distance. Coming to terms with painful memories overshadowed those happy, carefree times.

"I don't like to think of those times," she said, turning away and looking around the small store. A strong odour from dried fish and oakum, mingling with the smell of a round cheese parcelled in waxed cheesecloth, was overpowering.

The shopkeeper came out of the storage room and called to Jamie. "I heard you're trying to get on a sealing ship."

"I've been wanting to," he said. "Seasoned men get first chance, but my time'll come."

"Don't be in a rush, dear boy. That ocean is not too tame this time of year. Dangerous times, it is, to be on the water, ice like dragons' teeth."

"Never you mind," Jamie said. "There's adventure and I'm wanting that."

Maggie turned from listening to Jamie, her lips tightening against a smile when she heard a customer say, under her breath, "I'm wondering if your wife is about. There's an article I'm keen for. Your wife knows what I mean, if you'll be kind enough to fetch her."

"Indeed, I'll get the wife," the shopkeeper answered, the colour in his florid face deepening.

The customer gave him a quick nod and turned her back to Jamie and Maggie.

Eli Butler's shop in Foxtrap carried almost everything a family could need or want, including a hair tonic peddled by J. J. Gozine, a Jew living on Bell Island. He claimed it could grow hair on a rock, though he hadn't been up to proving it.

Eli also carried *unmentionables* known as "open fireplaces." A lady would come in, look around, and, if there was another customer in the shop, quietly ask for an open fireplace. Eli's wife would reach behind the counter and pick up a box from which she lifted the article. It wouldn't be good for a merchant to be seen holding, in his big hands, underdrawers with a waistband and two legs on a string: open-forked drawers, a wonderful piece of clothing. It meant that a woman could straddle outside and let her water run in a stream discreetly, pick up sticks for a fire, and breastfeed a baby—all at the same time.

The shopkeeper cleared his throat and called, "Chelsea, dear, a young missus is looking for a certain article."

A small woman who was filling a barrel in the storage area hurried out, pulling her shawl tight around her shoulders. She looked around as if to make sure there were no children about.

"Get out of the way, Eli," she said. "I'll handle women's business."

Her husband stayed put and she raised her eyebrows. "Eli!"

He got the message and hurried to other business.

Chelsea shook her head. "As long as women have tongues, men have ears and eyes when it comes to delicate matters."

The woman at the counter made her request in a low voice: "I'll have a pair of fireplaces."

"Sure you will," Chelsea said. "I'll get them." She looked the woman up and down. "A size large, I expect."

Maggie piped up, "I'll have a pair while you're at it—a size small." She gave Jamie a quick look and added, "For me aunt."

When Chelsea was finished with her other customer, Maggie passed her a dollar her uncle had given her when she left Bareneed.

Jamie bought a bag of nails. He lifted an eyebrow as he held the door for Maggie on the way out. "Keeping warm, I suppose," he said, nodding toward the purchase in her basket.

Maggie's words rang in Jamie's ears as they parted. "Now James Maley, I'll be thankin' you to keep your mind on your nails and the wood you're likely to hammer them in."

Jamie wondered why women's underwear were called fireplaces. An open fireplace was for putting a poker in to stir a fire, one that could get quite hot. Underwear was a less suggestive name. He'd like to hear what his father had to say about fireplaces; he wasn't brazen enough to ask.

Jamie told Elizabeth he had met up with Maggie at Eli Butler's shop.

"I'd love to see her," was all Elizabeth got out before Jamie, on impulse, said, "We could have her for supper."

Their mother smiled and raised an eyebrow. "Yes, Jamie, the next time you run into Maggie, ask her to drop by one night for supper."

William was out by the woodpile when Maggie came over the hill a week later. It began to rain and she started running to get shelter. William put out his hand. "Stop yourself there. You're runnin' so fast the freckles's bouncin' off your nose."

Elizabeth stood on the doorstep. She leaned forward, her eyes squinting. "There's a little bit of yourself in there from years back. But the size of you! You're up there like a steeple. Sure, you've changed."

Maggie let out a self-conscious laugh. "So's yourself. I'd pass you as a stranger, I would."

Elizabeth frowned. "All that time you've been gone and not a word."

"You did show up in me thoughts now and then," Maggie said. "I was lookin' forward to gettin' back home."

Elizabeth took her hand. "Is yer on for stayin', then?"

"I'm hopin' to. I'm lookin' after Aunt Liddie's family in the Bight for now, but I want to get back to Pappa's house."

William gave her a quick look but didn't say anything.

Maggie thought there was concern or something else in his look. *He has to know about my stepmother*. She eyed Jamie coming up the path. "Look at Jamie," she said, turning to Elizabeth. "Sure, he's all grown and fine-lookin', to be sure."

William winked at her, thinking, *Before long that boy of mine'll have his feet worn flat goin' to see her.*

At supper Maggie hooked her small finger around one end of the chicken wishbone and Elizabeth hooked hers around the other end.

"Pull when I say. Not before!" William said.

The girls looked at each other and grinned.

"Now," he said and the girls pulled.

The bone snapped, and Maggie rolled her eyes as Elizabeth held up the shortest piece, declaring, "I'll be married first."

Jamie let out a chuckle and Maggie glanced his way.

He faced her, his look purposeful. "I'll be hoping for a berth on a sealing ship this year in the hopes of saving money to get married some day."

"Berth or no berth, who's up to marrying the likes of you?" Elizabeth retorted.

Jamie looked at Maggie and winked. He laughed when she looked away. Jamie loved the look of the girl, her smile, her walk, the way she spoke.

William Maley eyed his two children. He'd soon be without them. He and Mary Jane would be left alone in their house by the apple trees. Elizabeth had already gone for walks with some young gaffers from

Long Pond, bringing a dark cloud to his face. He hoped Jamie would stay close by.

"My son's a fine lad," Mary Jane told Maggie as she lifted a bedsheet and spread it on the clothesline. She squeezed a clothes peg open and pinned it. "Young Jamie is old William on the spot. Sure, you won't likely tell them apart if the old fellar lives long enough and Jamie catches up. He'll be bald like his father's gettin.'"

Not with that thick head of honey-brown hair, Maggie thought as she said goodbye.

She glanced toward the house she once lived in. She didn't know then that her stepmother's son would claim the house, and she wouldn't care. It was no longer a home. It was just a house, its windows a reminder of her stepmother's evil eyes looking out at her.

Never a home after Pappa left, she thought with a shudder. *I'll bide where I am for a while.*

Mary Jane tried to discourage Jamie from making plans to go on a sealing voyage. She told her son, "We've got enough land to plough and enough sea from our door to give us plenty of food."

"As long as it's only us," he answered, "but I'll be having a family to take care of and I need money laid by to build me own house."

His mother tilted her head to one side to look at him. "Maggie is moon-eyed over you. You won't leave to go live away from this place, will you?"

"I'll stay and bring a woman here. I won't go away. I won't," he promised.

That October, Mary Jane noticed that, when Maggie came to gather a basket of apples from the tree, Jamie pretended not to see her wide grin and the perky nose in her brown berry face. She filled her basket and then she stuffed the two big pockets in her dress. She dropped a big penny into Jamie's hand. He held it against his palm, fancying that it was her skin his fingers were touching. She looked at him as she dug her teeth into an apple. Her lips looked soft and moist as her small white teeth closed over a chunk of the apple.

"Off you go," William said. "Let Jamie get about his work."

Maggie gave Jamie a quick look and hurried toward the gate. She turned the block of wood keeping the gate closed. The gate swung open and she pranced up the hill without a backward glance.

"As wild as a loon by the brazen looks of her," William said. "Still, she's restful on the eyes, me son. Sure, she is."

"If by wild you means she skips about showin' a bit of life, that's a good thing. A day's work comes easy to someone with so much life."

The night Jamie left home to walk to Middle Bight, his father called, "Don't give her too many kisses. You'll fry your lips."

The sea strummed the beach, its music drawing Maggie and Jamie together under the moon's silver gaze. They slid down on the warm sand along the shore. By the way Maggie's lips pursed to his, Jamie figured she was ready to be courted.

She pulled away, her eyes holding a distant, tender look. "I never forgot the time on the beach when I laid my shoes on a rock and waded out into the water. Your cousin, Thomas, called me a ragamuffin and ran off with me shoes. You chased him, but not before he threw the shoes into the water. You brought them back dripping wet. I remember you buckling them on my feet."

"I never forgot you," he said softly.

She smiled. "I could never forget *you*."

11

Mary Jane was turning the feather bedding in Jamie's room when she saw her son trudging down the narrow path past the graveyard with its tipsy-turvy headstones. Her heart lurched like a berg turning over in icy waters until she realized that his step was heavy. Jamie had not secured his berth on a sealing vessel. *Please, God, don't let him go to the ice, ever. Save him!* She watched as he picked up an alder branch and pulled it along the pickets of the graveyard fence as if he had nothing else to do, as if he were going nowhere.

Last year Jamie had seen sealers go out the road on their way to meet up with other men going on a sealing vessel. He had come home long-faced.

Mary Jane told him, "Your father makes a bit of money selling eels and frankum to the St. John's crowd. They clamber for the fresh taste of tree gum. It appeals to their palates and sweetens their breath after they've eaten your father's eels. There's all kinds of ways to make money besides seal hunting."

Jamie's face was sullen as he unlatched the door and came inside. He admitted that he had been turned away and sent home. A sealer with no experience had bumped him. "It was likely someone in with the captain," he said, his voice bitter.

He'd get the experienced boys from Foxtrap to speak for him next year. He had several cousins who had gone to the ice. Adrian, a distant cousin, went only once. He didn't get the chance to go again after he'd complained about having to drink rusty tea. Any sealer who complained while on the ship risked losing his share of the voyage. Adrian got his share but not another ticket. Jamie had hoped to get Adrian's ticket. Someone had beaten him to it.

Jamie gave his mother a determined look. "I'm still goin' to the seal hunt the first chance I gets."

Mary Jane didn't look up from where she'd started shining the stovetop. "Mind you don't, now. Grief is already sewn in the linings of more than one heart in this place."

He shook his head. "You wouldn't let the wind blow on me if you could help it. Harm can find a mark anywhere. I'm goin' sealin' as soon as I gets a ticket."

She looked up. "You won't want Maggie handy to you when you comes home stinkin' of seals and blubber. There'll be nothing else to do with your clothes but burn 'em. A good scrubbin' down with steel wool is what you'll need yourself. The merchant will have his money and the rich and fancy ladies of St. John's will have their lips painted from the scented oil of baby seals. They'll have soap for their baths but you'll have little for your toil."

"I'll be goin' yet, and nothin'll stop me," Jamie mumbled.

"I know that, me boy," Mary Jane conceded.

He grinned and threw his arm around her shoulder. "Take heart, Mamma. You won't have to worry about a thing."

Even though he didn't know it, he was right.

* * * * *

Winter overriding spring finally lost its strength and the place opened up to warm days and soft evenings. Spring grass crept up through rich, dark earth in baby green newness. The soft air came alive with the songs of birds flittering among the bushes. Maggie and Jamie spent evenings beside a stream, up from the beach, listening to the tickle of the water over rocks while they made plans. Daydreaming they were, seeing only a rainbow above calm, blue waters of the bay.

Maggie did not tell Jamie about a dream that had repeated itself night after night for a full week. She was lying in bed staring up at the sky, in it a pattern of illuminated stars forming a cross, the width of it angled against the length. One after another the stars fell on her, finding a place all over her body, icy stars imbedding themselves in her skin. The sky went black. She woke shivering, a dread inside her that took a while to be swallowed by sleep.

12

Elizabeth had been delighted to see Maggie all grown up and courting her brother. She was seeing a young man herself, despite her father's disapproval.

After a walk along the beach, Tim kissed Elizabeth at the gate and made a swift departure for fear William would fire a shot above his head and he'd been running for his life.

William stood by the kitchen window and watched his daughter fasten the gate and walk toward the house. "She's only a child," he said, "with not a clue about the wiles of men."

Mary Jane put down her needlework. "She's a woman! She won't learn how to handle men if you don't let her."

"By the time she learns she'll have done things she might not be able to undo," William said. He had tried to scare Elizabeth into staying home. One night he rigged a sheet between the apple trees to make her believe a ghost roamed the place. Another night she came home after her father and mother had gone to bed. Her experience with William's tricks had taught her to be cautious. She crept up the stairs, smiling as she ducked to avoid the bag of nails her father had hung from the ceiling. He could forget it! She was on to him.

"Silly man, you is!" Mary Jane said. "No one in his right mind would hang a bag of nails above the stairs. If Elizabeth bangs in it, all it'll do is wake us up."

"Then we'll know what ungodly hour she comes home," William retorted.

"A little after ten, most times," Mary Jane said.

"He's got the old Irish trait," Mary Jane told Elizabeth after one of his shenanigans. "He seems to forget that Maggie, Jamie's coosie, is much the same age as yourself."

Soon after, Elizabeth told her mother, "Store owner Caleb Butler on Bell Island wants a woman to do light housework and run some errands. I'm eighteen now."

"You're getting out from under your father, that's what you're doing," Mary Jane said.

Elizabeth gave her father an impish look. "You can save your bag of nails for when I haves a man who wants to build me a house. He'll need a few nails to keep the boards together."

"Ump!" William said.

Elizabeth eased out of her family's life by boarding the passenger vessel for Bell Island. Her mother's last words reverberated in her ears as she got off the ferry. "Never give a man more than you're willin' to lose. You could pay for it the rest of your life."

Caleb Taylor had offered Elizabeth a job, though she hadn't known why at the time.

One day she asked Caleb if he ever went seal hunting. A strange look crossed his face. "Agards er me shootin' ere seal, it'll stay in the sea," he said.

Caleb's wife told Elizabeth, "Caleb never picks up a gun, not after what happened."

Caleb came back into the room and she stopped. "What're you two gatchin' about?"

"Maybe the weather!" Elizabeth said quickly.

Caleb's wife kept Elizabeth busy. She was often sent around Bell Island selling chickweed and other vegetables to Jewish merchants and fishermen. In time she drove a horse and carriage carrying passengers and parcels to the ferry. She took pleasure in the sight of the horse's brass-trimmed harness glistening in sunlight. She liked to listen to the tinkling bells around the horse's neck. Clods of dirt flew into the air, leaving splatters on a little girl's fancy dress on one trip and the mother reproached Elizabeth even though it wasn't her fault. Elizabeth passed the child a Newfoundland penny and her eyes lit up.

She never whipped the horse. She touched it lightly and it pulled forward, its hoofs prancing. It knew its route to the boat: a heavy load going down the steep hill, a light load returning, if it was lucky. The uphill climb could tax a horse's strength when the carriage was loaded. One day Elizabeth was taking passengers to the ferry going down the steep incline when the breeching around the horse let go. Elizabeth called, "Whoa!" with a downward snap of the reins. The horse whinnied and came to a halt, its ears twitching against a swarm of flies.

A passenger jumped down and caught the horse's bridle. "It pays to be kind to animals," the man said. "I see that you are. We don't know what could have happened had the horse bolted and dragged the carriage. It may have overturned down this steep hill. You're clear-headed for sure." His eyes lingered on Elizabeth's bright young face.

He was handsome, and a bachelor. Elizabeth knew that much. She wasn't interested. A young Bell Island miner had caught her eye, though there was no chance of a relationship. Nathan Mills was friendly and charming. She noticed how his eyes lit up when another miner engaged him in conversation. She might as well melt into the ground.

One morning Elizabeth drove him to the wharf. He was on his way to Montreal to work on Grand Trunk Railing. They sat waiting for the boat to board passengers.

"You'll find a woman to marry," she told him.

"You won't understand, not ever," he said, getting up and dropping her hand. "I'm leaving for a place where I can live life anonymously. I'm attracted to me own kind."

She'd never known of such a thing and she didn't let his words sink in. She watched him go, lifting her hand to wave and call, "Just be yourself." Then he was gone. She wondered what it would be like to go to Montreal. Nathan had told her that people there lived in buildings that housed apartments, rooms like boxes. Other people lived in single houses that stood in neat rows with smooth roads and green lawns. If she'd gone to Montreal she might have found a job in a store selling clothes that came from Europe. She might have found adventure.

Another miner soon had all of her attention. Jacob Kennedy was a young fisherman who had left Hibb's Cove to mine ore. He had a tall and lean look, his flesh tight and smooth over his bones, not fallen, stretched, and wrinkled like her father's skin. Maybe that was the way her mother had seen her father in his day. She watched Jacob hurry toward her and her heart quickened, a wave rippled through her body from her head to her toes.

The first time Jacob laid eyes on Elizabeth he had just come up from the Bell Island mine. He stared at her abundance of hair, like warm mahogany under firelight. Her laugh pealed out like the strike of a bell in fresh, crisp air. He stopped and took in her length. He smiled. "Usually when I come up out of the mine I get that first glimpse of daylight. The sky opens like a window to heaven. Today that window got a beautiful girl in it."

And I thought Nathan *was charming.*

She crinkled her nose at the rusty scent of the young miner. "You smell like the earth," she said, her voice girlish and playful.

He raised an eyebrow. Then he hurried across the path, stooped, and picked a wild rose from a bush. He crushed it in his hand and crossed the walkway. He placed the petals in Elizabeth's hand. With a wry smile he lifted his hand with the scent of rose petals to her nose. "I suppose that smells better."

Without waiting for her reply he added, "Sometimes a flower needs to be crushed before it can give off a sweet scent. I hope that never happens to you—to us."

"Us?" She tried to hold in a laugh but it burst out. "Mind yourself."

When Maggie and Jamie took William's boat and rowed across to visit Elizabeth, she told them about Jacob and then about Isaac, the handsome son of a Jewish jeweller and his wife. She often went to their home to sell chickweed and other vegetables. Isaac eyed Elizabeth as he rubbed a cloth over a gold ring or gave her a wink as he examined a diamond. He was trying to get between her and Jacob. "I'll have my father's business some day," he told her.

Maggie smiled. "You can't go wrong with marrying a Jew. Jews are related to none other than Jesus. They're God's chosen people. He'll always take care of them."

Jamie, listening to the conversation, asked, "What does that make us Gentiles? Dogs, eh!"

"Shush!" Elizabeth pinched his arm. "You can't be sayin' things."

"God's people, too," Jacob said quietly.

Elizabeth looked toward Jacob and Thomas, another miner, coming over the hill.

Thomas grabbed hold of the conversation. "English people are the lost tribe of Israel. I'd be ashamed of me life to be Irish, like Jacob here."

"There's worse a person could be," Jacob said.

"And what might that be?"

Jacob came close and looked into his face. "Someone who acts like a pig."

Elizabeth pulled Jacob back, giving Thomas a defensive look. "Jacob got the best of everything. He's of Irish and English stock and he got a Jewish name."

"Sure, the name of a man who had a rock for a pillow," Thomas answered. "There's likely nothing else Jewish about him." He sneered. "He's not been cut down there, has he—like Isaac and the other Jews?"

Elizabeth drew back, colour suffusing her face. "How would I know? I've never seen the heels of his socks, let alone anything else."

"You wanted Nathan, didn't you?" Jacob said one day after they'd strolled together along the beach.

"His sense of adventure, not him," she answered.

She forgot everything she liked about Nathan when Jacob lifted her chin and traced his finger over her face. He lowered his lips to hers.

Jacob might be the kind of man who would give more than he would take. She hoped she could give more than she would take.

Late September, Mary Jane lifted her head from a bruised apple tree she was trying to cure with a mixture of wet clay, fresh milk, and cow dung. She hadn't known Elizabeth was coming home and would have never guessed her news.

She stood in front of her mother smiling. "I'm getting married. I'm marryin' Jacob Kennedy, the fellar I brought home in June."

A shadow crossed Mary Jane's face. She sighed. "The house will be empty in no time. Sure, Jamie's that knotted with Maggie from the Bight he spends his time goin' and comin'. He's bent on gettin' his sealer's ticket to make a quick bit of money to be married himself."

Elizabeth patted her mother's cheek. "Don't worry yourself, Mamma. Sure, everyone does the same. You left your mother and went with a man. My half-sisters and half-brother left home."

Mary Jane straightened her brin apron and stood up. "I know. Come on in for a cup of tea and a slice of blueberry cake."

She remembered William's first kiss, how he had pursed his lips in a quick buss, not soft and holding like Edward's. "A man must be taught," she said, "to be the man with whom a woman will find satisfaction." She said this in a quiet, steady voice without turning her head to Elizabeth.

After they had eaten, Mary Jane filled a pan with water, stirring in soap. She rolled the cloth over a plate she was washing. She lifted it to a place on the cupboard and washed a tumbler, letting her hand ease down over it and up and back down in a gentle motion around the base, saying, with a keen eye on Elizabeth, "A woman must find pleasure in helpin' her man toward satisfaction while seekin' her own pleasure and teachin' him how to add to it. When a couple sits down to dinner, both of them leave the table satisfied. It should be the same when they comes together as man and wife. Don't be ashamed of the gift God gives a woman as well as a man."

Elizabeth stared at her mother. She didn't answer but she tried to fasten her mother's words to her mind for when she would need them. She felt their significance in how her marriage to Jacob would be in making two people in love feel loved over and over.

William scuffed across the floor breaking the moment. "Sure, I overheard what you said outdoors. You've gone and got yourself a man to keep. You don't say."

Elizabeth laughed. "I do, then. I had him home once when you were gone to St. John's. He's a miner, sure, workin' on Bell Island. He's from around the bay. Jacob Kennedy, it is."

William's eyes widened. "I know of that crowd. His father was born not far from here. It's a likely mix. You're like your mother, marryin' a Kennedy. Look at the luck she had with that, and the one you're holdin' to marry had his beginning on a cliff."

Elizabeth pinched his cheek. "And survived. Jacob is a kind man."

"The worst of it is that you're marrying a miner," her father continued. "I'll be weary with worry. There's always the chance of the earth founderin'. You never know when a miner is goin' to come home from Bell Island with a part of him blown away—if he comes home. Men are rarin' to be miners until they get the work and then they see how the earth could bury them under a rugged, ribbed roof, or machinery take a part of 'em."

She patted his back. "There you is, Pappa, looking a dragon in the mouth before there's even a dragon."

When Maggie came to see Jamie one day, Elizabeth told her she was going to be living in Hibb's Cove.

"Hibb's Cove!" Maggie exclaimed. "You'll be down over a few hills and around a few turns from Bareneed where I grew up. Sure, it was Jacob's own father who brought me back home in his boat."

Elizabeth smiled. "Edward John, me half-brother, went to Hibb's Cove and brought back Flossie Porter, Jacob's first cousin, and married her. He built her a house and, though the floor wasn't covered, Eli Reid, the fiddle player, and the neighbours come to dance at the weddin'. Their feet beat the clay floor smooth. 'Mats will do for now,' Flossie said, 'but when the fall comes I wants the feel of wood under me feet.'

"'And you'll have wooden floors,' Edward John promised as he sat enjoying a bowl of her mussel chowder. He was as good as his word. Flossie got her wooden floors. She painted them red and laid white hooked mats over them."

Elizabeth let out a contented sigh. "Jacob is a piece of good stock, too. I'll be marrying a miner whose father's a fisherman, somethin' he'd be himself if there was a steady harvest."

"Men finds a way to do what they wants," Maggie said. Her look turned pensive as she thought of Jamie and his strong will to go sealing.

Elizabeth turned to the wedding gown she was sewing. She cut the petersham for the collar and fitted it in place.

Maggie beamed. "The dress'll be a beautiful fit. You've got nothin' for a waist."

Mary Jane laughed. "The old grannies'll be takin' note. Whenever there's a wedding there's as many fingers waitin' to count the months as there's tongues flapping. But never mind." She handed Elizabeth something old, the lace from her christening dress to sew on the bodice of her gown; something borrowed, Gran Martha's handkerchief, one she had mended over and over; and something blue, a blue cord she bought from Simon Swartz, the peddler.

Elizabeth slipped the thick, silk cord through the high neck of her dress and tacked it. Then she stood up holding the gown against her. Sunshine, through the window, spun it into a golden sheen. She swirled it around in front of the mirror. Her eyes shone. "I'm gettin' married."

Elizabeth walked down the aisle of the Church of England on her father's arm to be married to Jacob, amid whispers.

The children who had lived close to the beach were all grown up, far from the fun and mischief of their childhood. Some of them had come to the wedding to watch Elizabeth marry a stranger. "Not from around here," Zachary whispered to Olivia. "She had to pick one from around the bay."

"Anything for a change," Olivia answered lightly.

Zachary's look lingered on Olivia's face. She was the most beautiful girl he had ever seen. He couldn't wait to marry her.

Olivia turned to Laura and remarked that Elizabeth couldn't have caught a more handsome man than Jacob. "Sure, he's so good-looking he'd take the sight out of your eye."

"Handsome is as handsome does," Laura answered.

Maggie turned to Jamie beside her, her own eyes dreamy. "They'll do handsomely together. Nothing to it."

Jacob's head of thick, dark hair was smooth as a duck's back above clear blue eyes. His face had a naturally sculptured altogether look, no part more pronounced than another.

Elizabeth's dark hair rose above her small face in a bouffant cloud. Below it her blue eyes were bright and optimistic, her face open and expressive.

During the ceremony the minister said, "For this reason a man will leave his father and mother . . . forsaking all others. . . ."

In her mind Elizabeth interjected, *I'm the one leaving, forsaking family and friends.*

After the wedding, William looked at Elizabeth. "Jacob's just like a frame, not an ounce of fat. You'll need to get the cookin' pot on boil. You're no more than a rasher of wind yourself." Then he muttered, "I don't want you to leave this place."

She answered lightly, "Pappa, a bird's got to leave the nest to fly."

"You're not a bird. You're me little maid."

She touched him lightly on his sleeve. "A woman. That's what I is."

After the dinner and dance, Elizabeth hurried upstairs and laid aside her wedding gown. She changed into a sensible warm dress, buttoned her gloves, and laced her boots. Then she donned her red merino coat and its matching hat and prepared to go with Jacob to meet his parents. She turned to look across the waters to Bell Island, a place where she'd had her day's work and her night's freedom. She felt a twinge of uncertainty. Until now she had owned herself. From now on she'd be giving herself to a husband and, later, if God willed it, she'd have children. She'd have no time for herself.

You'll have love, the wind whispered against her window.

Love. She smiled. *It is everything.* She touched a wooden ring alongside her gold wedding band. Jacob had given it to her, promising to be as strong as a tree in wind, as sheltering as a house in a storm, and as adventurous as a boat on the sea.

Jamie grinned as he hugged his sister goodbye. "I'll have the loft—two rooms—all to meself."

"Until Maggie takes you over," she teased.

Maggie smiled at Jamie and hugged Elizabeth. "I'm looking forward to it."

Mary Jane could hardly bring her voice to the surface to say goodbye as William outfitted the horse and sleigh and made ready to take the couple to the train station in Manuels. She bent toward her daughter and whispered, "A wonderful thing it is to belong to another person's love, to live in it and create children out of it. But be careful not to fall in the family way too soon. Give yourselves a chance to know each other and, if you can't bide the place and Jacob is not who you thinks he is, come on home to your own bed."

Elizabeth's eyebrows furrowed. "Now, Mamma, don't be talking that way." Her lips brushed her mother's cheek. Then she climbed up to the seat of the sleigh.

Jacob hugged Mary Jane, shook William's hand, and then hurried up beside Elizabeth. He lifted his hat to Jamie and Maggie.

"It's snowing in fits," William said, "but the train can cut through anything." He lifted Elizabeth's hope chest, packed with her personal belongings, and stowed it.

William drew back quickly as the cacophony of gunshots resounded through the frosty air. The acrid smell of smoke and gunpowder spread. A pause and more shots reverberated through the night.

Mary Jane grabbed William's arm, exclaiming, "Using good powder to startle people. The fools!"

Elizabeth settled back against the seat and smiled at Jacob. Sometimes she had eyed him from her boarding house coming along the road to see her. She had pushed up a window and called to him. She got his answering wave. Her body had stirred and quickened, her flesh rippling with desire. The first time it had happened she knew why a man and a woman would want to belong to each other.

At the train station William lifted his hand to wave goodbye. It dropped to his side like a weight. The family home he'd built had lost a side. It had been taken by a good-looking young miner. A dark cloud descended and a chill spread through his bones as the train pulled out of the station. *Who will I lose next?*

As the train hurled itself along the tracks going around mountains and down valleys, Elizabeth thought of her mother's promise to give her—come spring—a sapling from her apple tree and a root of boy's love to be set in the soil of her new gardens. She visualized the boy's love growing, wind stirring its scent while she sat outside her home with Jacob. She thought of her parents' marriage as one of the finest kind, a kind to be emulated by her and Jacob, their children caught up in their humour. When she was six and had swallowed an apple seed she had lifted an anxious face to her father and asked, "Will it grow a tree in my belly?"

Her father had given her a serious look. "That depends."

"On what!"

"On how much earth you ate with it. It needs soil to grow."

He chuckled, and her face relaxed. Then they both burst into laughter.

After the train had long gone, taking Elizabeth, William stood on his doorstep looking across the waters separating him and his little girl. "I hope Jacob can make you laugh at your own words," he whispered into the cold air, "and that he can spell you a happy long life."

That night Mary Jane lay in bed, her loosened grey hair, still soft and silky, spread across her pillow. She drifted to the time when she had married Edward Kennedy. Now her daughter was gone off, married to a Kennedy, relating them on both sides.

She kept busy the day after Elizabeth left for Hibb's Cove. She had to, telling herself, *It's the way of the world, children leavin' home.* She straightened up from the mattress she was fluffing in Elizabeth's room and glanced out the bedroom window. Jamie and Maggie were coming down the hill holding hands and swinging their arms. They tripped over lumps of snow in their path and pitched forward. They threw their heads back and laughed merrily. Mary Jane could see that they were at ease with each other. She had been like that with Edward. That kind of completion was so strong and yet so fragile. *They're full of life now, bless 'em. They never think of the hourglass drainin', time peterin', every day spent meanin' fewer days left.*

"Smile at each other and laugh often," Mary Jane told them when they came inside.

She had better get to work and bleach some flour and sugar bags for pillowcases and bedsheets for Maggie, as she had done for Elizabeth. She would embroider flowers on the pillowcases so that when winter winds howled and the land holding flower seeds lay in storage, the bright flowers would lie under the young lovers' heads, catching their eyes now and then. She planned to embroider Maggie and Jamie's names on the wide hem of the pillowcases. She knew Maggie's young face would flush to know her mother-in-law could foresee her and Jamie between the sheets, loving each other, holding each other in sleep. It was what Mary Jane cherished most about her and William's time together. She had been amused to overhear William tell Jamie, "Now son, the main difference between men and women is that they have bumps in different places. How these bumps are handled will make all the difference in how you get on in married life."

Jamie had looked at him, his face reddening with embarrassment.

Mary Jane shook her head against her musings and went downstairs. She touched Jamie's face on a snapshot he had taken in St. John's. He told her about the large box on a tripod and how the photographer had poked his head under a black cloth. He saw a flash like lightning from the black, hooded camera and then the photographer pulled back from under the cloth and smiled. "You've been snapped," he said. "Come back for the photograph next month."

Mary Jane murmured, "A flash of light and there you were, your likeness set. Something to behold. When you're in your grave you'll still be there, the young face and eyes of you."

Jamie had come inside in time to hear her add, "You'll never grow old." He gave her a startled look.

She shook her head. "Oh—my! I mean on the snap. It will always keep you this age."

13

The train rumbled, jerked, lapped the miles to Brigus Junction while Elizabeth lay with her head on Jacob's shoulder. In her mind she composed the notice of their marriage for the social events of the Southern Shore newspaper: *Jacob Taylor Kennedy (of William James Kennedy and Sarah Ann nee Taylor) married Elizabeth Emma Maley (of William James Maley and Mary Jane Maley née Bussey, formerly Kennedy) Jan. 3, 1912 at Foxtrap. The Right Reverend E. Petten performed the wedding ceremony. . . .* She would post it for the next week's news.

Elizabeth fell asleep and woke to the lonely *whoo-ooo* of the train as it rushed toward the station, and then rough braking as the locomotive screeched and slowed. It pulled into Brigus Junction and stopped. She quickly came to life as cold air entered the coach. She pulled her heavy woollen coat around her against a cold wind drifting through the train car. She slipped her hand inside Jacob's arm and he squeezed it tight. He lifted an eyebrow. "Happy?" he asked.

She nodded and he reached to cup her other hand lying in a fist on her lap.

"For better or worse," he said. "I'm hoping for better. By being together we'll half whatever worse comes."

She and Jacob stepped down from the train to a waiting horse and sleigh. The driver from Port de Grave greeted them and helped lift their luggage onto the sleigh before clearing a seat behind him for the couple to sit. He drove down through the Dock, over Bareneed Hills, down Happy Jack's Hill.

Port de Grave stretched above the sea like a knuckled and bent finger. Along the finger stood houses, cottages, and fishing stages. The sleigh bumped over hardened snow along the rugged edges of the jagged highland. Below them the sea thrashed about, flinging itself against the cliffs, white spray rising and falling.

They rode past Pond Road to the cove and up under a fish flake roofing the road halfway up Porter's Hill. Rails bordering the edge of cliffs stood askew like a drunken man. The horse's nostrils flared, its hot breath steaming against cold air as it climbed the steep hill to Cliff Path. While it stopped for a spell Elizabeth refrained from looking to the edge of the road, for fear the skidding sleigh would slide over and down into the dark sea below. The driver urged the horse across and down Cliff Path and along the foot, then up Kennedy's Hill beside Jacob's home. The sea breathed through the air an exhalation of a dark ghost whose heavy, salty breath had journeyed through eons from the mouth of the earth's beginning. It touched Elizabeth's face, its mystery enveloping her.

Fleeces of snow stretched across headlands rising above the cove like colossal beasts, their rugged backs holding ochre-red sheds, barns, square and rectangled yellow and white houses, fish flakes, and outhouses looking as if they could easily be lifted away by a strong wind.

Fishing stages jutted out from small beaches necklining the cove like the rugged throat of an old man.

"This place in winter is not the best," Jacob said with a warning glance. "But you'll adjust. We'll spend the night at Ma's and then tomorrow we'll start gettin' the house in order."

Elizabeth's mind dragged details to the surface. Jacob had told her about Sarah Ann, born of Jacob Taylor in Ship Cove on December 28, 1853 . . . married William Kennedy on January 23, 1879, at St. Luke's Church when she was twenty-six . . . could read and write . . . a great hand with the needle and fancy work, especially in her after years . . . a strict Church of England member . . . tall and a fair size, though not fat . . . long legs which came in handy.

At the sound of sleigh bells Sarah Ann opened the front door. She took in the length and breadth of Elizabeth as she alighted. "Goodness!" she said. "Will she be able to work?"

On the train Jacob had remarked that a fisherman's wife needed legs on her like longers to have the strength to climb the steep Kennedy Hill from the stage, and strong arms to bear the handles of a wheelbarrow holding soaking wet fish.

Now Elizabeth cringed at her mother-in-law's words. *They think their sons have to answer to them on the qualifications of a wife.*

"I can do whatever Jacob requires of me," Elizabeth answered primly. She followed the woman inside. Then a bit of her father crept to the surface and she added, "As long as he does what I require of him."

Jacob's brother, George, leaned back on his chair, pulling on his braces. They snapped and he came forward, his face lifted. "Who's you, a'tall?"

Elizabeth answered, "I thought you knew me. I'm Jake's wife."

"I know of you, me maid," George said. "Come on in and bide."

A young woman leaning on the baluster of the stairs stepped away and came through the hall.

"'Tis Vine, there," William called. "She's George's woman."

Alvina was short and soft-faced with an easy smile, though a sour look crossed her face at the sight of a slim bride. "Not hardy, that one!" she said under her breath.

"Have a bite," Sarah Ann urged. "There's pea soup and doughboys on the stove and none the better for having to wait."

* * * * *

That night Elizabeth held Jacob's hand as they climbed the stairs to their bedroom. She was unsure how she would handle seeing Jacob in nothing but his small clothes. Perhaps she'd put out the lamplight before then. She moved to turn down the counterpane and flannelette sheets. She drew back when she saw an apple-pie bed. Someone had made the bed with the sheets folded short so that it was impossible to stretch the length of the mattress.

"At least there's no rice or pickled fish," Jacob said just before he saw movement at the foot of the bed.

Elizabeth screamed as a mouse scurried to the floor. Jacob's shoe dropped the fleeing mouse dead in its tracks.

"Wait until I get the chance," Jacob promised. "I'll give George a bedtime story."

George, in the next room, wrapped his arm around Alvina and whispered, "That's the most we'll be hearin' out of that room tonight."

"You're the funny one," she answered, pushing away his hand.

"Now, now," he coaxed. "Don't be trying to get over me time."

That night Elizabeth dreamed she saw a field of flowers tight in their bulbs, suddenly bursting open with children, their arms and legs like white petals, faces round and cheery. Cliffs were nowhere in sight. But there were clouds, heavy and black, an ominous presence bearing down.

14

The next morning Elizabeth woke to the sound of the sea below the cliffs taking in great gulps of breath and whooshing it out repeatedly as it beat against the towering cliffs siding small patches of beach. She slid away from Jacob, got up, and stood at the window, its pane crusted by salted sea air.

The house of Jacob and George's grandfather had been built on a 200-foot cliff, a lofty distance straight up from the sea, the dwelling a cliffhanger in raging winds. The brothers and their sisters were born in the little saltbox house that always held the sound of the sea, the music of the wind, and the serenade of birds, or—as Sarah Ann told it—the ruction of the sea, the tantrums of the wind, and the crackle of wild seabirds.

Some days a northeasterly wind beat at the house like a bare-knuckled boxer bent on knocking the building down over the cliff. There the sea waited with a ferocious, frothing mouth and bared black teeth. Other days wind blew through open windows like hefty arms hooked through a window on one side of the house, through to the other side, as if trying to lift the house and let it sail out and down to a boiling sea. The house stayed strong. Its front porch, opposite the cliff, hugged the dusty narrow road at the top of a hill that levelled off to a small meadow and on to more cliffs and more homes built on their edge.

George, the oldest son, had helped his father replace his old house and the weathered fence along the cliff eaten into by sea-salted winds. A whitewashed picket fence now bordered its edge and went back toward a knob of hill where it was fastened. George gave the new house a fresh start with a wife. Alvina often complained about the chute under the fence, which was used to empty the slop pail. George had promised to hook a fishing net over it but he never did. "Two generations have been raised mere feet from the cliff without incident," he told her. "Children have two eyes in their heads, don't they?"

Jacob followed Elizabeth to the window. She gave him a sympathetic look. "So this is where you were born, on a cliff so close to the edge a sneeze could knock you over. Foxtrap is a tamer place."

Jacob slipped his arm across her back and squeezed her shoulder. "Ah, but I'm not there."

After breakfast they walked down the hill and up a bank of land to the framed house Jacob was building in the shelter of high, cragged hills. "Up from the beach and in from the cliffs," Jacob said with satisfaction.

Elizabeth drew in the scent of new wood. Then she took in the sight of fish flakes standing at the edge of the cliffs, one down from William's house and another on the outreaching cliff.

"The flakes are bare now," Jacob said. "They'll be loaded down come summer."

"And I suppose I'll be expected to stand atop the flakes on the cliffs and spread fish to the edge and not a fence to catch me if I trip."

"You'll get used to it," Jacob promised.

He looked toward the Kennedy fishing stage fitted haphazardly into the cliff, its square, dapple-grey skull holding openings like black, sightless eyes. Strong winds swept over the water, gathering its salty mist as it beat into the cove. Water lashed the head of the stage jutting out over the beach.

Jacob pointed to *The Hunter*, an eighteen-foot punt. "Ours is the last one out, sitting like a tongue in the mouth of the cove. See it?"

Elizabeth followed his gaze to the anchored boat with a sail tight to its aft mast like a man along for a lazy ride. She nodded and turned away, lonely for her home in Foxtrap and her real family. Jacob had to be enough to keep her here—Jacob and the life she was bound to live in sickness and in health.

And in loss! The words leaped up before she could stop them.

"You built our house in a graveyard," she said as she made her way to the back of the house.

"Not in—outside of." Jacob gave her a wry smile. "The headstones were here before we were and they'll likely be here after we're gone. The livin' should live beside the dead to remind us that we're sojourners on earth."

"I'm sure there's reminders," Elizabeth said. A sensation, like cold fingers, pressed the small of her back.

When night fell she looked up at the stars twinkling above a dark sea heavy with an aloneness that stretched from the cove straight across the bay to the dim lights of Foxtrap.

The shadows of the dark cliffs haunted her sleep.

15

Jamie heard a rush of footsteps and a voice calling: "*Titanic* has sunk! It hit an iceberg."

He lifted his head from where he was leaning to plane the side of a boat model. He stared at Lavinia, his young cousin, her small face flushed from running. "Go on! Who dreamed that?" he asked.

"Well, it's true then," Lavinia told him. "I heard it as I was passin'

Rideout's lumberyard. The men sittin' on the rock wall outside were all abroad with the news. A newspaper was passed around with accounts of what happened. She hit an iceberg on the fourteenth of April and sank on the fifteenth."

Jamie laid aside his boat model and walked down the road. Men were marling about, taking each other's comments with a spit of tobacco and a headshake and adding their penny's worth.

One skipper, off a fishing schooner, umped, "Thought it was mightier than an iceberg. Sure now, that's how much its captain knew about sea mountains."

"What did it think it was gonna do a'tall, stare it down," another man said, spewing a mouthful of tobacco into a bank of corned snow.

A sea captain from a Labrador voyage narrowed his eyes and gazed out into the bay. He shook his head. "Only the sun can stare it down."

On and on went the conversation. The men talked about the ship's passengers caught in the hold like a net load of fish, and others cast into the sea, flapping about like fish tails.

"And how many were saved?" Jamie asked.

"No one knows yet, me son," the old skipper said. "She was a great ship."

The truth of the grave news took hold of Jamie from the top of his head to the tips of his toes and he ran down the rough path to the shed beside the beach. Red-faced and gasping for breath, he stopped when he reached the shed. His father was outside making an eel trap. He looked up. "You're all in a tear. For what, me lad?"

Jamie leaned, his palms on his knees, and got his breath. He swallowed, settled himself, and spilled his news. "The ship that wasn't supposed to sink has sunk!"

William straightened up. "What ship might that be?"

"*Titanic* is her name. I read about her in the newspapers while she was being built. I remember tellin' yer all about her."

His father stood up and wiped the back of his hand across his forehead. "Aw, not a'tall. That ship can't be gone. Sure, 'twas said God couldn't sink her."

Jamie shook his head. "Well, He made something that could, and it did."

"That's little to do with us," William said, though he felt a shiver. He turned to pick up his work.

Jamie continued, "She sank off our shores and a load of people gone to the bottom with her."

William dropped his trap, shaded his eyes, and looked out to sea, riveting his gaze along Kelly's Island and across the far stretch of blue waters as if he was expecting to see debris and corpses.

"Not that close," Jamie said. "According to reports in the newspaper, *Titanic* sank about 372 miles from St. John's on the best kind of a moonlit night, the sea smooth as water in a jug. The ship scattered passengers who hadn't made it to lifeboats—all fallin' from great heights to the calm sea spotted with pans of ice. There was hardly a chance of survivin'."

William was reminded of when he was a child and an ice pan had drifted in over Foxtrap beach carrying the body of a young man, his legs trailing the water. He appeared to have struggled against the steel cold net of sea closing in on him and had stretched across the pan, both arms above his head, his face like a porcelain dish, his hands like carved stone—like Johnny might have been had he not been shot and saved by Caleb. Grown-ups had raced to the beach and waded into the icy water to bring the man to shore. They lifted him, a cold junk, his clothes stiff like garments pinned on a clothesline in the dead of winter. The victim was buried in All Saints graveyard, a wooden cross above his grave. For a long time after, William often glanced toward the ocean, his mind uneasy.

When Jamie told his mother about *Titanic* she gave him a sad look. "It must have been an adventure to sail on such a fine ship, but what a terrible end to a fine beginning. Don't you and Maggie be goin' far in that boat you're on for buildin'. You wouldn't stand a chance."

Jamie grinned. "Don't you worry. Any boat I build is not goin' to take me under."

News of the 1912 tragedy spread along the Southern Shore, settling like a fog around seaside communities as updated newspaper accounts were passed around.

Jamie took pity on his uncle, stuck on his stool by the fire, and he often went to read to Johnny from newspapers he borrowed from Samuel Butler.

Sam, a man with a thick, grey beard and heavy eyebrows to match, kept all the reading material he bought. He stowed newspapers, gazettes, books—anything with words. He took a keen interest in news near and far, gathering it like a farmer his hay. The stories he could tell, all kinds that were happening every day in faraway places. Jamie got hungry thinking about them and, whenever he couldn't hold himself back, he went down the road to Sam's house.

Sam sometimes sat in his deceased wife's rocking chair, pulling on his beard and ruminating. He was philosophical about *Titanic*. "Man's foolhardiness is what sank the ship," he said. "A captain can never be too confident. He needs to be aware always of the ghostly reach of a colossal iceberg, its massive cliff under the sea."

Jamie learned from Sam that the minute *Titanic* hit the iceberg, awesome stories were made. An Irishman in St. John's had been expecting his daughter. The night *Titanic* sank he dreamed Colleen was in the water. He awakened startled to see her standing before him dripping wet. Then she was gone like the blink of an eye.

Jamie imagined the Irish lass standing by a rail in Queenstown, Ireland. She looked out to sea and then back at the home she was leaving, her eyes large and deep-set, as if in shadows. She lifted her shoulders and turned her back, ready for a journey to a new life. Her last night closed in around her like a damp blanket as she stood on the deck of the tilting *Titanic*, shivering from the cold, and news that an unsinkable ship was sinking—taking her and her dreams.

Jamie and Maggie were reading a newspaper Jamie had borrowed from Sam when William turned to Jamie and asked, "If you had been on *Titanic* and had the chance to get into a lifeboat, would you have given a woman your place?" Then without waiting for Jamie to answer he looked at Maggie and asked, "Would you have let another woman go in your place?"

Startled by his question and unable to imagine herself on a sinking ship, Maggie took her time answering, her green eyes thoughtful. "It's easy enough to say I would, knowin' I don't have to prove it. It might depend on another woman's circumstance and mine." She gave

William an impish look. "If I'd gotten on the ship in Queenstown, during those four and a half days it would take to get to New York, I might have found my eye on an Irish boy. Two eyes on him and I might have gone wherever he went—into the lifeboat or into the sea." She turned to Jamie. "If he'd looked like you, Jamie, me man, I'd've gone wherever he went."

After he had listened to all the talk about *Titanic*, William spent a restless night. Turbulent dreams caught hold of him, smacking him awake. He lay thinking, *For the love of God, I hope Jamie stays away from the icefields. If mighty ships can sink there's less hope for smaller ships against icebergs and storms in a sea that shows no mercy.*

He forgot his dreams once daylight broke abroad. Everything seemed safe. Jamie was home—for now.

16

William lifted a log onto the wood horse and Jamie kept it steady while his father sawed through the log and dropped it to the ground in lengths cut to fit the kitchen stove. He was setting another log in place when he noticed Jamie looking out over the water into the distance.

Jamie couldn't help thinking about the majestic ship that had sailed into Atlantic waters unaware of a beautiful, mysterious leviathan veiled in the dark night, the ocean's salty tongue on her icy body. Most captains of small and large ships were keenly aware of her, aware that only ten per cent of her showed above the surface. Beneath the water she was a solid, formidable threat that could not only wound a ship but destroy it. Jamie sensed the terror the captain and passengers must have felt standing on the decks of the wounded *Titanic*, silvery moonlight unable to cut through the darkness of the sea outside the periphery of the ship's lights.

"What's your mind holdin' in, me son?" William asked.

"I think I'll paint *Titanic*," he answered.

William straightened up. "So you can. It'd be nothing at all for you to do."

"I'll get me boat built first."

Jamie never saw a tree without visualizing its potential to become part of a boat or a house. He took his father's horse and cart and went into the woods early one May morning. He was soon cutting trees, opening their sweet fresh scent. After tramping through thick brush he found what he'd hoped for. He came out of the woods with a log that had a good sweep for a stem. He sawed timbers and set the planed strips to dry in half-hearted sunshine, careful not to lay them under too-strong sunlight that would split the boards. He was happy as he slid into his chair at the table and lifted a cup of hot, bare-legged tea. His mother had made him a plate of toutons and covered them in molasses.

"You need a little sweetener this mornin', Jamie, after all your work," William said as he sat pouring tea from his cup into his saucer and slurping it. "Molasses makes you run uphill, and if you ever go to see your sister in Hibb's Cove you'll be going up a few hills."

Jamie dug into his toutons, his mind on his boat. He looked at his father, his young face alive with anticipation. "I'll be riding hills of waves once my boat is built."

The boat would be patterned after one of his father's models. He imagined her settling on the ocean as if she owned it and slicing through temperamental waters as swiftly as the steel blade of a knife. The boat would be big enough to voyage to Kelly's Island to get a load of wood and rocks for the foundation of his and Maggie's house. Maybe they would use the boat to take a jaunt over to Hibb's Cove to see Elizabeth's new home.

After breakfast Jamie rubbed his hand over a boat model his father had taken down off the wall. He turned it in his hands and nudged his mother. "See what I wrote on this side."

She read the words: A TREE MUST BE SET FREE TO RIDE THE WAVES.

Mary Jane gave her son an affectionate look, grateful to have one child still at home. "Sure, you got a way with words."

William grunted. "Words and paint won't feed him. I'll tell you that."

By late spring the punt was built, witch hazel laid in the stern for good luck. The boat didn't look big from the sides, but when Maggie looked from the stern to the stem she imagined it full of children—a family load. Jamie took strips of oakum lying like fairy hair on the workbench. He pulled the oakum apart, its strong tarry smell on his hands as he rolled it and pressed it between the seams of his boat. The Old World permeation made him think of ancient ships, sailors, rum, and bilge water. He and his father filled its cracks and nailheads with putty and tar.

William's rough hand slid over the underside of the boat, which he had helped Jamie plane smooth as an egg and hard like the belly of an expectant mother. In time it would mate with the sea, its belly growing heavy with a day's catch.

The men rigged the boat with a sail and removed the shores holding her up. Cousins Noah and Thomas Bussey came to help haul the boat down to the beach. They watched the *Mary Jane* face the waves with a gentle roll before righting herself on the water.

Noah, the older cousin, shook his head. "Ah, me boy, you must'n be goin' far in her. The sea is a tempting wench. Be mindful of her wiles. She'll play with you, pull you to her until you're under her skirts, twisted in them and smothered."

"I'll stay on top of her," Jamie replied. "I'll ride her like a master."

"So do," Noah said, slapping him on the back.

The cousins turned their backs to go up the lane and Jamie's look followed them. He was thinking how lucky they were to have had a ticket on this March's sealing voyage. He turned back to tending his boat. *I'll have one next year.*

William was a farmer who loved to turn the soil to sow vegetables, but he also loved the feel of fish flopping about his feet as he sculled home with a fresh fish for supper. He and Jamie took time from farming to net codfish and salmon and salt them for the winter. By July they had enough codfish to fill a flake for drying. They caught so many fish one morning when the sea was rough that the boat almost swamped. Jamie was bailing as fast as his arm could swing. "It's hard toil, this is," he muttered.

"Cutting the spade through soil without rain to soften it is hard work, too," William answered as he sculled the boat through the wild sea. "It's hard on the spirit when the crop can't make it to harvest. Still, a man can hold a piece of land. He'll never own a piece of the ocean."

* * * * *

Maggie leaned against the risings of the *Mary Jane* for her first ride. She listened to the rhythmic knock of Jamie's oars against thole-pins, waves swimming along the boat like porpoises. White sparks flew against salty tongues of baffling winds licking her skin. They sailed to Kelly's Island, where Jamie took a *piggin*, stuck in the boat's gunnels for bailing, and waded into the water. He filled it with blue mussels. Maggie walked on the sandy beach gathering driftwood. Wild birds soared above the sea, dipping as Jamie made a fire and boiled the mussels. He and Maggie ate the succulent morsels while they watched birds settle on the diamond winks of blue water. Afterwards Maggie nestled against Jamie, closing her eyes. She didn't feel the need for conversation. Silence had a gentle conversation all its own.

After they came ashore in Foxtrap, Maggie went down the lane and out of sight. William let out a laugh. "You got yourself a fine woman there, Jamie." He whacked him on his back. "I saw you kiss her goodbye." He leaned close with a twinkle in his eye. "You know you're in love when you kiss a woman and it goes straight to your heart. If it goes down farther it may be lust, not love."

Jamie blushed. Then, realizing his father was teasing him, he grinned. "Can't it be both?"

William let out another laugh and slapped him again. "That's me boy."

Jamie set out to paint the ill-fated *Titanic*. He cut a piece of plywood. Then he took matchsticks and softened them into brushes with his teeth. He would use leftover house paint. A little white paint was left in the bottom of a can after Mary Jane painted the kitchen wall, some blue paint after she painted the pantry walls, and enough black paint after she painted the floorboards. If necessary he'd prick his finger for a bit of red in the flags.

The first time Maggie came to take a pattern off Elizabeth's wedding undergarments for her own, Jamie didn't see her until she touched his shoulder. His teeth were bearing down hard on a spent match, breaking its end into a fine brush as he leaned over a piece of board, his lips tight, his expressive, smoky eyes intense.

She ran her fingers through his thick curls and joked, "There you is, chewing on a match. Anyone would think there was no food in your mother's cupboard."

Jamie lifted his head slightly. He was too intent on what he was doing to answer. He closed his eyes for a moment, trying to forget the newspaper sketch he'd seen of *Titanic* off-balance, and then the drawing of her with her jaws raised in the air, people caught in her throat.

Maggie watched as he painted meticulously and sparingly, not wanting to waste a drop of paint.

"You're paintin' the ship cutting through the water," she said. "I'd paint her goin' down."

Jamie looked up, his voice firm as he said, "I don't want to paint her goin' down like a drownin' animal. I'm paintin' her whole, majestic, as if she owns the ocean."

Maggie didn't voice what she was thinking: *No one owns the ocean; it answers only to God.*

A black *Titanic* took shape, bold and confident on a blue accommodating sea under a dark sky. Jamie painted her as if she still carried passengers with great expectations: children, parents, young lovers, people alone, rich and poor, the poor with only a few coins tucked in a valise, looking to fulfill dreams of finding a home in a new country. Other passengers were going to meet loved ones: a wife to meet her husband, children to meet a father, sweethearts to be united; all from different ranks in society. He imagined the steamer's occupants, all enjoying a measure of comfort on the luxury ship, unaware that an iceberg could loom out of the waters like a ghost ship and turn their greatest adventure into a tragedy.

Jamie painted a man in the crow's nest, the first person who would have seen the iceberg.

When he finished his painting, he hung it above the stove to dry.

His mother wiped her hands on her apron and looked up. "You've done some job, son. There she is, upright on the sea, moving along like she was meant to do. Still, I don't want you goin' out beyond the bay, maybe close to where *Titanic* sank." She reached up and gave his ear a sharp nip.

He drew back, lifting an eyebrow. "Not that far. Never! Still, I suppose you'd rather I stayed in bed, the place where most everyone dies sooner or later."

"Only because they're sick," she said. "It's also where most people have their beginning."

17

Jacob finished building a fine house for Elizabeth, an eight-room, two-storey dwelling. Below Kennedy's Hill and in from the road, a gate opened to a lane going up to the house in a reach of land beneath sheltering hills. Just in from Cliff Path stood a storehouse built on large flat rocks beside the narrow road and a water well beside it. To each side of the house Jacob fenced land for a vegetable garden.

The new house was sheeted with wide pine boards that came from Jacob's uncle, Samuel Taylor, after his storage shed on Taylor's Hill in Ship Cove was torn down. To the side of the house facing Cliff Path was a porch entrance. Another door at the front of the house led into the hall and faced the sea. Around the corner, facing Jacob's childhood home, Jacob had built a landing and a second porch, the storage area holding buckets of clear, cool water. Elizabeth made porch mats from ravelled-out brin bags for each doorway.

"A woman's kitchen window usually frames the sea," Jacob said, taking a jug from a row of jugs, gifts from the cove women, hanging along the kitchen shelves. He went to dip it into the bucket in the porch. "Ours don't. It will be your choice to look out through the hall door facing the sea."

He slipped his arm around Elizabeth's waist and they walked through the kitchen and in through the hall, passing a room on their right and one on their left. They made their way up stairs covered in canvas fastened by brass rods across each of the fourteen steps.

Jacob nodded toward a room, its window facing the sea. "A bedroom for us and there's three others to fill with children or company," he said.

"Is that so?" Elizabeth murmured. She laid her head on Jacob's shoulders as if it had become too heavy. She had started on a journey that was no longer her own, a haphazard one. She had ceased to belong only to herself with the freedom to make her own choices. Her life had merged with Jacob's and together they would face tomorrow, next year, and whatever time and their own actions brought.

Through the upstairs window Elizabeth looked toward the beach, above it a row of weather-grey stageheads, their sprawling legs in rocks protruding up from the seabed. Wooden walkways led to stage rooms built to store bedded pickled fish. The stageheads held roughly made tables, hooped barrels, puncheons, and, during the fishing season, men, women, and children. Through a side bedroom window she viewed the steep, narrow road leading up to Cliff Path. Beside it Jacob's father had built a shed, one side shored up with rocks as it leaned against the rocky hills. The bottom part was used to store hay. A ladder led to a loft where William and George worked at fishnets during the winter, mending some that had been torn by sharks or eaten into by mice. At the bottom of Cliff Path a lane led to Petten's store, the other to William's store. The doorstep of its stage was a plank against cliff rock beside a two-storey shed, another loft on top.

Elizabeth walked under the shadow of netted, bough-covered flakes at the bottom of Kennedy's Hill and along an oblong, partitioned building—a red, rectangular two-door chicken coop attached to a coal pen, which was fastened to an outhouse rimming the cliff. Elizabeth went in and leaned to look down a hole. She drew back, startled that the toilet holes were hanging over the cliff. Waste going down the holes dropped into the sea's whirlpool flush.

In the calm of softly falling snow for two days and nights the cove lay in a dazzling white blanket, hills and cliffs in soft curves and rumps. Nothing moved. Sound was hushed, the sea distant and black, swirling snow swallowed as fast as it fell. Suddenly there came dark figures in long woollen coats lining up with shovels to cut through snowdrifts, leaving walls on both sides of the road. On they came, faces whitened, moving like sealers against pinnacles of ice.

Late January, snow that had settled on the cliffs was blown away by strong winds. Hailstones pelted windows facing the sea. Elizabeth imagined them as pieces of cliff the wind was tearing away and flinging at the house.

Each winter night Jacob lifted the large oval rock he had warmed in the oven and carried it up to their bed. They pressed their feet against it, snug under flannel sheets and woollen blankets. Wind raged against the house and lashed the windows, whimpering at times as if it were the ghost of a lone fisherman left on the sea in a small boat, a man with no hope of finding his way home.

Tight in each other's arms in the warmth of their bed Jacob and Elizabeth drifted away from the day, away from any thoughts of the sea and the wind, away from everything.

Elizabeth awakened in the dark of late winter mornings sometimes spooned in sleep, Jacob's strong chest against her back, his hands cupping her soft belly. Other times they woke sharing each other's warmth back to back, Jacob reaching for Elizabeth's hand and twining his and hers, warm in the cold air. They were two people lying, smiling, wanting to belong to each other for the rest of their lives.

Their bedroom window framed a long stretch of water to where the sun's first light splashed. Elizabeth walked to the landing and looked out from a house that seemed as high as the sky. The sun was so bright against her window she imagined going down to the sea's edge and warming her hands by its fire flickering on the water.

Mornings when the wind softly brushed its tangy tongue against the windowpane she opened the window, letting the sea's breath permeate the house.

"Men came from far away to live here, to own land and grow livin' things from the soil, and have a net in the sea," said Jacob. "This is our piece of land to have and to hold and our sea to harvest until kingdom come."

"Until death do us part," she had replied.

And my belly will grow hard with children. Elizabeth's hands went to her flat belly. *I hope.*

Spring came, its winds like a razor some days and soft as fur other days. It was heralded by sounds of hammer and maul against wood ringing over the still waters of the cove as fishermen repaired fishing stages. Others lifted nets into large iron pots hung over a fire. The strong odour of boiling tar and bark, used to preserve the nets, drifted to open windows. Curtains danced in the breeze like the veils of June brides.

The season brought a brightness to the land above the jagged cliffs. Soft, wispy grasses stirred in gentle winds and bent to the ground as if the ghost of a pirate was tramping through, his heavy boots bending the grass as he passed on by to the lighthouse on Green Point where it was rumoured he lived. The seemingly barren point of land held patches of moss hiding berry treasures for winter jams and pies.

Nature had found a way to bring its spring song to cliffs bared by winter's burn. Out of scant soil blown into crevices, fragile-looking bluebells, buttercups, and dandelion flowers sprang up to dance in soft winds. Birds filled the air with trilling calls to mates as they sought cliff nooks and shrubs to nest in. The sky squeezed its mild spring rains on wild peas and hop clover and into hand-ploughed land. Soil was turned and seed sown for vegetables to be ready for a fine autumn harvest. Days grew bright and Elizabeth forgot the cold face of winter.

Sometimes, on a dull morning, she fingered the gold band on her finger and gazed through the upstairs window to the smoky image of land across the waters and back to the wild cove where tongues of wind off the sea spread a briny scent over the seaside gardens. It mingled with the damp smell of the earth roused from winter's sleep, its heart beating with life. Elizabeth's vegetable gardens slanted up to the hills on both sides of the house. She dropped the eyes of cut potatoes in beds and turned the soil over them. She coaxed life out of the sparse soil and the ground miraculously responded to her touch. Jacob fertilized the gardens with animal manure, trenching each drill.

Gardening reminded Elizabeth of spring in Foxtrap, when the scent of scythed grass drifted up from her father's inland meadow. She remembered running barefoot across the ground, soft grass tickling her feet. Her father and her uncle ploughed their farmland, its rich, dark earth breathing under their feet, its soft belly laid open to receive seed.

By autumn the ground delivered out of its great, pregnant belly lacy green ferns holding clusters of carrots as orange as a sunset forecasting a good day, potatoes as white as a new moon, and cabbages as green as new grass. Only the parsnips looked strange, ancient and knobbed, like aged fingers. Still, they sweetened stews and soups. After a day's harvest Elizabeth's mother stirred lemon crystals in a jug of water. Elizabeth remembered running up from the beach, her throat parched, and lifting a glass to draw in the smooth, velvety taste of the cool drink.

Jacob had already gone down to his store loft one morning when Elizabeth woke, her stomach feeling full of bilge water. She reached for the pot under the bed and retched. The room whirled and she sat back down on the feather mattress, her mind caught in a terrible thought: *I hope I don't have influenza. Not now, when there's so much work in the garden and soon on the stagehead.*

She tightened her lips in resolve. *If bluebells can survive in the cracks of cliffs, I can survive anything! I will!*

Elizabeth came down the stairs one morning, turned the glass knob on the inside door, then unlatched the storm door. There came a flutter inside her like a little bird going to wing. She touched her belly, felt its hardness. She had been too young to notice her mother's growing belly before Jamie was born. She had not heard anyone talk about the first signs of life. Now and then there had been talk about the first signs of birth—a neighbour murmuring behind her hand to her mother that so and so was sick, meaning she was in labour. No one had told her about the unexpected instant when the baby moved inside a woman's body. Nothing could compare to that moment of awareness. Her body, like the earth in spring, was awakening to new life. It was her strange, unbelievable secret to be shared, for now, with only one other human being.

Jacob, coming up the lane, took in her stunned look and knew that nothing else in the world could create such an expression. Elizabeth's hands went to her belly. She whispered, "Our baby."

Jacob smiled, his eyes moistening. He reached to cup his hands over hers, his words tender. "A child of two hearts, yours and mine."

Jacob had decided not to go back to the iron ore mine. He would fish with George instead of his father, who wasn't well.

"I'll be falling back on me father's ways," he told Elizabeth. "You married a miner but you'll be living with a fisherman."

"And helping with the work of a fisherman," she said as she

sat cutting Jacob a suit of oil clothes from flour bag material to be waterproofed with two coats of linseed oil. She used an old pair of oilskins for a pattern, but the briny stench of fish offal ingrained in its cracks and seams nauseated her. She picked up the clothes and went out on the landing to work just as Alvina and Sarah Ann came up the lane.

"Soon Jacob won't have time to draw his breath," Sarah Ann said.

Elizabeth had cut out the new coveralls and was lifting the old jacket to make a pattern for the new one when she began to urge. She ran behind the shed and threw up.

"That's it," Sarah Ann said when she came back. "Your belly is on for rising. I'll get you some hard bread to suck on. That'll help when you're on the stagehead."

Elizabeth felt the colour rise in her face as she became aware of what her mother-in-law was saying. Soon everyone would know.

18

Jacob and George left most mornings, except on Sunday, to go far out into the bay before sunrise.

Some mornings, when Elizabeth got out of bed and looked out, a grey sky appeared to have dropped around the house. She went downstairs and unlatched the door. Salty, damp wind breathing through thick fog and cold as the belly of a fish pressed against her face. Other times the easterly wind blew so fierce that when she opened the door it slammed shut against her face. Those mornings Jacob stayed on land and helped with the gardens.

One clear morning in early June, Jacob eased out of bed and lifted the curtains to the window. It had blown hard during the night and the men had delayed their trip. Elizabeth lay in bed gazing at the clear view. In the distance the rim of ocean held the blazing sun burning its way above the sea. Its saffron glow spread across the bedroom wall like melted gold. The wind had blown itself out and now it was the finest kind of a morning.

Soon skiffs and punts were sailing out of the cove under the watchful eyes of women standing at their windows. As the day warmed, windows were opened to sea breezes, lace curtains dancing in the breeze while the women went about their work, washing, mending, cooking, and baking, always with an eye on the bay, knowing that their men's work would be their work as soon as the fishing boats came home.

Often windows holding the sheen of evening light became dark lengths of glass in evening shadows before fishermen arrived home after fighting rough seas. Elizabeth, Alvina, Sarah Ann, and other women and children of the cove gazed out over the bay intent on spotting their men's voyaging boats, hopefully low in the gunnels, their barked canvas sails full and billowing, coming home laden like a woman about to deliver. If they were late Elizabeth felt shaky as a fishing flake in a storm of wind.

Jacob and George came home often with a load of codfish, tails flapping against each other, their gills showing a pink under-plate as they panted for water, black eyes staring, light fading. Elizabeth had once asked her father if fish cry. He had shrugged and told her, "If they do it's not loud enough to get anyone's sympathy."

William Kennedy, no longer strong and vibrant, hobbled down the hill to the stagehead where Jacob had pierced a tin can and set in it a light that outlined the figures like a phantom scene etched on the night. He watched his sons prong fish and throw them up on the stagehead. Then he hobbled back to his house satisfied to snuff his lamp. He dragged himself to bed and lay beside Sarah Ann to wait for tomorrow, hoping his health would not worsen.

Under light glowing on the stagehead above a dark sea the couples worked hard, their faces weary. Alvina and Elizabeth filled a puncheon with buckets of clear spring water flowing by the side of the stage. Elizabeth's hands slid into the cold water without her realizing its bite. The jolt surged through her whole body, settling like a pain in the pit of her stomach.

Alvina took in her drawn, white face. "This is life as it is in the cove," she said. "You'll get used to it just as you'll get used to the stench of fish blood on days when the sun is strong enough to burn your skin."

"Ump! You women's too nish," George said, grabbing a fish, thumb and finger in its eyes, and slapping it on the splitting table. He cut it across the throat and down its gut, straight to the tail. Biting wind veered into Elizabeth's face and eyes as she gutted the steely cold cod. There was no shelter from it. Elizabeth's mind often drifted away to other chores that needed to be done. They piled inside her head, making it heavier than her hands holding the dead weight of a codfish. She slid the fish to Alvina, who took it and banged its head against the side of the table. The body came off, cut clean, and the head slipped down a hole in the stagehead. Seagulls rose from cliffs and dropped to the water with maddening cries.

Two swift strokes of Jacob's knife and the sound bone was out, leaving the fish as flat as a maple leaf.

"Cold enough to skin you, that it is," Alvina told Elizabeth as they changed places.

It was also cold in the stage when there was an upwind as they wheeled barrows of split white flesh over the long grey platforms into the ash-grey stage. They bulked the fish, piles and piles of it, sprinkles of salt raining down on each layer. Despite the cold, Elizabeth was sweating. She lifted a weary wrist to wipe her forehead. Lamplight, a misty halo around it, flickered on the stage walls like shadowy ghosts. She glanced at the light. A tiny flame could cut through the darkness of night. Only sleep could push away the weight of a day's toil.

Finally, Jacob dropped a pail on a rope down into the water, filled it, and drew it up to wash the stagehead. George put the boat on collar and came back to the stagehead in the flat. All across the cove, one by one, stages were emptied of people as lightened vessels were put on collar. Doors opened and closed as houses gathered tired fisherfolk.

Elizabeth could hear the rumbling noise of the stage rails under the tramp of her and Jacob's feet as they dragged themselves up the path, crossed the road, and trudged up the lane to the house. Elizabeth tended to water blisters that had formed on Jacob's chafed palms, dressed them and the sores on his back. The sweat of hard work and salt spray were tough on a fisherman's skin. Jacob never complained. One more time he'd made it home from the capricious ocean thankful not to have come home with a water haul—all water and no fish.

Elizabeth's voice was heavy. "Land is strong and steady beneath our feet. That's why me father is a farmer. I fear the sea. It got power the land knows nothing about."

"I know," Jacob admitted. "Once I let go of the land and go on the water in a flimsy craft I'm at the sea's mercy. It teases me, rocks me, fights me, but it don't swallow me."

"Not yet," Elizabeth said.

"The mines, too, take their victims," Jacob reminded her. "When I'm out on the water, away from shore, and I looks in on the land, it becomes a different place. Houses and stages are dabs on the landscape, unfamiliar and mysterious. I see children spreadin' fish on flakes, a man rakin' his garden uphill, a mother wheelin' a child, and I feels thankful to be a part of this earth, part of this place."

He stopped and smiled. "There's nothing more wonderful than to stand in a boat miles from shore, draw in the crystal clear air as if it's comin' from a far land and a distant time, its winds sweepin' the ocean. Often I watch the sun rise and blaze over the water until I'm caught in a glorious light. Other times when I don't get home until after sunset and the moon's a crescent reflecting earthshine from the sun, the sea and earth takes on a magical aura. Other times when there's no moon our lamp's light beams over the water, dancing like silver stars on the slate-black sea. Not a'tall like bein' down in the mines."

Elizabeth listened, keeping silent.

In bed she lay thinking about the weight of water on her husband's nets and his struggle to harvest fish against tides and winds, sometimes in foul weather. She had chosen Jacob. He had chosen their way of life. She closed her eyes. Morning would come fast.

Soon, Elizabeth and Alvina barrowed the salted fish bedded in the stage across to a dank cavern with a pebbled floor slanted toward the stage. Sunlight sometimes made rainbows in the trickle of water running down over the rocks. Here, with the sounds of waves crashing on the beach below them, the women washed fish in water cold as ice. An old sail against the mouth of the opening kept out wind and the rain.

Once fish was washed it had to be cured. Day after day Elizabeth and Alvina loaded the hand barrow—a four-handle flat tray—with wet fish and bent their backs to tighten their hands on the handles. The barrow swayed under their tired hands as they lifted it. They faced the climb up the steep, rocky path to the road, where they tramped up Kennedy's Hill, their heels bearing the weight of the barrow. Atop cliffs, extending to a brink more than a hundred feet above the sea, fish flakes spread out like tables covered in boughs and secured with fishing nets. Elizabeth and Alvina locked their legs as they leaned to spread wet, flattened fish.

They carried barrow after barrow of the heavy fish to catch a mellow sun. If the sun grew too hot the fish had to be shaded; if it rained it had to be covered. At night it had to be bundled and wrapped tight against the chance that fish flies would leave eggs to turn to maggots. Most times the women were fortunate to have the white flesh turn golden under a warm sun and gentle winds. But there were times when fish had to be washed of maggots and spread to dry a second time.

"You're speckled like a codfish's back," Jacob teased when freckles sprang up over Elizabeth's arms like summer flowers. Her breasts were filling, swelling, her belly rising. She loosened the strings on her apron, not caring who knew she was *in bungalow*.

She kept herself busy and tried not to worry about Jacob out in rough weather. Her side window faced the meadow holding Charlie and Diana Kennedy's house and a side garden across from the house where Jacob was born. Some nights she looked up to see the warm light in Alvina's window. Alvina, whose eyes weren't as good as she would like, squinted to look back to the light in Elizabeth's window. It made the women feel less lonely when the men were on the sea and late returning home.

During the day Elizabeth often looked through the window up to where Alvina and Diana faced each other over a white picketed fence and chatted, taking moments to rest and commiserate on the day's happenings. The women's white aprons lifted in the wind. Beside them clothes on the line dipped and danced under the sun's smile. Their work was long and tiring, moments of idleness sweet.

From her upstairs window Elizabeth could see two grannies farther up in Lear's Cove sitting outside their houses in ambient conversation. Curtains flapped against screened windows above their heads. Old women they were to Elizabeth. Sun lines traced paths through their faces and at the corners of their eyes, ingrained from lively looks piercing the distance out over the water for the dark shadows of their men's boats coming home. Above the hill against the sky she made out the black, slanted roofs of houses built against the cliffs above Lear's Cove. The women in those houses waited, too.

Elizabeth walked up the hill to visit Alvina and Sarah Ann. A lone lilac tree was in full bloom outside the front of the house, its scent welcoming. Sarah Ann was out on her step bundling sprigs of flowers. When she saw Elizabeth she called, "I'm gatherin' lilacs for me table. They'll clear the house of the salt fish smell from dinner."

Elizabeth nodded. She went toward the door, stopping to turn and stare down into the throat of jutting black cliffs, and farther into the open mouth of the sea spitting tongues of foam. *How can any woman have the nerve to raise children on those cliffs?* she thought. *Alvina will have to. My situation is not much better.* She felt a fierce determination to protect her baby.

By fall, in the stage a narrow path had formed between the layered walls of salted codfish. The hard edge of the flat, headless fish fanned out, hitching the clothes of cove children running through the stage. The briny smell of offal nipped between rocks under the stagehead spread through the air as the sun beat down, and the damp, raunchy smell of fish flesh was so strong Elizabeth could taste it. She was thinking it was spoiled, the lot of it.

"The gulls would throw that up," she told Jacob.

He gave her a boyish grin. "Not a'tall. It's a relish."

Handling fish guts wasn't something she had imagined doing when she fell into marrying Jacob. She thought of how she'd starch and scent crisp white sheets and huddle against Jacob in bed, their feet entwined, feeling his strength, and listen to the strong rhythm of his heartbeat. She'd mistaken life with Jacob for love without labour.

Early November, fish was barrelled and sold to Harold Andrews, the harbour merchant. Fishing boats were pulled up on the launch and left like gulls with their heads under their wings.

Winter came early, and when its first snow swirled in the mouth of strong winds and shadowed the hills, Elizabeth felt its chill and with it her first labour pang.

No one had told her that she'd have to bear down and push out, her own life force caught in a maelstrom of pain. Nor did anyone tell her that it would be forgotten once her newborn lay snuggled against her breast.

19

Elizabeth had heard women say that an unborn child does not exist for men; the baby becomes real only when they hear the first cry. Jacob wasn't like that. Before the baby was born his rough hands had gently cupped Elizabeth's belly. Sometimes he had pulled up her nightgown and waited for movement, hardly believing his eyes that a living human being could be cradled inside another body.

After Elsie was born Jacob stood in the doorway of the bedroom. He ran his fingers through his rich brown hair, sleek and thick above his handsome face, and looked at her. His tone was mockingly solemn. "Looks like we've made an entirely separate human being. I don't think anyone has done that before."

Elizabeth held her stomach while she laughed. "You think so, eh? Well, let me tell you. No one has made a child exactly like this one."

Jacob rushed then to lift the baby into his arms, all the while looking into Elizabeth's eyes. "Well, now," he said. "I guess we're Mamma and Pappa."

Elizabeth looked at her child and at Jacob and felt complete for the first time in her life. She smiled. "I've put the first limb on my father's family tree. Maybe Jamie will put on the next one."

"Indeed he might," Jacob said.

"Nine days abed," the midwife told her. "After a woman's body is torn it needs time to heal. That means time away from the household and husband's needs—time to get to know the little stranger."

Elizabeth looked toward the window in the early morning light, the sun rising quietly and as beautifully as a flower opening, the new day dawning as pure as her sleeping newborn.

Three months later there came the sound of chatter and laughter. The upbringing cake was ready and the cove women were coming to tea to watch as Elsie was shortened. Alvina, Diana, and others came. Elsie's barrow was untied and the sheet binding her legs lifted off. She let out a chuckle as her legs kicked the air. Then she stopped as if puzzled that she didn't have to push against the cloth binding. The bellyband was removed and the coin holding the healed cord given into the keeping of Elizabeth's dresser box to await the next child. Elsie was dressed in a white woollen gown, bonnet, and long stockings Elizabeth had knit for the occasion. The baby's wrinkled skin had unfolded plump and smooth, her blue eyes clear and focused. Once she was shortened the wide-eyed, dark-haired baby preferred to suck on her toe rather than take the breast.

Sarah Ann hadn't been well for a few months. Now she ambled down Kennedy's Hill. Elizabeth spied her through the kitchen window and thought, *She'll never get back up. I would have brought her the baby had she waited for me to get my strength back.*

Sarah Ann came on down the path and up the lane clutching her chest as if to squeeze the pain away. "I couldn't wait," she gasped, her face drawn. "I wanted to get me hands on the child and remember how it was for me, though I never really forgot."

Elizabeth opened her arms and Sarah Ann gathered the baby to her. She put a finger to her cheek. "She's healthy enough. John William, my first baby, was born November 6, 1879. He wasn't quite the colour he should have been. He struggled to breathe and he lived until two days past Christmas of the next year. Then Henry William died when he was born in 1890. Now these babies live in my heart." She looked away but not before a tear slipped from her eye. She caught it with a worn finger. "Death is like a wild creature, not only waiting on the rise of an ocean wave near and far but also at every turn in the road."

Elizabeth rushed to tell her, "The year Henry William died was the year I was born and here I am now givin' you a grandbaby to hold. Life has many wonderful surprises."

"Indeed," Sarah Ann answered. "I'm grateful for God's mercies in givin' me the children I have." She reached to give Elizabeth back the baby, and when she left to go back up the hill it was with a smile, if not a quick step.

Elizabeth watched her go, hoping never to have to live her years with the memory of a dead child. She would never want to carry a baby only in her heart.

20

The January Mary Jane took sick she kept going as long as she could. Then one evening she climbed into bed away from what was left of her day's work and closed her eyes. She lay deep in the folds of the featherbed, her flesh burning the cold air around her.

William brought wet cloths and wiped her body. He drew his lips tight as he listened to the croaking coughs and wheezing breath.

When he told Jamie his mother was sick and had taken to her bed, Jamie crept up the stairs, the creak of boards blending with the hoarse sound of his mother breathing.

Caroline came to administer the herbal remedies she and Mary Jane had often used to help other people recover. Nothing worked. Mary Jane slipped into a deep sleep.

On her last evening Mary Jane lay in bed forgetting, for a moment, her struggle to breathe. William placed his hand on her head and she felt its warmth. Her greying hair lay across the pillow. She opened her eyes as William reached to loosen it from a braid, still silky soft and wavy like the sea. She imagined it dark and flowing and not a grey hair in sight. She had just met Edward Kennedy . . . just had her first child . . . her second child . . . her third. Then she lost Edward. She was lying on the floor crying, believing that tomorrow was empty. Then the children had tightened their hold on her and their little bodies had given her strength to stand on her feet, to look beyond what she had lost, and to think on what she had left: three children who needed her. Then William came and they were blessed with two children of their own: Elizabeth and Jamie. *It's hard to get into this world, difficult to stay in it any length of time, hard to believe we have to leave it.*

Her heartbeat was slowing and her breath no longer had an easy pull. Someone else was going to handle the worries between the birth of each day and the sleep of each night. "Hold me gently," she planned on telling God. "These old bones are brittle and tender."

She knew He'd smile and answer, "Not anymore."

* * * * *

Jamie had gone to the beach to gather kelp washed up by strong northerly winds. He'd have it dried by spring to fertilize the vegetable gardens. Joe came for him.

"Pick up your feet and get on up to your house," his uncle called. "Your mother don't have enough breath to cool a bowl of porridge and not enough time, if I'm any judge."

Jamie trudged along the path trying to shut out the news that his mother was failing. He looked toward her bare apple trees remembering the sweet taste of apple pie soaked in sugar and cinnamon. He staggered into the house feeling weak.

Joe put his hand on his shoulder. "She'll be goin' soon, Jamie. There's nothing anyone can do. Her pulse is struggling and her lungs—" He shook his head. "They're aflood with double pneumonia. Your father made a mix of kerosene and molasses and got it to her lips but no further. Her stomach's too weak."

Jamie's steps were heavy as he climbed the stairs to the sounds of his mother's breath rasping her throat like a saw. Jamie and his father's eyes met over the bed of a woman they both cherished.

She's only sixty, not old enough to die, Jamie thought, touching his lips to his mother's eyelid as soft as swansdown. Under it he felt the slippery ball of her eye quivering. Her eyelashes, like thin threads, fluttered.

Trying not to cry, he left the room. Later he wondered why he hadn't stayed to hold her hand while it was warm and soft. Maybe she would have wanted to hear him say, "Mam, I love you."

William was left like a bicycle knocked to the ground, its wheels spinning in the air going nowhere. His head dropped into his hands as the anguish of losing Mary Jane sliced through his heart.

Hours later, Edward John and Fannie, who had been called from Kelligrews, hurried down the road holding each other and sobbing as if their hearts would break.

Caroline brought a boiler of soup and fresh bread. "Your poor mother went quicker than we'd expected," she told them.

William was unable to eat. He sat smoking his pipe and thinking he had to be dreaming. Mary Jane couldn't have left him forever.

Caroline called midwife Melinda Tucker, whose task it was to bring out the newborn and lay out the dead.

The next morning Jamie came downstairs not wanting to go near the back room, where his mother lay, hands folded over a still breast like a fork and knife over a plate after a meal is finished. He leaned against the door facing. "We'll have to get Elizabeth over for the funeral."

"You can't be wearying your sister," William said. "She's full of work tendin' to Jacob and the baby. 'Tis not fit this time of year for her to be in a boat or knockin' around on a train. Joe already sent someone with the news."

Jamie turned to a familiar sound. The door was ajar and wind swept in like a gentle hand setting the rocking chair in motion. For a moment he thought his mother was sitting there.

William said, "It's her ghost."

"It's the wind, Pappa, just the wind finding a crack and blowing in to stir the rocker."

"The wind never rocked it before she died," he said hopefully.

Mary Jane's sturdy rocking chair had been, like many rocking chairs, made to the specifics of the woman who would use it. William had made it to accommodate her height so that her feet touched the floor to rest exactly where they should.

Maggie went to sit in it before the funeral. The chair didn't match Maggie's long legs for a good reach though the headrest was a perfect fit.

"I'll make you your own," Jamie promised.

She smiled up at him and he leaned to kiss her. "You're the only woman who loves me now."

She shook her head. "Not true. Your sister thinks the world of her brother."

21

Who's coming now, and what for? Elizabeth strained to see through an upstairs window, shading her eyes to make out the man in the small skiff. She watched as the painter was thrown up and tied to the stagehead.

She saw that it was Sam Bishop from Foxtrap. The man was

wearing a black armband on his sleeve. Her hand went to her throat and she let out a gasp. "Pappa—Mamma—Jamie." She ran downstairs, took off her apron, smoothed her hair, and braced herself.

"My mother! My mother!" Elizabeth cried when Sam took off his hat and solemnly relayed her father's news. Her legs wobbled like a young foal's as Jacob folded her in his arms—Jacob so strong holding her, she so weak leaning into him.

Alvina helped Elizabeth get ready to go to her mother's funeral while Jacob went to turn over the punt pulled up on the launch and put on its cuddy, a shelter for Elizabeth.

"It'll get easier," Alvina said as she gathered warm blankets and packed Elizabeth and Jacob's belongings. When she was finished she reached to hug her sister-in-law.

Elizabeth stared past her and spoke softly. "My mother never told me she loved me but I knew she did."

"Sure, she loved you," Alvina said. "Now go on. The baby will be left in good hands."

Elizabeth stepped down into the boat remembering the sound of her mother's quick step to open the door to her knock when she was too little to reach the latch, her smile after she bit off the last piece of thread to a dress she'd finished making. She'd pull the dress over Elizabeth's head and Elizabeth would push her hands out the sleeves feeling like a princess. Her hair was combed smooth with her mother's gentle hand. Her mother may have held her words in but she had been generous in meeting her daughter's needs.

Jacob was a good hand at making sandals and coffins, the first to wear while one was very much alive and the other to lie in when one was off one's feet for good. He used pine for his boxes, the wood gentle to his saw. He and Elizabeth left for Foxtrap, his boat carrying a pine coffin.

Jamie was standing on the stagehead watching Jacob tie up. "We already have a coffin," he said, "but Pappa and me's much obliged."

"It won't go astray," said William.

"No, indeed," Caroline said as she came down the path. "There's always someone—" She stopped and turned to Elizabeth. "I'll come with you to see your mamma. She'd been laid up for only a few days after she caught a chill hangin' out clothes."

Elizabeth nodded.

Inside the house Elizabeth turned to acknowledge Edward John standing by the coffin, his eyes swollen. Mary Jane looked young, her face unlined in death. Elizabeth bent to kiss her cold face. She cupped her cheek and it was like holding a beach rock in her hand.

Fannie came up behind her, her small brown eyes red. "Our mother," her half-sister sobbed, and gathered Elizabeth into her arms.

Lavinia pushed open the door and came in with her mother's dish of stew. "Poor Aunt Mary Jane," she said, her voice shaking with emotion. She laid down the dish and left quickly.

Fannie turned to Elizabeth. "I remember when Mam was havin' you. When she'd sit for a spell her belly moved under the flower print of her apron and the flowers seemed to nod. That was you wantin' to get out." She gave Elizabeth a weak smile.

Elizabeth kept that fresh image of her mother as she came back to the cove and pulled up the window shade Alvina had pulled down. She sat at the kitchen table and stared at the leaning, lichen-crusted headstones in cracked stone like an open palm holding the commandment: THOU SHALT DIE. A few surnames were legible: Grealey, Bishop, Butler. . . . She drew the window shade back down and went upstairs while Jacob went to bring Elsie home from Alvina's. A yearning for her mother came as strong as any she felt for Jacob. She remembered her mother washing her face tenderly with a warm cloth when she was a child. She retraced her footsteps down the stairs to where Jacob was laying the sleeping baby in her cot. She gave Jacob a plaintive look. "Likely no one else will ever wash my face, like my mother used to do." She broke down sobbing and sniffling like a small child.

Jacob got up and, without saying a word, went to the stove. She watched as he picked up the kettle and took it to the porch, where he poured warm water into the face pan. He dipped a cloth and wrung it. He came back and, placing his arms around Elizabeth's drooping shoulders, he sat her down. He washed her face with the warm cloth, lingering over her swollen eyelids, his voice steady. "I'll be your husband and your mother. I'll give you children and they will fill your heart until you'll hardly have room even for me."

She looked at him, and then at Elsie in her cot, and for that moment it was only Jacob and her baby she thought of, only Jacob and Elsie she wanted to think of. They were enough.

22

William hardly lifted his feet as he trudged back to the grave after Mary Jane was buried and everyone had left. He wanted to be alone with the only woman he had ever loved. The gravedigger had cut into a beautiful blanket of snow and turned up dirt for Mary Jane's grave. A fresh fall of snow had given it a new covering and filled the lines in headstones beside the path, leaving blank faces. Scarves of snow shadowed them just as sorrow now shadowed William. The rosy cast to his face and the twinkle in his eyes were gone. He wished he could be gone with Mary Jane, away from the pain of losing her. His footmarks left long, deep trenches in the snow as he made his way home. He sat alone, the *tick-tock* of the old Clinton clock grating on his nerves. He had wound it with its heavy brass key days before. He reached his hand inside the glass door and stopped the pendulum. He wondered if this was how God felt when He held a person's heart in His hand and stopped its ticking. He could almost hear Mary Jane say, "Fancy how you talk about God when you don't believe in Him."

He sat in the silence waiting for Jamie to come home. The silence grew loud against his ears and he muttered, "That young scallywag is gone courtin' and left me alone."

He could hear Mary Jane answer him, "What else would you expect?"

He curled up on the settle. Though it was hard on his bones it was close to the fire he left lingering through the night. Sometimes it sputtered and crackled. A log rolled and he awakened startled.

Jamie came home, but it was long after he walked Maggie to her aunt's place. He came on down over the hill through thick snow falling around him. His shoulders were bent into the wind, his tears like rain falling into his open mouth. He swallowed them, warm and salty.

Instead of going into the house and following the lamp's light upstairs he turned up the path to the barn. He squeaked open the door and went inside. Curling up on a bundle of hay he fell asleep and dreamed that St. Peter reached down from heaven and grabbed his mother. He looked at Jamie out of fiery eyes and threatened, "I'll get you later." Then his mother and St. Peter disappeared into the clouds.

Jamie's cry, "The scoundrel!" woke him. It was pitch black. He heard the shifting of the horse in her stall, imagined her lifting her head to the sound of him getting up from his straw bed. He left the barn, closing the door and sliding the latch in place. He hesitated before going into the house. A cold silence swept toward him as he opened the porch door and entered the kitchen. He spied his father sitting beside a lit lamp. The naked pate of his head looked alien in the lamplight, his eyes shadowed like caves. The fire had gone out and William sat with Mary Jane's quilt around his shoulders. He had the look of a man who had lost everything.

William croaked, "I thought you had left me, too."

"I won't leave you," Jamie said, believing it at that moment. He passed his father and forced himself to go upstairs to his room. A wave of hunger for his mother's cooking assailed him. He longed for the warm breath of her baked bread and the aroma of meat covered in thick gravy along with new potatoes and cabbage. He remembered her small, worn hands reaching up to pick an apple from the tree, straining to grab one after another. He'd never forget the scent of sugar and cinnamon caramelizing inside her apple tarts and its sweet juice bursting up through the crusts.

He swallowed hard and looked toward his window facing the bay. *I won't forget you, Mamma, the way you lived, the good you did. You'd forgive me for gettin' a berth and goin' to the seal hunt next year. You thought sealin' was dangerous, but here you is gone at sixty. Livin' is dangerous.*

From where he was sawing wood William's head jerked up at the sound of laughter pealing out like a song on a clear day. He'd forgotten how a house could fill with laughter, how it could burst with energy as Maggie's feet danced up and down the stairs like a bird in swift flight. He remembered how easy it was for a woman to bring a man to life.

Mary Jane had done that to him, a bachelor, and added life through a pair of children. Now here he was again with a young woman in his house soon to be married to his son. He was hoping they'd give him grandchildren to fawn over.

Maggie and Jamie took the train to St. John's. Places appeared to gallop past, keeping Maggie's eyes busy as she sat by the window. Once off the train she took in the look of the place. St. John's was like a hooked rug of colourful architecture against a background of hills hung on a blue wall of sky. She and Jamie eyed electric streetcars with wonder as they strolled down cobbled Water Street. Tall stone and brick buildings held black windows of mystery. Foreigners and locals swarmed the sides of the street, strange tongues and laughter a cacophony. A sign outside a shop read

READ YOUR FORTUNE TODAY FOR TOMORROW
—ONLY TWENTY-FIVE CENTS.

Maggie turned to Jamie, lifting her chin as if to defy an objection. "I'll have me fortune told, so I will." She put her hand on the black wooden door and Jamie, willing to indulge her, pushed it open. Its heavy hinges creaked, startling them. They went in to the tinkling of a silver bell. The boxed entrance was lit by a candle in a black sconce; its golden light splashed the tin shield behind it. They hurried up narrow, planked stairs away from the candlelight to the blackness at the top of the stairs. Maggie grabbed Jamie's arm. "What if this is Satan's workshop and the woman is a bad spirit?"

Jamie let out a hearty laugh, his eyes alive with anticipation. "Go on with you! It's all in fun."

Maggie pulled him back. "If she tells us somethin' awful about the future it'll play on me mind."

A heavy-set woman stepped from behind a thick dark curtain in misty lamplight. The woman's face was trenched, hair grey and wispy around it. She wore a variegated scarf across her forehead. It hung down on one side to her neck. She introduced herself as Madam Tuscan.

"Come! Sit down," she urged, her smile engaging. They stepped inside and Maggie dropped to a chair and held out one hand quickly. She closed her eyes as if it was going to hurt.

"Don't be nervous, dear girl," the woman said, leaning forward. "Fortune favours the brave. You've got a fairly smooth hand." She looked intently. "There's going to be a loss—a deep loss, not only for you but for many people."

"And I suppose you knows what it is," Jamie said lightly.

"You'll be marrying a man whose surname is Christopher," the fortune teller said.

"Indeed I won't, then," Maggie snapped. She pulled her hand away and stood up. "This is my man and he's a Maley."

"There's not many with that name in this country," the fortune teller said. Her brows crinkled. "There's trouble and sorrow brewing off land and none can tell how great its sweep will be."

Jamie gave the fortune teller a skeptical look. "We came for a good fortune to be told. You're a misfortune teller. Only God knows the future and He's not tellin'. I won't be mistrustful of voyages in the sea." He tossed a few coins on the table and grabbed Maggie by the arm. "You shouldn't be wantin' to know the future," he said. "We make our own." He squeezed her arm as they made their way down the steps. "We missed our senses in coming here. If the fortune teller had foreknowledge she'd know I'm not a Christopher. It's easy to read her future. She's growin' old fast, her face so wrinkled a mosquito could crawl into a furrow and smother before it got its belly full."

They came outside laughing.

Maggie turned quickly at the sight of Emily Penny from Foxtrap, all neat and crisp in a dark cotton dress and starched white apron. She'd heard that Emily had been given a position by a St. John's merchant. "I haven't seen you for a long time," Maggie exclaimed.

"Nor I you, and here you is, you and Jamie all grown up." She eyed Jamie from head to toe with a smirk.

"Hello, yourself," Jamie said.

She wasn't finished. "I remember once when you threw a rock in a puddle of water and splashed me."

"A long time ago," he said. "We'll be seeing you." He hurried Maggie along.

A few months before, Emily had climbed on the horse wagon of a Foxtrap trader going to St. John's. She sat atop a sack of potatoes beside crates of salted dry fish until the trader stopped at the waterfront where a merchant spied Emily and offered her a position.

Emily turned back to look at Maggie and Jamie going down the street. A dark cloud crossed her face.

23

Despite the fortune teller's prediction, Jamie was determined to get a ticket on a sealing vessel. Edward John had gone to the icefields twice while he lived at home. Mary Jane had tried to coax him away from his plans, confiding, "William's got money laid away." When she saw that he couldn't be persuaded to stay home, she knitted a shiften of woollen drawers and blanketed them with red flannel to keep the wool away from his skin. After he came home from the ice front she had stayed awake night after night with him while he cried from pain in his legs and hips.

William had cursed the captain of the SS *Newfoundland*, cursed the ship, and the dangerous ice that had killed or maimed many of Newfoundland's crop of strong young men in their war against poverty.

"If I tell you what it's like out there, do you think you'd want to go?" Edward John asked Jamie.

"I will!" Jamie answered.

He had listened to Edward John and other sealers' stories about the adventure of the seal hunt as they sat around fires in sheds and on docks during long winter nights. They appeared undaunted by the deathly cold sweep of March winds and ice raftered by wind and currents, ice pans unpredictably separating, leaving space between sealers and the icefields.

"The ocean bed's strewn with the bodies of ships and people who didn't make it to port," Edward John told Jamie. "Sealers were lost when ice jams cracked wooden schooners into matchsticks. Other sealers were lost in the sudden sweep of blizzards that had many ways to kill. Of the first fifty wooden steamships to go to the ice beginning in 1863, forty-one ships were lost at sea." He shook his head. "The ocean surface is like a graveyard in winter, ice sticking into the air like blank headstones, a memorial to the sealers who died on icefields a thousand or more unnamed."

Jamie didn't tell anyone that he was having bad dreams. He had a repeat dream of running down a road to get on a sealing ship, the road stretching longer and longer the faster he ran. It gave way under his feet and he woke shivering, his bedclothes on the floor. One night he dreamed he was on a vessel that was listing; someone's hand was on his face smothering him.

His father cautioned him. "If you get a berth on a schooner goin' to the Gulf of St. Lawrence, stick with experienced sealers. Don't be goin' off on your own to try to prove yourself a great sealer. You're not goin' to the icefields where there is solid whiteness. You'll be goin' on ice that is loose and threatening. You'll need to be quick and nimble not to fall between the pans where the deep blue waits to pull you under. Keep your gaff and mind your step. A sealin' voyage can turn a boy into a man, a man into a corpse. If God wills it you'll be successful in gettin' yourself back home as good as when you left."

William knew he could caution his son but he couldn't tell him what to do. Other years Jamie had gone out to the turn in the lane and watched sealers leave, excitement filling the air as they laughed, pushed, and shoved each other. Voices of fathers left behind rang out, "Here's to bumper crops and bloody decks."

William set his mouth, mindful that this was the long and hungry month of March. Sometimes it became a march of death and April a month of mourning.

24

I got a berth on the Southern Cross *for a voyage to the icefields.* Jamie's words sang through his head. He'd gone to the St. John's waterfront with his cousins determined to get a berth. Once he got confirmation he couldn't wait to get home. When the driver's horse and dray got to his lane he jumped off and ran up the slope and down the hill calling, "I got me berth!"

Jamie found William standing at the wood horse and lifting his hatchet to come down on a junk of wood. The hatchet and wood fell to the ground as William, seeing his son's grin, hurried to slap him on the back. "I can't be keeping you back," he said, his face working through mixed emotions.

William picked up his hatchet without saying another word, nodding as Jamie told him he was going to Joe's place to ask for the use of his Labrador box.

When Jamie was little he had pressed his forehead against the palings of the picket fence outside his grandfather James's house. He eyed the old fellow and called, "What is it you're doin', Grandda?"

The man lifted his head from a length of wood in his hands. He placed it on the wood horse to saw and turned to his grandson. "I'm repairing a board in me Labrador box."

"What's it for?" he asked.

The old fellow answered, "It's to the Labrador your Uncle Joe will be goin' with this box."

"Won't you be goin', Grandda?"

James shook his grey head. "The work is for the young and strong, lad. I had me day with the crowd when I was younger. I even had me time with the seal hunt."

The old man got a faraway look in his eyes. "Nothing is ever the kind of adventure you hope for." He straightened his back and pushed his hand against it. "You'll find out fer yourself."

"I'll have a good kind of adventure," Jamie said in a strong, determined voice.

He smiled, remembering the old grandda as he ran over to Caroline's. He opened the gate and hurried up to the house. Johnny, hearing the door open and Jamie's light step, lifted his head. "Have you brought the young colleen with yer?"

"Not this time," he answered.

The first time Jamie took Maggie to meet Johnny, sitting on his stool by the fire, the sightless man reached his hand into the air. "Give here your hand, me lass, and tell me somethin' so I can get a speakin' likeness of you."

Maggie looked into his eyes, still pools in a small face with enough expression to make up for what his eyes lacked. She reached to grasp his hand, her long, shapely fingers touching his. She held his hand between her soft ones. "Jamie told me about you," she said.

Johnny pulled down his mouth. "Did he now? I can tell you somethin' about him. He's lost his heart to you. Don't *you* be losin' him on a ship."

"I won't if I can help it," she had promised.

Johnny added, as if to himself, "That Atlantic Ocean is a graveyard, the deepest and longest and widest graveyard there is—more dead people in it than live people on it."

Jamie had shrugged away his uncle's warnings not to go.

Now his uncle said in a resigned voice, "Ah, I know why you're here. You've come for the Labrador box."

Jamie grinned, forgetting that his uncle couldn't see him. "I'll have the box to hold some food and a few belongings if it can be spared."

"It will have to be spared for such a one as yourself, though your aunt will be reluctant to let it go. The box means the world to her."

Jamie knew that the box had been promised to James Butler, his cousin, who had drowned while casting for caplin. James had a fashion of holding the balls of his casting net between his teeth and throwing it overboard whenever he saw a dark swarm of caplin. One day he went headlong over his boat with the caplin seine.

Caroline called from the pantry, "I'll spare the Labrador box this time. Come back with it and not in it."

Jamie hurried to squeeze his aunt. "I'll bring back the box, I promise." He winked. "Sure, I'll have to, or be haunted."

Jamie hauled the pine box home on small wooden wheels Joe had attached to it. He packed his canvas knapsack containing hard bread, a bag of rolled oats, and a jar of molasses. William had corked a pint of rum. "In case you're on the ice too long and needs to warm your blood."

Later that day Caroline and Joe showed up. Caroline was holding hot buns in a cloth. She passed them to Jamie, saying, "Now, me boy, if your mam was here she'd do some fussing over you. She'd have molasses toutons in your armpits if you had no room in your box. Seein' she's not here to look out to you I'll do the best I can."

Joe passed him medical supplies Caroline had gathered: friar's balsam, a salve of sulphate of zinc for curing sores and cuts, and black gauze to attach to his headgear to protect his eyes against the crystal light of the icefields.

Joe warned, "You have to be prepared. Experienced sealers know well enough to protect themselves against ice blindness and sunburns on their lips and face."

"Don't be staying on the ice alone," Caroline added. "You could find yourself sailing away on an ice pan and it too stormy for anyone to launch a rescue."

Jamie gave her a steady look. "I know that."

Joe nodded. "I know you do," he said, "but knowin' is not enough. Sealers like you knowed it and where's they? Sunk in the deep for the fish to have for a spring meal and the women on land gone mad from the pain of never more layin' eyes on 'em, their ghosts haunting their dreams. We don't want the likes of that with you and your cousins."

That night when Jamie went upstairs he hesitated at the open door to his father's room. He thought of his mother dead a little more than a year. Her colourful wedding shawl, as soft as cobwebs, lay on a pile of clothes folded on a nightstand. He went in and picked it up. He smiled as dried rose petals floated like blossoms in a summer wind and scattered to the plaited mat on the floor. His mother had hated to see a flower die and its petals disappear. She gathered flowers and pressed their petals between cardboard covers. When they dried as light as a butterfly's wing she placed them between the pages of books. Sometimes she used rose petals to make rosewater for her morning wash. Jamie pressed the shawl against his nose drawing in the gentle scent. He remembered his mother walking in the shawl, its fringes dancing off her heels as she hurried up the road to a wedding, a christening, and other outings. He held a faint, long-ago memory of her taking it away from her shoulders and wrapping him in it as she sang him a lullaby. He folded it, intending to take it downstairs and place it in the Labrador box for good luck. Instead, he lifted it to his face again. Then he laid it back on the nightstand. He would leave it at home away from the blubbery smell of seals. Maggie could wear it after they were married. He spoke aloud to his dead mother. "I'll come back to Pappa, truly I will, Mam. The old fellar don't have a spirit in him since you left. I'll lighten him up when I comes home with me share and stories of the ice."

Maybe he'd go sealing again next year if Maggie got with child. A baby would bring a spark back to his father. He couldn't leave his father alone, not with his mother just gone and Elizabeth not long gone across the bay. In time Maggie would have her own home. Jamie had promised her that, telling her that in the interior of Kelly's Island there were long-standing trees called snags to be dragged from the grove and brought back in boat for their new house. He could almost smell the new wood and see sawdust fall like gold specks as he sawed through a tree trunk.

The next morning Jamie donned flannel-lined, knitted drawers. Over the drawers he wore moleskin trousers, and a red flannel shirt under a guernsey his mother had knit. It would hug his body under his fustian jacket throughout the voyage. He pulled on heavy woollen socks and vamps casing them, his feet in leather boots. When he came downstairs William looked at him and then turned to the open box. "Make sure you got all you needs for your voyage. Don't be wantin.'"

William helped him drive steel slivers a quarter-inch deep, three in each heel of his boots to keep him from slipping on the ice and falling into the open ocean between pans. "Your legs are young and strong but it takes concentration to jump from pan to pan on floating ice, some of it soft and honeycombed."

William saw to it that Jamie had a rope a quarter-inch in diameter and three fathoms long to tow his seals, a large sharpened knife, and a steel to sharpen it. "Keep your tools handy at all times," he cautioned.

Jamie took a charcoal pencil and some paper scraps left from what William had used to mark out his models and pushed them inside a blue bottle. He jammed the cork tight and tested it in the water bucket in the porch. It bobbed along keeping to the surface. He made room for it beside a change of clothes and a red blanket. He hoped he wouldn't get sealskin fingers. They'd be hard to heal and he wouldn't be able to use his pencil and paper to sketch the *Southern Cross* with her pile of seal pelts.

William leaned against the door facing and looked toward his son as he pulled on a lined woollen cap and fisherman's mitts. A cold feeling wrapped around him. Elizabeth, his only daughter, had gone far across the waters of Conception Bay. Now Jamie, his only son, was going to the danger floes. He couldn't forget the night Mary Jane had awakened from a deep sleep calling weakly that Jamie was falling into the sea. Her strange premonition clung to him and held on. But then whenever he saw Jamie healthy and full of life, his arm slung around Maggie's shoulder, the premonition drifted away like fog. Jamie would get married. He would farm and jig a season's supply of fish to salt for the winter and on times he'd likely paint pictures. There'd be children.

William, now almost fifty-seven, had never been to the ice. He didn't have the steadiness needed for sea legs. His eyes had a far-off look. "The Maleys have been here a long time, Jamie. You're the last man in these parts to carry the name after me and me brothers. Don't lose your life to a wooden boat or on icefields, where death always stalks a sealer's life, lookin' for his weakness." He let out a heavy sigh. He didn't let on that he was thinking about the 1898 seal hunt. Forty-eight men from the *Greenland* had died on the ice. Wind wraiths swept across the seascape caking the men in heavy, wet snow. The air like ice crystals stung them while their eyes under iced lashes stared into the blizzard trying to see the lights of their ship. Their warm blood chilled and their hearts stopped beating as they stood, knelt, crouched—did whatever they could to stay alive. Their faces froze in an expression of despair. Other sealers watched in horror as a relative tumbled off the ice and disappeared into the dark depths of the ocean.

Jamie drew in a deep breath as he strode up the rock path to the graveyard, pulled open the gate, and hurried to his mother's grave covered in snow. The earth had been cut into, leaving scars the snow hid, scars grass would heal in spring. Hearts would take longer. "I'll see you some day," he said and felt a splash of tears on his face.

Maggie had come up the path in time to hear his last words. She felt an icy claw of apprehension down her back. *Not too soon, please God.*

He turned to her. "I'm packed and ready." He squeezed her tight and she watched him hurry back to the house to claim the Labrador box.

Maggie had tried to talk Jamie out of going on the voyage. "Never mind the seal money," she coaxed. "We'll have love in a cottage."

His mouth was set, determined. "Just this once."

His father slipped a few coins into his hand. "Get the things you need. You've been a farmer. Now you'll be a sealer. I'll be home waitin' for a flipper to grease me innards."

They tried to make their goodbyes lighthearted. William cocked his eye and cautioned Jamie, "Mind the weather and stay with the other sealers. You don't want to end up in England before your supper."

Jamie laughed. "I think a few suppers would pass before I landed there."

Jamie's mind was on the wonderful time he would have standing on ice sparkling under the sun, thousands of crystal plates around him, many holding the coveted seals.

His father had one more caution as he clasped his son to his chest. "Watch the ship's deck. When it's aglitter with ice you'll feel like you're walkin' on a floor of slippery eels." His hand tightened into a fist against Jamie's back. "Don't be gettin' big in your boots, me boy. You could come back with just yerself."

Jamie pulled back and punched his father's shoulder. "Go away with you. I'll come back with money enough and a taste of seal meat to strengthen your blood."

When Jamie went to say goodbye to his father's family Joe looked at him and said, "We old fellars with our game legs would never stand up to the shifting ice, not like you young gaffers."

Johnny threw him parting advice. "Oh, 'tis not good to be too confident, me son. Mischance can dig a hole in a full pocket."

Maggie went with him to the end of the lane, one hand clutched in his while his other hand pulled his sea chest on its wooden wheels. She kissed him goodbye. "Come back to me," she said.

He gave her an amused look. "And why wouldn't I? Sure, you're me very heart. The icefields may be a hundred miles from St. John's but there's no distance between our thoughts." He teased, "You'll be able to buy yourself a sealskin stole once I'm done on the ice."

"The fur skins can warm the ladies in Europe," she said. "I'll have you to warm me."

As soon as Jamie's back was turned, Maggie ran after him for another hug. He dropped the strap on the Labrador box and cradled her in his arms. She drew in his scent and the feel of his face on hers. Loneliness washed over her as Jamie disappeared over the hill, distance lengthening between them. Her hand stayed lifted in goodbye after he had gone out of sight. A cold wind touched her face as she dropped her hand and turned back. Her thoughts followed Jamie. *While you roam the icefields looking to have the warmth of coin in hand for our wedding you will live inside of me, in the warmth of me heart.* She was suddenly reminded that March had come in like a lamb. She had heard it said that when it comes in like a lamb it goes out like a lion.

She hoped Jamie got home before the lion roared.

25

Jamie met up with several other young men going on the voyage, five of them his cousins. The Bussey boys included young Alfred, who was big for his age. From the time he could haul on a pair of rubber boots, stumbling awkwardly, he would run down on the stagehead to grab the painter of his father's boat and try to fasten it. He was eager to grow up and be a fisherman like his big brothers Noah and Gordon. Other cousins were Joseph and Thomas. There were several Butlers, including Zachary, who appeared downhearted since Olivia Porter left to go to the Boston States without an explanation. He told Jamie that he planned on saving enough money to eventually sail to Boston, find her, and bring her home.

The Foxtrap sealers filled the air with their laughter as they trudged out Church Road to go by horse and wagon.

"A voyage you'll never forget," said Sam Rideout, the wagon driver, banging Jamie on the back. "It'll be over in a few weeks and if luck will have it you'll be foldin' bills and twirlin' coins. You'll have money to put by for your wedding."

The men didn't mind being jarred and shaken, their tongues rattling in their heads as they sat in the wagon, some dangling their legs from the open back as they held on to the open slats on the sides. The horse half-heartedly dragged the loaded wagon, its unsteady wheels going over the rutted and muddy road to St. John's and on down to the harbourfront.

Once the men jumped down from the wagon and waved goodbye to their driver, Jamie and his sealing buddies clicked along the cobblestones of Water Street in their sealing boots, hurrying to get the berth promised them. The sun had slipped from under a lid of cloud, a bright eye, naked and piercing, while Jamie and his cousins were on their way to St. John's. Now it sank back, looking small and uneven in the face of a dark cloud.

Jamie's old buddy Ted, whose family had moved to St. John's, touched his shoulder as he unfolded his brin bag to fill it with hay stored in a shed beside the wharf. Jamie stopped at the sight of him in street clothes and carrying no baggage.

Noah called, "Issin you goin' to the ice, me man?"

Ted looked toward the barque and the black smoke billowing out of its stacks into the crisp air. He shook his head. "I've a bad feelin' about the *Southern Cross*. But don't let it bother you." He hurried away.

Jamie tried to convince himself that everything would be all right. The 325-ton whaling ship had handled other voyages. A dark cloud hovered and then descended over his happy mood as a memory flashed of the fortune teller's prediction that Maggie would marry a Christopher. He shook away her words as he hurried across the wharf to the ticket office. *Maybe she will marry him when I'm 100 and dead.*

After waiting in line for some time Jamie stood in front of a large oak desk and took off his cap. He dipped his head toward the clerk sitting behind the desk. He cleared his throat. "I've been wantin' to get a sealing ticket for a while," he said. "Now it's me turn. I've got the money right here."

The clerk took the money, giving Jamie a scant glance. He ran an ink-stained finger down the pages of an open ledger and dipped his pen in an inkwell. He lifted it and proceeded to place a check mark beside JAMES WILLIAM MALEY in the large ledger. He looked up. "So yer pa's name is William James—the reverse of yours—if there should come the need to contact him."

Jamie shrugged. "I don't think you'll be doing that."

To the question of where he lived Jamie answered, "Foxtrap, sir, and proud of it."

The clerk rolled his eyes and scowled. "I've seen der place."

When Jamie had procured his ticket and crop note marking him for a gaff he'd secure on the vessel, the clerk nodded and dismissed him. "Be along wit' yer, then."

Jamie stood up and put his cap back on. "Thank you, sir," he said with another dip of his head.

A seasoned sealer from Foxtrap, waiting in line, called to Jamie, "Wet your ticket for good luck and wet the other eye. God save us from makin' widows and orphans."

When Jamie came outside, one man who had been unlucky in obtaining a berth tapped him on the back and remarked, "'Tis a risky business, b'y, to be goin' on the *Southern Cross* to the Magdalen Islands. The ice is loose, not packed. There's less risk on tight ice, and this year Newfoundland's got a fleet of icebreakers, the first country in the world to have it. It'll be safer on the SS *Newfoundland*."

A sealer from Kelligrews let out a hearty laugh. "God willin', me son, we'll be sleeping in the fat soon and there won't be a berth left for someone else next year, as there's one for you because a sealer was injured on last year's voyage."

Jamie felt as if someone had kicked him in the stomach, but his voice was steady as he answered, "We're sailin' with Captain Clarke, a man who knows his business."

Another sealer nodded. "Yeah, b'y, Captain Clarke's been to the ice fourteen times. The *Southern Cross* is able to bring home bumper crops. She's done that off and on for a good many years, so I've been told. Captain Clarke intends for his vessel to be the first back in port. That's somethin', that is."

No one said anything about the ship having a wooden hull and that it did not have wireless, should it find itself in danger of ice and blizzards or an engine explosion.

Cold, salty sea air blew against Jamie's face. He squared his shoulders. *No matter what, the sea will not be the master of my fate.*

26

The waters of St. John's harbour were calm under sheets of ice around several sealing ships preparing to sail to the icefields. Sealers filed up the gangway of the *Southern Cross*. They dropped down to a deck covered with plywood that extended from stem to stern to take the marks of the sealers' boot picks.

Crowds stood on the wharf as the barque's lines were loosened and cast off from the dock. Women at home, who had sons and husbands on the vessel, looked out their windows and smiled as horns and whistles blew to announce the sailing. They had hopes that there would be money to buy food for their children crying for nourishment. Bedridden elders, with bellies distended for the want of a good meal, turned to the sound. They licked papery pale lips remembering the taste of fresh seal in gravy. There were blasts from muzzleloaders shooting blanks of oakum and powder.

The 140-foot-long barque carried men from St. John's, Torbay, Conception Bay North and South, Trinity and Placentia Bays. Surnames included Butlers, Clarkes, Kennedys, Porters. . . .

The *Southern Cross*, its sails unfurled and engine engaged, shuddered and scrunched against ice barring its way out of the harbour. A call rang through the crisp air: "Everybody off the ship and on the tow line!"

The sealers, some wearing scotch caps with long tassels, others in canvas or sealskin caps, rushed off the ship. Jamie joined the string of men moving across the ice like a long shadow. They dug their hobnailed boots into the ice and strained on the tow line to pull the heavy vessel through the ice and out into the open sea.

"It's cold but I'm sweating already," Jamie grunted to the sealer behind him, who, like other sealers, was undernourished this time of the year. Still, there was strength in hope and expectation and the men pulled hard.

Seasoned sealers who had retired from going to the ice stood onshore watching the vessel break through the ice and the men swarm aboard. They pictured them finding a place to bunk, a spot they would occupy sleeping, yarning, playing cards and checkers and eating from a meagre supply while the ship steamed toward the icefields. Families and friends of the sealers from St. John's and the surrounding area waved though they could no longer see the men. Finally they turned back to their work.

The barque passed between the frosty face of the Southside Hills and Signal Hill with Cabot Tower, a grey sentinel above the harbour, its southeast windows framing St. John's. The ship sailed out through The Narrows past its black cliffs, out into the Atlantic Ocean on its way to the seal hunt.

Fortune teller Tuscan had pushed aside the red curtains at her window and watched the men free the *Southern Cross* from the ice.

She shuddered as they reboarded the vessel and disappeared below deck.

"Their coffin," she said, turning away.

27

In the early morning darkness Eddie, a stowaway, had snuck down to the wharf and made a run for it onto the steamer when the boatswain's attention was elsewhere. His pockets were heavy with cakes of hard bread and a flask of water tucked inside a gunny sack. He knew where to go, having listened to sealers who had previously sailed on the boat. He drew a canvas over him in a far corner below deck and lay still. If sealers had known there was a stowaway aboard before the steamer weighed anchor they would have reported him and he'd have been thrown off the ship. The sea carried enough threats without the added jinx a stowaway could bring to a voyage.

Eddie had heard that a stowaway was never allowed on the ice to kill seals and claim a share. He planned on being the best lackey the captain ever set eyes on. No matter what his punishment on discovery, it wouldn't be as severe as what he had endured from his stepfather. His face was pinched and pale as if something under his skin was sucking its goodness. His light brown eyes were wet-looking, glassy, and under his lower lids the skin looked bruised and translucent. He would never have gotten a berth. He had a crippled hand. His stepfather had held it over hot coals under the damper of the stove and had smiled during Eddie's blood-curling screams. The burned skin had not recovered and Eddie's fingers were drawn up against his palm. Whenever he sat in church and the minister preached on hell, waves of fear shook his body. He wanted to believe in a God who would not do worse than his stepfather. He stopped going to church. Instead he spent Sundays on the beach firing stones into the water, pretending he was hitting his stepfather.

Twenty or more men had been assigned tiered bunks in the overcrowded forecastle. Jamie and the other sealers dropped from a rope into the makeshift space in a hold below deck. Here sealers would idle away time and sleep four to a berth when they were not on the ice. It was a confined place, dim in lamplight. Missing home already, Jamie breathed in the damp, barbed air of the ship.

Thomas took in his lonely look. "The women will be waiting," he said, thinking of his wife, Esther, who had lost their infant son last year. It would be a long voyage.

"We'll be the first in port," Joseph Butler said, slapping Jamie on the back. "Then we'll be in the money."

Thomas Bussey stretched against a post. "The merchants would skin a man like a seal if they could get a dollar for his hide," he said. "We won't get much when they've finished our account."

"B'y, don't be blaming the merchants for everything," Zachary Butler said. "Sure, we'd have neither ship to come aboard if the merchants didn't risk their money." He was excited to be on the *Southern Cross*. It would take his mind off Olivia. His boyish face clouded when he thought about her.

Both Zachary and Jamie had been fascinated with the *Southern Cross* ever since they'd learned that she had sailed on an Antarctic expedition in 1898, going through the Great Ice barrier to the unexplored Ross Sea.

Joseph Bussey looked at the other sealers. "In 1901 the *Southern Cross* was the first ship to arrive in port with a full load of more than 26,000 pelts. That can happen ag'in."

Jamie nodded. "I hope so."

"And she a smaller ship than others at the ice," Joseph added.

A seasoned sealer piped up, "I hope you all got your *hardtack* and black tea, a bit of oats and such. We do our own cooking. There's a man among us who cooks fresh meat, potatoes, and turnip hash for the captain and officers. He'll be lucky to get a bit of fat for himself. Hard bread and porridge with tea and molasses is the most we'll eat until we're in the swiles. Then there'll be a meal of fresh flippers in onions, pork rinds, and gravy."

One sealer drew a bottle of rum from his bunk. "Here, Alfred, take a lick. Just don't tell your mother. She'll be on her knees with the Bible."

Alfred shook his head while another sealer prodded him, "We're men here. Down the hatch, me son."

Alfred glanced at his brothers. Then he opened his mouth. He gulped the fiery liquid and let out a screech when it hit his throat. His eyes watered.

The sealers clapped their hands and stomped their feet. "You've been screeched, b'y," one of them said.

Thomas shook his head at his younger brother. "You'll learn, Alfred, to make your own choices." He glared at the other sealers.

John Bishop from Kelligrews lowered himself to a berth. "If we get a good crop," he said, "we might have to give up our bunks for seal pelts and fat. Perhaps sleep on them. But we won't be killing seals on Sunday. The captain don't owe with that kind of disrespect. When God rests, he rests."

"The Commercial Society presents a silk flag to the St. John's captain who brings in the most seals," Noah said, his eyes bright. "Some day I'll be a captain and get a silk flag fer me ship."

Joseph laughed. "There'll be a long day before that."

"And a long night gettin' to the seal patch, and a tirin' one if we don't get some sleep," Thomas said. He blew out the lamplight.

Conversation gradually quietened as, one by one, the sealers settled into sleep amid the steady beat of the ship through cold, dark waters.

part four

28

Simon Swartz, a wiry little man, lifted his burlap bag to his shoulder and walked down the frozen path like a soldier. He had hitched his horse and cart to a post at the end of Church Road. Other peddlers waited until later in the spring to go from door to door selling their wares or making an exchange. Simon knew well enough that women who had hoarded a few coins in a jar all winter were ready to part with them if there was a sealer in their household expected to return with cash. Sometimes Simon accepted knitted goods in exchange for items a woman didn't have the money to buy. He had been born with a flipper left hand—no fingers, just a thumb. He kept a glove on it so he would not be accused of causing a woman in the family way to be frightened and thus have her unborn child cursed with the same malady. He showed respect for people's superstitions and they were grateful for his caution and allowed him their hospitality.

On and on from house to house he went, his bag getting lighter as he pried what money he could from the jars and purses of careful mothers. He always smelled of something grand and women were known to have invited him in just for his scent. They were drawn to his quick, easy smile and bright brown eyes and seduced by the scent of new cloths and soaps that smelled like a field of flowers. To the children the sight of pearl, silver, and gold buttons, shiny as money and in all sizes, intrigued them. They gathered close to the peddler's knee. He wasn't a heartless fellow and, sometimes, if he was satisfied with the jingles in his pocket and he saw a child's dress apart for want of a button, he willingly parted with a bright one just to see a little girl's dull eyes shine. He thought of it as wiping the clouded windows of a soul to show its gleam.

Other times the peddler gave a family a coin or two in exchange for heirlooms he knew had value for a wealthy customer but meant little to hungry families trying to survive *hard scrabble days*. His eyes held a glint like new coins as he carried off items from an old fellow's shed: treasures to antique dealers, useless to him. After the death of an elderly member of a family, goods of little value to those left behind were often tossed into the sea for wild birds to pick at—gold brooches, figurines, baroque framed paintings, and other articles—unless Simon got there first. He opened his bag in the homes of wealthy people, hopping from one item to another like a leprechaun, grinning all the while, persuading the lady of the house to buy a *must have* item.

He lifted the latch on the storm door to Joe Maley's house and cautiously entered calling, "Missus."

Caroline hurried toward him wiping her hands on her apron. "Come in," she said and he followed her inside to the large kitchen. He lowered his leather cap to the table, its crown sunk into a bowl holding white pools of light coming through the kitchen window. He flicked his right hand through loose black lines of wavy hair and scratched at needles of black beard pushing through white skin. He dropped the ragged-edged bag, burlap sprouting threads, and bent down leaning back on his haunches, black boots under him.

He looked up at Lavinia, who had come to stand by her mother. "I suppose," he said, "you want to see what's in me bag."

"I'll thank you to empty it on the table," she said, her eyes eager.

He bowed. "Just for you." He carefully lifted out a soft brown cloth and spread it on the kitchen table as if it was a tablecloth made ready for food. Caroline watched as he lovingly lifted items she wished she could afford. She wondered aloud if he had a flowered plate, one to hold a nice cake for company. She'd keep it for Lavinia's hope chest. She looked at him hopefully.

"Indeed," he answered and lifted an exquisite plate wrapped in a flour bag.

Lavinia let out a startled breath. She swallowed in longing.

"I've got a few ten-cent pieces," Caroline said.

The peddler had thought his prospects good. Now he was disappointed. "It's worth more than a dollar," he told her.

Caroline's look pitched on a paisley scarf hanging on a nail that her mother had left her. She hated its bruised colours and seldom wore it. She offered it to the peddler and he reluctantly accepted it and her ten-cent pieces. To be sure she was fair Caroline handed him some buttons she'd cut off a dress she was using for mat rags.

She saw him look toward the kettle boiling on the stove. "You'll have a cuppa. Sure, you will," she said.

"You are unthinkably kind, ma'am," he said as she set a cup of tea before him and laid out a dish of bakeapple jam and a thick slice of bread.

The man lashed into his bread in silence. Then he asked for another slice. When he was finished he looked up with a slight smile. "I'll thank you for the cup of tea, such as it was." He got up, gathered his bag, and left the house without a backward glance.

"That man can put away a turn of grub given the chance," Caroline said. "He's got goods but nothing he can eat."

Lavinia held her wedding plate up to the light and read the gold lettering: LIMOGES, FRANCE. "How far it's come," she said, rubbing her finger over its wide gold edging. She could already see the plate holding fresh blueberry cake dabbed with cow's cream as she sat at a table, just her and Joshua Rideout, her future husband.

The peddler trudged back down the road not suspecting that before the day was over lives would be changed, secrets made and kept for a while. He had no idea how lucky he would be this night after a day with a disappointing turnover of coin and article.

29

Maggie was at William's house the next day sitting by the table drinking tea when Caroline rushed in exclaiming, "There's bad news but it's not anything to do with the *Southern Cross*."

"What is it, then?" Maggie asked. She laid down her cup.

"Laura Rideout was found frozen to death outside her grandmother's house in Manuels this morning."

Maggie's hands gripped her cup. "Oh, no!"

"Indeed!" said Caroline. "Ebbie Miles looked through his window and saw that there was no smoke from the chimney. He went to check on the trouble and found Laura outside on the ground, a bloody gash on her forehead. Phoebe, her grandmother, was inside huddled under her counterpane."

"And little Lily? Sure, she's the very spit of her mother," Maggie said.

Caroline shook her head. "He never found her."

Maggie gasped. She thought of Timothy gone to the seal hunt on the *Southern Cross*. He'd come home to find his wife buried and his daughter gone.

Caroline had seen a wolf around the place the week before, a large, white animal with a black stripe down its spine. It had let out a high-pitched, mournful howl during the early hours of the morning. Then it had run off down the road.

"Such a sad situation, the child likely carried off by a wolf," Caroline said.

Joe heard her as he came into the house. He stood in the doorway. "I doubt that's the way it was," he told her. "The mother's coat was missing. Whatever that means we might never know."

Maggie hadn't seen much of Laura after they grew up but she remembered a silver scar on Laura's arm after she was married. Laura had confided, "Timothy and I did it in secret after the wedding, cut along each other's arm to let our blood flow together, with the hope it would sneak into each other's veins. It's an old Scottish custom."

Maggie had looked at her. "A blood tattoo?"

"Kind of." She giggled. "We have matchin' scars. Matchin' wedding rings can get lost."

"I never expected you to be married before me, Laura," Maggie had said with a mock pout. "Now here you is soon to be a mamma and Timothy these past two seasons gone on successful seal voyages."

As Laura thickened with child she gained weight everywhere. Her scar widened. It no longer matched Timothy's. But it didn't matter. The two were a true match.

* * * * *

"I'm gone," Laura had called to her mother, who was busy banking the fire for the night. She pulled the hood up around Lily's face and drew the two-year-old to her bosom as she closed the door and started up the hill to her grandmother's house. The night was crystal cold, the air still, and the road hard and slippery.

Ebbie later surmised that she was almost to the door when she teetered on the icy path. Her feet gave way and she hit the ground, cushioning Lily.

Maggie imagined Laura lying motionless, eyes closed, the child screaming. Lily would have seen her mother's face in the silvery light of the moon, blood leaking from a cut on her temple. She likely looked toward the house as if longing to get inside, where it would be warm. Then she would have burrowed down beside her mother, searching for the warmth of her mother's body against the cold air seeping into her bones.

Phoebe had grown tired waiting for her granddaughter. She had climbed the stairs to her room and gone to bed. Soon she was sound asleep, warmed under a mound of quilts while her granddaughter and great-granddaughter lay without shelter beyond the reach of their home.

Wind came like a ghost, its fingers slithering up and down the child's spine. Someone heard her cry long and loud, breaking into sobs as if she realized she was all alone, abandoned by a mother who refused to answer her, hold her, save her from the cold. Someone found her tugging on her mother's hand, as if to urge her to get up and take her inside, a mother who lay silent, unheeding her daughter.

It would be years before the mystery of that night would unfold to the satisfaction of Laura's family.

30

More than a year had passed since Emily Penny left Foxtrap and went to St. John's to become a servant to Adam Dixon, a merchant on Duckworth Street. When the horse and wagon carrying the young girl had drawn up in front of a beautiful mansion she had thought, *If only the other girls from Foxtrap could see me in this mansion!*

The driver got down and tied his horse to a post and she followed him along a cobblestone walkway and up brick steps that led to wide double doors. He pushed a button and a ringing sound echoed inside.

"This must be heaven," she said, looking at the doors as if they were pearly gates.

He laughed. "If heaven has an attic it's likely where you'll be sleeping, or in the basement with other housemaids."

She turned to look at the street crowded with colourful buildings. She drew in a deep breath, the eateries with foreign spices and other goods mysteriously potent.

A door to the mansion was opened by a straight-backed, elderly man who gave her a stern look. Emily passed him, fastening her gaze on the woman descending the carved oak staircase beside windows in wide casements. "Oh!" she said. Her hand went to her mouth.

Mrs. Abigail Dixon stopped at the foot of the stairs, her hand resting on a brazen figurine golden under sunlight shining through the bubbled glass windows. She nodded toward Emily and disappeared into the oak-panelled drawing room, leaving the door open for her to follow.

Emily hesitated in the doorway of the room while the mistress, now in a wing chair by the fireplace, eyed her with disdain. Emily turned to take in the room with its bevelled glass windows and high ornate ceilings.

"Pay attention to my instruction; it won't be given twice," the mistress said with such a sharp voice that Emily knew she would no longer belong to herself but to this woman, who likely had a covey of housemaids ready to drop a thought or a night of sleep to rush to her whims.

Emily went to say, "Indeed, ma'am," but her tongue seemed to be stuck to the roof of her mouth.

Every morning Emily hurried down to the kitchen, where the cook was preparing Abigail's breakfast. An egg was placed, like a clouded moon in white edging, between two halves of rye bread on a gold-rimmed plate. When the meal was ready Emily brought her mistress breakfast in bed on a tray holding an image of the late, sour-looking Queen Victoria, not someone she'd want to be facing during her morning tea. Her knuckles were white from her tight grasp, her cheeks flushed as she climbed the winding stairs careful not to slop the tea and juice.

She was the only servant in the attic. Others had a bed in the basement and were scurrying in all directions without a thought of conversing with her. Even the cook scarcely glanced her way as she came into the kitchen to help with the peeling of vegetables after she had finished the beds and dusting. She scrubbed the kitchen floor afterwards feeling hot and faint. She grumbled under her breath, "To be a servant is less than living."

She never told a soul her secret; soon it would tell itself.

One night the persistent ringing of a bell woke her. She imagined the merchant's stout finger on the button. It kept ringing as she drew on her clothes and followed its sound three flights of stairs down to the library. Cline, the elderly father of the merchant, was sitting in a Queen Anne chair. He held out a small book. "Read to me, my dear," he said, his voice crusty. He cleared his throat. "Me eyes are old and rheumy."

She drew in a startled breath. "But sir, I can't tell how to form the black marks into sounds. I have no meanin' for them."

"The late Queen Victoria didn't raise subjects such as ourselves to be ignorant and unlearned," he said. "You, too, will learn. I shall teach you."

She gave him a level look. "I might be ignorant of your ways and the Queen's ways, sir, a queen gone beyond words and life itself, but I'm not unlearned. I know how to mix barm and raise bread. I can draw a mean flower and embroider it on a pillowcase in a clear stitch that the ma'am can be proud to show off."

"Then you shall add to your learning this instant. Your voice will fit pleasantly over words. There's no end to what you can do with them. Words can fill reams using only twenty-six letters."

True to his word the old fellow drew a sheet of parchment from a desk drawer and dipped a pen into an inkwell. Then he began to show her how to form letters to be coupled into an unlimited number of words, and words into sentences with periods, question marks, and other markings.

She eyed the bottle of ink intently. Then she turned and asked, "How many words can be made from a whole bottle?"

He gave her an amused look. "That depends on how large the words are."

Once a week for months the old gent called her to the library. He patiently taught her how words she spoke every day looked on paper. "Ah," he confessed one day, as if she hadn't already figured it out, "it's loneliness that bothers me more than me old eyes."

She smiled. "Don't I know it."

One day after she finished work, she went into the library intending to find a book. Instead she climbed upon a high bed against the wall and lay down, her body settling into a feather mattress thick enough to give her the sensation of floating. She stared at the stained glass windows, hardly able to turn from them to study the white plaster ceiling and its adornments: circles wreathed with fruit, leaves, and swirling ribbons. A green basin holding candles hung from the centre of the ceiling. She drew in a deep breath picturing the lovely bowl of light cutting through the darkness at night. She wondered how one man and woman could have all this and her mamma and pappa have hardly a door to their thin-walled house.

She turned, startled, as the door opened and her mistress came in. "How dare you lie on your laurels and your work undone?" she asked.

Emily swallowed hard and sat up. "But ma'am—"

The woman rushed forward. Her hand cut across Emily's face. "You're nothing but a blundering bay girl."

Emily fell backwards and landed on the floor rug. She jumped up and ran past her mistress and through the hall toward the outside door. She grabbed it hard and pulled it open. She ran down the street crying.

A white-haired, distinguished-looking man passing by asked, "What's the matter, young maid?"

"Nothing a'tall, sir." She drew back from his hand as it reached for her arm.

"I could find a spot for you," he said, his voice low and coaxing.

Abigail watched Emily run down the street in her bare feet and saw herself as the ragged young girl who had left Conception Bay years before. Adam Dixon, buying her father's fish, had been so taken with her he had employed her for a month. Then he had married her. He didn't tell her that he'd been stricken with a severe case of mumps as a child. It went down in his cuffs.

"Your seed has been damaged," his doctor told him.

"Children?" he had asked, his mouth dry.

"Possible, but not likely. You have deficiencies in your nature."

Above everything Abigail wished she had a child. Now she watched the servant's clumsy movements, the thickening in her body, and a plan was hatched. With all her might she called, "Emily! Come back!"

Emily turned, relieved at the change in her mistress, the sound of desperation in her voice. She looked down at her belly. "For you," she said, and started to walk back.

Late one night Emily was summoned from her bed by Abigail and told to follow her into the drawing room out of the hearing of the other servants. She closed the doors. "We know your trouble, girl," the mistress told her. "Is there any chance you'll marry the father?"

Emily shook her bowed head.

The mistress smiled. "We'll keep the child as ours. It will make me happy."

"You have a big house and a handsome husband. Don't that make you happy?" she asked.

Abigail's eyes grew moist, her voice quavering. "I'd pay anything for that squirt of joy that allows people to laugh with ease. Sometimes I feel a quiver inside as if I'm foundering and there's nothing to hold me together."

"No one could tell by lookin' at you."

Abigail's voice dropped to a whisper. "And I don't want you to tell. This is my burden. I wouldn't wish to bring sadness to my husband."

"I thought you had the world," Emily said.

"I have everything a woman needs. My illness is part of me. It can't be cut out or lessened with time. A child will help. I know it will."

"As long as this roof stays over me head," Emily answered quickly. She'd be getting the best of care for her baby and seeing the child grow up.

"No doubt about that," the mistress said. "You'll stay."

Adam opened the door and Abigail grabbed her husband's hand. She pulled him inside and told him that Emily had agreed to their plan.

His face relaxed as if he had let go of a burden he'd been carrying. "It's settled, then." He didn't look at Emily.

Emily had heard the other servants talking, saying the master had been damaged in the lower field and had no chance of producing a crop. He was letting his wife have something she wanted and he couldn't give her. She knew different.

The mistress turned to Emily. "You can nurse the baby and meet the child's needs but he'll be mine and we'll have no more talk."

Emily nodded, unable to speak. She was having a baby by chance; it was her child's destiny to be raised in a fine house with the baby's very own father.

It was a comfort to be caught in the benevolent eye of her mistress who saw to it that Emily was given light duties and rested often. She even allowed her a key to the locked buffet so she could help herself to any food she might crave. That all changed one night when a storm seemed to brew in Emily's belly. It caught her up in a whirlwind as she lay in bed unable to call out. She felt ripped from stem to stern as blood and her child burst out into the bed, a red blob slipping after the tiny, still creature. She crawled down the stairs leaving the baby behind, crying as she went, a bloody trail following her. The mistress found the baby dead and took it away. "Where?" she had asked but the mistress told her it didn't matter where the child's body was buried. God had taken the child's soul to heaven where it would have a new body.

Soon Emily was back to heavy duties, her mind bursting with sorrow for the baby she would never hold.

Every year Simon Swartz showed up at the merchant's door, the same peddler who made his rounds along the Southern Shore. This time he came with his bag holding a surprise, the sound Emily wished she could have heard on the night of her child's stillbirth.

Emily was on her way to her attic bed when she heard the doorbell ring again and again, an urgent clapping, and then footsteps. She stepped back on the stairs and listened. She could hear only a murmur of voices so she made a stealthy climb down each flight of stairs from the servants' side to the landing. The door to the kitchen was ajar and she got close enough to recognize the peddler she had seen in Foxtrap. "I've come with somethin' your mistress would want if she saw it."

"You won't be waking the mistress this time of night," Emily heard the cook say.

"But you will," the usually mild peddler said. "Do it quick if you don't want to be at the end of her tongue and a whip besides."

The peddler seemed so sure of himself that the cook set up over the stairs with a hurried step.

The peddler's face lifted as he heard the heavy creak of Merchant Dixon's feet on the second landing. He stood at the top of the stairs pulling off his nightcap and calling down, "There better be a right good reason for this disturbance."

"There is, sir, and you'll be glad for it."

"Aye, then, what is it?"

"Hasten down, sir. I've brought a bundle, a child who doesn't need the breast, maybe a little pap."

Abigail came out of her bedroom and stood on the landing. When she saw the baby she rushed down.

The peddler looked at her with a grin. "I've brought you a child, ma'am. There's been a chance event and the mother is gone beyond help."

He told Abigail how he had been walking back to his lodging along a path on the outside of a rock wall when he heard a weak cry. He dismissed it at first as the sound a cat might make. But then he stopped to investigate. He followed the cry growing fainter and came upon the sad scene, moonlight showing the figures of a woman and a child. He'd been to the house before and knew that Laura Rideout, with Lily, her daughter, was staying with her grandmother while she waited for the child's father to come home from his sealing voyage on the *Southern Cross*. He had bent toward the mother feeling for her pulse. She lay dead, the child huddled beside her shivering uncontrollably. He lifted the coat from the mother and wrapped the baby in it. Then he sheltered her with his greatcoat. He didn't go home that night. Instead he huddled in a shed with the child trying to soothe her with a lullaby:

"Cosey down, little one,
Sleep until the night is done."

Her body shuddered then settled into sleep while he stayed awake wondering what to do with a treasure more valuable than anything else he had to peddle.

The peddler smiled at Abigail. "I thought of you and Mr. Dixon wanting a child and I knew what I had to do."

The little girl opened her eyes and sobbed, "Ma-ma! Maaaaa!"

Abigail took in the child's tiny face, the shiny, golden ringlets. "Poor baby," she said softly holding out her arms. The little girl began to cry more earnestly.

"I'm going to take care of you until your mammy comes," she said softly.

The child leaned away from her and she hurried to the pantry. She came back holding out a bright red apple. The little girl took it and put it to her lips.

"I'll peel it for you," the cook offered.

Abigail shook her head. "No, no. Leave it." She watched as the child's tiny teeth bit into the fruit. She smiled when the child's shivering subsided. "You'll be warm here," she said.

The cook rushed to stir the fire. It leaped high in the fireplace and Abigail picked up the little girl, careful to face the fire so she could watch the flames and forget everything else.

The peddler went away, his guilt assuaged by the look on Abigail's face. In time, he told himself, baubles and toys would take the little girl's attention; her mother's face would become vague—a dream she had long ago. She would cry less and less for her mother, finally giving Abigail what she wanted.

When Emily saw the child her heart fluttered. She pictured how her own child would have looked. She would make sure this child would not take the brunt of the mistress's low moods.

She crept back up the stairs feeling her loss all over again.

31

"Be yarry and get your gams in gear!" Captain Clarke's voice boomed out firing instructions rapidly. "The swiles won't lie waitin' for yers. Over aboard you go with your gaff and gear. Jump from the rope leaning forward so you'll fall flat on the pan. A misstep could put you under water. Ice doesn't make for a comforting grip. Don't get close to the seals unarmed."

The captain made sure that each man had a gaff shod with iron, a bat, a coiled tow rope slung over his shoulder like a sash, and a sculping knife at his waist. Every man carried his knapsack holding food and supplies. A canteen of water was also belted at the waist.

Jamie had been warned that when the sun shimmers as if it is dipped in a bowl of crystal and there are mare's tails in the sky bad weather is on its way. There were no mare's tails today. He stared at the endless field of floating ice, its undersides reflecting the blue sea. He glanced beyond it to the clouds of ice in the distance and pinnacles of it reaching into the air, golden pillars under sunlight in the pure blue sky. "Ah!" he exclaimed. "This must be the crystal sea come down from heaven's celestial city the reverend preaches about. A heavenly city not made with hands."

A sealer behind him growled and gave him a push. "Over you go, greenhorn. Move. The day won't last. The captain'll call yer down for being a hangback."

"Yeah," said another sealer. "You could end up in the bowels of the ship stoking the fires."

"And miss this view." Jamie shook his head. "Never!" He hurried down following a skein of sealers. Shivers raced along his spine as he stepped on an ice pan. He was soon sweating trying to hold his balance on the cakes that danced on the churning sea. Far from land he felt as if he were floating in the sky.

Soon the dazzling white seascape was stained with bloody footprints and the bloody shadows of seals. A bed of whitecoats mewling on the ice was easily killed with a light blow from a gaff. Older harp seals, dark on the back and light on the belly, were killed with a bat or shot by gunners. The blue-grey splotched hood seal was scarce and prized. The captain warned the sealers to be careful of hoods. If they killed the mother and pup the male hood might kill them. Jamie was elated to have killed several male hoods.

Thomas could skin a seal in thirteen seconds without damaging the skin. It took most sealers a minute.

"I'll learn to be that fast," Alfred bragged, his young face freckled and burnished from ice glare.

"We'll see," said Noah. He raised an eyebrow. "Don't make vows hard to keep."

Seal skins were laced together three at a time and towed across the ice to the steamer or, if the men were far from the ship, to a collection point. By the end of each day sealers came off the ice with their faces and hands greasy and bloodied. Skin chafed or cut was treated with carron oil and wrapped in gauze.

There was much to weary a sealer as the days went by. Loose ice was easy to fall through. A sealer needed to keep his gaff handy to pull himself out. By the end of the day there were strained muscles, cold tremors, diarrhea, and dizziness from fluxing ice pans.

Firemen had it no easier. They hauled coal out of the pounds day and night carrying it in baskets to the stokehold and hauling ashes up on deck. Mittens blackened by coal dust were cleaned by rubbing them on the ice leaving marks that looked like shadows of black birds.

Each sealer received a ration of rum at eight o'clock to relax sore backs and shoulders from hauling pelts, weighing thirty to fifty pounds, some carried as far as a mile to the vessel. The sealers spent long hours trimming carcasses, stowing pelts, and chopping ice to cover the harvest once it was stored in the hold of the ship. They stowed and iced seal sculps until midnight and fell into their berths exhausted.

Jamie drifted into sleep murmuring, "If you could only see me, now, Maggie, you wouldn't come anighst me."

The men had little water for washing. It was needed for cooking and drinking. A galley was fixed to the deck just aft of the forecastle scuttle and near the scuttlebutt—a drinking fount on the ship. The kitchen had a forty-gallon puncheon filled with rocks used for wood fires to cook grub and boil tea on each watch for the crew and captain. The sealers mostly lived on molasses, porridge, hard bread, and bare-legged tea—raw without sugar and cream. Some ate salted fatback. On Friday, after a long week's work, the sealers were given salt fish to boil or roast.

Captain Clarke had warned the sealers at the start of the voyage, "If there's a stowaway among yers the scoundrel had better get off the ship now. If we find him he'll go head over heels over the side. We'll have no jinkers."

When Eddie was discovered on board the ship the captain was beside himself, first berating the boy as a jinker and then taking pity on his looks. Beside his scars he had the bearings of an undernourished youngster. The captain put him to work as an unpaid helper for the men on board. Eddie was so busy inside the barque he hardly looked outside.

One evening the sealers came in out of the weather with faces like whitecoats. The snow had found every crease. "We'd've been done fer if we'd stayed longer," one sealer muttered.

The sealers spent time in surly weather playing cards and checkers in their bunks with boots on in case they were called out. At night tales of ghosts were told and music played. The men danced to an accordion or mouth organ. A warning came from the captain: "You can fiddle and tap your toes but don't let a whistle out of yers."

Now and then a sealer glanced at Jamie, who was often seen sitting by candlelight sketching. "Sketching and writing letters to his coosie, I s'pose he is," one sealer teased.

Jamie slipped his rolled paper and pencil into his bottle. He blew his breath into the container and sealed it. *For you, Maggie, my breath off the icefields.*

The deck, which had gleamed white with ice by the time the vessel had reached the icefields, was now covered with bloody seal pelts. Beyond the ship pans of ice floated like porcelain plates holding dark seal flesh, morsels for wild birds and fish.

As the last of the weary men climbed aboard the ship the sun carried dusty reflections.

"A sun hound—a bad sign!" Jamie exclaimed. He lifted his tongue to barbs of ice, his body moving awkwardly in clothes caked in hardened seal blood and fat crackling in the cold air.

Sealers cheered at Captain Clarke's news that enough of the prized fur had been winched aboard the ship and stowed to meet the ship's quota. The sealers were going home and the *Southern Cross* was expected to be the first ship to arrive in port. The captain's announcement rang in Jamie's ears as the men made a feast of seal meat. He was going home to sink into a tub of warm, soapy water. He was going home to keep his promise to his sweetheart. He'd have a little money in his pocket. Unlike some of the sealers who had paid three times the cost of their supplies on credit from the steamer owners he had brought most of his provisions. He lay down among the other men on seal pelts. He didn't need drenches of liquor or a charm to dwall off.

Sleep was deep and waters calm when the barque left the icefields. Soon the ship's boards began to creak and heave in seas gone wild.

* * * * *

32

The first morning after Jamie left for the icefields Maggie woke with a start. Night had fled, taking whatever strange dreams she'd had, leaving her unsettled. It lasted only a moment and then the day opened to what was real: a safe place for her to daydream about her life with Jamie. She ran her fingers through her hair feeling comfort in its long tresses, soft and silky from the shampoo Jamie had brought her from St. John's. She slipped out of bed and pulled the corked stopper from a bottle of perfume. Last year Simon Swartz had agreed to take two pairs of her aunt's knitted cuffs in exchange. She dabbed the sweet scent on her wrists and neck and turned to look toward the shelf, at the white satin material that her aunt had bought from the peddler for her wedding undergarments. She had started to knit her wedding dress from worsted white wool. Elizabeth, who was looking forward to having Maggie as a sister-in-law, had promised to help make a grand stitch for the Victorian collar trimmed with *something blue*, a remnant from the blue cord Elizabeth had used for the collar of her wedding gown. *Something old* was a piece of purple heather now brown after many years lying alongside a shamrock between the pages of her mother's Bible. Jamie's tie clip would be *something borrowed.* She let out a lingering sigh thinking of Jamie and their wedding night. She gathered the satin against her soft breasts and felt her heart race. Her body longed for Jamie, ached for him. She no longer wondered how a couple got around to coming together. Now she knew that if there was love there was a passion that pulled a man and woman tight to each other without shame and regret.

She hurried downstairs and swept her young cousins Bea and Melanie around by their arms until they complained of giddiness. She fell back to the table bench breathless. All she had ever wanted in life was for someone to love her forever. Jamie was going to do that.

She shaved lye soap into a tub of hot water, washed her petticoats, and hung them out on the line, her glance straying as if she could see the lonely stretch of sea that had taken Jamie—as if to see the ship that would bring him back. Jamie wouldn't be fit when he got home. She blushed to think of him lowering his naked body into a puncheon of soaped water in his father's shed. "Sinful thoughts!" Aunt Liddie would say as if she'd never had such thoughts about men.

"I've had ten youngsters and kept my modesty. Not once did their father see the stretch of me," she boasted one day as she sat knitting her husband's drawers to be lined with cotton she'd cut from flour bags.

A pity then, Maggie had thought. *Jamie might want to see the length of me, and—* She blushed with the thoughts of what she and Jamie could do to each other.

She looked up thinking that God could be reading her thoughts. *You can strike me dead now if you don't want me imagining us together.* She closed her eyes and smiled. God believed in love. Wasn't He the one who made it?—and good!

Even a woman like Aunt Liddie, her body gone doughy, had to think about love sometimes.

Daylight stretched longer now. Through the window Maggie eyed a tree's vein-like branches cutting into the cold orange blush of white sky. Another night closed in over the heavy, darkening skin of water. Fewer days and nights to wait for Jamie. She counted them away.

Twenty days went by and there was talk that the *Southern Cross* would soon be sailing home. Maggie passed several men sitting on a rock wall leaning against the shed of retired skipper Jed Porter.

"Likely the *Southern Cross* is on course," Jed said. "The weather's been civil so far."

"I hope it stays that way," a farmer said looking up into a sky of furled clouds.

It will, Maggie thought. *Jamie can't be kept out, delayed by bad weather.*

Maggie stood out on her aunt's porch step, her arms folded around her body to keep warm as she eyed the clear sky. Stars twinkled like ornaments on a velvet black curtain and she thought of the Southern Cross constellation: a silver diagonal cross formed from a group of stars for which the sealing ship was named. Jamie had told her about it, saying, "Only people who live in the southern hemisphere can see the Cross."

On Sunday, March 29, a cold, starry night, Maggie looked

through the window and saw a thin slice of moon lying on its back. She shuddered.

"Lovesick, she is, you know," Liddie said to Aubrey. "Her fellar gone on the *Southern Cross* and she with such a wild imagination that he'll bring home a pocket of money."

Maggie went up to bed and closed her eyes to shut out everything but thoughts of Jamie. "I'm a mind traveller; it's the cheapest way to travel," Jamie had mused as he and Maggie sat against a wall of smooth stones beside William's gate last summer. "I close my eyes and imagine whatever I want. I like to imagine Boston, where Avery, me cousin, went last year. He's helping build buildings high enough to scrape the clouds. Maybe Avery and Olivia will run into each other," he said.

Maggie had frowned. Olivia had left Zachary to go to Boston and Jamie was leaving her to go on the ice. Zachary didn't know if Olivia was coming home. Maggie was sure Jamie was.

She drifted into sleep imagining Jamie's arms around her. Long before morning she woke, darkness wrapping her like a cold blanket. She slipped out of bed and blindly reached for her water jug. She held it as she made her way carefully down the stairs for a drink. She stayed by the kitchen window until the black fog of night petered out. Morning brought a strange calm under a blushing sky. A tiny stir creased the bay water. A brooding, heavy silence filled the air outside. It seeped inside until the room felt heavy and smothering.

That night the moon, a silver, unfettered vessel, sailed through straggly clouds. Maggie couldn't help noticing the dusty, golden ring haunting it.

William was awakened out of a deep sleep to the sound of footsteps, then nothing. *Jamie is wantin' to be home in a warm bed*, he thought. He lay for a while and then pushed back the bed covers. Through the window he looked toward a bright red sun and a leaden sky bearing down on it. Gulls were flying in from the sea and drifting high above the land like charred bits of paper. His eyes narrowed at the sight of the reddening sky. Nasty weather was on its way. He hoped the *Southern Cross* would stay out of its path. "When a halo is around the moon look for rain or snow quite soon," he said quietly, remembering an old saying. If the wind pitched northeast he knew there'd be trouble.

He hurried downstairs and tapped the barometer. The needle was falling. Screaming gales, fog, and pellets of ice above wild seas were all part of a sealer's lot while hunting seals, but when a vessel was on its way home with a load of seals William knew it made for a harrowing journey.

When Jamie was a boy he had asked him questions as if he had all the answers. Now he felt small and vulnerable as he asked a question hooked in his heart: "Is my only son safe?"

"A storm is brewing," a fisherman said as several men gathered in store lofts to knit new nets and mend old ones.

"Ah," sighed Ned Porter as he sat hooking a needle under a strand of twine, "the potter spun this island in anger. He left it jagged with cliffs and rugged shorelines and at the mercy of a sea with as fierce a mouth as any lion and an appetite as strong."

"We've got the softer part of it here on the Southern Shore," someone answered.

William met Maggie on the road to Eli's shop to pick up a bag of white beans for her aunt. He touched her shoulder. "Come down, me maid, and stay with me. See if I'll eat yer."

She shook her head no and pulled away.

Undeterred he said, "There's no need for you to be off lookin' after a tribe of youngsters belongin' to someone other than yourself. Sure, 'tis no hard labour I'll put you to. You can do the wash and cook a scattered meal. A feed of brewis will stay me when there's not much else."

Maggie went on by, her mind on the bad weather coming. She bought the beans and by the time she reached her aunt's place the air was damp and heavy under a swollen sky. She spoke aloud, her voice strained, "The ship *is* comin' home, Jamie. I know you're comin' home to me." A deep, shivering pain shook her body. She whispered, "A kind sea, please God, a kind sea."

part five

33

THERE WAS NO way to warn Captain Clarke that a storm was on its way. Families cringed in fear that the *Southern Cross* would plough into the heart of the gale. A full day passed without a report that the vessel had been sighted.

Maggie hurried down the road to where a crowd had assembled outside the post office located in the back of Porter House. Their feet made restless scuffing as they waited for their weekly mail. Maggie scanned the posting on the outside of the door giving the arrival time for all the sealing vessels. There was no news.

Abe Petten, beside her, said, "Old Hattie's inside making clickin' sounds on a gadget that'll bring all the news. When she's finished she'll post it on the door. I hope it's not all bad."

A man behind banged him on the back. "Away with yer and feel your head. That captain and his ship knows each other full well. There's worry for naught."

The post office door was finally opened and then the wicket. Maggie pushed close. Men and women gripping their children's hands stood outside waiting. The calm weather had not eased the storm brewing in their hearts, dread suspended above their heads like a sword.

William scuffed along the path to the site of a dozen men gathered around. People pushed to get close as the postmistress read a cable: "At 7:00 p.m., Sunday March 29, a wireless message from Channel–Port aux Basques, on the southwest corner of Newfoundland, informed

St. John's that on Saturday, the twenty-eighth, about 6:30 p.m., the *Southern Cross* was spotted passing about seven miles out. She was down in the head with all flags flying, a signal that the barque was going home with a bumper crop estimated between 17,000-25,000 pelts."

William's mind settled at the news that the *Southern Cross* was finally on her way home. Families cheered the captain on with their prayers knowing he was racing to be the first in St. John's harbour, a distinction every captain dreamed of claiming. She had her load of pelts and flippers and she should be in port Tuesday evening or Wednesday morning.

The strain of waiting eased.

"She's coming," one man said running down the road and throwing his cap into the air. Off to one side a father stood silent. He was waiting for news of his son who was on the SS *Newfoundland.*

All along the Avalon, Butlers, Battens, Busseys, Pettens, Taylors, Stanleys, Bishops, Kennedys, and Porters waited, spirits lifted now that the *Southern Cross* was on her way home.

"There'll be some fiddlin' and whistlin' now," someone said.

Families' hearts grew light and expectant. Floors were scrubbed and pots shined and filled with stews and soups from food garnered from their sparse cellars. The men went about sawing and laying in wood with renewed energy. Having been anchored with fear for what seemed like a lifetime, families now waited with welcoming hearts. Still, their minds weren't far from the men on their way home; there were uneasy glances at the sky and furrowed brows for signs of a weather moon.

The storm erupted on the last day of March, swells swallowing each other over and over, while the sea opened its mouth with sprays of white spit. People standing outside their homes and looking out to sea felt the sting of snow pellets against their skin. Then heavy, wet snow pelted down. The spring snow had a name.

"Sheilagh's brush," a farmer said as he settled his horse in his stable.

"I'd say it's not," his son answered. "It's Sheilagh's fleece-lined white drawers hanging low and heavy."

They laughed, forgetting for a moment the vessel on her way home.

Caroline sat inside her house, her lips pressed in a grim line. Room windows were darkened with snow. *The shades already drawn.* She shocked herself with the thought.

A day later, the first day of April, the storm had worsened. Maggie pulled on her grey woollen coat to go see if William had any news.

"Stay put, me maid," Liddie urged. "There's a living screecher out there this mornin'."

When she saw Maggie determined to go she shrugged. "If that's what it takes to settle your mind, go, though it won't be an easy tramp."

Grateful for her aunt's understanding, she drew a blue knitted cap over her head and tucked her long light hair into her neck under a thick, varicoloured scarf. She pulled on a pair of double-knitted blue cuffs. Her aunt wrapped hot biscuits in cloth and tucked them in her pocket.

She thanked her and hurried out the door and down the road through driving snow. The wild wind swung like an iced rope in the hands of a madman. A ribbon of silver skin from a birch tree sailed through the air and hit her face. Barbed ice crystals shot up her nose sharp enough to bring tears.

After a long struggle she reached William's house, her stiff fingers clumsy in lifting the latch on the porch door. The door swung at her like a beast pushing her backwards. She lost her balance and fell while the wind banged the door against its hinges. She dragged herself to her feet, grabbed the latch, and pulled the door back. She got inside and stood shivering in the porch. It was no day for anyone to be out, no day for a ship to be on the ocean.

William seemed to have shrunk inside his shabby clothes. Maggie looked at him sitting by the stove, his face drawn and heavy, his mouth down. Pouches, red and sore-looking, had formed under his eyes. He drew in a heavy breath. "Jamie is unchancy, that he is, to be out in this weather."

Maggie said nothing as she shed her ice-encased coat, cap, scarf, and cuffs by the stove. Then she took a chair and sat by the fire listening to the screech of wind around the house, its sharp whistling against the windows. The silence between her and William became so heavy that she jumped up. "I'll make you a fine cup of tea," she said. She reached into her coat pocket and pulled out her biscuits. She laid them on the table and set the kettle to boil.

When the tea was ready William lumbered to his seat and lifted his cup in shaky white hands. He took a sip and put it down. Then he dipped his biscuits and ate them. He didn't speak. His mind was crowded reliving stories of men caught on the ice and frozen as solid as statues, others surviving by wrapping themselves in sealskins and lighting fires with blubber. He thought of the many sealers that had disappeared in icy waters never to be heard of again. He hoped that the *Southern Cross* had left waters too rough for the wooden ship to handle and had found shelter in one of the bays along the coast.

Maggie gathered her belongings where they hung beside the stove, dressed in them half-dried, and went out the door wanting to be away from William sitting silently, brooding.

There was no gentleness anywhere. Wind shrieked and trees swayed in its grip while snow smoked the air. Maggie trudged along like a blind woman feeling her way home, wind and snow like steel needling her skin. She was relieved to get to the house and hurry inside.

Liddie looked up from knitting a sock, worry creasing her brow. She said nothing as her niece hung up her wet clothes beside the fire and went up to her room. The warmth of the wood stove rose to fill the small space with coziness.

Maggie pulled back heavy quilts and slid into bed hauling the quilts back over her shoulders. The stove heat had not reached under her sheets and she shivered until her body heat warmed her. She drifted into sleep and woke with a jerk. She lifted herself on an elbow and stared through the small window. Wind and sleet smacked the thin pane, beat against the house in twists and turns. Her heart lurched. Jamie was out on a vast ocean in contrary weather. "Be safe, Jamie," she whispered. She remembered Jamie's mother saying, "Worry is a thief not to be let in."

That was easier said than done. She could not lock a door or shutter a window against it.

* * * * *

34

Sealers hurrying up the makeshift ladder to the *Southern Cross* on the last day of the hunt had noticed, in the distance, whitecoats taking to the water, a sure sign of stormy weather. Still, it was fine and fair when the ship left the Magdalen Islands for St. John's with its prized load of seal sculps and barrels of seal flippers.

On the last day of March the *Southern Cross* headed into the path of the storm. Wind screeched through the rigging, ice pellets like claws tearing into the steamer. The men, their clothing stiff as canvas, lay abunk on bloody pelts heavy with thick layers of fat. They smiled wearily pushing away memories of twelve-hour days lifting the gaff over and over to kill seals, the back-breaking work of helping load pelts on board the deck and in the hold of the ship. A sweet, heavy feeling blanketed them as their bodies relaxed. They drifted into sleep.

Jamie dreamed he was placing his mother's gold wedding ring on Maggie's finger. He was jarred awake by a lurch of the ship. He sank back trying to sleep but he kept reliving his first time as a sealer: buckling on a sheathed knife, razor sharp . . . grabbing a tow line and gaff . . . pulling seals over ice . . . eating his aunt's buns, hard bread, and oatmeal on the ice, and a few raisins Noah had given him. Voices and scenes gathered and scattered as Jamie slipped in and out of sleep . . . the turn of pelts he'd dragged across the ice, his blood warm with thoughts of Maggie . . . John Stanley calling him a young greenhorn, and teaching him how to lace up six seal pelts to a tow.

"Cut your holes in the edge of the sculp, me man. Pass it right through back and front like this," John Clarke from Brigus called, holding up a pelt. "Then tie a knot. Make a turn of rope to grasp in your left hand. Here, watch. Pass the long end over your right shoulder and take it in your right hand. . . ."

A blue gulf of water was rising . . . Jamie was losing his balance . . . unwittingly flinging pelts into the water. James Lynch from Harbour Grace grabbed him, pulled him to safety, both of them wobbling on a small pan, the tow of six pelts gone. But he'd worked hard and made up for the loss.

* * * * *

It would be a stormy voyage home. Already clouds of wet snow had drifted into the nooks and crannies of the ship and along the deck of the crowded *Southern Cross* lurching in contrary winds.

Jamie heard the faint sound of a whistle and then his ship's answering siren. He dozed and when he surfaced it was to a sharp shift. His heart quickened at the memory of his sweetheart brushing her long, thick hair. He had spent twenty days away from her, twenty days with thoughts of them together. He imagined her arms around his neck, the sweet scent of her perfume. Coins would soon jingle in his pocket like wedding bells.

Screeches and moans mingled. Jamie's breath was caught in his throat, his face under a heavy, suffocating weight as bloody, oily sealskins broke through the decking. Trapped sealers slid and tumbled against each other under creaking and breaking boards. Water rushed over the ship like demons running into every crack, into every open mouth, into every nostril. Maggie's name rose gargled in Jamie's throat. The icy ocean pressed inside him and he, unable to resist breathing, felt the burst of pain in his lungs as he was hurled into the darkness of a deep, icy grave.

35

William's apple tree branches clawed the air like skeletal fingers spelling a message of misadventure. Ghostly hands of wind urged them on. William looked out the bay at the drifts of snow disappearing into water. Winter was muscling spring out of its way. A chill snaked its way down his spine. "Mary Jane," he said, "I'm glad you're gone from the world, away from the torment of Jamie in this storm."

Caroline and Joe were at home sitting by the table, the lamplight flittering from wind breathing around the windowsills. They turned startled at a loud bang, as if something had been flung against the outside of the house, making a scraping sound down the side before landing on the ground with a thud.

Caroline let out a cry, her hand going to her mouth. Joe grabbed the lamp and ran to open the door. He stared into the dark night. There was nothing there. He closed the door and for a while nothing was said. Then there came Caroline's whisper: "It's an omen. Poor Jamie promised to return the box and he's done it in the only way he could."

Joe turned in anger. "Hold your tongue and don't be talking trouble. It's enough to see what is when it is."

"As sure as daylight he'll be home," Johnny said in a trembling voice from his place by the fire.

"As sure as night he won't," Caroline answered, her look grim. "This is an omen."

The next day, all day, Caroline waited, unable to dismiss the fear that Jamie was dead. In a rush of anger she sputtered, "I don't know why men have to go to sea usin' up energy they could have saved for the land. Widows and children are left crying over men dyin' without reason."

Joe looked at her, his face drawn. "Stop your blathering and wait to see what will be."

Johnny's sightless eyes closed, lashes trembling as he recalled his time on a rocking pan of ice. Heavy, suffocating despair came back black as any night. He bowed his head in silent prayer. He had wished many times that he could have his time back before he went on the ice. Now he wished that Jamie had his time back.

Maggie sat by the window in her aunt's kitchen and fell asleep. She dreamed she was running on light feet to Jamie coming up the path. His look lingered on her bosom, the buttons on her silk Sunday dress straining against the buttonholes. He turned away and laughed as if embarrassed that his mother might notice. She woke murmuring, "Mary Jane is gone." She got up and went up to bed.

The next morning her bare feet hit the cold wooden floor as a rush of apprehension assailed her. She parted the white lace curtains and looked through the window. She let out a laugh. April the second had come and the storm was over. The day had opened crystal clear, the blue light of the sky like the clear eyes of a child after a tantrum. The land lay mute under dazzling snow played on by golden sunlight; the ocean's fury was gone. Two crows on a fence picked at each other's feathers. Their beaks dipped into caps of snow on posts and then touched each other. Snow kisses. She turned to a small mirror on the wall. Her soft green eyes were bright and brown-flecked in sunlight as she smiled at her image. Thick, light hair capped her head and flowed down her shoulders. She pulled it back in the tortoiseshell combs Jamie had given her for Christmas and gathered it in two looped braids. Her mouth formed the words: Jamie will soon be home!

William woke smelling sea air and tasting salt on his lips. He wondered where he had been in dreams he could not remember. He dressed and hurried over to Joe's. The men sat silently around Joe's wireless radio hoping for news of the *Southern Cross.* All they heard was a crackling noise.

"Dang useless!" Joe grumbled. "I shouldn't have let the Water Street merchant talk me into buyin' it."

Caroline took in William's white face. She couldn't tell him about the omen. "Hold on to hope," was all she could say as he left to go back to his house.

William dropped on a chair by his table and cut through a loaf of bread Caroline had given him. He was slathering a slice with butter and partridgeberry jam when Maggie hurried inside and sat down. He didn't look up until after he had poured milky tea into his saucer to soak his bread.

Maggie met his droopy eyes, relief showing in hers. "It's a nice day for the men to come home. They should get in today."

William pushed back his chair. He hurried outside and came back with an armful of junks for the stove. They slid from his arms into the woodbox with a bang. He stirred the fire and threw in a log. He looked at Maggie, light from the fire grate flickering over her face. "'Tis time someone told us something," he said gruffly.

She nodded. "Indeed it is if they've heard. After the voyage Jamie will need a long rest." She stood up. "I'm on my way to the Quilting Bee. I'll need to be makin' quilts for our home."

Maggie stopped by the post office on her way down the shore to the Quilting Bee at Etta Whalen's house. She heard people who had gathered by the post office say there was no news about the *Southern Cross.* There were sketches about the SS *Newfoundland*, rumours of sealers dying on the ice. She hurried on, not wanting to listen, not wanting to know anything about another ship until she had news of Jamie.

She dropped her coat on a hook in Etta's porch and went inside to the back room where the coals in a Ruby stove glowed. She nodded at the other women and took her place. They all turned to the sound of footsteps slow and dragging coming down the stairs and a pause when the landing was reached. Evangeline Snow, Etta's mother, came out to where the Quilting Bee women sat around a large oak table fitting pieces of material for a quilt. She had a lost look. "Dear, dear, I'd like for someone to take me home. There's bad news on the go."

There was a sharp gasp in the room among the women quietly stitching pieces. Maggie tightened her lips.

"You are home, Mother." Etta's voice was soft and cajoling. "You need to go back up to your room."

"I'm home?" She looked around bewildered. "I had a dream that there was a sealing ship out on the ocean that wasn't comin' home." She put her hand to her mouth as if to hold in something she wasn't meant to say. She turned back and went out and up the stairs calling, "Blue of sky; blue of sea, soon, my love, come back to me; black sea seething 'neath black sky, never thought my love would die."

Maggie listened to her pacing the floor of her room.

Etta shook her head. "It's sad to be living with your mind half gone—worse than losing a leg."

She cautioned the ladies as they resumed their sewing that it was best not to mention sealing around her mother. "Ever since she lost my father in the 1898 sealing voyage she dreams that he's on an ice pan driftin' away from his ship. She hears him callin' and cryin'. At night this time every year she kicks all the clothes off the bed as if she's tryin' to get to him. Then she lies in bed shiverin' like someone freezing."

Julia Porter's voice wavered. "There's been lives lost on the *Newfoundland*, I heard. I know my Luke is not among them. He can't be." Her voice ended in a low tremor. "I'd know it if he was."

Melinda Butler's hand stopped in mid-air. "My man's on the *Southern Cross* and he's coming home."

"And mine!" Maggie's words leaped out before she could stop them. She gave Julia a guilty look. "I'm sure Luke's fine."

* * * * *

The next day was clear and sunny. Maggie walked to the post office hoping to get a letter from Elizabeth in Hibb's Cove. Instead there was one from Olivia in Boston telling her she was coming home. A few months before, Maggie had opened the door to see Olivia standing on the porch bridge. She was in muffs and a long, shabby green coat, its large astrakhan collar turned up around her quivering chin.

Maggie had looked at her in alarm and asked, "Where is it you're off to?"

"I've come to say goodbye," she said in a tremulous voice. "I'm goin' to the Boston States to Great-Aunt Lila's. She's not fully recovered from the effects of bein' in the water after *Titanic* sank."

Maggie was puzzled. "I thought you'd be marryin' Zachary."

She hesitated. "I was—I is." She passed her a piece of paper. "Here's me address. Write once in a while and tell me how Zachary's doing."

"You can write him yourself, sure."

Olivia shook her head, her voice muffled. "I can't." Looking distressed she hurried away.

Maggie had met Zachary on the road a few days after Olivia left. His toe pushed against a rock as he told her, "Maggie's gone and left me." He kicked the rock hard and added, "I don't know why."

Maggie wrote Elizabeth with the news:

> *You remember Olivia? You would, for sure. Who wouldn't! A china doll among us plain Janes. She took off to Boston, leaving Zachary waiting to marry her. He's gone to the seal hunt on the same ship as Jamie. You remember other children we played with on the beach. Laura, poor thing, slipped and fell outside her grandmother's house. She hit her head and died. Lily, her little girl, is missing (someone must know where she is). Emily Penny, the bold one. Well, she went off to St. John's and got herself work with a rich family. I'm not sure if she knows that her two brothers went on the* Southern Cross. *If not it's best this way, her not having to worry. Other men along the shore went on the* Newfoundland. *Your baby must be a treasure.*

After Jamie and I gets married we'll be over to see you. Write when you gets a little spare time.

Your future sister-in-law,
Maggie

Maggie left the post office and carried on to Etta Whalen's house to help finish a quilt the women were making for a poor family who had infant twin daughters and hardly a stitch of coverings for their beds. They were cutting good parts from worn clothes to make a second quilt when Maggie arrived.

"I hear Olivia's comin' home from the Boston States," Bessie Rideout said as she pulled a dark thread through two pieces she was sewing together.

"Home! Is she, then?" exclaimed Amy Moss, a plain-faced girl. She looked disappointed, as if she'd hoped there'd be a chance for her with Zachary if Olivia wasn't around. She lifted her square to the brin bag backing and asked, "Is it to stay?"

Minnie Marshall lifted her head from her sewing needle. "Or not! Who knows! She'll come back too highbrow for Zachary, a farmer."

Amy shrugged. "The high and mighty thinks themselves a cut above the rest: the penny looking down on the halfpenny."

Shy Jessie Young lifted her head, her long, thin nose sticking into the air. "Beautiful women miss out in other ways. God made us all equal, so if she's got one favourable trait she's missing another."

Amy nodded, looking relieved.

Minnie said, "The young ones go off to Boston, put on airs, and come home speakin' in broad Boston tones for a day or two. Then they settle back to their usual speech." She drew herself up straight, her needle in the air, and said in a hoity-toity voice, "Is it Boston, Boreston, or Bosston?"

"There's as many sounds to one word as there's voices and any number of ways to say it," Jessie offered. "Still, some people think of themselves higher than the rest of us just because they've seen a smidgen of the world."

Minnie bit off her thread and went on, "I thought Olivia wanted Zachary. That's what everyone believed until she went away leavin' him to wonder why. I said to meself when I heard she'd gone away, 'There's sleek shanks and a long carriage on that one. The maid's too comely for her own good; maybe something untoward happened to her.'"

Amy's eyes narrowed. "All Olivia wants is a man with a hearty jingle in his pocket. She went off and left Zachary and he pining for her—wouldn't glance at anyone else. She likely got herself disgraced in Boston and she's back to break Zachary's heart and bring shame to her poor mam and pap. Dandelion fluff is all she is. When Zachary gets home from the *Southern Cross* he should put his mind on someone else."

A heaviness settled around the table. Everyone's thoughts turned to the sealing ship now overdue.

On Maggie's way home lines skipped through her mind like rope through the air. *He's comin' back; he's not comin' back.*

36

Olivia returned from Boston wearing a pair of high-buttoned boots with a silk rose on each instep. She held a floppy black hat beside the long skirt of her fashionable red suit as she stepped off the train, her blue eyes defiant as they met the uneasy looks of women standing around. She donned the hat over fine hair long and braided like white sheaves.

One farmer remarked, "As good as a sail that contraption is. I wouldn't mind boardin' that wonder-wench's boat."

His neighbour nodded. "I'd say she's a one for red shoes and no knickers."

Months before, Johanna, Olivia's mother, had found her retching in the chamber pot. She had given her a hard look. "You'll not be wanted here in the condition you're in. You might consider havin' the father marry you."

"He's already married."

"Then you're worse than I thought any daughter of mine could be. Here I was thinkin' you'd been considerin' the Butler boy."

Johanna turned quickly as Jabe, Olivia's stepfather, passing through the hall, stopped in the doorway of the bedroom and glared at Olivia. "Do I have to shoot the Butler boy in that slack backside of his to get him to marry me daughter?"

Olivia lied. "I don't know him *that* well."

"He knows you, then."

"Not as good as you," she said.

One quick step and he was in the room. He slapped her face. "You whore."

She answered him then, right in front of her mother: "If I'm a whore, I'm yours!"

His face hardened and, without looking her way, he left the room and went outdoors.

She got another slap in the face, this time from her mother. "You're not a very good daughter."

"You're not a very good mother."

"I do what I can. You shouldn't look so pleasin' to a man."

Olivia's big eyes, blue as the underside of an ice floe, clouded. "I wish I didn't."

"You could have told me about him," her mother said, her face white and strained.

Olivia looked at her without wavering. Only the month before she was making jam from freshly picked partridgeberries. The berries and sugar began to boil and when she stirred the liquid and bent to taste it the juice splattered on her arm and on a side of her neck. Her stepfather came into the kitchen and slid his tongue along her arm and licked the juice. She pulled clear. Her mother, standing in the doorway, saw and turned away. Months before, Olivia had seen her mother's face at the window watching as she ran from the barn, her blouse torn, a button hanging.

Now she answered boldly, "If I had come to you you would have shown me the door."

"I'll show you the door right now. Out!"

"I'm having your husband's child with no will of mine. I was forced."

"Liar!" The icy accusation stung her ears.

She turned back and in a quiet voice asked, "Do you believe in God?"

"More than you ever could," her mother said.

"Then you tell Him I'm a liar and see what He'll write in His judgment book about you bearin' false witness and about you keepin' silent. Gina knew what Jabe was like."

She left the room without waiting for a reply and ran out of the house slamming the door.

Johanna hesitated. Then she followed her daughter, calling, "I can't weigh him with blame. I did far worse."

Olivia looked back, her voice heavy. "What do you think could be worse?"

Johanna caught up with Olivia and grabbed her sleeve. "I didn't want you. I tried to keep you from bein' born, an intruder—"

Olivia pulled away. "I was an intruder?"

"Not to God you weren't. He meant for you to be."

Olivia kept on running out to the barn. Inside she curled up in a ball on the damp clay floor. She had never forgotten what she had overheard when she was a child. Her mother had been kicked out of her home for getting in child. The father had vanished and she had nowhere to go. Jabe, an older man, had married her.

When she was little Olivia had taken black thread from a reel of cotton and strung it through the eye of a silver needle. Then she had pushed the needle under the skin in her hand, making black stitches all the way across. When she went too deep her hand bled. She did this often during the summer after she had overheard her mother, more so after her stepfather bothered her. Then she would rub her finger over her palm with its broken skin without looking at it and sit there as if she were reading disturbing words in braille: My mother doesn't want me; my stepfather does.

"I know what to do," her mother said coming into the barn. "You'll go away to Boston. I'll write your father's Aunt Lila. She'll know what to do about this."

Maggie had felt that something was wrong when Olivia abandoned her mother and stepfather's comfortable home and left for Boston. Now she was home and keeping to herself. They were both living with the worry of their men surviving the sea hunt. She knew she should go visit her. She wasn't sure why she hesitated.

* * * * *

37

"The Ides of March came and went," William said as he sat boxing the compass listlessly, going to each of the thirty-two points as if one of them would point him to Jamie's whereabouts.

Maggie looked up from stitching a square of material from one of Mary Jane's dresses to a flour bag backing for her wedding quilt. She smiled. "One day you'll be saying Jamie went and came back and we were foolish for worrying."

William's face relaxed. He lifted his head. "I know, me maid. Worry buries the living before they're dead."

Winter should have lost its hold with the sun crossing the line. Instead the world was soft and newly white, brown skeletal branches white-veined against a clouded sky. The snow-capped land held its inhabitants in a comforting stillness. The bright sun casting its dazzling light almost penetrated the dark place within those prisoners of hope.

A wild wind soon raked the land raw, dark earth showing through the sprinkling of snow. Maggie laid aside her stitching, dressed in her coat and boots, and went outside. The land lay cold and unyielding under her feet as she ran down the road looking to find the least bit of news. The train had come and there would be mail from St. John's, perhaps a newspaper report.

St. John's prepared for the return of sealers who had left in merry expectation. Snow banked the roads and hills—a frosty, deathly presence for families standing silently, wind lashing their drawn faces. They squinted and lines deepened around their eyes and corners of the lips as they waited for a sign, a speck in the distance, that the vessel carrying their loved ones would be the first to arrive. Some families were unsure which ship their men had gone on, they having secured a berth at the last minute.

Bowring Brothers Limited had a stock of new hats and coats. This store and others on Water Street had been built with money earned by sealers and merchants. While their men were on the icefields women often pranced in front of their bedroom mirrors imagining themselves in bright spring hats, their children in spring coats and new shoes. This year, during the March storm, windows facing the St. John's waterfront were filled with worried faces. Women were petrified with fears they'd be wearing the widow's veil, their children fatherless. When the ghostly sweep of violent wind had heightened with ice in its teeth the frosting panes flexed and rattled. The families could no longer see out; they pushed hot breath against the glass making an opening to look for signs of a ship battling its way to port.

Merchants in their well-heated St. John's homes gazed on the sea, eager to inspect and count furs and oil. They would weigh the fat, measure the furs, and think of the lucre the lot would bring. They began to pace the floor, an unease setting in. There was no way a ship could make its way through the seething mouth of The Narrows in this weather.

After the storm had abated Lawrence Bigby, a merchant, sat in his heavy mahogany chair. He papped on his pipe and leaned on his massive desk facing the window framing St. John's harbour. He squinted through a trail of pipe smoke hoping to see a speck of the *Southern Cross* sailing through The Narrows. Now the ship was two days overdue. He expected that Captain Clarke had sniffed out the weather and had put in to some harbour. He could not think the ship was lost, all the pelts gone, while a voracious market waited. Customers were already gathering, waiting impatiently for seal flippers. He'd have his share. He could taste the flippers now, the way the cook prepared them in gravy and pastry. He would salt a barrelful for the summer.

His thoughts shifted to the sealers. He knew some of the families. If anything happened to the men they'd be looking for a settlement. Still, nothing could replace the loss of a sealer. He sighed and turned away from the window. He'd stop courting the worst before his mind slipped into a grunge. He settled in his comfortable chair and reached for a glass of port. It was the only spirit he'd let haunt him.

News came confirming rumours that more than fifty sealers from the SS *Newfoundland* had frozen to death on the icefields. The 568-ton wooden ship built in 1872 had left St. John's midnight on the ninth of March cutting through thick ice to make her way out through The Narrows to Wesleyville. She sailed from that port March 14 for her voyage to the ice. Shocking details of the disaster coming out of St.

John's seeped into homes along the shore shrouding the residents in its fog. Families numbed by fear gathered, some at the Manuel's railway station, others at the Foxtrap post office.

Subsequent news was more horrifying. Seventy-seven sealers had frozen to death and one sealer was on his deathbed. Eleven sealers were maimed for life all while trying to jump across loose pans of ice in a snowstorm. Some of the SS *Newfoundland*'s sealers had been inadvertently left on the ice for fifty-three hours and had wandered around lost, suffering cruelty beyond words before they froze to death, toppling where they stood, lifeless sealers piling up on each other. Others had wandered aimlessly in the blinding snowstorm, stepping off ice pans into the black sea. A few sealers had built gazes of ice for shelter against the icy blow only to have southwest winds veer to northwest leaving the resourceful men defenceless and weak. Through snow falling thick as fog some sealers managed to kill a seal and smear its warm blood on their face and hands to lessen frostbite. Others cut flagpoles into shavings with sculping knives. Using tow ropes and gaffs they lit a fire, adding seal fat.

"Waylaid by trouble, this year's hunt is, and there can be no good end to it," a farmer said as he stood on the St. John's waterfront. "I pity the mother and father with one son on the SS *Newfoundland* and a son and father on the *Southern Cross*."

Another bystander assured him, "Captain Clarke can bring his sealers home. He survived before when his ship was driven out to sea and his lifeboats were dragged off the deck and into the boiling waters. No worries about him. He'll be home. He may have been born in Paradise, Newfoundland, but he's not goin' to the other paradise yet, not with a wife and daughter waiting at home."

"We'll see what Ethel got to say about her father when she grows up," the farmer replied. "She won't think him such a great captain if she learns that he pulled out in a storm and sank the lot of poor sealers."

A sharp voice called, "For God's sake, man, give it up! The poor child is eight and there's no word on the ship's fate and no proof of Captain Clarke's misadventure."

They didn't know that on the night of the storm Ethel's uncle, Harold Perrin, a good Salvation Army man, had gone outside and stayed a spell. When he came back in he spoke what he believed to be the truth: "Whoever is out on the water in this weather will never be heard from ag'in."

"Pappa is out there," Ethel had called from where she was leaning on a rail at the top of the stairs. "What is Uncle Harold sayin'?"

"Shush!" her mother said. "Your uncle's talkin' about no one in particular. Back to bed now before the bully boos takes you."

Reports were read out to people gathered at several post and telegraph offices around the bays that a wireless operator in Saint Pierre had wired St. John's with the message that a three-masted black sealing steamer with a yellow funnel had been seen crossing Cape Ray in the Cabot Strait and continuing on past Saint Pierre and Miquelon, going southeast. It was thought to be Baine Johnston's *Southern Cross.*

Captain Thomas J. Connors of the SS *Portia* also reported seeing the *Southern Cross* pass his ship about five miles west-southwest of Cape Pine on the southern end of the Avalon Peninsula. He claimed that he and his chief officer were on the bridge sizing up the course of the wind when they saw the big ship looming out of the snow and going about five knots. The barque was heavily laden and rolling into the swells. The captain said that the seas were high and visibility was nearly zero. The SS *Portia* blew her whistle making sure the vessel kept her distance. The *Southern Cross* responded and sailed on. Despite the blizzard the ship kept going on to Cape Race. Captain Connors took his mail and passenger ship into the shelter of St. Mary's Bay, where a lee shore provided shelter from wind and swells. He believed it wasn't safe to round Cape Race and risk the shoals off Cape Pine.

After reports that the *Southern Cross* had been sighted not far from St. John's, Maggie waited believing she would see Jamie soon. She smiled remembering a moonlit night when he had walked her home. They'd stopped outside and Jamie's long, slender fingers, golden tufts springing on their backs, had reached to cup her face. He blew the hair off her forehead, his breath sweet and warm against her eyelids. She reached up and kissed his lids. Then he slid his lips over her earlobe. It was the kind of intimacy she'd never forget, an intimacy that may have gone further if the door to her aunt's house hadn't opened. Jamie slipped away into the night.

She smiled, remembering. *My earlobe! I never thought a man would want my earlobe, though it was pleasant enough.*

That night she pulled the bedclothes over her ears and burrowed deep down inside herself, stilling all thoughts of doom that might threaten her peace of mind. She slept well, the best she'd sleep for a long time.

38

Elizabeth had her hands in her bread pan when the door was pushed opened and Nathan Petten, a Pick Eyes fisherman, stood in the porch, his face tinctured in shock. "Have you heard the news?" he asked.

Elizabeth's hands flew into the air scattering bits of dough. Her voice came out like a thin thread. "And what might that be?"

"There's bad news about the SS *Newfoundland*. She's on her way home with some of her sealers frozen ter death. They'd been left stranded on the icefields for more than two nights. I got the news from Brigus. Oh the state of affairs there and whereabouts. I was wonderin' about your brother."

William had not sent news to Elizabeth that her brother had gone to the ice for fear she was delicate again. He didn't want her worrying about her brother while she was expecting a child. Elizabeth knew it anyway. Tucked in her apron pocket beside a bag of peppermint knobs was a letter she had received from Maggie the day before.

Dear Elizabeth,

Jamie is not home from the sealing voyage. The boat is overdue. I tell myself not to worry. The possibility of him not coming home is a thought too unbearable. I spend time with your father when I can. When fear comes over him he stretches out on the settle staring. I wish I could put worry aside. Olivia is home from Boston. Likely you didn't know she had gone. Did I tell you? It was only for a few months. She is still the beauty among us. Not many people bother with her. The women at the Quilting Bee believes she was mean for going off to Boston, leaving Zachary. There is still no news on the whereabouts of little Lily, poor Laura's little girl. Timothy will be beside himself, losing Laura and Lily. Hopefully by the time you read this letter Jamie and the other men will be home and we'll be laughing all our fears out the door. It's just not possible that he and your cousins won't come home.

Forever your friend, Maggie.

Elizabeth had laid down the letter. For sure they'd all be home.

"We'll get more news later," Nathan was saying. "I'm relieved to know your brother wasn't on the SS *Newfoundland*. No one from Port de Grave was on that schooner or the *Southern Cross*. But there are relatives." He shook his head. "There's so many rumours. We never know the truth without the evidence. I'll be back if there's more news," he promised.

"So do," Elizabeth answered.

After Nathan left she stood at the window, her face clouded. Until now she had never imagined that her brother could be lost. She planned on going to her brother and Maggie's wedding.

Jacob passed Nathan going down the path. He stopped with his news and Jacob hurried home, his face heavy. He pulled Elizabeth into his arms and she settled against him. After a while she raised her head to look at him. "Surely the *Southern Cross* wasn't out on the ocean in the March storm. Jamie must be on his way home."

Jacob held her a little tighter. "We have no reason to think otherwise."

Elizabeth wanted to believe him. She went outside and listened to the ocean run against the land. Its heavy breath stirred through its massive belly. Far out, sky and bay seemed to hold a communal breath. She knew that beyond the bay white mouths, formed by ice pans, were yawning and gnashing like jaws opening to gulp sealers making one misstep.

Jacob thought, *Nathan need'n have come with news to make Elizabeth heartsick. Grief can wait another day. Once it comes it got a long life.*

* * * * *

39

On the fourth of April the iron sky cast its gloom over the St. John's harbour entrance while the sea squeezed in through, spitting against the piebald cliffs. On the rugged, bald head of Signal Hill glimmers of sunlight shone through fog.

A sea of relatives and neighbours hurried down side roads into main streets connected to the waterfront at King's Beach and Harvey's premises, facing The Narrows, its open mouth blowing a polar breath in over the land. On they came, grim-faced men in long, dark greatcoats and quiff hats and others in sealskin coats and hats. Some wore shabby coats and pants, their white, weathered faces under flat, round caps peaks shading fearful eyes. Women, too, some in veiled black hats, stayed back behind the men, a flicker of hope in their solemn eyes, hope that it was not their son or husband who was dead. Others gripped the hands of their children as they waited in silence. They stood rigid in the damp, grey air, stunned people, hope and fear flowing and ebbing like ocean tides as they cast grave looks toward the ocean with its hostile temperament. Hands were clenched at their sides or lifted to their face as the SS *Bellaventure*, under Captain Robert Randall, her Red Ensign at half-mast, steamed in, cutting through the boiling waters of The Narrows.

As the schooner got closer young men climbed poles, wrapped their arms around them, and held steady, their long coats hanging like black flags. The thoughts of everyone who had a relative on the SS *Newfoundland* were the same: *Who are the survivors? Who are the dead?* Relief filled the minds of some onlookers: *I'm glad my son . . . my husband . . . my father . . . my uncle is on the* Southern Cross.

The crowds moved closer as the schooner docked at Harvey's waterfront premises amidst the gloom of the falling night. There were cries of relief as loved ones caught sight of sealers leaning against the ship's rails; others, frostbitten and injured, leaned on another sealer or on a gaff. A survivor lying on a stretcher lifted his hand.

The sight of three layers of canvas-covered corpses, stiff as dried fish ready for market, laid on the fore hatch in the well of the ship, cast a long shadow over the faces of those watching the gruesome scene. Men wept uncontrollably. A mother screamed when a tarpaulin over a frozen sealer slipped and she saw it was her son, frosted brows and ice-fringed lashes around pitiful open eyes burned by the glare of the sun on ice, his mouth wide open, his reaching fingers in a frozen pose. Cries of despair rose louder as the marble faces of the frozen dead came in view and were recognized. A son and his father lay with their arms wrapped around each other. Sealers who had struggled across acres of ragged ice, and survived, their blistered faces grainted with blood and oil, left the schooner, limbs drawn up, crippled with nerve pain. Others had swollen limbs blackened by frostbite. Their faces mirrored broken spirits. Instead of caring for their families, their families would have to care for them. Still, laughter and weeping mingled when mothers and wives saw a loved one walk off the schooner. Women at home caring for babies and the elderly hurried to prepare hot meals for the survivors as best they could from a sparse larder.

Ambulance corps, city physicians, Drs. Mcpherson and Campbell, and nurses rushed to take the injured sealers to hospital. Brigade boys saluted and citizens lifted their hats while a cortege of stretcher-bearers passed by with the dead sealers.

The SS *Newfoundland*, carrying a crew of 189, had lost seventy-eight sealers out of 132 men left stranded on an icefield for two days and two nights. Some of them were undernourished before they left for the voyage and under-nurtured during their hard days of relentless labour.

One old captain, a black cap shading his weary eyes, muttered to an onlooker standing beside him, "Ah, me boy, 'tis a wonder anyone survived on ice pans in open water, the relentless claw of ice-laced winds, threatenin' seas, hunger and sleeplessness, their hearts beatin' while every other part of 'em was turnin' ter ice."

The onlooker didn't turn. His gaze was steady, his words convincing: "It's a testament to the will of the Newfoundland sealers. They've proved to be iron men in wooden ships."

40

News of the SS *Newfoundland*'s tragedy spread fast and a foreboding fell over communities like a black pall. Along the shore, in every household missing a man gone on the sealing schooners, hope for the

Southern Cross was tenuous, suspended as if on a thin, tight wire ready to loosen in any direction by the least bit of news. Tearing at the minds of people waiting for the late *Southern Cross* was the fear that evidence of her loss would remain buried in the deep waters of the Atlantic.

"Don't you be maisin' yourself with worry," Joe told William as he sat on the step of his shed whittling a boat model. "The SS *Kyle* and two other boats, the *Fiona* and an American patrol vessel, the *Seneca*, are gone to search for the *Southern Cross*. Other ships are keeping a keen eye. If something untoward had happened there'd be signs on the water and somethin' would have rocked ashore."

That night William left his house and sat in his barn talking to his tired old horse. "You're likely all I can depend on. Me wagon's idle in winter and me sleigh idle in summer but you're there to take me anywhere through all seasons."

The horse bent her head and nuzzled his hand. He moved away, curled up under a horsehair blanket, and fell asleep. He dreamed that Jamie was on the *Southern Cross* in a violent storm and that the buoyancy that had begun on the return voyage had evaporated as sealers curled against each other, seasick from the stench of blubber and blood and the rolling of the ship as she thrashed about. He tried to shut his eyes against the scene but it carried on. The ship groaned, split, its sealers screaming, falling. A net of icy water spread over bodies floating like dead fish, Jamie's face a shocking sight.

William was awakened by his own voice calling Jamie. He lay shivering in the darkness crying without shame.

On Monday the notice of steamer arrivals was posted on the outside door of the Foxtrap post office. The SS *Southern Cross* was not among them. Maggie was tending to a bowl of soaked hard bread and salt fish when her uncle came home and told her that on Saturday the *Daily News* had listed the names of all the men on the *Southern Cross*.

"Not to say they're dead," he added.

Maggie's heart lurched like a ship on surly seas. She tried to hold it steady as hope dipped and rose on each wave. *Please, God, let Jamie be safely stowed, the ship sheltered in a harbour, maybe staying there to make repairs.*

That night dreams grabbed her. She swam through oceans, her

feet nibbled at by little fish. A whale swallowed her, then spat her out in water thick as cold molasses. A lifebuoy of morning light drifted near. She grabbed it and swam to shore—relieved to be awake.

There was no safety there. The *Southern Cross* seemed as distant as the star bearing its name.

Words from the Song of Solomon she'd read in her mother's Bible galloped through her mind: *My lover is gone and I don't know where to find him.*

The next morning, her eyes heavy and swollen from crying, she made her way down to the post office. She called to William shuffling to where a crowd had gathered. Instead of answering he went to lean against the building as if his body was too heavy to hold him up. He listened to Ned Porter's words to those around him.

"A sealer sove from the ice floes will live through a sealing tragedy a thousand times," he said. "He'll wake from dreams believin' he's on the ice fighting for his life, his hands clenched as if frozen. He'll remember other fellars lost on ice pans and how he was near enough to try to save a sealer fallen into the sea jammed between ice pans. He'll wonder if he wasn't a coward for not offerin' a gaff, afraid the drownin' man would drag him in and both of them sink. His family will wake to his cries and try to settle his mind and stop his shiverin' by wrapping him in extra quilts."

No one answered the skipper, his eyes glazed by his own awful memory.

The land line to Cape Race that had been knocked out during the storm was restored and a rumour that the *Southern Cross* had sheltered at Trepassey in St. Mary's Bay was dismissed by the American Telegraph Company. There were fears that the barque had foundered in heavy swells and steep waves in the vicinity of Freels Rock, two miles off shore.

Days-old news that the *Southern Cross* was on her way home had lost its optimism. Awareness that something had gone amiss came like a thick fog creeping in over the land until the air was weighed down heavy enough on the inhabitants to bend their bodies into a slouch, their eyes dark with worry. Fear crept over the whole bay from Carbonear to St. John's and into one community where it found the mother of a young boy, his mother's sole supporter, a lad who by chance or destiny had acquired a berth on the *Southern Cross*. Long past midnight she, like other women, sat in her rocking chair running the rockers back and forth over hard floorboards, praying fervently.

A week passed and still there was no sign of the *Southern Cross*. Residents in shock from what they had already witnessed at the St. John's waterfront spent long periods there almost perishing from the wind's barbarous bite as they gazed out to sea, squinting under the sun's cold glance. After a time all of them, their lips stiff and blue, went home to sit by their windows looking for a speck on the horizon. Hope like a filament of light often rose as a ship was seen crossing the ocean. The ships went on their way, their captains unaware of the expectation their sighting had aroused.

After a second prolonged search for the *Southern Cross*, the *Kyle* returned to port on the twelfth of April.

Without success.

41

In Foxtrap, time wore away and yet it seemed suspended, a portent like a black moon showing no light. An outward calmness settled over the place as men worked in their lofts and sheds and women tended their homes. Still, uncertainty spread like a plague, sickening the hearts and minds of relatives waiting for a confirmation that their men were living or gone.

All through the long nights, echoes of disturbing news that the *Southern Cross* had not found safe shelter kept Maggie awake, hope washing away, drifting back like flotsam. Hours stretched as long as days and days lingered like weeks. She pushed at fear present like a black intruder and went to see William who reasoned that if the storm had driven the barque out to sea it would take days for her to make land.

Maggie glanced out the window and saw Caroline carrying a crock of stew in her apron. Lavinia came behind her mother, her face pale, her eyes dark. Caroline nodded toward Maggie and laid the stew on the stove. Lavinia dropped a steaming loaf of bread on the table.

"You've got to eat, me man, and you, too, Maggie," Caroline said. She stirred the stew and gave William a critical eye. "Do you find it cold?"

"Not altogether," he said, his voice logy.

"A sweater would do you just the same." She got up and took his sweater from a nail on the back of a door and laid it on his bent shoulders.

Lavinia touched her uncle's back. "It's a terrible loss, all those men on the *Newfoundland* perished, but Jamie is coming home." She lifted her head stubbornly. "There's no one says he's not."

Caroline drew her lips into a hard line. She said nothing. Then, seeing her daughter twisting the tail of her pinafore in her hands, her eyes wet, she put her arm around her. "We can't borrow tomorrow's trouble. Wait and see. There'll be news soon."

Maggie left the house without waiting for a dish of stew. More than ever she and William remained prisoners of hope.

That night she curled in bed beside Melanie and wrapped her arms around the tender body. She woke the next morning to hear voices from the kitchen. She jumped out of bed and slipped down to the stovepipe opening in the floor and listened. She heard a neighbour's grave words: "The *Southern Cross* would have been in port by now if she hadn't met with trouble. She headed right into the mouth of the storm and was likely swallowed."

"Don't tell Maggie right away." Her aunt's voice came strained and hoarse.

Maggie's heart galloped, her ears buzzing. What were they saying? She dressed and crept along the landing and down the stairs holding to the bannister. Her stockinged feet hooked in the clips holding the flower-patterned canvas in place and she almost tripped. She pushed open the door to the pantry just as the neighbour closed the door to the porch behind her. Her aunt was already reaching for a pot and rolled oats.

The porch door opened and Maggie turned startled. It was only her Uncle Aubrey coming inside.

Liddie frowned. "Don't be jumping like a scalded cat. You'll be gettin' news soon enough. I'll be thinkin' it's not good news, so don't rush it."

Maggie's lips quivered. "Even if there's some bad news there got to be good tidings with it. The *Newfoundland* brought good news with the bad. If the ship foundered and lost some men a passing ship may have rescued Jamie and other sealers."

"The Christian thing is to pray for the needs of others above our own; there's the tragedy of the *Newfoundland* to think on," Aubrey said.

After breakfast her aunt urged her, "Occupy your mind with work. Scrub the clothes and hang it to dry. Put the sunshine to good use. The day won't wait."

Liddie brought water already heated and poured it into the grey wooden tub in the porch. Maggie took down the washboard and settled the wood-framed glass board against the inside like a ladder. She spun soap into bubbles and kneaded a petticoat in sudsy waves, bringing it up over the washboard, water cascading like a waterfall turning dull, rope-patterned glass into diamond ropes. She washed the children's belongings, driving her reddened knuckles over the washboard with such intensity that she rinded them out. She rinsed the clothes and pinned them outdoors on the clothesline. She came inside and hung the washboard on the porch wall. Work had not settled her mind. Sorrow was coming. It was already pressing in around her heart.

She caught a glimpse of people hurrying past the window. Trembling she grabbed her coat and raced down the road still wearing her apron. A crowd had already gathered by the post office.

There was talk of several sightings of wreckage from the *Southern Cross*. Jack Kearsey, a seaman who worked on a small boat doing depth soundings in Placentia Bay, had told how he had been using a heaving line with a ten-pound weight to measure depth. It had a wax core at the bottom to collect material from the ocean floor for observation. He brought up a piece of white fur with fat attached. He wondered if his heaving line had dropped into the sunken *Southern Cross*.

Captain Gate Winsor of the *Bloodhound* reported that on his return from the icefields he had sighted wreckage on the Saturday morning after the *Southern Cross* went missing. When his ship was ninety miles southeast of Cape Broyle he had seen a large mass of floating debris at the edge of an ice floe. There were deck sheathing, pound boards, flagpoles, prizes, pieces of timber, a seaman's chest, a cap, and a bottle tightly corked bobbing in the water. Other debris had been spotted by cutters *Fiona* and the *Kyle*. No one could be sure any of it was from the *Southern Cross*.

Still, the *Southern Cross* had not been declared lost and people outside the post office waited for the door to open, waited for good news. The listing for ship arrivals placed on the door hadn't changed and didn't once the postmistress unlocked the door. She went back inside the mailroom and people pushed their way in as close to the closed wicket as possible, ears cocked to the mysterious movements and shifting sounds inside. They waited, talking out their fears.

"If the sealers's gone I hope the bodies don't wash ashore here," a nervous-looking man said. "That would be a terrible thing."

"Unlikely to happen—too far away," said an old farmer emptying and refilling the bowl of his pipe. He lit it and papped on the stem. It was a warm comforting smell to anyone standing beside him in the damp weather until he muttered, "All's not well, not handy to it. No news is bad news."

42

People now weak in sorrow and bearing faint optimism felt compelled to go to a service on Easter Sunday. Moth-holed Sunday suits were pulled from wooden chests and pressed. William wore a black suit over a starched white shirt and tie. The suit looked as if it had been hanging on a nail for some time. The pook was still in the back as if God had grabbed him like a cat grabs her kittens and planked him down in the church.

William's father had not paid for a pew. William took a place anyway, hoping for tolerance from whoever had paid for it, maybe someone gone under the sod. He needed to be sitting in the same place as other people suffering the same loss of hope, all wondering what God was going to do about it. They were hoping for His mercy and a miracle.

* * * * *

Reverend Petten stood, his arms outstretched, palms open, and intoned: "These two things shall come to you in a moment, in one day; the loss of children and widowhood shall come upon you in full measure." He carried on. "Isaiah wrote, in the forty-fifth chapter, verse seven, 'I form the light, and create darkness: I make peace and create evil: I, the Lord, do all these things.' We don't dismiss nature when we are caught in her destruction. Neither should we dismiss God, the source of all life, when we are caught in what we see as the evil of death. We are born with the promise of life and no guarantee of its length. The old graveyard with its many headstones bears the testament to the certainty of death. Unfortunately, headstones to the many people lost at sea from one calamity or another are invisible to us. We suffer a phantom loss when we can't view the bodies but—" The minister's finger pointed upwards. "—the day shall come when God will move His mighty hand over the ocean. The temperamental sea will churn like a cauldron of boiling water and rumble like an earthquake. It shall give up its dead—every man, woman, and child, red and yellow, black and white bodies brought to life and spit out of the great mouth of the sea, a surge of humanity on every beach around the island—on every beach around the world."

"We've had no confirmation that the sealers are lost," William muttered to Joe as they scuffed their way back home. "No one told us anything. Until they do I'll wait for Jamie."

Mary Jane had gone. He couldn't lose Jamie and Maggie. Maggie's name rushed through his head like a whirlwind. Her quick laugh let out like a stream rippling over rocks had stirred the life Mary Jane's death had frozen. Her face had settled into a contented pose as she sat on the floor and leaned against Jamie. The girl was good to have around. If Jamie were gone she wouldn't come near. He'd lose her, too.

For days after Jamie was presumed dead the world fell down around Maggie like a smothering cloud. Sometimes she sat staring, lost in hope and expectation that any minute Jamie and the other sealers would break over the crest of the hill and hurry along the path singing their jollies. All along the shore in welcoming homes there'd be dancing and singing boisterous enough to threaten the floorboards.

She went to see William and found him sitting in the dim evening light. She reached in across the table and turned the knob on the Aladdin lamp to brighten the room. She took in William's heavy look and said, wanting it to be true, "Jamie *will* come home."

He placed a hand over hers, just the barest of touch. He quickly withdrew it. A woman's hand beneath his was not something he'd have to cherish ever again. "Caroline brought a pot of cooked dinner," he said. "If you're up to sharing it I'd thank yer."

She nodded, unable to get words past the lump in her throat. She ladled the food on their plates and bowed her head in Grace. They ate in silence. When they were finished and she had washed the dishes she stood up to leave. "Parson Petten would tell us we should pray," she said.

William's look was dark. "That good fellow can tie his advice to the underside of a cow's tail."

Caroline, coming in the door, overheard him. "You can't be saying that. Indeed not. Whatever happened is an act of God."

"Sure," he muttered. "The Almighty looked down and saw the ship and her proud happy sealers eager for the dollars they had earned to feed their families and He acted."

Caroline patted William's shoulder and he grunted. A splinter was caught in his heart too deep to ever pull out.

43

The news was made official in newspapers on April 14. Joe brought a newspaper home to Caroline. She stared at the black headlines:

THE *SOUTHERN CROSS* IS LOST

And underneath an article stated that the *Southern Cross* vanished in the vicinity of Freels Rock.

"You have to tell William," Caroline urged.

"I can't," he said trying to control his emotion. He pushed the newspaper under the mattress of the daybed and spoke as if he was dreaming. "She was last sighted near St. Shotts. That's the place where settlers used to put lanterns on cows' horns to misguide them and lure ships on the rocks, a trait brought from the Old Country." He reared up in anger. "By gad I hope they didn't interfere with the *Southern Cross*."

Caroline put her finger to his lips. "Hush yourself. You can't be makin' accusations. All the roamin' beams of lighthouses along the coast couldn't get through the white death envelopin' that ship."

News spread like a black plague. People rushed to the post office, their panicky voices seeking confirmation for what they had heard. William stood among them, his head down.

"Is she found?" a young fellow who had wanted to go on the vessel asked.

"No, me lad," an old sealer said, swallowing hard.

The young fellow jerked a shoulder up as if to ward off bad tidings and left mumbling, "A night in ashes, this is."

The wicket of the post office finally grated open and the postmistress lifted a bundle of letters tied with a string, the borders of the white envelopes in black edging. The truth of that terrible moment ran through the people standing near the counter. They let out a gasp and moved back. The restless movement of the crowd and their chatter came to a halt.

"Let anyone through who's got a sealer on the SS *Southern Cross* and anyone who had one on the SS *Newfoundland*," the postmistress called in a solemn voice. Her hands shook as she slid the string off the bundle and the letters settled on the counter. Her voice cracked as she began calling names. No one moved and the letters were passed hand to hand to a reluctant relative, passed like a raised axe to descend with a swift blow to split their hearts. The weekly mail was seen as a means of connecting in a letter with a relative or friend in Canada, Boston, or elsewhere. These letters would disconnect families from hope.

Peggy Green had two sons on the *Southern Cross*. When she opened her letter and read news of her sons gone forever she ran out the door of the post office and up over the path stumbling from side to side. She flung herself on the ground crying and pounding the hard earth.

"Hurry! She'll break her wrists," someone yelled.

Her brother ran and hauled her up. She fell back down on her knees, her knuckles blood-crusted.

"Adam's name's not on the letter with his father's," another mother cried. "He has to be alive." Hope was dashed like a wave against a rock when a voice asked, "Then where would he be all this time?"

"I was dying to get the news of the ship's whereabouts," a wife sobbed. "Now it's come to kill me."

William's name was called. He felt the blood drain from his veins and fear clot in his throat. His face drawn and grey, he teetered back on his heels as if a north wind had come up and driven into him with a terrible force. Then he straightened up and reached to take the black-bordered letter passed over the crowd to him.

Finally, after the postmistress, her face solemn, had distributed all the mail, she closed the wicket. It was as if a blind had been pulled over a window in a building where death had occurred. The people standing outside holding black-bordered letters knew that letters carrying the same news were arriving in St. John's and in communities beyond the Avalon. Church bells began to toll and a black flag was run up the public pole, a chilling sight. No lamplight showed in any window to break the night in ashes.

William did not open his letter. Along the lane curtains were pushed aside, eyes wide behind them watching as William slewed around and staggered home. He sat all night by the fire holding the envelope in his fist as if news not acknowledged would go away. The fire threw its last spark and the embers died. He did not feel the cold air seeping into his bones as he waited for daylight, his eyes open in the darkness. He finally curled around himself on the settle pulling a blanket over his shivering body. He had learned that life was both beautiful and terrible, beautiful when a child is born, terrible when he dies before his father. An image of Jamie as a bright-eyed smiling baby flashed before him. It was quickly replaced by an image of him packed among other sealers below deck in the black pit of night caught in the turbulence of the *Southern Cross* battled by a raging storm. Jamie and the other sealers would have prayed or let out a rhyme of oaths as they heard the crack of boards and fell against each other facing the smothering load of seal pelts.

* * * * *

Maggie cranked the arm of the Victrola and dropped the needle to the phonograph disc to listen to music. She was swinging Melanie in a dance when through the window she noticed people gathering on the crest of Church Road. She hauled on her gaiters and coat and hurried down the road. When she saw people huddled over letters, their looks drawn, she started to run. She tripped over a trench made from the grid of buggy wheels and went headlong. "What a sight you is, then, full of mud!" a farmer called as he hurried by. He turned back and reached to pull her to her feet.

"What's the news?" she asked.

The man's answer—"The *Southern Cross* is lost"—twisted deep inside her like an auger. Her knees buckled and she fell in a heap feeling as if her bones had shattered and pierced through her skin.

"Come on, then, get up," Minnie Marshall standing on her doorstep called. "You can be sorrowful but it's not as if you and he've started a life together."

Maggie looked up, her eyes wide in shock.

"You're not in the family way, is yer, then, fallin' like that?" the woman asked.

Maggie didn't bother to answer. She strained to get to her feet, steadying herself on weak legs. She had been daydreaming about leaving her aunt's place to be with Jamie. The truth cut her. It was never going to happen. She turned back and started to run as fast as she could toward William's house, her breath coming in gasps. She had to see William. She came to an abrupt halt. *Not tonight!*

She hurried back to Liddie's, passing her aunt in the hall and the children calling to her as she clung to the rail taking her upstairs. She rushed on, away from everyone, away to her bed. Shock settled in her like pooled blood as the black fog of night drifted around her. She lifted herself up on an elbow to look through the dark window. The moon had died and left the sky in black sackcloth.

Daylight came before she fell asleep.

Morning sounds of a family's hushed movements surfaced. Maggie's eyes opened, stared without comprehension of where she was and what day it was. Her aunt's hand touched hers and she blinked. Yesterday's news crashed against her, waves of it enveloping her, drowning her. A wrenching cry tore up through her throat. Jamie wasn't coming home—he was gone.

"Not even his body," she whispered, her voice choked in tears.

Liddie looked at her. "You poor girl. Don't let yourself get down in your nerves. It'll be hard to get back up. You need to think of what you have, not what you have lost. The parson once preached that we must'n think of half a glass of water as half empty, but half full."

"My glass is full—full of emptiness," she answered, her voice toneless.

The blazing sun burned its way across the water and spread light on the wall of Maggie's room. The wind's rush outside her window was cut into by the rapid chirping of birds fluttering about. Inside, the house was warm like a blanket, the air still, voices soft. Maggie's body felt weighed down, too heavy to move.

Liddie came back up to her room just before noon. She coaxed her downstairs for a cup of tea and a warm biscuit. "In time," she promised, "the tragedy will fade into a dream."

Maggie pulled her sweater tight. "I don't want Jamie to fade from me mind."

Myra, Liddie's widowed mother-in-law, had come from Canada to stay with the family. The old granny sat in her rocking chair, her eyes whitened from cataracts in a face wreathed in wrinkles. She cautioned Maggie in a quavering, thin voice. "There now, me child, we must never let ourselves be so overcome by sorrow that we slip under it and stay there. Everything in life is connected to loss. We lose the comfort of a place inside our mother's bodies once we are born. We lose our place in childhood, grow up, marry, give birth, and in time lose our children as they make their own lives. We lose our health as we age. We are all on a journey and we must make the most of every moment as best we can, enjoying what we have while we have it."

Maggie voice was leaden. "You can't know what it's like to grow up missin' the love of a mother, though I hardly had her, and sufferin' the loss of a father's love though it was short-lived—and now Jamie. I was strong when I had the love of a man, when I knew I was in his thoughts. Now I'm alone."

"Ah," said the old lady, "we all suffer one thing or another at one time or another. God never leaves us alone."

She got up from her chair and felt her way along to where Maggie slouched. She took her hand and in a firm voice said, "In time you'll think of yourself as someone *you* haven't lost. The most important person in your life is you. You lived a long life before Jamie and you will live long after him. This is not the end of your story. Your life story is larger than this."

"My story?" Her chin lifted and her eyes widened.

"Your life story didn't begin with you. It reaches back to the beginning of time. All that makes you a person was carried in the bodies of your ancestors. You're the witness to their existence."

Liddie poured Maggie another cup of tea and gave her a keen look. "You're not in trouble, are you?"

"I wish I was carryin' a bit of Jamie," she answered, her chin up, a fierce look in her eyes.

"You'd be a fallen woman," Liddie said.

Maggie looked past Myra and Liddie, her voice distant. "I'd be fallen in love. Jamie had me heart. He deserved the chance to carry on our family tree. Our future is lost."

"It is Jamie who is lost, not you and your future. There's more fish—"

"In the sea," Maggie snapped. She turned and ran upstairs going to her dresser. She pulled out a drawer and lifted the soft wool wedding dress, its bodice half-knitted. She slipped the needles out of the stitches and slowly unravelled the dress until there was only a pile of white yarn on the floor, her dress unravelled like her future as a bride, shapeless like her life had become.

She slipped to the floor, her body shuddering like water in a pond stirred by a cold wind.

William woke, realization like a hammer slamming against his head. He groaned as he sat up and eased his feet over the bed. He poured water from Mary Jane's flowered jug into a wash pan and sluiced his face in it, ignoring the blueberry soap. Then he lit the fire. He poured porridge and a pinch of salt in boiling water as usual and stirred it with the wooden spoon Mary Jane had brought with her. His hand trembled as he lifted the first spoonful. He stopped, his gaze on Jamie's painting of *Titanic* on the wall. He cringed remembering how that loss had swept over the place. Now sorrow had come closer, dug deeper, to last forever.

Caroline sent Lavinia over to see how William was faring. "I'm going to get married next year," she had told him a few months before.

"And who might you be marryin'?" he had asked. "I know you've been in service down the shore."

"Joshua Rideout," she answered. "I can't wait."

"I suppose then there'll be a batch of young ones comin'."

She let out a giggle. "People make batches of bread, not batches of babies, though one here and there would be to my liking some day."

When she said, "Well, I must be goin'," he answered, "There's scads of time."

She gave him a bold look. "Yes, but I don't have to spend it all here."

William raised his hand. "So long, then. I'll hear tell of you another day."

"Don't be a black stranger yourself," she said. "Uncle Johnny likes to see you."

Lavinia had always had the fresh, full look of an unblemished white apple in the Maley orchard. Now William noticed how drawn and thin she looked. He kept silent though he was thinking something he didn't dare say. His son was gone and his brother's daughter was going.

44

A jagged, heavy stone had slipped inside Maggie's heart. She couldn't breathe without it hurting. She had looked forward to becoming part of the Maley family. Instead she was an outsider.

"Go back and see the old fellow some more," Liddie urged. "He'll want to see you."

Maggie slogged down the road past the graveyard. When she turned up Church Road she let out a strangled breath. She tried to steady herself to go into the house where she knew William held the official letter informing him that the *Southern Cross* had been declared lost.

William sat with his elbows on the table, his fingers under the sides of his head as if to hold it up. He turned to acknowledge Maggie. Then he spoke as if he was dreaming. "The boats spent ten days looking for the *Southern Cross*. She was a fine steamer, not like the rotting ships that brought me forebears to this land. There was no way to know she'd be the biggest coffin of all." He lifted his head, his face heavy and bloated in anguish. "I don't believe there'll be any sighting. Jamie's gone and Mary Jane's nephews and other far-off relatives lost." He dropped his balding head into his cupped hands, his shoulders heaving from the deep sorrow surging through his body.

"I thought men didn't cry," Maggie said, her own eyes wet and bright. Then waves of grief rushed against her and her fingers pressed against her mouth to hold in her anguished cries.

William didn't answer and she set the kettle to boil, her tears splashing on the black spout. Boiling her tears for tea is what she'd be doing if she wasn't careful. She turned and flopped down in Mary Jane's rocking chair and stared at Jamie's painting of *Titanic*.

William followed her look. "He got her likeness," he murmured. "She looks real enough to board."

"Why did Jamie paint *Titanic*?" Maggie asked.

William drew in a deep breath and let it out before answering. "Jamie got caught up in all the talk about her: her magnificent beginning and her tragic ending. The young lad's fingers always itched to paint, and paint he did as you can see, makin' some job of the ship."

He nodded toward a wooden box on the table. "Jamie made you a wedding box. Go ahead," he said, looking away.

She reached to take it, her hands trembling. A cross was carved on the outside of the cover. The words MY LOVE FOR YOU HAS NO QUESTION MARK, AND NO PERIOD, JUST AN EXCLAMATION! were carved on the inside. She lifted a gold wedding band and held it on the palm of her hand thinking, *A wedding ring I'll never wear.* On the inside bottom of the box Jamie had carved a tree with MAGGIE and JAMES on the first branch.

"His mother's wedding band," William said. "I remember the day I put it on Mary Jane's finger." He struggled to his feet grabbing Maggie's shoulder as if she were his anchor. He mumbled, "It's a blessin' Mary Jane's passed on. She'd be some way knowin' Jamie's gone and she not able to lay him out and give him to the ground."

Maggie pulled away. *What does he think he's doin' lettin' the weight of his grief fall on me, and me with me own?*

She set William's tea and a slice of bread and jam in place and left him there alone.

She came back to her aunt's house, the wooden box held against her breast. She sat on her bed still holding it. How could she have been sitting down eating, maybe laughing, and not feel the jolt of the ship, hear Jamie's gasp for breath as his lungs filled with water? Shouldn't she have felt something as he drifted to the bottom of the ocean? Surely he reached out to her, put his mind on her as he faced his end.

Evening shades slipped over the land. Night fell, its darkness soaking through her. She lit a kerosene lamp. Its flame like a tongue reached up to lick the darkness. She felt alone inside this pool of light—the whole world outside.

Saturday morning Liddie called up the stairs, "Haul yourself out of bed. There's children to be tended to and readied for tomorrow's Sunday prayers."

The sun sent a gentle light into the room and she opened her eyes to a world too bright against her sorrow. She held a small pillow, HAIRLOOM PILLOW embroidered on it, to her heart. Mary Jane had given it to her saying, "It's a pillow made of Jamie's hair from when he had his first haircut and every haircut thereafter. He had such a head of golden curls." She had looked toward William, her expression mischievous. "Now you know where William's hair went."

She watched the clouded sun with its partial aura of rainbow, its arc broken like Jamie's promise to come back. Bay waters laughed and winked under sunshine. How could the day be so cheerful and life go on as if nothing had happened?

She dragged herself downstairs pretending she could go on even though she wasn't sure it was possible. She, like a ship sailing on sunny seas, had been hit by a prowling iceberg breaking her, sending her to the bottom of a deep ocean. She didn't know how to haul herself back up.

One night she woke rearing up with a terrible cry. Liddie hurried up the stairs to settle her back on her pillow. She lay there, her eyes wide open, afraid to sleep and fall into the same distress.

Liddie rushed downstairs and back up, urging her, "Drink this tonic. It'll help you get past your troublesome sleep. Life don't give you a choice. You have to keep goin' day by day until your mind gets further and further from your grief."

Some nights Maggie dreamed about Jamie. His arms reached for her and she caught the scent of his skin, felt the touch of his lips, the surge of life through his body. She woke with a start, the room cold and empty, her voice begging, "Be with me, Jamie, and I'll stay asleep forever."

45

Wind screeched against Jacob's house as if it was trying to carry it off as a Pick Eyes fisherman lifted the latch on the porch door and made to go in. He hesitated, then stood with his back to door and looked out to sea. He turned slowly to face Elizabeth as she opened the door. She smiled. "It's Len Bishop from across the cove, is it?"

"Indeed, and you're Elizabeth come from over on the shore to marry Jacob." He scuffed his toes against the landing and mumbled, "A good many black sheep will be losin' their wool this year." He tightened his hands on the bib of a cap he held in front of him, trying to steady them.

Elizabeth felt her heart quiver like a little bird in strong winds. She asked, "Why this year more than any other year?"

He shifted his look to the ocean, choosing his words carefully. "Women all over will be knittin' black stockings and shawls for the year ahead."

Elizabeth backed away, her hand to her breast. Dried mint hanging in the porch scraped against Len's face as he went past her and into the kitchen, where Jacob stood putting a shovel of coal into the stove.

"The *Southern Cross* is lost," Len blurted. "There's sealers gone from everywhere. St. John's, Foxtrap, Kelligrews, Long Pond, Brigus,

Spaniard's Bay, Harbour Grace. . . ." As if too overcome to finish he dropped to the settle. "Joshua Taylor's punt just left the stagehead. He came from Cupids to tell us there's black flags hangin' and window shades down in ever so many houses. Every family in the place'll be keepin' their window shades down until after a memorial service."

Len's words pierced Elizabeth's heart like a needle of heavy black thread drawn through it and knotted. Her mouth and tongue felt stiff. Then her tongue came loose as if freed from the spell of the Old Haig. Her brother's name came out in a lament: *"Jaamiee."*

Jacob reached and caught her as she was falling. He held her trembling body against his, murmuring, "Liz, I'm sorry."

"Hard it is," Len added, "the sorrow deep when there's no bodies to bury."

Elizabeth caught sight of the century-old headstones outside the window. *Not even to have that for Jamie*!

Her voice was muffled against Jacob's chest. "My father needs me—Maggie, too! My my, what must she be feeling! I have to go, Jake."

"Not yet," Jacob answered.

She felt him tremble as if he was reluctant to risk taking her in boat after such a calamity.

She pulled away. "I could go by train. Me father's got no one."

Jacob promised, "He was alone before he had a family. We'll ask him to come to the cove and stay with us."

Elizabeth's hand moved down her belly to answer a quickening inside her. *If you're a boy I'll name you Jamie Maley. I will,* she vowed, *a brother for Elsie.*

Elizabeth changed Elsie and settled her in the cradle. Then she went through the hall, her eyes clouded and burning with grief. She slid her hand along the window leaf and felt a draft of cold air as she looked out over the bay, light playing on it bringing varied shadows. Those waters reached toward an ocean in which Jamie had disappeared. There was nothing more alive than the sea, nothing more deadly.

By nightfall she felt as if her mind was on for carrying her away like a wave never to bring her back. Jacob came up behind her. She turned and smiled wistfully. "Maggie and Jamie got on well." She swallowed hard. "She and I are bonded in our loss. She lost a coosie and I lost a brother. She won't have the chance to become a mother of Jamie's children and I'll miss my chance to be an aunt to them."

In bed Jacob reached his strong arms around her and pulled her body snug in the crook of his. She fell asleep to nightmares that Jamie had washed up in the cove, a piece of wreckage stuck in his throat. She thrashed in her sleep, awaking intermittently.

"There's always hope when there's no evidence," Jacob said softly, "but if worse should come I'll be your husband and your brother. I promise. You got me for always."

He snuggled against her back, her arms together and her legs curled up to her stomach as if she had folded herself around her lonely heart.

The next day they stood on the porch landing looking out to sea. Jacob said, "The sea is dangerous on its own but when it and the weather join forces man is a leaf without a tree. Still, we can't forget that the sea, a graveyard for many, is also a generous giver of life."

Elizabeth turned away. She resented the sea for what it had taken and for what it might take. On late spring nights she stood on the landing outside her porch door and listened to a resonance rising from the deep, dark belly of the ocean. During a calm night when a full moon rubbed its tongue along the sea's dark back its skin lay like a sleeping body.

She felt its deadly silence, its metallic taste in the air as wind brushed her face.

Elizabeth picked her words carefully in a letter to Maggie. She rewrote parts of it.

> *. . . it's important not to keep the past in front of you as if you have the means to change it. You can't dwell on me brother's death. You have to remember his life. Visit me dear old father often if you can. You share the same heartache.*
>
> *In fond memories of you,*
> *Elizabeth Emma*

Elizabeth lifted her cup of tea cradling it with both hands, her gaze wandering to the large headstones outside her kitchen window like grey ghosts, letters on the stones like eyes peering in. Its truth cut through her mind: "*As you are now so once was I. . . .*" The refrain would come often as she sat having breakfast alone and Jacob gone on the water.

46

A tightly corked bottle bobbing in the water! That's what was seen. Who's to say it's not Jamie's message sent to me? Maggie drifted into sleep thinking about this possibility. In a dream she caught sight of a bottle in the sea amid fields of ice like diamonds sparkling in the sun. The stoppered bottle neck rose above the water and danced to the dulcet sounds of lapping waves holding carey chicks and ice partridges. Waves muscled the bottle toward the beach, the lip of a tide nudging it ashore. It lay like an exhausted body dying in the sun. A child picked it up, held it in mid-air as other children watched a dead whale on the beach, driven in by a storm. Gulls swooped down for a pick. The child threw the bottle at a gull. It smashed against a cliff and pieces of paper floated into the air like feathers and drifted down on the sea. She ran into the water to gather the pieces.

Maggie woke, her body in a sweat. She lay digging her feet into the feather mattress imagining another possibility. The bottle rolled against Paddy's Beach. She pulled the cork and unrolled a sheet of paper from the bottle. "*Dear Maggie, My hands are trembling from the cold but my heart is warm with thoughts of you. We've cleared the last patch of seals from the ice, leaving a field of carcasses for sea creatures wanting a ready supper. I'm coming home. There's a storm brewing and there's worry talk all around. I'm not joining in.*" He would feel a lurch of the ship and then he would add, "*If perchance I don't survive the voyage I will live in the air you breathe, on the land you walk, and in the sea you sail. I will live on in you.*" He'd sign his name and push the paper into the bottle and press the cork into the neck.

She curled around herself. Daydreaming was all she was doing, waking the dead that couldn't be waked.

There was a creak in the house, a stir of wind at the window, and for an instant she thought Jamie had come. The wind swept in like a bird, ascended as if with a mighty rush of its wings. Leaves outside her window lifted and rose, dropping gently as the wind passed. She gasped, "Jamie's ghost! There has to be a sign of him somewhere."

She crept downstairs to sit by a window facing the ocean. She wondered what Olivia would do when she got the news of Zachary's drowning, and Emily when she heard that her brothers were lost. *Carefree children on a beach we were once, never thinking beyond the next day, never expecting misfortune.*

She grabbed her woollen coat from a hook and pulled it on. She left the house and hurried along the road rushing to get to the beach where she and the other children had spent the early years of their childhood. Heavy snow swirled like a veil around her as she ran squishing wet snow under her feet. She stumbled across the beach tripping in rocks. Finally she stopped and stood trembling in winds strong enough to buckle her knees and take her breath. Their fierceness reddened her numbed face. Still she stayed taking in the sweeping chaos of seafoam, kelp, stones, and seashells swept ashore. It was not easy to forget the sea's tantrums, its dark moods and killing ways. Not easy to forget that Jamie and other sealers lay cradled in its wild belly beyond the reach of those who loved them. She lifted her head to where the old house stood abandoned by her stepmother's family, its windows now boarded up as if blinded.

The snow cleared, the sky brightened, and the sea grew quiet. Sunlight twinkled like stars on the sea's shiny blue coat.

"Wish upon the stars of the sea," Jamie had told Maggie, promising, "We'll be together as husband and wife come fall."

Wind came in a gentle brush against her neck. She turned startled as if Jamie had touched her with his lips.

47

"My brothers!" Emily screamed when she heard her mistress say that the *Southern Cross* was lost.

"Your brothers?" Abigail stopped still. "I didn't know." Then she charged her: "Off with your apron and hurry to get the truth."

Emily went out the door still wearing her apron, a dust mop in her hand held out as she ran stumbling and catching herself. She rushed down the street to where other people waited. The wharf swarmed with people whose solemn faces bore the heaviness of a shocking truth: the *Southern Cross,* carrying her brothers, was lost. Her father was home alone waiting for sons who would never return.

When Emily got back from the wharf Lily was sitting on the deep window leaf, its casement wide open in the oak-panelled drawing room. She had a pensive look as if she was still wondering why her mamma hadn't come to get her. Now her pappa wouldn't come for her either. He was gone forever on the *Southern Cross.* She'd soon forget all of them.

Emily had overheard the peddler and the merchant talking about Lily and had been shocked to learn her identity. She had struggled with her secret but no longer. If she took the orphan back home, who would care for her? At least she was growing up in a family who would feed her out of its many fancy serving dishes, a lot more than comes in use in the run of a day in many outport homes. The peddler did her a favour. He would think that, too, as he went about bringing yards of bright cloth, soaps and buttons, and dishes to homes around the bay. It was just as well to let the secret bide. *I have other things to think about. I have two brothers who will never come home.*

She started up the stairs, her eyes moist. An epitaph she'd seen on graves in All Saints graveyard dug its engraving pen through her thoughts:

ALL, ALL ARE GONE, THE GOOD, THE FAIR
ALL LOST IN LIFE'S SWEET BLOOM;
THEIR GRAVES OUT IN THE OCEAN DREAR
GOD WILLED TO BE THEIR TOMB.

A black net of grief lay over families from St. John's to Conception Bay South and Conception Bay North. Bloodlines twined like the perennial trailing vines of morning glories. Descendants of Butlers, Walshes, Kennedys, Porters, Conways could all lay claim to losing a part of their family on the *Newfoundland* and the *Southern Cross.* Few of them were more than six generations apart, making it a communal loss. Hearts and minds from far and wide were hung on hooks of grief tangled on the same trawl line.

Wherever relatives and neighbours of the victims gathered, beside rock walls of sheds, outside post offices, or inside railway stations, they all carried the same mesmerized look as they listened to stories that connected the living to the lost.

It was a stormy winter night when Mathilda Roach saw Charlie's ghost pass her and go into their bedroom. Another sealer's wife woke to see her husband standing soaking wet at the foot of their bed. Josie Maidment scrubbed her hands raw on her washboard while her plaintive voice could be heard: "Philip, Philip went to sea. Someone bring him back to me." She sang the same words over and over as she hung her clothes to dry. She didn't seem to notice that her clotheslines were heavy with sopping clothes not wrung out. Another widow went around the yard calling, "Poor, poor I. What will I do?" She lifted her apron and slapped it down. She did this over and over until her arms dropped with tiredness. She ran back inside her house and sprawled back on a chair pushed under her. She moaned and cried, "I loved the junk of a man." Her neighbours agreed he had been kind to her, hardly letting her bring in a stick of wood when he was around, flouring the fish for dinner while she heated the pan and rendered scruncheons. He didn't mind turning his hand to a dirty dish either. He was as good as a maid. "Surely God had better things to do than take my man," she murmured over and over.

One father told his daughter grieving for her lover he didn't care for, "Get yourself to rights and stop this—" His voice skidded to a stop as his wife gave him a withering look. He jutted his chin defiantly and the word he wanted to say stretched through the air like a hiss. "Nonsense!"

Mona Rideout had been promised to Jack Smith and they had their future planned. But on a cold morning after hearing her father's words she slipped out of bed and took a steady and purposeful walk out over the beach. She kept on going into the ocean, her face a mask. Those who saw her said she was sleepwalking. She had to be. The water would have knifed every pore. She walked out as if she felt nothing, as if she heard nothing as people ran calling to her. Little bergs of ice swirled around her dark skirts as she went deeper. She slipped beneath the water, her dark hair streaming like a school of caplin just as a fisherman ran to grab her. He was too late to save her life. The parson was called to her bedside. "A sinful thing!" he said. "Only the devil calls one to such a deed."

Her mother's voice rose in her defence: "It was the grief that wrung her heart and she drownin' in love for him. She wasn't goin' out to die; she was goin' out to be closer to him." Her voice cracked.

The parson admitted, "Sometimes grief is so demanding and impulse so strong a tide that there is no logic in a person's behaviour. For that reason she shall have her place in consecrated ground."

In one house a mother had a premature child born at seven months without help. She and her children couldn't eat for poverty. Weak from childbirth and hunger she became desperate. The mother pulled a blanket over the baby's face and turned away from her frantic movements. When there was no stir she lifted the blanket and looked into the peaceful face. "Go with God where there is no pain. I had you inside me for a few months; God will have you for eternity." When a neighbour said, "You lost your baby," she answered: "She's not lost. She's in heaven."

The sire of a son and grandson who were lost on the sealing ship suffered a stroke when he heard the news. He saw the *Southern Cross* coming every evening. "Make haste!" he'd call. "Go to the boat and bring home Eddie and Wilson."

These were other stories: some confirmed, some denied.

Beyond the east coast a family scattered here and there had lost a sealer and mourned alone.

Olivia was like them. She grieved alone in a house she now shared with her grandparents. She was unable to discuss her loss with anyone, knowing she would have little sympathy from those who judged her for leaving Zachary. If only they knew.

48

Woodsmoke drifting out of chimneys along the Southern Shore trailed in the wind like flags of distress. Joe sat in William's house and wiped sweat from his forehead as if the strain of bad news had exerted him more than a day's hard labour.

"The loss of the *Southern Cross* and the loss of life on the *Newfoundland* makes this our greatest sealing disaster on record," Joe said, "though it's been told that the worst disaster was in the spring of 1838 when a fleet of fourteen vessels went to the icefields and got caught in an ice tornado. They disappeared takin' over three hundred sealers. Now here we is, then, with the deaths of two hundred and fifty-four sealers from the *Newfoundland* and the *Southern Cross*, counting a sealer killed on the *Bonaventure* and a stowaway aboard the *Southern Cross*."

William didn't answer and after a while Joe left and strode down the road and up a ladder to a shed loft where men had gathered knitting twine into nets. The men were speculating on the cause of the *Southern Cross*'s disappearance. There were rumours from sealers who had sailed on the ship the year before that the pound boards were rotten. Other people blamed Captain Clarke, accusing him of testing fate, gambling his life and his men's lives for the glory of reaching port first. They believed that the captain had forced his heavily laden ship through the storm into heavy rollers. The strain of the ship pushing against head-on winds with a large amount of unused coal and a heavy load of seal pelts slugging back and forth may have broken the rotten bulkhead causing the seals to fall into the forecastle, smothering the sealers. The vessel would have rocked and heaved causing a hard list from which the *Southern Cross* could not recover.

The next day Joe read in a St. John's newspaper that mariners believed other factors contributed to the sinking of the *Southern Cross*. The ship had a low-mounted engine. High bulwarks and pelts floating like cork in an inch and a half of fat may have blocked the water holes. Deck boards made of oak would have become waterlogged. The rush of air going backwards may have blown the hatches off the ship. Once the hatches were off and the ship plunged forward the heavy seas boarded the ship pushing her nose under. Her heavily laden body would have slipped under high seas and disappeared.

Sitting on a keg at the end of the Foxtrap wharf, Eli Reid played his fiddle, its mournful dirge like a wail out over the sea as if he was still waiting for news of the sealers.

"Put up the fiddle," a fisherman said, laying his hand on his shoulder. "Your woman's got the soup simmerin'."

Eli dropped his head over his fiddle and wept silently. He had been absorbing his bad thoughts of his brother's loss in his music and now there were only the breaking sounds of the sea reminding him that there was no solace.

Southern winds swept in chasing away the harshness of earlier spring days. Water trickled off house eaves, chimed against nails sticking out of boards, and laughed as it ran through the throat of streams let loose. It was easy to wonder how the sun could beam down, wind caress the land, and the world look so bright. Didn't nature notice that strong young men who had once turned the soil, set a boat on the water, lifted a child to a cheek, put an arm around a sweetheart, wife, or mother, were absent, their silence loud inside the mourners' hearts?

Though the etched images of sealers' foot and body prints in ice had been eaten by black water, images of frozen sealers from the SS *Newfoundland* remained in the dark archives of people's memory and in newspaper photographs.

There were no images of sealers from the *Southern Cross.*

49

James Butler, sexton of the Church of England on Church Road, used his one arm to pull on the rope in the belfry of the church with all his might. The deep sounds knelled through the place, an echoing sadness swinging wide. People stopped what they were doing and listened, knowing that the *Southern Cross* was officially lost.

Church bells had sent out their dolorous dong for victims of the *Newfoundland*, those brought home and those left to the sea. Now they tolled for sealers lost on the *Southern Cross.* They kept on tolling through April as memorial services were held in each community that had lost sealers. Ships in St. John's harbour kept flags half-mast.

Families of missing sealers of Foxtrap and neighbouring communities frapsed themselves in black attire and, to the resounding ring of church bells, came by horse and wagon and mare's shanks. They kept a stiff upper lip as they made their way past headstones and along the footpath to the door of the little white church. Inside there was not a single coffin, not a single body to look on as evidence of the tragedy.

Heads turned but only for a moment as Olivia swept in wearing a long, black velvet dress under a shoulder cloak, her waist pinched tight, a little purse to the side. Her coiffured blonde hair was swept off her neck revealing soft white skin, her eyebrows arched over swollen eyes under a netted black hat. She slipped into her stepfather's pew toward the back, one he and her mother had left empty after she left for Boston.

William entered the church like someone lumbering with a ball and chain around his ankles. He was wearing his weekday clothes and clutching a woods cap in his hand as if he was about to haul it over his head and be gone. Mary Jane would be ashamed of her life for a husband who went to church in such a getup.

Relatives of the missing sealers scuffed down the church aisle on leaden legs to sit and rise in accordance with the service. Hymns were sung but they could not push aside thoughts pounding in the minds of mourners that the sealers should be coming down the aisle in their new scroopy boots and dropping a coin in the offering plate in thanks to God for bringing them home safe and sound.

Reverend Petten began his sermon. "On a clear night, when The Dipper is sprinkling the sky with the seven brightest stars of its constellation, the *Southern Cross*, a ship proudly named for a southern constellation, lies beyond starlight and moonlight, akin to a greater and more powerful ship—*Titanic*. It is for its silence that the *Southern Cross* will be remembered as it lies deep in the belly of the ocean holding the secrets of its last voyage. *Titanic*, in a rush to make a transatlantic speed record, ignored the risk of a silent white threat. The *Southern Cross* ignored the forces of nature in trying to get ahead of its fellows in reaching St. John's. It took one hundred and seventy-three men and perhaps a stowaway, leaving widows and orphans and sweethearts. We have to look for a lesson here for our own lives.

"When a ship disappears into the ocean, its young men gathered like fish in a net by the sea, and church bells ring out to announce the calamity, farmers in their fields take off their caps and women in their kitchens bow their heads. They have all felt a loss in one way or another through the years. All Saints graveyard carries the ending to many earthly lives. In its hallowed ground lies the calligraphy of bones until the resurrection unites soul and body. It is the same for those sleeping in the ocean."

The minister quoted the Bible, his voice rising loftily: "They that go down in ships . . . do business in great waters. These see the works of the Lord and His wonders in the deep." The minister lifted his palms. "For He commandeth and raiseth the stormy wind, which lifted up the waves thereof. He shackled the sea by His might. He maketh the storm calm, so that the waves thereof are still." He paused and then continued as if triumphant: "Then they are glad because they be quiet. So He bringeth them until their desired haven."

The minister's voice came against Maggie's ears like an ocean swell. She wanted to tell him that home was Jamie's desired haven; heaven could wait.

Amid intermittent sobs from distressed parishioners the minister carried on, lowering his voice. "There is peace for souls in the valley of trouble. Storms rage but God's love is a shelter. The sealers died in the sea they loved with its sounds washing over them, sounds like the waters that once cradled them in their mother's body. Their souls have found rebirth in an eternal home."

The minister named the men missing from each place: "Captain George Clarke will be missed from Brigus, and Paradise, where his family resides, James Kelly, Noah and Thomas Sparkes from Brigus. . . . Then, from this place, there were Noah, Thomas. . . ."

Maggie pressed her fingers against her ears. She didn't want to hear Jamie's name listed with the dead.

When the minister was finished he reached his hand out over the congregation as if to bless them, his lofty ascension of words funnelling up into the heavens: "The death of saints is precious in the sight of the Lord. . . ."

"Excuse me, ma'am," William said to a woman sitting beside him with her husband and two sons. He stepped over the feet in his way and hurried down the aisle and out the door. He rushed down the road, his body shaking with sobs. He turned up the corner of the graveyard and over the hill down to his empty house. Someone had hung a black ribbon on his door. He went inside and up the stairs to the bedroom where his church suit hung. It was a suit he had worn with joy at his own wedding. He had meant to wear it at Jamie's. It would be his burial garb. Soon, he wished. Soon.

The service ended with the doxology, the congregation raising mournful voices in singing, "Praise God, from whom all blessings flow. . . ."

The minister caught Maggie's hand at the door. His voice was solemn. "You are not alone. Whole families are swimming through the seas of sorrow."

She imagined them all in an icy ocean swimming for dear life.

"So much crying, people washing their throats with their eyes and no evidence of a tragedy," one woman mumbled as she left the church. "I've never seen the like of that in all me born days." She had to be caught from falling over the steps.

The minister shook his head. "Grief can coil inside a person and then let go unexpectedly. Her grandson was on the *Southern Cross*."

Maggie hurried down the steps to go back to Liddie's. She began to shake, her teeth chattering against each other. When she got to her aunt's she climbed the stairs to her room, where she dropped to the floor and curled into a ball. She'd think of their times together, their last time going out in Jamie's new boat, the sail billowing in a lazy breeze. The boat had rocked through water steered by tides and wind. Jamie had rested the oars across each other like folded arms and bent to kiss Maggie, his eyes bright, his lips hard against hers full and yielding. Her soft body and the hardness of his body came together. "We have to wait," she had cautioned him. She had drawn back, her lips wet from his. There had been such a longing in his eyes. Now she felt defiant. She shouldn't have waited to express their love. The minister would tell her she was sinful. Human! That's what she was.

Hours later she rose to her feet and plodded to William's house. She went past him up the stairs to Jamie's room and stood there, her body weighted like lead. Her hand touched a shirt lying on the foot of his bed. She held it to her face drawing in Jamie's smell and whatever breath he had left in the room.

After a while she went downstairs and, without a word to William, put the kettle to boil. She had no sooner poured the strained tea into William's cup and set it in front of him when a knock sounded on the porch door. The door was opened gingerly by William's neighbour, an Irish woman who lived at the far end of the road in a two-room cottage. The woman crossed the floor and hurried to stand in front of him. In a sorrowing voice she said, "Ah, there you be drinking a cup of tea all alone." Her lashes wavered above grey eyes.

William gave her a chary look and took a long drink of tea. He then raised puffed eyelids, his face sour. "A cup of tea is a measure of hospitality a man gives himself," he said. "You're not someone I clap eyes on every day, Merna. What wave washed you up?"

"'Tis mindin' me own business I am on a usual day. That takes up me time, me a poor mortal. I had to come. Oh my! Me mind's knocked astray with the latest news. The young fellar gone and I wantin' to offer my condolences. Sure, 'tis the least I could do."

William frowned, but she kept on. "'Oh yoo-u don't mean it,' I said to someone. 'Sure, it can't be. All these lovely young men gone to a watery grave.' But 'tis true for sure. I can see it is. I minds the time I said to Jamie, 'Your mudder won't allow you to go to the ice, you, her babby, with all the punishment the hunt gives the fellars who go. She'll be wanting you home stacking firewood and filling the coal bucket.' That's what I said."

Jamie's framed picture stood on a shelf above her. A groan lumbered up her throat. "Ah, Jamie Maley. I loved the sight of the young Maley, so I did."

The woman took the picture in her hands and tilted her head. "Ah! The boy was lovely, so he was. It's terrible. So it is. And I there with a christening dress made of proper Irish cloth. I would have loaned it for his first child, so I would have, me with no children."

Maggie came out from the pantry and the woman shook her head. "Take heed to yerself, dear girl, and don't be burdened with nursing a snap of a man gone for all time. Mindin' grief brings no solace."

Maggie shook away the woman's words and asked, "Would you mind a cup of tea?"

"I'd be foine with a cup of tay to mimpse," she said with a dip of her head.

Maggie poured her tea and Merna sat cradling the cup in her palms and murmuring, "Sure, we've all lost someone, so we have. My oh my but it's pitiful, the sight of poor Margaret Jane Bussey down the road, tears streakin' her thin face, calling, 'My sons, my sons,' and she after losin' one son in an accident and another shoved off a train in a lovers' spat and killed. I always said there'd be no good come from havin' the train."

She bit into a raisin biscuit Maggie had placed on a plate. "Be glad they didn't bring young Jamie home, dear girl. You'd not want to cooble his cold, decayed face. Hold the memory of him warm, his grey eyes alight, and lips parted with that roguish grin. So do."

Unable to bear the woman's chatter Maggie went outside. She folded her arms and leaned on a rail. A snow mist drifted up from the ocean. *The breath of the land's lost souls.* She turned as Merna called goodbye to William and closed the door behind her.

"Straighten up, me maid," she admonished Maggie. "You'll be down in a crump time enough. So you will."

"So I will, then," she answered, staying where she was.

The woman went out the lane and William came outside muttering, "The old biddy is fishing for gossip to shovel into the ears of anyone wanting to listen."

"So she is, then," Maggie mocked, her smile thin.

50

Joe finished sharpening a garden tool. Then he went to see William. He found him sitting at his table, elbows down, fists under his chin. He didn't speak.

"Mr. Corbett of Otterbury must be in some tear," Joe said trying to break William's silence. "His oldest son Patrick was on the SS *Newfoundland* and a younger one—I can't mind his name—is on the *Southern Cross.* Ah! I remember now. Joseph was his name. Patrick was brought home a monument of ice."

"There is no God," William said quietly.

Caroline, coming into his kitchen with a crock of stew, was blunt. "Other fathers' sons have been dying since the world begun. Why does it take the death of your own son to wipe God out of existence?"

Joe added, "God didn't overload the ship."

William buried his head in his hands and Caroline reached her arm around his shoulders. "There got to be a power greater than us, a power that gave birth to everything. It's all too vast for mortals to understand. The Bible asks, 'Shall not the judge of all the earth do right?' Trust in yourself to handle anything life brings."

Caroline's words stuck in William's ears like bees after she'd gone home. He didn't want to hear them. He was sick of life going on.

The next morning he hauled himself from his makeshift bed by the stove and went outside. The terrible silence that came with loss was broken by crows *ku-cacking*, their harsh cries renting the air. William restrained himself from getting his gun and sending black feathers flying. Instead he hit the side of the rock wall by his shed, his body in a cold tremor. As the day wore away William went around stunned as if someone had hit him with a mallet. Jamie had been like a seed he'd set in the soil for a future harvest. His life was to have gone on in him and his children on Maley land. Jamie's drowning was likely quick. Drowning in the pain of losing him would never be over.

On May 11 the Halifax *Chronicle* contained disturbing news from Charlottetown, news that made its way to Foxtrap. It stated that on Sunday morning, May 10, a lobster fisherman found a body thought to be a Newfoundland fisherman floating on an ice cake a half-mile from land. He had no way to cut the body loose; it drifted out to sea.

"It could have been Jamie!" Maggie said when a young farmer brought the news. She dug her fists into the dough she was mixing, turning it, folding it, slapping it, tears clouding her eyes until she couldn't see. She imagined Jamie splayed out across an ice pan he'd managed to drag himself aboard only to freeze to death. She wouldn't care how she got him back. To be able to bury him close by would have brought some comfort. She willed her mind back to her dough and finished kneading it. Then she wrapped it with cloths to keep it warm for rising.

She tried not to think of Jamie adrift on an ice pan as she rounded her bread into buns and settled them against each other in pans to rise. Her heart lurched against the image as she later pulled the baked bread from the oven, the heat smarting her eyes. Her young cousins watched her and waited to hold out their hands for a steaming slice of buttered bread.

"We love you," Melanie said, her blue eyes shining.

"And not just because you make us bread," Bea added solemnly.

The community built a memorial in All Saints graveyard to bear the names of the sealing victims. Families gathered for a memorial service.

After it ended Maggie stood among other mourners by the tall stone pillar. William joined her, his mouth tight, eyes dry. Jamie's name on stone sent a shock through him. He traced it with thin, shaky fingers. "Jamie should have had his place in the heart of the earth beside his mother," he said.

A neighbour passed and tipped his hat. "I say, it's a pleasant day, what. A nice one to be above ground."

William gave the man a surly look. "More pleasant than it deserves to be with all those men gone and the ocean licking its chops."

Caroline, coming behind, tapped William on the back. He turned to meet her troubled look. "Perhaps we should have asked the parson to bless the *Southern Cross* so it need'n show up on the water, a ghost ship holdin' the spirit of dead sealers to haunt fishermen goin' about their work."

"Go away with yer," William said. It wasn't something he was going to worry about. He was already haunted and he would be for the rest of his life.

When Maggie closed her eyes that night she visualized stinging cold liquid washing over the *Southern Cross* like acid eating into Jamie's bones, globs of the smothering water filling his mouth and nostrils. His last thought had to be of her, their last kiss, his lips slipping over hers, a kiss that must have awakened his body as it had hers.

Sometimes she broke free from troubling dreams and came to the surface. She rose up in bed, her mouth opening and closing as if gulping water. Other times she woke with a scream.

Liddie's voice rushed against her ear. "Hush! Whatever Jamie suffered he's not sufferin' now. Imaginin' his end will do you no good. You need to think on the time you had him and not on the time you lost him. You need to carry on with your life."

"There is no future without Jamie," she said flatly.

"There's a letter for you," Liddie said passing her an envelope.

Maggie slit it open. Inside she unfolded a single sheet of paper. A stranger had written in an unsteady hand

> *I, too, have lost part of myself in two boys who will never give me grandsons. They are in the deep with your Jamie. When I learned of your loss from Elizabeth Emma, who would have been your sister-in-law, I decided to write you. We free ourselves from pain by not concentrating on it and by doing something good for someone else. I'm not into the emotions of religion but I know that God is with us in our darkest hour when we can't see the stars and moon. He is with us on our darkest day when we can't see the sun for clouds and when we can't see the rainbow after rain.*

A stain had blotted the word "rainbow" as if a tear had fallen.

> *God is with you and so am I in thoughts and prayers. I remain a companion in hope of a future bearing a moon to make you a silver path to romance, the sun to give you the fragrance of flowers, and enough rain to make a rainbow of promise.*

The letter was unsigned.

Maggie whispered, "Hope, for me, is like a light in a blind man's hand. It may be there but I can't see it." Still, she read the letter over and over wondering if there could be a rainbow in her tears.

Maggie looked at Jamie's photograph on William's kitchen wall. It showed him straight-backed in a suit, his look purposeful, his face strong and healthy. He could have become a sealing captain in time. He had the mind for it, always keen on boats large and small. His own small punt would never have looked aged as long as he could repair a rotting plank and fix a nick in the risings.

She walked down the path to where his boat was pulled up on the beach. William must have turned it upright.

"We could take a scull in the boat." She hadn't heard William come up behind her as she bent to rub her hand along the gunnels. She straightened up and shook her head. She went on past him. When she looked back he was standing still, his arms slack by his side. The common thread holding them together was breaking.

William had held an expectation that Jamie and Maggie would give him grandchildren. Now he grieved for what could have been. The loss of Mary Jane's warmth in his bed still brought cold shivers around his heart. He lumbered up the path and stood by Mary Jane's apple tree. It leaned toward the whitewashed fence that separated his land from Joe's. The trees had begun to leaf out and the memory of apple scent wafted across his nose. He slid his body down to the stoop, where he sat with his head in his hands. He got up and pulled a rickety barrel chair out from his doorstep and scooped away last year's tree leaves settled in its corners.

Spring, a time for new life, had become a season of death.

51

The perfumed scent of spring breathed through the ground, its sweetness permeating the air. Sweet young shoots pushed aside ragged, coarse grass and skeletal grey branches of trees were infused with the rich growth of pleated green leaves. Residents stirred to the task of preparing their gardens and boats. Farmers and fishermen along the shore began their work with heavy hearts. Not only had they lost part of their family; they had lost good, strong workers.

Then, overnight, ice swept in choking the bay and shifting into peaks and pinnacles as if wind and currents had made enough headstones for every sealer ever lost from the place. A sad reminder! William sat around the blazing fire in the grate pushing away thoughts of a glacial ocean holding his only son.

Maggie remembered the minister saying it would help everyone in their sorrow if they prayed for others. She prayed hard for herself and all the people she knew who had ever lost loved ones and the tide of grief went out. When she finished her prayer sorrow rolled back and dashed against her heart like a mighty wave. Jamie was gone and there was no way she could sneak around her grief. She dragged herself to the window at her aunt's place and looked out. A neighbour waved as she went past the house on her way to the Quilting Bee. "Come on," she beckoned, her mouth silently forming the words. Maggie turned away to face the room, sodden, it seemed, with her despair.

"You ought to come to the Quilting Bee," Minnie Marshall had urged when she had passed her on the road a week earlier. "We're making quilts for all the families on the shore who lost a sealer. Our project is called The Sealer's Patch."

She had nodded half-heartedly. "I'll try to be there."

She pushed herself to get ready, slipping on her long-sleeved white blouse and over it a dark paisley gimp, all the while wondering what she'd do if someone let out a laugh as if the world were fine and joyous. She hauled on her coat and shoes, closed the door behind her, and hurried along the path, branches reaching out and hooking her stockinged legs. She pulled free and went on, deaf to the stir of leaves, rustling branches, and birds singing. A season bursting with new life and fresh breath could only bring a mockery to her grief. Jamie should be here sauntering up the path to grab her and fill her mouth with his kisses.

"I'll have her, sure," one old widower said aloud as he leaned on a fence and eyed Maggie passing.

His neighbour let out a laugh. "You wouldn't want her in your bed with Jamie's ghost between yers."

She felt like turning her tongue on them. Instead she kept on going.

Quilters were gathered around the table at Etta Whalen's house when she got there. Etta explained, "We're making a quilt for each family who lost a sealer." She looked at Maggie. "We'll be making one for William."

Her voice came out low and scratchy. "What about me?"

Selena Petten from Kelligrews opened the door and hurried in just in time to hear the remark. She called to Maggie on her way to the table. "You wasn't married. We don't know for sure if that would've happened if—" She stopped at the look on Maggie's face.

"We won't be doin' one for Olivia either. She went off to Boston leaving Zachary without expectations and come home without an explanation to anyone," Susie Porter said. "The sealers should have gone off to Boston. That's the thing to do, help build skyscrapers, not chase seals. Americans are building skyscrapers the like we'll never see. They're well-to-do, their families livin' in fancy brick houses beside cobblestone streets, motor cars runnin' along 'em all day long."

"Not all the people's well-off," Selena said.

Maggie hardly heard their idle chatter, hurt that the women weren't sewing a quilt for her. When she could stand it no longer she left a patch half-cut from a worn dress and stood up abruptly. She turned her back on the table and hurried to the porch, where she dragged on her coat and shoes and left.

Minnie watched her through the window, her slow drag up the hill, her shoulders heaving in sobs. She turned to Selena. "You should've had more tact than to suggest that Maggie and Jamie might not get married."

"Yes," said Etta. "Sometimes a tongue is so long it reaches a destination long before the common sense that should have gone with it." She got up and opened the door calling after Maggie, "Come back, me maid! Don't twine grief and spite."

Maggie didn't turn her head. *I'd like to be finished with that crowd.*

The women looked toward the window as Susie said, "There's Amy comin' down the path. She's disgraced herself with a sealer who went on the *Newfoundland* and froze to death. Now she's got to carry on with what he's left her. Be sure your sins will find you out."

"Is that so?" asked Selena.

"It is, then," Susie answered.

"And I suppose your sin found you out when you got yourself in bungalow," Selena said.

Etta shook her head, her voice sad. "We cut pieces of clothing belonging to each other and sew them together to make a beautiful quilt, yet we use our tongues to cut and tear each other apart."

The quilters fell silent and turned back to their patches.

Maggie went on up the road thinking that only a few months ago the women at the Quilting Bee had told her they had saved their brightest pieces and were starting a quilt for her wedding before they got busy planting their gardens. Bright patches were coveted and not so easily gathered. There were more black and dull patches to be had from dresses worn to pieces from all the mourning done each year in communities where death came often.

Now there would be no wedding quilt. But there would be a quilt. She'd quilt pieces from Jamie's clothes. A piece of shirt worn over his heart would be quilted in a spot that would lie over her heart. She'd use London Smoke for the backing.

Late spring Elizabeth came to see her father, holding him tight while she cried. She stayed to cook, clean his house, and wash his clothes without a sign from him that he cared.

"I have to get on home," she told him after she had stayed more than a week. "Work is pilin' up and the lambs born need care."

William nodded. He squeezed her tight and let her go, his droopy eyes swollen.

Before Elizabeth left for home she went to visit Maggie. She found her working the treadle on her aunt's sewing machine, going as fast as she could. When the thread broke from the strain she kept her foot going furiously. Finally she stopped and burst into tears.

Maggie hadn't heard Elizabeth come in and stand motionless, eyeing pieces of Jamie's shirts cut to be sewn into Maggie's memory quilt.

"Maggie," Elizabeth said softly.

Maggie looked up and her face opened in wonder that Elizabeth had come. The women embraced, holding each other—friends who had become sisters in a common grief.

"Jamie loved you, Maggie," Elizabeth said, standing back.

Maggie nodded.

"I know you loved him," Elizabeth said, "but you can't be givin' up on love. Sure, I had me eye on Nathan Lear, another young miner, before I met Jacob. There was only affection exchanged. He went away."

"Do you love Jacob?" Maggie asked.

Elizabeth ran her finger along the seam between two patches. "With me whole heart," she answered, "but marriage is not always easy to handle, not as romantic as we expect it to be. Life itself can get in the way."

"I wish I had the chance to live through the good and bad of it," Maggie said, picturing Elizabeth and Jacob with a baby in their home beside the sea. She imagined Elizabeth's little girl climbing onto her lap and looking up into her mother's face, her face alive with wonder, her eyes shining, her little hands reaching to palm her mother's cheeks as she leaned in to touch her mother's nose with hers. A child's love must be the most precious love of all.

Maggie broke open with grief, weeping uncontrollably. It was not just Jamie's love she missed. She'd lost the hope of having his children, their love, pure and binding.

"You have to get on with life," Elizabeth said gently. "Bear up and think about others who have lost both husband and sons."

"Their great sorrow can't lessen mine."

"No, but it can remind you that you're not grievin' alone."

She lifted her chin, hardness in her eyes. "Jamie promised to be back with jingles in his pocket."

Elizabeth stepped back. "You're blamin' me brother?"

Maggie gave Elizabeth a defiant look. "He didn't have to go."

Elizabeth shook her head and leaned to touch her hand. "Dear, dear friend, Jamie was me brother and I miss him every day. Blamin' him won't make you feel better."

"No," said Maggie, misery filling her face. "I need your courage and your strength."

Elizabeth gave her a steady look. "We have to believe that even if things don't turn out the way we expect them to we can go on and live the life meant for us." She let out a weak laugh. "I don't know when I'll have to swallow me own words."

Maggie said, "Never, I hope."

"Come visit me," Elizabeth urged Maggie as they said goodbye.

"I will," she promised, feeling the soft touch of Elizabeth's lips on her cheek long after she was gone. *Skin of Jamie's skin*, she thought and felt comforted.

52

Summer had come and gone and autumn was letting go. Light was weakening, days shortening and nights lengthening. Intermittent winds blew stubborn tree leaves onto their backs showing tiny brittle veins. Under sunlight suffusing an autumn evening glow, yellow and scarlet leaves lifted and flared like tongues of fire. The wind running on the wispy feet of fallen crisp leaves moaned as it swept the leaves into nesting hedges. Flowers, too, were closing up and bending tired heads in relentless winds. Soon early morning air would be sated with frost.

A pain had slid under Maggie's ribs and wouldn't let go. Now she knew how bitter this season could be, how cold winter would be, coming to stick like an ice candle inside her heart.

"My wedding month," Maggie whispered to her face in her bedroom mirror, "and no sign of a groom." The reality caught in her throat like a chicken bone.

Love at first is pleasing like an apple on a tree, a hearty colour infused with a fresh, sweet aroma. The apple is to be explored by biting into the skin tasting white flesh satisfying oneself with it. That's how she imagined it. She had only gotten to the first bite. That realization added to her sense of loss. Last fall she had twirled the stalk of an apple A-B-C-D-E-F and the stalk had come loose before she got to J. She had let out a hearty laugh. "I'm *still* going to marry you, Jamie."

"Know it!" he said and reached to taste the apple juice on her lips. He'd whispered a line from the Song of Solomon: "Under the apple tree I awakened you."

Afterwards she had found the Song of Solomon in her mother's Bible and read: "How fair and how pleasant art thou, O love, for delights! This thy statue is like a palm tree (*more like an apple tree*) and thy breasts to clusters of grapes (*apples*). I said, I will go up to the palm (*apple*) tree, I will take hold of the boughs thereof: now also thy breasts shall be as clusters of the vine (*apple tree*) and the smell of thy nose like apples; and the roof of thy mouth like the best wine for my beloved that goeth down sweetly. . . ."

He would never again take her hand and hold it against him, their lips bent to each other's, their bodies quickening. All their dreams taken by a ship swallowed by a hungry sea.

Neighbours urged Maggie to move on as if she were in other people's way, they tripping up in her.

"Let the dead rest," Selena told her.

Maggie wanted to retort: "The sea doesn't let a fish bone rest."

"You'll forget on times. Then grief will pool around your heart and you won't be able to breathe." That's what a mother from the Quilting Bee had told her she was like after she lost two sons and a husband on a sealing ship years ago. "Still," she said, "life never leaves us stuck in one spot. Our emotions are like the ocean, always in motion. No matter what we lose and who we lose we have ourselves and keeping ourselves whole is a promise we make to God, whose breath we hold."

At night she lay in bed, her body a heavy stone while her mind yearned for what she could not have: Jamie beside her, his warm body folded into hers, his breath on her neck, his arms cradling her. Her imagination became unbearable and she pushed it away and tried to accept the truth. There was only misery in imagining something you never had. A thought pushed back: *But I could have—I should have had Jamie, if he hadn't been the fool he was to go on that ship.* Other women were lying beside their men, manhoods rising, bellies promising. She stirred against silence, a heavy ringing in her ears.

Sam Butler had told Jamie that the Southern Cross constellation contained what was known as a coal sack—an empty dark place.

"It's where you are now," she whispered, "the kind of place I am—alone."

One day when William found Maggie eyeing Jamie's painting he gave her a rueful look. "Sometimes it was just as well to yell out to a man six feet underground as it was to call Jamie when he was paintin'. 'Twas a strange thing the way he went to work on the board paintin' with such fervour he had a like to put his teeth through his lip. A forebodin' it would seem now. What a hand he was wantin' to paint *Titanic*, a ship no one would ever see ag'in. 'I'll set her in paint,' he'd said, 'to show everyone that she still exists if only on the bottom of the ocean.'"

Jamie had offered Maggie his painting and she had refused it. "I don't want a reminder that ships disappear."

The trace of a smile reached his grey eyes. "A ship can disappear but a painting of it can hang on a wall long after. I'm going to make enough money to buy brushes and paint. I'll paint more than ships. I'll paint our babies."

She blushed. "Who says we'll have children?"

"We'll have fun trying," he said, mischief in his eyes.

Now William offered her the painting and she told him, "I don't want it. Jamie put adventure before our love."

"Mind, now, me maid. You couldn't be keepin' him back. If a man won't venture he'll never have adventure. Everyone knows that terrible things can happen at sea but no one believes they will happen to them. Too many people like meself hove away the chance to go beyond our own comfort."

"Was it because of Johnny almost dying on the ice pan?" she asked.

"It was a hard reminder of the dangers," he answered.

He took in her downcast look and said, "Jamie's life may be over but yours isn't. He won't hurt if you don't think about him. You'll hurt if you think about him too often and too long and if you let his death get in the way of your livin'."

He was good at telling someone else how to mend a broken heart; his would never be mended.

A raw feeling sliced through Maggie late October. She overheard Liddie talking about Lavinia Maley getting married. Anger cut her so deeply she could almost taste blood. *I should be married!*

She walked to the beach where she and other children had spent so much time collecting stones odd-shaped and sharp, blue-speckled and smooth, pink-veined and flat. There was no end to the patterns and shapes telling the story of winds and tides. The children of the beach were all grown and scattered—some lost to an ocean that had lapped their toes. She picked up an ebony stone. It cut into her hand marking it. She tightened her hand wanting it to hurt.

She turned to the sound of a voice calling her. She thought at first that Elizabeth had come to visit her father.

It was Lavinia who had spied Maggie coming up from the beach. She offered her an apple from a basketful she had picked.

Maggie took it and bit into the sweet fruit. Another bite opened it up to a cluster of brown seeds.

Lavinia smiled softly. "I can see Aunt Mary Jane holding the apple seeds in her hand and saying, 'We can count the seeds in an apple; God counts the apples in a seed. We're each like a seed and inside us are children only God can see.'"

Lavinia offered Maggie an apple to take home. She shook her head.

"Come inside, then, and see Mam makin' me weddin' cake."

Maggie gave her a miserable look and Lavinia drew back murmuring, "Sorry."

Maggie turned on her heel and walked away. She didn't want to think about wedding cakes.

Lavinia hurried to empty her basket in a barrel by the side of her father's house. She went inside, where her mother was mixing her wedding cake.

"We'll lace it with rum and wrap it in a rum-soaked cloth and it will be perfect by May," Caroline said. She gave Lavinia a thoughtful look. "The wedding night is like a cake. Put your best into it and you'll get the best out."

Lavinia's pale cheeks flushed. She managed a faint smile.

part six

53

SINCE JAMIE'S DISAPPEARANCE Elizabeth had a greater mistrust of the sea, anger and resentment rising against it every time Jacob went on the water. She watched for signs of storms and mad seas, her prayer constant: "Please God, my mother's first husband drowned in the ocean, Maggie's father was lost at sea, and my brother is still out there. Don't let my husband die on the water." Her mind settled once she saw the boat turn in by the point, settled more once Jacob's feet were on land.

Jacob never complained about his day on the water even after summer gave way to a cold autumn. More mornings than not, damp, cold air lambasted his face and continued penetrating his bones through the day. Sometimes by the time the boat reached the cove the sea hissed under darkness thick enough to swallow a man. He came home chilled, his weariness so heavy it weighed his feet like anchors.

Nine days into November Elizabeth gave birth to another girl and named her after her mother. Jane was tiny and dainty and in a few months her head held a mass of golden curls.

"The whole world is at war," Jacob said coming into the house and stooping to touch little Jane's cheek. "I don't suppose we'll see any of it. Joseph and Nathan Bishop and young Josiah Porter left for Europe. I expect Josiah won't get his coveralls changed every week over there and he won't have his mother to clean out his ears. He'll grow up fast."

"And be fortunate if he gets back home with liver and lights," Elizabeth answered. "Young men are urged to join the war and see the world. They're not likely to see this part of it ever ag'in."

"Our babies will be saved from goin' to war," Jacob said, looking down at Elsie playing on the floor beside Jane in her crib.

When Jane was baptized the minister quoted Isaiah 61:3. ". . . give unto them beauty for ashes, the oil of joy for mourning, the garment of praise for the spirit of heaviness. . . ."

Jacob nodded and Elizabeth smiled. The spirit of heaviness following Jamie's death had lessened with Jane's birth.

By the new year of 1915, Lavinia had grown pale and thin. Often she let out a long, dry cough that kept on and on making Caroline cringe. "Sit in the fresh air," she urged her as she bustled about making plans for the wedding. "Joshua will be none the happier if you beat yourself into an invalid before your wedding night. He'll want you all fresh and full of vim."

It was already too late.

"This is an active disease for which nothing can be done," the doctor said. He closed his black bag. "She's in God's hands."

Joshua Rideout lifted the latch on the porch door and faced Caroline. She'd seen him coming and had hurried to waylay him.

"Lavinia is sick, Joshua. You must have noticed her coughin' before you went bird hunting last week. She strains herself against it. If it was summer we'd make a chair for her in the sun. But the weather's nasty and she feels the cold right through her bones when we opens the window. She don't have the stomach for the cod liver I gives her. More comes up than stays down."

His young face looked hopeful. "Can I see her for a minute?"

"It's best not. You wouldn't want to breathe her sickness and carry it back home, not after your mother's loss of your father on the *Southern Cross*. It would be hard on her if you fell sick and needed care. Now go on home to Kelligrews."

"I'll see her when she's better," he promised. "I'll go help me mother cleave some splits for tomorrow's fire." He strolled jauntily down the road as if he had all the optimism in the world that Lavinia would be better soon.

Caroline felt sorry for not telling him the whole truth. She hoped for Lavinia's life, but, after the doctor's words, she feared the worst.

Johnny sat by the stove, his head lowered. He heard what was said, felt it zip through his nerves like a hot wire. The sound of Lavinia's musical laugh, her quick step, her energetic presence had buoyed him ever since she was a little girl but lately there had been a quiet weariness in her walk. He lifted his head to the sound of harsh coughs from the bed above the stairs. He knew what was coming, knew it as if the coffin lid had already been drawn over his niece's face.

The next day it was as if something inside Lavinia had broken. Blood spilled over her lips, so much it could hardly be stayed. She lifted her head off the pillow and turned to her mother, her eyes dark and frightened. "I'll never get married."

"You won't need to be married in heaven," her mother said. "There'll be enough happiness there without it."

February 15, with the snow falling gently, Lavinia died. The coffin that Jacob had made for Mary Jane's funeral was painted white and cased inside with the white satin Caroline had planned to use in making her wedding dress.

William stood above her grave, snow already covering the mound of earth over the coffin.

"I knows full well the punishment you and Joe's sufferin'," he told Caroline.

"'Tis a grief I never thought possible," she said. "Johnny, too, is beside himself. He sits there on his stool, his arms hangin'. He cries without making a sound."

Joe gave William a haggard look, his voice subdued. "When we was born held upside down and slapped to get a wail out of us we'd knowed then if we'd had sense enough that life's goin' to be rough terrain to navigate."

When Elizabeth received a black-edged letter with news that Lavinia had died she felt her heart lurch. *Who's next?*

Out in the bay a fish hawk swooped down to bring death to a fish. Its *chewk*, *chewk*, *chewk* echoed through the air.

Late one evening Jacob stopped mending salmon nets in the twine loft. Elizabeth heard his heavy step on the landing, a different tempo to his walk. He opened the door, came inside, and took the baby from her arms. He cradled her, letting out a heavy breath. "I'm motherless," he said. "George just came with the news."

It was the fourteenth day of September 1915. Sarah Ann was sixty-two.

Elizabeth slipped her arm across Jacob's shoulder. "You know she was poorly for a while, too proud to let on how sick she was."

Elizabeth and Jacob climbed the hill holding their children tight. They walked into Jacob's childhood home. "She never got her three score years and ten," Jacob said, weeping into his hands at the sight of his mother laid out.

"I suppose you know that Sarah Ann was a wonderful hand at embroidery," Diana Kennedy said as she sat in Elizabeth's house for tea after the funeral. "You should take it up."

"Maybe I will," Elizabeth answered, "when I've no weans underfoot."

She had enough winter work. Clothes were wearied from use year after year. There were garments to be made and mended. Jane's clothes were Elsie's hand-me-downs and often needed alterations. There were the hens and the sheep to feed and care for and wool to spin besides the fish curing and the gardening.

A few months into 1917 Elizabeth knew there was another life on the way. Labour pains came prematurely. Doris Elizabeth was born on November 13, a tiny, shivering creature letting out a wild, belligerent cry as if she were too early and too small to be let out of a warm place. Alvina took one look at her and declared, "There's nothing to this child. Sure, she'd fit into a water jug."

Elizabeth's first son was born February 12, 1920.

"There's no time a'tall since Jane came and here I am with a boy," Elizabeth said as she brought the chubby baby to her breast. She smiled at Jacob standing in the doorway. "A son for you, Jacob. We'll name him William James Maley after your father and mine and after me brother."

Jacob raised an eyebrow. "That's a load for a little mite."

Elizabeth's half-sister, Fannie Eason, died from influenza less than two months later—six years less a day after the *Southern Cross* disappeared.

* * * * *

Maggie came to visit Elizabeth that spring. Her sad look lightened at the sight of Jamie's sister. The corners of Elizabeth's eyes crinkled like Jamie's when she was amused. She turned a shoulder with a lift like Jamie and rattled her teacup with her teaspoon the same way.

The friends talked about their memories of Jamie and for that time Maggie's terrible hunger for Jamie lessened.

54

Maggie had stayed with her aunt though the children were no longer in need of her help. She pushed open the kitchen window and drew in the zesty sea breeze, long and deep, and breathed out, over and over, her mind lightening. She went outside feeling alive for the first time since Jamie's disappearance. She had framed his memory as if inside the covers of a photo album, her mind's eye gathering scenes of their times together. The taste of Jamie's lips and the sense of having been held in his arms had left unrequited love lying heavy inside her. Now and then she forgot the ache. It returned whenever she saw a couple strolling down the road on a Sunday afternoon, sweethearts sidling against each other, shoulders rubbing, voices low and secretive as if the whole world were contained in the space they held.

The year passed and another October came reminding Maggie of her planned wedding month. She had been working in the kitchen garden all morning pulling potatoes from the ground, damp clods of earth clinging to them. She shook the potatoes from the stalks, dusty brown and speckled like sandpiper's eggs, and laid them on brin in the cool, dry air. She would gather them tomorrow.

She lifted her head to watch children play. The leaves had left the apple trees next door and the neighbour's children were running through coppery coins, tossing them, laughter bubbling through the crisp air. She turned to see a young fellow tall and strong-looking, his gloved hands in the pockets of a dark woollen coat. Their eyes met, his watchful, hers narrowing.

"And what might you be staring at?" she asked.

"You," he said with a lazy smile.

"I'll not be looking at you, then," she said turning back to her work.

He came closer and leaned in, eyes squinched. "The green eyes on you. That's a Taylor in there if ever I saw one. I know all about you though I haven't clapped eyes on you for years."

He turned and casually walked away.

She shaded her eyes from the sun with the back of her hand and called, "You're not a peddler, I suppose?"

"No, then. Not the least." He lifted a finger to the side of his face. "On second thought, I've got a heart I should be peddlin' though I'm not sure what I'd get for it."

"There's no one here to offer anything for it. Not a red copper."

"I'm Ben Christopher. Your aunt said she'd mention me to you."

"Did she, now?" Maggie shrugged and turned away.

"You're missin' Jamie, to be sure. 'Tis sympathy I'll offer first."

"And then?" she asked, not sure she wanted to give him the time of day.

His eyes twinkled. "Well—we'll see—"

She went into the house and shut the door. She leaned against it wondering where she had heard that name before.

In the middle of the night she bolted up in bed wide awake. The fortune teller's words—"You'll be marrying a man whose surname is Christopher"—sounded through her head. She frowned and snuggled under her bedclothes. What did she know!

A few weeks later, on a Sunday afternoon, she lowered a bucket holding a bowl of jelly down the cold well to set for supper, and went to sit on the veranda.

"Maggie!" She was startled by the strong, energetic voice coming from behind her. She swirled around to face Ben Christopher. He stood straight and tall holding a bowler hat in his hands. Strong work hands, she noted, the veins large on their backs like blue tributaries.

"Yes?"

"It's a nice day for me to take a dodge with you as far as the beach and back."

"You can walk along if you mind to but don't be thinkin' anything more." Her voice was defiant, belying her need. Her body ached, her heart ached, and she knew it would be hard to turn away a man if he proved to be decent.

One night after several walks, neither of them saying much, she looked up into his face, into his soft brown eyes, and asked, "What would you be wanting with me?"

He smiled and answered lightly, "What every man wants: a woman to come home to."

Her heart warmed under Ben's gaze like a beach rock under sunlight, warm but hard and unyielding.

55

Maggie didn't mean to marry Ben Christopher. Her heart was too full of Jamie.

"Stay shuttered and you'll grow old while doin' it," Ben said. "Don't deny me a chance to help your heart to mend. I'll do me best to be a good husband learnin' as I go if you've the mind to teach me. I'll take what you can give and be thankful for it."

She gave in to his persuasion.

I'm getting married, she told Elizabeth in a letter. *It don't mean I think less of Jamie, only that I need to carry on with me life. . . .*

She wanted to be part of someone's life, someone who would consider her needs. She longed for a man who would have her in his thoughts no matter what he was doing, wanting to be home with her no matter where he was. She wanted him to feel for her what she felt for Jamie.

She looked in the mirror silently asking, *Will Ben be able to do that?*

Her eyes looked back at her. *Will you be able to do that for Ben?*

"I got your letter and I had to come," Elizabeth said. The tips of her fingers touched Maggie's cheek as she stood in a plain grey muslin dress and rimmed black hat. "I want you to be happy, but don't forget me brother!"

Maggie squeezed out words. "You know I can't. I've found a man who says he has enough love for me to make up what I might not have for him. He's a good man." She gave Elizabeth an even look. "A fortune teller said I'd marry a Christopher. I'd gone for fun to have me palm read. Now I know it was meant to be."

Elizabeth's face clouded. "A fortune teller can't cast your fortune or your fate. You're in God's hands. Don't marry Ben for that reason."

"I'm not, but Jamie's memory won't warm me bed or provide for me. I don't want to spend me life cleanin' other people's dirt and helpin' raise their children. I want to be the mistress of a place. I want to be a mother like you."

Elizabeth swallowed a lump in her throat. There would now be one less person to hold Jamie tight. When her father died there would be only her. Still she squeezed Maggie's hand and urged, "Go on and marry him."

"I will despite my dreams."

"Dreams?"

"Sometimes I'm in church and walkin' to the altar where a man waits. I can't see his face even when we are pronounced man and wife. When I turn Jamie is standin' in the aisle wearing his sealer's greasy clothes. He is soakin' wet. He moves toward me, his hands held out. There is a terrible yearnin' in his eyes. Our hands almost touch and then he sinks beneath the water. I turn back to the man I just married and there's no one there."

"Maybe marriage will cure you of your dreams," Elizabeth told her trying to hold in her own mixed emotions.

Maggie married Ben. Her heart raced through the wedding ceremony. *What if Jamie comes home!*

She settled her mind. *He's been gone too long to be alive.*

Ben's house, one he'd built himself, was plain but kept warm. The several rooms downstairs included a large square kitchen with a pantry holding long shelves with jugs and cups on hooks, a rectangle porch beside it. Upstairs led to four bedrooms.

"All for a large family," the groom said.

Maggie blushed when Ben, big and imposing, stepped naked from the tub in the porch. He grabbed a towel and grinned. "You can dry me off and rub me down."

"I could never do that," she mumbled, turning away before she caught the whole sight of him. After he hauled on his clean long johns Ben reached for her hand and tucked it inside his. They made their way upstairs.

At first Ben's kisses were gentle as they lay together, lamplight snuffed. She faced him shaking, her hands folded over her silk nightgown, her knees drawn up. "I can't let you near me."

It was too dark to see his eyes when he asked in a quiet voice, "Then why did you marry me?"

She had a fleeting image of her mother's white flesh against crimson-stained sheets and the tiny creature on her breast, a grey rope trailing it. "I don't want to die like me mother."

He turned his back and she whispered, "Don't you want to know about me mother?"

"Not tonight."

He was soon snoring.

Maggie lay wondering why she had not felt fearful all the times she had thoughts of being with Jamie once they were married. She woke the next morning to Ben sleeping in bed beside her, a white shadow in his long johns, every manly part of him safely stowed.

The next night she asked Ben, "Could I have me own bed?"

He looked at her.

"Only for a while," she said.

"Only for a while," he answered, turning away.

He climbed the stairs and went next door to the room they had shared for one night almost as sister and brother. She shut the door to her room, hesitating before she pulled the key from the keyhole and laid it on the bureau. She had to believe he wouldn't disturb her.

Soon she heard the creak of the ropes under the mattress as he lowered himself to the bed and the whispering stir as he turned over and over. She lay awake for a long time and then she crept along the hall to his room. She listened to the sounds of his breathing and then she went back to her room and fell asleep.

Ben didn't say much in the next few days. She took hold of the work in the house and he spent time outside repairing nets and fences.

One day she watched the golden light of the sun shine through autumn leaves under the stir of the gentle wind. Ben was beside the wood horse, sweat beading on his forehead as he lifted a log and placed it between the crossed posts. He drew his saw against the log cutting into it back and forth. Chips of wood and dust flew into the air and settled at his feet like discarded leaves. He stopped and lifted his arm across his forehead taking a long look at the house, his countenance kind and tender. She knew he couldn't see her standing back from the window. New wood and tangy oakum scents mingling in the cool air awakened her to a beginning. She felt a stir through her body as she imagined Ben waiting for her to yield to him. She sensed it in the longing in his face as he sawed through a log and it thumped to the ground. It was what a man and a woman expected from each other, a willingness to become one self.

She lifted her pot of berries jamming on the stove and put it aside. She untied her apron strings and lifted the bib over her head. She ran out the door, her eyes alight and her lips parted. Ben's face creased into a smile. He laid down his saw as she came closer. She tasted his lips salty with sweat. He pulled her tight, his hand on her bottom. She felt him hard against her, felt her own body respond. He reached for her hand and led her inside the shed and up a ladder to a loft permeated by the heavy scent of twine and oakum.

Ben found her deep inside herself, curled like a periwinkle in its shell. He gently spread her with his thoughtful words. The sound of his voice, his kiss on her earlobes, down her face and neck awakened her to her own need. He murmured, "The men around here says a woman likes to be explored." He trailed his fingers down her skin reaching and finding a sweet spot that sent shivers through her body. Feelings inside her rippled like water, exploded like waves.

She put aside the memory of Jamie, then, like she'd lay a prized piece of jewellery too heavy to wear, in a dresser drawer, not too far that she couldn't take it out once in a while. She'd be a wife and lover. God willing she and Ben would have children. She tried not to think about her mother and the baby that caused her death. That couldn't happen to her. She wasn't going to die like her mother.

That night she lay against Ben as he slept. Her toes curled against his leg skin to skin. She ran her hand up his back resting it on his shoulder, heat rising beneath her palm. Ben stirred slightly. *To be with someone I can wake up to every day, to not feel alone. That is something wonderful.* She smiled and spooned against strong buttocks; then she fell asleep to dream of Jamie.

Months later when Maggie felt the stir of life she thought of the chance she had taken—the risk. She pushed her fears aside and ran outside calling to Ben, "We're having a baby."

She was met with frowns by Ben's next-door neighbour on her step beating out a mat. "Here you is merry as a weddin' bell. You're not the first woman carryin' a child."

Maggie ignored her and went toward Ben. He took her hand, his voice tender. "You're the first woman to carry *our* child."

The neighbour, a mother of two sets of twins, gave her mat a last shake and called, "You won't be dancin' when your breasts bes in an infant's mouth one after another for the next twenty years."

Maggie went to lie in a hammock Ben had rigged between two trees. She lay watching a butterfly alight on a flower, a bee nestled inside its cup. She listened to the whispers of the garden, the *chee, chee* of a yellow warbler, a gentle wind rubbing against a leaf, grasshoppers rasping in the grass. She'd take whatever sweetness she could get from life. She'd do everything to make up for any thought of Jamie. She'd be everything Ben wanted.

One morning as Ben turned to her in triumph and moved his body over hers he spoke as if unaware that his thoughts were loud enough for Maggie to hear. "I've got something Jamie never had and never will."

The words stunned Maggie. Her hand flew up and hit his face. He let out a gasp and dropped down beside her. They lay in silence, a wall between them. Maggie realized then that she was not the only one who carried Jamie in her thoughts. He was a shadow in Ben's life.

Finally Ben spoke, his tone brittle. "There's room in your heart for both of us but there's only room in our bed for you and me."

He'd never know that sometimes she pretended it was Jamie giving her the love he would have given her in marriage.

Once after she and Ben had quarrelled she ran down the road to tell William about it.

He rose from the settle saying, "Don't worry none. A quarrel is not uncommon in a household. Mostly it comes from tiredness, yours and his. Then any little difference in opinion can start a spat. You puts a log in the fire and Ben puts a log in the fire and soon you got a cracklin' blaze. Tongues leap and lap threatenin' to burn everything black. If you wants to straighten up you have to lay down your logs and let the fire out."

Maggie kissed his rough cheek and went to leave. He looked at her and a tear slipped from the corner of one eye. "Still, quarrel or not I'd take Mary Jane any way if only I could bring her back."

"I know that," she said. She was thinking, *I'd take Jamie any way I could have him.* She felt guilty as she hurried home to Ben.

Maggie laid a newly plaited mat on the floor, but when Ben came in from the barn and wiped his boots on it, she ran and grabbed it, rushing to explain, "It's too good for here. I'll make a brin one. This mat can lie across our bedroom floor."

Instead she scrubbed it clean, dried it on the garden fence, and laid it across the foot of their bed to warm their feet in winter. She didn't tell Ben that six months after Jamie's loss she had gone to William's house and gathered some of Jamie's clothes. She made a quilt and when she had finished it she plaited a mat from scraps left over. She had wanted to bring the quilt with her. Instead she had decided that it wouldn't be fair to Ben. Now the mat was at the foot of Ben's bed and she knew that wasn't fair either.

One morning Maggie woke with a rush of memory stabbing her heart. Ben felt her body go rigid and he pulled her into the comfort of his arms, his sleepy voice against her ear. "What's the trouble?"

She couldn't answer, wouldn't tell him something that would hurt. She held the pain as steady as she could until it subsided. She fell back asleep and dreamed about Jamie dying in blackness under a sea of bodies.

Ben nudged her awake. "You're talkin' in your sleep. You're calling, 'Jamie.'" He tightened his arms around her.

She jerked away and sat up drawing her knees to her chest, her arms around them.

Ben gave her a keen look.

"It's the day," she said in a flat voice, "another anniversary of the *Southern Cross*'s disappearance. . . ." Her voice drifted like a thin trail of smoke.

Ben lifted up on an elbow. He spoke, his voice heavy. "Sometimes I wonder who you would rather have gone, him or me. Well I'm here and Jamie isn't. He lost his life. I intend to spend mine."

She felt a kick and looked down. Ben was giving her something Jamie hadn't. She leaned to touch his forehead with her lips. "I was meant to have you and our children. God willed it that way."

56

"Alvina won't be doing much on the stagehead this June," Jacob told Elizabeth. "I saw the midwife go up the hill. On her way down she told me there's a sweet baby girl born this very morning, a frail little thing. I met George on the turn to Ma's house. He said that the midwife told him Alvina will be able to help with the outdoor work after a couple of weeks."

Elizabeth looked up from the baby she was holding. "'Tis a blessin' to have it over, not to have to carry a baby while on the flakes."

Jacob sighed. "Pappa is no good to work. Let him exert himself er bit a'tall and his heart fair beats out of his chest. He can look after the baby. That will take his mind off poor Ma's passin'."

William nicknamed his granddaughter Spindle Shanks because of her long, thin legs. While Alvina was on the fish flake he often sat outdoors beside the lilac tree rocking the deep-eyed little girl in an alder chair he had made. Her tiny hand clung to his fingers chafed and scarred from years of fishing.

Alvina detected something wrong with Nellie after she was only a few weeks old. She sent for Dr. Pritchett, who examined the baby, taking note when his touch made her whimper. He'd seen enough: soft bones, deformed ribs. He snapped his black bag shut. "My dear woman," he said, "your child is crippled with rickets. Handle her gently. Her bones are soft and easy to break."

Alvina stared at him as he went on. "She needs the sun when it is highest in the sky. Keep her head shaded. Cod-liver oil may improve her condition."

Now and then while she and Elizabeth spread fish on the flake down from her house Alvina straightened her stiff back and rubbed her hand down her spine. She looked toward her house, a longing in her face. "Nellie Rita," she called, her voice winging its way with love kissing the little one's ears.

She pulled the old fellow's scratched and dull monocle from her barbel pocket and slipped it against her eye. Her golden baby, a bonnet shading her head, lay fast asleep, tucked against the old fellow's strong chest, blond curls spread on his shoulder.

Alvina smiled and turned back to the fish, hurrying to reclaim moments lost in catching precious sunshine. There was so much to do. In an hour the sun might withdraw behind a cloud and black clouds drop rain and the fish would have to be gathered, piled together, and covered.

William spent a second summer caring for his granddaughter. Whenever William heard Nellie Rita's weak cry after she woke from sleep he lifted her from the pine cradle he'd made. The straw stirred ever so lightly in its casing. The child smiled weakly, her blue eyes meeting William's faded ones. He straightened and cooed, "You be good, little one. Your mam's on the fish flake."

The little girl let out a sharp, whining cry and he told her, "No one knows how long you'll be with us, no one but God and He's not saying." He cradled her against his chest, her head leaning into his arm. "Here you is lily-white and weak-legged," he said. "You should be walkin' around." He held her tight. A salty tear splashed on her face and she let out a whimper. His rough finger wiped it away. "You'll be all right," he soothed her. "Sure, you will, then." He took her outside past a honeysuckle bush with its sweet scent. He caught Alvina's look shifting from the fish flake to him and Nellie.

He gazed out over the water from the walkway along his house on the cliff. "Here we is, then," he said pointing to a steering. "That old fish bird in the water is a sure sign for a good haul." He settled into his chair and pointed to gulls flying low. They were like flashes of silver under a bright sun as they dived letting out a relentless cry. "Look, little one, see the gulls," he said.

Nellie Rita's look followed the birds and then her eyelashes dropped like tiny gold threads against her face. The little girl fell asleep, her little chest barely rising.

William laid a finger on her cheek and she stirred. He blinked back a tear. "You and I will soon be goin' beyond the vale of tears to heaven, we've been told. You'll be up there, for sure. No muddy roads for your little tootsies. You'll walk on streets of gold. Not even a princess gets that close to so much gold here on earth."

One November morning Jacob looked through the window and gazed up the hill to George's house. He felt a stillness about the place. "The clothesline is bare at Vine's this morning," he told Elizabeth. "I think I'll go on up and get the news."

Elizabeth nodded, her heart racing. "Vine is earlier than most women in having her lines full on a Monday."

George was opening the gate when Jacob got to the top of Kennedy's Hill. "The little one's gone," he said and then his cheeks puffed to hold in a sob. His large hand brushed across his eyes, moist and heavy-looking. Jacob squeezed his arm and went inside the house.

Alvina looked up from staring at the cold face of her child, her eyelids red.

At the funeral the minister said, "The Lord giveth and the Lord taketh away. Our children are His. We have them for as long as He wills."

On their way back home George said bitterly, "We'll get nowhere arguin' with God. I've got me bottle. What do you have?" he asked Alvina.

"I have me hope," she answered.

George stopped outside their house and said, "If I could believe little Nellie is an angel I wouldn't grieve as much. It'd be our loss and her gain."

Alvina rubbed his arm, her voice crusty. "That is as it is. Believe it."

William heard their heavy steps and rubbed his chest to ease a pain. "I hope to hold Nellie when I gets inside the pearly gates," he murmured. "For now Sarah Ann is holding her."

Elizabeth and Jacob followed Alvina and George inside. Elizabeth, feeling the loss of her mother and brother resurface, hoped she would never know the pain of losing a child.

* * * * *

57

“Sometimes I wish I could die a tragic death. Then I would be carried forever in your heart,” Ben said one day as Maggie stood looking through their kitchen window to a wild sea.

Shocked at his words she didn’t reply at first. Then she turned to him and saw the depth of pain and despair in his eyes.

“How many men married to widows of sealers live day after day in the shadows of ghosts! They deserve better,” he said. “I deserve better.”

“I love you, Ben,” she said, startled at the truth of her words. She was beside him, then, bringing pent-up passion to her embrace. His arms hung at his side as if he were too stunned to lift them and wrap her in his embrace. His hesitation made her realize what he had felt all the times he’d wrapped his arms around her and she had not reacted. Now she tried to explain believing it for the first time. “Jamie is one memory, an old memory that surfaces. You’re not a memory. You’re here.”

Then Ben did something unexpected. He took her hand and, without explaining, urged her out the door and along one road and up another. They came to the gate of All Saints graveyard. He unlatched it and led her inside.

“We have what we have and it’s got to be enough,” he said stopping at the *Southern Cross* memorial where Jamie’s name was carved. “Wish him goodbye,” he said, his voice terse.

Maggie looked at the memorial, really seeing it for the first time. She ran her finger along Jamie’s name and then she dropped to her knees, her head bowed. She tried to say goodbye. When she looked up at the hopeful look in Ben’s eyes she almost did.

He lifted her by the hand saying, “It’s time to let go of someone gone. Today and tomorrow and for as long as God wills the days will be ours, yours and mine. What we have together is enough.”

“It is,” she answered. “Having you is enough.”

On long winter nights when winds blew strong and heavy around the house Maggie would say, “Hold me, Ben!” He’d hold her, his face against hers like a hot water bottle. Her mind reached for Jamie.

Already he was drifting from her mind. A wave brought him back, slamming hard, knocking her off balance and then he was gone again. She tried to let him drift away and be at rest.

Cyril, their first child, was born in 1919.

"Yours and mine," Ben said bending down to kiss Maggie. He took the mite in his strong arms.

Other children followed: Joseph James, Harris, Wilhelmina, Gladys, Laura, Hayward, and Eric, all by 1929. She held the children in her arms and they cuddled against her as if she were the most important person on earth. She watched them run about outside, their clothes in varied colours, each child different from the others. *Like a rainbow!* She smiled remembering the letter from a stranger, her words about a rainbow of promise.

Now her rain of tears had been wiped away by a rainbow of children.

Maggie lay in bed in the softness of a spring morning and let out a satisfied sigh. For a moment her feet nestled against Ben's warm feet skin to skin, her lips brushing his back and lingering. The children were asleep. Not a stir.

She slipped out of bed to make breakfast. It would be a busy day, the start of the planting season.

She had made porridge and set a bowl for her and Ben by the time he came into the kitchen, his face thoughtful. She was pouring their tea when he looked at her, his voice steady. "Johnny Porter has outfitted an old skiff he bought. I'll be off with him to look for fish to salt for the winter and some to sell. I can't always depend on the land."

Maggie's hands tightened into fists, her nails cutting into the skin leaving red scalloping on her palms. She didn't say anything as Ben got ready to work the land. He knew the land like Jamie had known the sea. Now he was going to know the sea.

For the next while when Ben wasn't working the ground he was off on the water as a hired hand helping with trawl lines. Summer came with hauls of fish.

Maggie touched his rough hands, rubbed powders into burst blisters and cracks from ropes and salt and trawl hook infections. The land was never as rough. Still she enjoyed the rich haul of food from the sea. Now and then Ben brought home a salmon and smoked it in a fire banked with sawdust and blackberry moss in a sod hut attached to the barn. She savoured its fresh taste, its flesh filling.

One day while she was on the stoop washing clothes she glanced at the sky. Dark clouds were gathering ominously. Suddenly the air came alive with wind. It struck like a birch broom sweeping up beach sand. Smoky winds cast a gloomy presence over the dark headlands. She stopped her fierce scrubbing on the washboard, leaned into her tin tub, and looked toward Johnny Porter's skiff beating its way in. Her heart lurched. *What if one day Ben don't come home?*

Later, after he had come ashore, she glanced out a window at him standing by the wood horse, his head lowered toward it as if he was deep in concentration. She wondered why he was still standing there.

She went to the stove to stir the boiling pot. She looked out again and saw Ben coming up from the Porter fishing stage. *Impossible! He was just by the wood horse.*

That night she looked at Ben sitting beside her at the table after the children had gone to bed. His jowls had softened and loosened but he was still fine-looking. She picked up his hand lacing hers with his. He slipped toward her and she fell under him, scared that she may have seen his token. She had missed her blood for six months. It was not a time to become a widow. She felt the heaviness of her ninth child.

When Harris was lost in the woods behind their house the next day Maggie thought God was punishing her for holding on to Jamie's memory. After a long search she and Ben found the little boy curled up against a tree asleep. When she rushed to wake him he yawned and rubbed his eyes. Then he looked up at his father and held out a pine cone. "Mamma told me that big trees grow from pine cones. I tried to open one to find a tiny tree." Then he looked up at tall trees piercing the sky and murmured, "Trees must get tired standin' on one leg all the time."

"It's their nature," Maggie told him. "They provide wood so we can make chairs to sit on when we're tired."

Harris nodded and Ben swept his arms under him. "Fathers have a place for tired little boys to rest their heads," he said.

Harris smiled and nestled against his father's chest.

58

Elizabeth hurried to fill the clothesline. She pegged the last article and then she leaned an arm on the fence. She'd been spoiled at home in Foxtrap. She hadn't known what work was—the little bit she had to do was nothing compared to this. Here she was with Elsie nine, Mary Jane six, Doris four, little Jamie fifteen months, and getting so big she felt like she had a front porch built on her. She'd been so taken with Jacob she hadn't thought about what she'd miss by marrying him. She missed the gentle roll of hills and lowlands in Foxtrap—the place where she belonged. She remembered her mother singing, "Simple life is very good. It keeps me oh so free." She began to sing it and Alvina, on her way down the hill with a solemn look, smiled. She crossed the garden laughing and singing, too. It was a good way to lift a down mood.

Jacob came up the path and leaned against the porch door facing looking amused. "There's something new under the sun," he said. "Glady Bishop got herself a bouncin' baby boy."

Elizabeth turned startled. "At fifty. Lord, don't tell me." Her hand went to her own belly. "I'd better be done before then."

"A woman'll have only what she's meant to have," Jacob answered, "one or a dozen."

"Pshaw!" she said. "I suppose Ida on the shore was meant to have eighteen, her insides stripped out by the time it was all done."

Elizabeth had made allowance for the baby growing inside her first by loosening her corsets. Then she laid them aside to free her belly growing full and hard like unripe fruit. This time was different, her body larger than before.

"I want my body back," she whimpered as she struggled to slide out of a cushioned chair. Jacob pulled her to her feet and her hands circled the globe of her belly.

Jacob smiled. "You're holding a world we created in your hands."

She nodded. Soon she would touch a fuzzy soft cheek and look into eyes as clear as a summer day or as warm as newly turned earth. That was worth everything!

One day as Elizabeth knelt to gather a yaffle of fish drying on the flake Alvina gave her a critical look. "You're swellin' something awful and it's past your time. We need to get the midwife."

"There's work to be done," Elizabeth answered noticing their boat coming into the cove, gunnels low. The women finished layering fish in piles on the flake and covering them. Then they laid aside their brin aprons. They hurried to the stagehead where they grabbed their barbels to cover their cotton dresses.

The sun beat hard on the women as they stood at the table. Jacob sent Jane to fetch a jug of cold water flowing down the hill from a narrow stream. Elizabeth took a gulp and Jane wiped the sweat from her mother's brow with a hand cooled from holding the metal jug. Elizabeth's mind drifted, her voice trailed in answer to a question. She was hardly able to keep up. The afternoon wore away and Elizabeth's hands grew heavy; dark spots clouded her eyes. Water pooled in the hollow of her neck and dried to a salty stain. Then, just as her hand slipped inside the split gut of the last cod, pain grabbed her stomach and dug in twisting her insides, squeezing hard. Her clear, wide eyes grew gibbous under tears. A moan slipped through her tight lips and her body bent away from the fish she was clutching.

Jacob turned at the sound, startled by the sight of Elizabeth's drawn face, her lips pale. He urged Elsie, "Run and get Aunt Ida Lear."

Children running along the stagehead stopped and stared as Elizabeth, moaning through gritted teeth, turned away from the table and started a painful trek from the stage up the steep hill to the house, Jane beside her running to open the gate. It swung wide and she trudged up the rough path of stones to get inside, to find her bed, and let the pain take her wherever God saw fit.

The midwife came with castor oil. She took a long look at Elizabeth's stomach and her lips stretched in a thin line. "This baby knows what's good for it. It's gettin' out while the going's good, not amid the ruction castor oil can cause."

A baby boy was born without a sound. Before Elizabeth could

catch her breath another pain ripped through her. She squeezed her eyes tight.

"Another baby," the midwife said grimly.

Elizabeth heard a weak cry.

Two babies! How can there be only one cry? The deep silence that came with the birth of the first child filled the air like a dark fog and Elizabeth knew that death had entered the room. Its cold sweep lodged in her heart. "My babies," she whispered.

"One son is gone," the midwife said wiping beads of sweat from Elizabeth's anguished face. "The other son is holding on." Her voice came calm and soothing from far away: "Here, take this drink of crowberry juice for afterpains."

Elizabeth was hardly aware as the midwife washed her face and body, and changed her clothes and bedding. She slipped into exhaustion and slept.

Alvina sat beside her bed, her face settled like stone. A lifeless baby lay in the crook of one arm and a gasping blue-faced baby lay in the other.

"What will be the name of the little one already gone?" the midwife asked Elizabeth as soon as she opened her eyes. She stared as the midwife took the still baby from Alvina and placed him beside Elizabeth. She squeezed her lids tight, her voice wet with emotion and defiance. "God can name him seeing He didn't give him breath so I could call him mine."

The midwife hesitated. Then she asked, "Do you have a name for the other little one? Reverend Tucker can baptize him just in case."

"His name is Victor," she said though there was no one in her family with that name. She wanted him to be a victor.

The midwife brought him to her. "The child is weak in his breathin'. He may not have strength for the breast. I've wrapped him in flannel sheets toasty warm from the heat of the stove."

Elizabeth took him gently, her heart already in mourning for the child lying motionless beside her. Victor's tiny heart quivered in his chest as she bared her breast and urged it to his mouth. The nipple opened like a flowering bud under his gentle tug. Translucent fluid dewed the nipple as his tiny blue lips let go. "Hold on, little one," she urged.

For the next three days she squirted milk into the little mouth. The cloudy fluid leaked out. His little body wasn't strong enough to swallow. She whispered "Victor" over and over, believing until the last minute he would live up to his name. He lived for three days and the chill that seeped into his little body also found her heart. She couldn't cry, not that day and not the next. *I should have known that when death creeps in to take one child it won't stop there.*

Jacob took a large, white handkerchief from his breast pocket and wiped her eyes. He kissed each eyelid tenderly and then he cradled her quivering body. "Try to think of what we have and not of what we've lost," he said. "I hope that's possible."

She stirred from a listless emptiness taking over her body and murmured, "I hope so, too." Then she drifted away.

She was awakened by children's voices. "We want to see the blue baby."

Elizabeth turned to see two of the cove children standing by her bed. She nodded toward the basket by the window. They tiptoed across. One of them gingerly lifted a white cloth and stared. "He's a lot blue 'round his lips, not so much his face," one of the girls whispered.

The other bent closer. "He's iceberg blue. I thought he'd be blue like the blue cloud he was floating on before the stork brought him here. He's not movin'."

"That's what dead means," the other child said.

"Pappa said he's gone back ter heaven."

"He's still here."

"That's his body. When he went to heaven he left it behind. He don't need a body in heaven. He'll have a soul to live in."

One of the children turned from the babies and pointed to a portrait hanging across the hall. A porky-faced woman in a black lace dress, her fat hand under her dimpled chin, looked sideways, her eyes bulging under heavy lids. A long white veil started at the front of her head and trailed down her back.

"That must be someone from long ago," the child said.

"It's Queen Victoria, don't you know?" the other child answered.

The girl rolled her head. "Hmm. Do you know her?"

"No, but we've got the same paintin' in our attic."

"She looks like she's got nothin' ter do but think about tomorrow."

"She don't have to think about it now. She's dead and buried."

They turned to the sound of hammering outside. Jacob was making the infants' coffin.

Elizabeth clutched the bedclothes and nodded to the girls. "Go home now. Go on and tell your mothers to keep you from comin' here while I'm abed. You can't be walkin' in on a sick mother with her heart torn."

They hurried away whispering behind their hands.

Elizabeth closed her eyes. Her teeth began to rattle against each other as the hope she'd had for one of her babies fell into a whirlpool of anguish. She pressed her hands against her ears to shut out the hammering.

Alvina met the children coming down the stairs and tut-tutted with a shake of her finger as she ushered them through the hall. They scampered out the front door to where Jacob stood planing wood for a square, pine coffin, tears streaming down his face.

There was hardly a sound from the bedroom. Elizabeth's wispy breathing rose slightly when she thought of her babies having to be taken away to a grave in over Hibb's Cove hills. She felt far away as if muffled in stillness. There came a creak on the stair landing and Elsie hurried in, her breathing quick and heavy. She put her lips to Elizabeth's pale cheek, her words strong, her eyes fierce. "You'll get better, Ma. Jane and me'll help." She tucked the bedclothes around her mother's swollen body. A flood broke and a sob ripped up Elizabeth's throat alarming her young daughter.

Alvina rushed upstairs and into the room. Elsie's voice was plaintive. "I was trying to make Mamma better."

Alvina didn't look at the young girl. Her words were to Elizabeth. "Hush, dear woman. We have to spend our thoughts on livin', not crying for what we've lost. There's no mendin' death."

Alvina took the children up the narrow, dusty road to her place. She placed a wall of pancakes on their plates and flooded them with blueberry syrup. "Eat," she admonished them.

When the children trudged back home their anxious looks met their father's forced smile as he finished the coffin. Jacob eased an arm across his forehead. He knew he could not protect the children from the truth that death carries off the young as well as the old.

Elizabeth tried to smile at her living children, the younger ones wanting to get close. All she could think of was how she would miss the joy of watching her twin boys unfold into growing children spilling laughter and delight.

Alvina came to her bedside. She reached down and took Elizabeth's limp hand. "I won't feel so alone now," she said. "You know what I've gone through losing Nellie Rita, how I felt." Her lips trembled. "How I still feel."

Elizabeth nodded and Alvina added, "When things get rough we women have to set our teeth and carry on. George was right when he told me I have to keep my pain inside." She picked up Victor and brought him to Elizabeth.

Elizabeth lifted him knowing, for the first time, what dead weight meant. The little head lay like a stone against her arm sending a terrible pain through her heart. Her eyes closed and she whispered, "It's bad enough that death ferrets inside a mother's body and takes the life of her son before he draws breath, double the injury when it stands by his twin's cradle hesitatin' long enough to allow a mother to hope and while that hope is alive takes the child. Even God seems to have stood aside to let death take its course."

Alvina chided her, "Now, now. Melancholy has you in its grip, else you wouldn't speak this way. Low-mindedness can come like a fierce animal, grab you, and knock you down. It'll gnaw at you until you're too weak to get up." Her eyes flooded. "I've had to fight it."

She hastened to bring little James to Elizabeth's side. He huddled against his mother sobbing as if he knew that something had gone wrong while he'd been kept away from her.

"I've been able to square me shoulders and take the blows of losing me mother and brother," Elizabeth told Jacob after he came upstairs. "This time is different."

The bedroom curtains had been pulled back from the window and she stared at the iceberg in the bay standing firm above a turbulent seascape. "I've always thought of a woman as an iceberg."

"Cold?" he said knitting his dark eyebrows. "That's not you."

"No, regal and strong with many sides and shades in the ten per cent showing above water. I didn't think of the tides nibblin' away at her below the sea line. It takes a lot to roll her over, break her. But it can be done. The loss of me babies has done it." She shivered. Despair rolled in like a fog and wouldn't burn off, not even with the touch of little James's face against hers. She had lost something and she couldn't get it back.

A shock ran up her arm when she touched Victor and his brother in their coffin. They lay pure like a first fall of snow. She whispered, "My porcelain babies."

When Jacob came into the room after the burial, she looked up, her voice strained. "Is there no name for parents who lose their children?"

"No word that can describe such a loss," Jacob answered softly.

He laid a tray of food on the bed and reached to smooth her cheek. "You have to go on for us," he said.

She didn't respond.

Elizabeth turned her back to Jacob at night and when her body healed and his body sprang to life against her she pulled away folding her arms and legs against her empty belly. "How can a woman know that when she carries life she may be makin' sorrow, a sorrow that will fill her body until it is burstin' at the seams?" she asked.

Jacob didn't answer. His need subsided in sleep.

For months they slept back to back.

Elizabeth's encompassing love for her living children had been broken into by her yearning for the babies taken from her. James, sensing a loss in his mother's affection, became fretful and demanding and she felt like a cow driving away her weaned calf.

After the children were in bed she often curled up on the settle wondering, *Did I do something to harm you? Maybe I forgot that carryin' you was the most important thing I was doin'. Did I forget you as I crowded me mind with tasks in the stage, bendin' against you in my body as I lifted a barrow of fish?* She clasped her trembling hands over her soft, empty belly as if to feel the familiar movement. Under her hands there was nothing.

Sometimes she stayed up late sewing and knitting. She heard the easing of her husband's body out of bed and his call from the top of the stairs, gentle and coaxing, "Liz, come to bed."

She went on unheeding him until her eyes felt heavy and then she crept up the stairs and slipped into bed at her husband's back. If he turned she held her arms in front of her like a locked gate, its key lost at the bottom of a deep well.

The weight of her sorrow shifted as she began to see the loss on Jacob's face, the loss of his sons and his wife. Her heart softened toward him. Gradually her body stirred to his. They held each other afterwards, his face in her neck, his lips on her racing pulse. He drifted into sleep while she lay staring into the darkness wondering if she had once again offered her body up to loss and sorrow.

One night she put the children to bed and went downstairs only to hear a plaintive voice: "Mamma, I wants a drink."

Elizabeth climbed the stairs losing strength with each move. Jane, who had been given a drink before she went to bed, looked at her with wide eyes. She took only a sip. Then she asked, "Why did me brothers die?"

Elsie said, "What she wants to know is if *we're* goin' to die and be put in the ground."

Elizabeth realized then that the children were not only grieving their brothers. They were fearing what could happen to them.

"Not today," she assured them. "You lassies'll likely live to be a ripe old age."

"I hope so," Jane said cuddling into her sister.

Elizabeth smiled and drew the sheets around her daughters tucking them snugly.

She came downstairs and willed herself to sit out on the front step and draw in deep breaths. Cool sea air settled her like laudanum. She stepped back into the hall, a sense of well-being returning.

A tremor went through Elizabeth's body when she knew another child was coming.

Jacob said nothing but one night she found him kneeling by their bed, his shoulders shaking. There was no sound. He leaned heavily on the bed and lifted himself up, his face drenched in tears.

"Jacob!" His name tore away from her throat like a cry.

"I just want us to have a healthy baby," he said.

Elizabeth laid her face against his. "God did not give you a stone for your pillow like He gave your Bible namesake."

The grief that had settled inside her as heavy as wet sand lightened with the birth of George Clayton on Candlemas Day, 1923. He was a child who would grow up trying to keep in a laugh, his cheeks filling and then his lips letting go in a burst of laughter at something said that he thought was funny.

59

"We'll have our cup of tea and go to bed," William told Alvina.

She gave him a vexed look. "You had your tea, Skipper."

"Uh?"

"Your cup of tea and a slice of lassy loaf. You've done with it."

His face seemed drawn and anxious. "Now Sarah Ann, you've muddled me."

Alvina tightened her lips. *Calling me Sarah Ann, now, is he? He's on for goin' clear out of his mind.* She led him up the stairs to his bedroom and pulled down his sheets. "Get yourself out of your day clothes and haul yourself to bed," she said.

He mumbled as she went to close his door, "Me mind is wearin' away. Memories all gone."

"I'll check on you before me and George settles into bed," Alvina said.

William gave no indication that he'd heard her.

It was nigh on midnight when Jacob and Elizabeth pulled the bedclothes over them and turned in bed to each other. A familiar sound cut through the deep silence. First there was the creak of the gate at the bottom of the path as it was unlatched and opened and then heavy steps coming up the lane, steps they recognized as those of Jacob's father. They listened as he reached the landing. Jacob made to get up expecting to hear the latch lift and the door open. Instead there was silence. The next night they heard the same sound with a different step. This time the latch was lifted and the door opened. George came into the porch and called out.

Jacob grabbed the lamp and hurried downstairs.

"Pap is gone," George said, his voice heavy, "gone to be with little Nellie and Ma."

Jacob took the news with a deep sigh. "I could see it comin'," he said. Then he told George what had happened the night before.

"Mourning I won't be doing, then," George said belying his distressed look. "He had to have had wonderful strength to be able to walk out of his body and up the lane. Someone who can do that got no worries about gettin' where he wants to go in the hereafter."

The hereafter was a place most cove people expected to go. Though they weren't in any hurry. Something was coming that would change that for many.

60

Jacob and Elizabeth were washing out salt fish readying them for the flakes when Elsie, now thirteen, came running and calling, "The Missioners is comin'!"

"Well they can keep on comin' and goin' past my door," Jacob answered swishing a fish around in the puncheon. "I knows everything I need to know about God and He knows everything about me."

"Shush, Jake," admonished Elizabeth. "You don't know when you'll be smitten by God's power."

"I don't know where you got so much religion," Jacob said. "It wasn't passed down."

He knew stories about his father-in-law. It was nothing for William to drive his horse and loaded wagon down to the sawmill in Middle Bight to have his logs cut regardless of the day. One Sunday morning when he knocked on the door of Lester Mun who ran the mill the man told him to go on home. It was the day of rest. William muttered that he didn't think Sunday should get in the way of a man's work. It never got in the way of woman's labour, which, on the occasion, meant pushing out a baby or two.

"You won't care about work when you're six feet under," the man growled.

William shook his head and muttered, "Under those same circumstances you won't care about Sunday either. God likely hasn't rested a day since He made man, not with all the wicked people keepin' Him on the hop from Monday to Sunday."

"What's your religion, then?" the man asked.

William pointed upwards and answered, "That's between me and the man above. I'm an atheist."

The man gave him a solemn look and asked, "A Catholic atheist or a Protestant atheist?"

Jacob liked to tell the story when Elizabeth wasn't around. It made for a good laugh.

Down at a gathering place known as The Tell on a day when heavy seas lashed the beach and rocked boats on collar every fisherman was on land. The men took a spell on the rock walls built against an ochre shed at the fork in the road between Hibb's Cove and Pick Eyes. They leaned toward each other chewing the fat, the bibs of their caps hauled down over their foreheads to shade them from the sun.

Jacob and George sauntered up over Cliff Path and down to the The Tell.

Henry Porter was saying, "There's a new religion on the go, so I've been told. A spinster calling herself Sister Alice Belle Garrigus come from the States back in 1910 and started up a mission in St. John's. Her converts have already invaded Clarke's Beach and they're on their way to Port de Grave. There's talk they've rented the Orange Lodge."

"Ump," said Esau Porter. "Give the Missioners—*holy rollers* to some people—their breakfast and they'll come back for their supper."

"Yes," said Steward Lear, "the Church of England's been here the longest. It don't take to other forms of religions stealin' their sheep. Renting the Orange Lodge to the Missioners is lettin' the fox into the barn."

"Alice'll have her work cut out if she shows up here. The French Catholics come a long time ago and burned the place twice," Tom Porter said.

A young Pick Eye's fellow lumbering along overheard the remark and grinned. "You minds it, do yer?"

"No, me son," he answered, "but tongues are like chains. They link stories from generation to generation and from century to century. The Irish Fenians from Harbour Main thought to tackle the place and help their Catholic friends take over. When the Church of Englanders got word of the invaders their sealing guns and whatnot come out. They sent a message warnin' them that if they come they better bring the pine for their coffins. They never come. Sure, the graveyard is all that's left of any of 'em."

"Look what happened to the Methodists," Silas Bishop said with a pull on the thick whisker above his lip. "They got their windows smashed, but they stayed. The Salvationists had eggs thrown at them. Only a few of them stayed."

"Aunt Maud over in Lear's Cove is one of those," Esau said. "She sings Ira Sankey hymns while she milks her cows. Sometimes she's skimmin' the cream off milk boilin' on the stove and toppin' it up with a hymn sailin' through the open window to where Uncle Abe is tying up his boat. She'll die a Salvationist."

Silas squinted against the sun. "Dan, me youngest son, spent all winter in St. John's doing carpenter work. He heard of the St. John's meetin's and went. He almost got himself saved."

"It wouldn't hurt Dan to get saved," Ethan Newel, who never went to church, not even to have his children baptized, drawled. "I hear he's been chasin' women, the wildest kind, in St. John's."

Silas jumped up, his face red. "That's not for me to say or you to know." He took off up over the school hill.

The other men turned back to their canting.

"Nothin' a'tall wrong with it," said Ned Morgan, who'd been quiet until now. "Gettin' saved gives people so much energy they dance about the church in a glory fit. Mind you," he added with a grin, "once when the glory fell at the St. John's Bethesda mission Sister Garrigus's petticoat fell along with it. She was dancing on the altar when it slipped down around her ankles. She picked it up and kept on dancin' without missin' a beat."

"So much for a woman makin' a fool of herself," scoffed Richard Newell, a grizzly old fisherman. "St. Paul would turn over in his grave. He wanted women to be seen and not heard in church."

"Yer," said Ethan. "He claimed to have a thorn in his flesh. Likely a woman. Either that or he sat on a bush and got a thorn in his hinder."

There were gales of laughter.

Esau lifted his cap and scratched his white head. "I hear that mission women must'n cut their hair. It's got to be battened down in a bun or rolled at the poll under a hairnet."

"Looks like they got to wear a black or navy dress with a white lace collar," Ethan said. He laughed. "I don't mind as long as men gets to wear the pants."

"Don't be argufying religion when you don't have the rights of it. What if Sister Garrigus got the full gospel?" Ned said.

Ethan drew himself up straight, his look disdainful. "Phew! I suppose the rest of us lives half the gospel."

"You don't," Ned snorted, "not even half of half." He banged his pipe against a slate, sparks flying.

The scent of salt beef, vegetables, and boiled raisin pudding in a bag wafted on the wind. Isaac lifted his head, drew in a breath and got up. "The woman's got the dinner on and 'tis calling me a lot louder than the mission preacher."

Jacob hadn't commented until now. "Elizabeth is on two minds about goin' to the mission," he said.

George, standing beside him, said, "The women's all for something new."

Esau quipped, "The next thing you'll be up to the Orange Lodge raising your handkerchief and singing, 'Hold the fort for I am coming.'"

George frowned. "I won't, then."

Richard let out a jeer. "Not until Alvina hauls you there by the ears."

"No woman'll get that privilege," George said. He went off in a huff.

When Jacob and George came home from fishing one Monday afternoon Silas Bishop was standing on the stagehead. He leaned forward and caught the ropes Jacob threw up to tie the boat.

"Have you heard the news, Jake, boy?" he asked. "Harry Petten is the first to drop himself at the Missioners' Mercy Seat and thinking himself none the worse for it. Pastor Bob English out from St. John's got him good with all the fiery preachin' a redhead can muster."

George pulled the boat close to the stagehead and lifted his arm across his sweating forehead. "Got religion, then, has he? That man raised his fist to the heavens at God for takin' his first wife almost as soon as he married her."

Jacob climbed the rails. "We'll see how his new religion works when he's out on the fishin' grounds lookin' for the buoys holding his spot and finds out that another fisherman've stolen his spot."

When Elizabeth went to the Orange Hall she met Sister Garrigus, who had come from St. John's for a meeting. She was a short, dark-eyed woman, her face dowdy and masculine. She had a broad forehead, a long, straight nose, and a chin that could balance a pearl if she had believed in wearing pearls. She was plainly dressed in a black dress with white lace at her throat. Her white hair was braided and, according to one convert, coiled on the top of her head under her black hat. Elizabeth had heard that she had one straw bonnet to her name. It got cased in white satin in summer and black velvet in winter.

During the boisterous singing Elizabeth felt an exuberance she hadn't felt at any other time. Joy whirled through her until she wanted to dance. But she wasn't one to make a show of herself, not like some of the cove and harbour women. Not like Sister Garrigus, who dropped her petticoat. Elizabeth's cares loosened and she felt swaddled in peace as she knelt at the altar and prayed quietly for Jacob to be saved.

After coming from a meeting Elizabeth told Alvina, "The world is due for a change. St. Paul had his say. Now it's a woman's turn." She convinced Alvina to attend a meeting.

"It soothes me grief at losing Nellie," Alvina told George.

"God giveth," Alvina said two years later when her second child was on the way. "I hope He don't take this baby away." He didn't and Alvina couldn't thank Him enough for Shirley. Later she would thank Him for Violet and Newman.

"I'm saved now," Alvina told George. "I must love God above everything and everyone else."

George complained to Jacob that he had to share Alvina with God. He sputtered that God should be satisfied that he and Alvina loved each other and they were making babies to keep the world going. What more could He want?

Alvina had dragged George to a service, one button of his jacket latched above a rotund middle. "I'm Church of England. Sure, that's good enough," he had argued. "I go, I listen, I drop in me dues, and leave. That's it unless there's a funeral or a weddin' to interfere in the business of the week."

He came home from the lively mission service and poured a drink. "You'll stop having rum in this house," Alvina warned. "Look at your gut. Sure, it's out like a keg. I could roll you down Kennedy's Hill and you'd go faster than a barrel."

George drained the glass and smacked his lips. "A drop of rum to make the spirit merry is no harm," he said.

"A drop!" Alvina was indignant. "You've been havin' more than a drop. Your stomach's so stogged it looks ready to blow."

Jacob liked a drink of rum on a Saturday evening.

Elizabeth eyed him and George up on the hill sitting out on casks and lowering tumblers of grog. Her dark brows drew together. "Jacob, get on down here," she sputtered to herself. After some time he made his way down the hill, up the lane, and across the path to the steps bridging the house, his steps slow and clumsy. "Mind the babies," he said coming into the porch and taking in Elizabeth's stormy look. "Don't upset their little hearts."

"You'll be stuck with ginger wine from here on," she warned.

On Monday while Elizabeth was pegging her clothes to the outdoor clothesline Alvina came down the path in a hurry. "I want to get George off the rum," she said. "Sure, his stomach's roundin' like a keg and when he's on the liquor he's got only enough sense to muddle me in me work."

"Well," said Elizabeth, a glint in her eye, "Jesus turned water into wine. Turning rum into water is something we can do."

"Now Liz Emma, what is it you're up to?" Alvina pursed her lips.

"Time'll tell," she answered, her blue eyes widening in mischief.

One day when the men were out fishing and the wind was offshore Elizabeth and Alvina rolled the rum barrels over the cliff and watched them bobbing and dancing on the water, on and on out into the bay.

"There'll be a dance in that for the one who picks it up," George said after he came home.

Alvina drew in her chin and raised an eyebrow. "Not likely! Maybe a few drunk fish in your nets. We pulled out the bung."

George clicked his tongue and shook his head. "No rum for your Christmas cakes, Vine, maid. Ah, then, I guess I've lost me job as a crank maker. The crowd of yers'll be losing the Christmas spirit."

George made the best ice cream: canned milk, sugar to taste, and generous shots of rum all placed in the ice cream maker with ice around it. He cranked out enough ice cream to serve everyone on the hill during the Twelve Days of Christmas.

She glared at him. "I'd rather no cake and ice cream than you drinkin' till you're spinnin' and your words stumblin'. We can have cake and ice cream without the rum."

The men at The Tell heard about the rum going over the cliffs.

Richard Newell dragged on his matted beard and grunted. He looked at the other men. "Jake's woman come from over on the shore and hove his keg of rum over the cliffs making the fish drunk and more glassy-eyed than they was already. Who's to say she won't throw Jacob over next?"

Susanna, Richard's wife, coming down the lane, wiped her hands in her white apron and called, "If he was anything like you he'd jump in after his rum."

"Pffft!" he said. "The new religion got Elizabeth bound up so tight her hinder end will soon be squawking hymns."

"Now, then," she said, "there's nothing like a mouthful of blaighard. The way men talks about women they should have their tongues circumcised. They thinks they're gold and women the baser ores. I've a mind to go off to the mission meetin' meself."

"Then I'll turn the key in the lock."

"Not if I take it with me."

"Go on, then, but don't be telling me I'm goin' to hell." He turned to the other men. "See, the woman preacher got the tongues of the women all loosened. Next thing they'll be payin' no mind to us."

"That'll be it," Silas Bishop said.

The others all nodded.

* * * * *

Jacob agreed to go to the Orange Lodge. "Just to see what all the fuss is about," he said.

Elizabeth washed, starched, and pressed his white shirt. He buttoned the high stiff collar and tightened a tie around his neck. He inserted silver links in the cuffs and pulled on silver armbands. His black serge suit now had a green cast from lying in his closet since his marriage. He had spread a little and his jacket was tight. He pulled on his black greatcoat as if he were going to a funeral. Then he and Elsie walked to the service. It was Elsie who tugged on his sleeve to go forward to the altar call. He dropped to the penitent's seat like a sack of potatoes, his shoulders shaking as he cried for mercy.

George eyed him the next day and asked, "What would Ma say, she a strict Church of England woman?"

Jacob gave his brother a determined look. "From now on it's what God says."

When Elizabeth and Jacob came downstairs the Sunday after he'd joined the Missioners he headed toward the window at the end of the hall and pulled white lace curtains aside. His eyes crinkled against the bright splash of sunshine. "What a day on the water. Not a breath of wind!"

The twenty-three boats on collar were settled in the calm water like ducks. Even fishermen who didn't go to church were too superstitious to fish on Sunday.

While Jacob watched, wind like a soft sigh moved across the water. It riffled the surface and the likeness of the boats painted on its face was washed from sight. The wind moved stronger and water sucked the keels of little boats rocking and nodding listlessly beneath a mackerel sky.

Jacob turned from the window and got out the Bible while Elizabeth stirred banked coals into a fire and set a pot of water on the stove to boil porridge for breakfast.

The children gathered around the table and Jacob read the Bible: "And on the seventh day God . . . rested—"

"And man," Elizabeth added placing a bowl in front of Jacob. "A woman can never get a day of rest."

Jacob glanced up at her. He said nothing as he turned back to the Bible and read about Jesus walking on water.

"Was it frozen?" Jane asked.

"No, silly," Elsie said.

"Maybe the ice pans were in the bay and he walked across them."

"Your mind is busy, Jane," her father said. "Jesus didn't need to make ice before he could walk on water. Anyone who can make the earth as fit as it is for people and other creatures can do anything. Close your eyes, now. We'll have family prayers while your porridge cools."

Jacob prayed for his father-in-law. "William only thinks he's an atheist. He can't know what atheist means. He believes in you in his own way."

"It can't be done, this figuring out things beyond our knowledge. That's like trying to hold the wind in your hands," Elizabeth's father had told her years before. "Enjoy what you can and forget the rest. If you feel you don't know enough think of all the people who lived believin' the earth was flat. That's *not* what killed them."

Church was an event for the God-fearing fishermen. After wearing the same overalls all week the men cleaned up on Saturday for Sunday. There was something refreshing and renewing about having a change of pace: men's hands idle from hauling nets and trawls and women's hands free from fishing chores. There was order to the day and gentility as families dressed in their finest. Women who stayed home from the morning service cooked a salt beef dinner for the men and children gone to church.

When the Orange Lodge was no longer available meetings were held in people's homes. Fishermen whose fists reached to drag in fishnets during the week now raised their hands, fingers open like sunrays. Jacob was at Harry Petten's house when he fell to the floor speaking in an unknown tongue. Thereafter speaking in tongues became part of his private prayer, emptying him of pent-up fears as he yielded to the loose flow of unknown words. He had found a place in his faith that gave him strength.

Soon prayers were held in the "upper room" of twine and haylofts as fishermen mended the lacy squares of nets strewn across the floor and seded hooks on trawls to be coiled in fish tubs. Converts found time to stop work while in their gardens or on a fish stage late in the night, all alone, to connect with a power they had previously taken for granted. Out on the water Jacob thought of God's greatness and burst out in sounds without the form of a familiar language. Willis Lear hung his cap on a garden post and knelt down to pray by a rock at the side of a hill. Women in their kitchens felt the after-effects of the prayer services and began singing until joy bubbled up and burst out in words of an unknown tongue. A curious child pulled on his mother's apron strings. She fell to her knees and held him tight while the sweet flow of tears baptized the child's cheeks.

"Terribly wonderful . . . people slain on the floor . . . wonderfully terrible. . . ."

That was the consensus of the converts who had the hope of The Rapture any day now, a hope that helped push back the certainty of death.

On Easter Sunday, 1926, the Missioners opened the doors of a little Pentecostal church they had built beside Ship Cove pond.

Men at The Tell who never went to church watched the Missioners hurry up the road a little earlier than the Church of Englanders.

"Mind now they don't get the smell of baccy on their clothes," Ethan Newell jibed.

The men turned to see Elizabeth go by, sprightly in her paisley dress, a flower in her navy straw summer's hat. Her face opened in a smile, her eyes bright as she acknowledged the men.

Once she'd passed, Ethan said, "She's the worldly one."

"Not a'tall," Silas Bishop said. "Jacob won't have Elizabeth dress frumpy. I heard him say that God made flowers bright and beautiful and women should wear the same colours."

Willis Lear went by and someone called, "We heard you got saved."

"Jesus is comin' in a cloud to rapture the saved," Willis answered. "You better get ready or you'll be left behind."

Silas looked up, his eyes squinted. "There's no cloud today."

"Jesus can bring his own cloud," Willis said.

Willis went on and the men shook their heads.

Silas said, "Accordin' to me young fellar who went to the Bethesda mission the Missioners do the Jericho March: walkin' around the church over and over. The next thing the altar is lined with people prayin' in unknown tongues."

Wilson Bishop from Pick Eyes shook his head. "It can't be French or Beothuk. They wouldn't know that."

"I never heard tell of people speaking without knowin' what they're saying," Silas said.

"They believe God knows what they're saying, that it's His language," Ned Morgan told him.

Silas scratched his head. "Makes sense. It must be Hebrew or somethin'. God's a Jew, iddin He?"

Richard leaned on his knees and looked up. "Not that I know fer."

"Foreigners off the European ships in St. John's have been goin' to the mission and hearin' their own language just like in Bible days," Wilson said.

Alf Petten, a new convert passing by, stopped at overhearing the men. "Sacrilegious, the whole lot of yers. God wouldn't hold with your kinda talk. Not a'tall He wouldn't. It's the Holy Ghost and don't make fun of it."

Silas scoffed, "I knowed you believe in ghosts, but a Holy Ghost?"

"Other ghosts can haunt you. The Holy Ghost'll make you feel light and the world look new and fresh," Alf said and went on up the road as if he had springs in his feet.

Ethel Porter attended the mission to disrupt the service. Instead she was drawn in by the spirit as the singing vibrated through the small building. She rushed to the altar praying for forgiveness. She left the mission exclaiming, "I feel so light I could float away."

When Silas heard about Ethel's change of heart he had a chuckle. "There's no doubt Ethel is gettin' ready to fly. The whole lot of converts is moulting like birds casting off their earthly flesh for spiritual bodies. Getting ready for The Rapture, me son."

Esau Porter shook his head. "I don't see their wings yet."

The mission became a place for converts to unburden themselves of sins and claim forgiveness, a refuge for fishermen from the tensions they carried while facing a ferocious sea. It was a sanctuary for a mother burdened by the cares of a family and the worry of her man on the sea.

Flora Bowering, a young woman, her face round and pleasant, her voice slightly husky, had come to hold services. The tail of her navy dress shivered around her thick, dusty-brown stockings as she told converts that Jesus was coming in the twinkling of an eye and Christians should not be weighed down with the things of the world. She quoted the Bible: ". . . women adorn themselves . . . not with gold or pearls. . . ."

Fearful that she would miss The Rapture if she was weighed down by worldly possessions one convert pulled on her string of pearls. It burst and the pearls went down inside her dress and rolled across the floor every which way.

Another convert knelt at the altar with tears streaming down her face. She let out a laugh like the clapping of a bell. One laugh rolled into another until, exhausted, she stood to her feet, her face shining, hands raised. The minister explained that she was laughing in the spirit.

That was the strangest thing to Elizabeth. She had never imagined anyone laughing in a place of worship, not even Jesus. She sat quietly, eyes closed.

One Sunday night after the sermon, the congregation was called to stand at the altar. The pastor went from one person to another touching each forehead and praying. There was the slight touch of fingers on Elizabeth's forehead and she fell backwards to the floor. There had been no measure of time and distance, no jolt from the fall. One instant she was standing and the next she was lying on a floor soft as a cloud under her. She was taken by surprise when unknown sounds unwound from her tongue and rippled forth, soft sounds, unrestrained, as if her heart had found its voice and was speaking its own language.

The mission children were sometimes hissed at and called *holy rollers* by other children. One child was attacked on her way to school, punched in the nose and swung around by her hair.

Elizabeth knew about the attacks. One rock thrown at the back of James's leg had bruised it. Another rock had hit Jane in the back of her knee.

"Persecution makes us strong," Elizabeth told them. "If someone smites one cheek, offer the other. That's Jesus's way."

To Jacob she said, "If the children don't react the other children'll get tired of their behaviour. But a prayer wouldn't hurt either."

* * * * *

Jacob didn't mind when there was no preacher. He felt at home in the pulpit, as if he was meant to be there. He tended to his sermon on Saturday night and on Sunday morning he dressed in his new suit. He wore it with a vest over a spotless, starched white shirt and coloured tie. Elizabeth put a white handkerchief in the upper pocket.

He stood in the porch ready for church in a polished pair of shoes and wearing a quiff hat and Elizabeth eyed him with a saucy glint. "Sure, I hardly knows you."

Away from the sounds of the sea, and the rush of winds over it, the little church beside a pond in the shelter of hills became a haven for Elizabeth to settle her weary bones and renew her strength each Sunday night.

Jacob stayed home with the younger children taking the chance for a nap once they were tucked away. Sometimes Elizabeth came home to find him leaning against the curved head of the settle, legs stretched along its body, their youngest child asleep in his arms.

Jacob was having the finest kind of rest on the Lord's Day.

One Sunday night she came home from the mission and the children were all asleep in bed. She pulled out her hatpins and lifted her hat away from her head. She shook out her hair.

Jacob glanced her way meeting her bright-eyed look.

She moved to where he was lying on the settle, stooped, and ran her tongue down his cheek, devilment in her eyes.

"Is this what you learn at prayers?" he asked.

"No, but it is what I can do after prayers. So many men in the Bible knew their wives. You need to get to know yours over and over."

He pretended to be serious. "Now, now. The Bible says thou shalt not work thy horse nor thy ass on the Sabbath—the fourth commandment."

"Ask any Jew and he will tell you that the Sabbath was yesterday," she lipped.

He slapped her behind and pulled her to him. They hurried upstairs. The chance for another baby.

* * * * *

Patience Kennedy, known as Aunt Pace, was up in her rocking chair mending her handkerchief when she heard that the Missioners were going to have an open-air baptismal service come Sunday. New converts were eager to be baptized before they left home to fish in Labrador for the season. Aunt Pace came outside to where Alvina was throwing feed to her hens. The day was calm and the conversation was carried down to where Elizabeth was hanging out clothes.

"I think the Missioners are *too* saved," Aunt Pace told Alvina.

"How can anyone be *too* saved?" Alvina asked.

"Gone in the head, then," she answered and went back inside.

The water is too cold, Elizabeth thought as she looked over the cove. She wasn't up to going into water that might still carry slivers of ice from floes not long left the cove.

Still, on Sunday afternoon she followed Jacob to the beach where converts had gathered. She looked around. The baptismal service had drawn people from as far away as Brigus. Onlookers lined the wharf and Cliff Path.

Elizabeth had sewn weights from a discarded cast net in the tail of her dress to keep it from lifting like an open umbrella as she stepped out, cold water gurgling in her worn shoes. Icy pain shot up her legs as she went waist deep. The preacher pressed a pure white handkerchief against her nose. His other hand on her back bore her weight as she went down through the blue liquid and came up, her wet eyelashes blinking, water falling away from her hair in beaded streams. She waded ashore and stepped through the crowd, her clothes sodden, her feet sloshing. She faced skeptics' mocking stares. Low in the sky crows cawed amid sounds of "Where He leads me I will follow. . . ."

Aunt Pace came out of her house to stand on Kennedy's Hill. She tut-tutted each time a Missioner rose out of the water, hands raised, bivvering lips praising God.

"I don't need a dip in salt water to prove I'm good," she muttered. "The Missioners'll be gone to heaven before their time if they catch their death. Sure, May water is cold as water lodged in the heart of an iceberg."

There would come a time when someone would whisper, "Death is in the waters of baptism."

More than one person would agree.

61

George wasn't one to talk about the loss of his little girl and his parents. So much dying could make a man forget about living. The rush of grief that often came made him feel he was in a punt without an anchor drifting in a stormy ocean that threatened to slam him against a growler. He could see his father sitting in the pine chair holding little Nellie, both of them frail. He was thinking this sitting in the mission beside Alvina wondering how he could fill the emptiness when the Missioners started to sing, "Come home, it's suppertime." He thought of when he was a boy and his mother called across the cove to where he was running with other boys playing lalleck and hiding under overturned old punts lying in the sand like beached whales. The boys may have been scattered from one end of the cove to the other but when their mothers called them they hurried home so hungry their stomachs were ready to eat their tongues. Now George was hungry for something more.

"It's wonderful to come home to God," the preacher said.

George felt as if a divine power lifted him off his seat and he found himself running to the Mercy Seat. He fell to his knees sobbing.

No one had seen George cry in public before. The men of the cove rarely cried. In the mission some of them became so soft-hearted they did little else.

More than an hour later George rose to his feet feeling lighter and free.

The preacher said, "The devil's been laughin' up your sleeve long enough. Now you can laugh back."

George nodded in relief though it was the first time he had imagined the devil laughing.

Alvina couldn't see well. "I can see as well as God meant me to see," she insisted. She didn't believe what Aunt Pace had suggested: God made earlobes to hold spectacles in place. She'd been straining to see boats far out into the ocean for a while not wanting to admit that everything was blurry. She could see Elizabeth's clothesline, the motion of her wash in the wind, but not as clear as when she was first married. "To wear glasses is nothing but a show of vanity," she insisted.

"There's nothing about glasses to make you feel vain," Elizabeth told her. "They'll only show God's world as He made it, not blurred as you see it."

One Sunday Alvina couldn't believe her eyes. The new minister was sitting on the platform as proper as you please wearing spectacles. She began to think about days when she wondered what was going on across the cove where people on the wharf were only a smudge. The next day the minister came down the hill to get a cod from the fishermen and Alvina got close enough to catch a glimpse through the side of his spectacles. Her eyes rounded in excitement. The world looked much brighter and clearer and everything at a distance was more defined, closer, which was exactly where she liked everything to be. She began to think that spectacles weren't sinful—not a'tall. She skimped to save money, a bit here and there from the sale of fish. She placed it in a small tea can. When she had enough money George took her to Bay Roberts to get her eyes tested. After weeks waiting for the eyeglasses they arrived by mail. She put them on and pulled them off with a sharp intake of breath. She gave George a shocked look. "I feel naked! It's as if everyone can see me more clearly now." She had not realized how comfortable she was behind her own eyes. Now she was open to anyone's stares. That lasted only for a moment. She looked through the window and drew back astonished. Elizabeth was coming out of her house and going down the lane. Alvina could see what she was wearing as plain as if she were standing beside her. She no longer cared about being vain. She went running down over the hill to tell Elizabeth that she never knew the sky was so close, the earth so sharp and beautiful, and the waters so lively.

She exclaimed, "What a world we live in!"

"Indeed," Elizabeth said, slightly amused by her sister-in-law's enthusiasm. "Come on up for a cup of tea."

She followed Elizabeth back to the house saying, "I'll have a clearer view of our men's boat coming home."

Jacob looked up from reading his Bible, the hint of a smile on his lips. "I don't say but you'll be taken with philistinism now that you got spectacles."

Alvina didn't answer. She knew Jacob was toying with her.

As the weeks went by and Alvina listened to Sunday's sermons she knew there was a reason God hadn't wanted her to have better eyesight. She saw too much of other people's business. She was sure God was calling her to give up her glasses to avoid temptation. She wanted to listen but her stubborn will held out. *Maybe some day*, she promised as she knelt at the altar. She looked out over her lenses and up at the platform where the minister was shining his glasses with his handkerchief, likely to better see sinners in the back seats.

She knew then that even God would wear spectacles—if He needed to.

62

"I figured I had my share of children," Elizabeth told Alvina as they stood on the stagehead tying on their barbels.

"For sure you have," Alvina said.

Elizabeth felt weary from all the times she'd had babies tugging at her breast sucking her milk until her blood seemed drained. Older children yanked her hands throughout the day wanting drink or food until finally it was night and she was relieved to be able to settle them in bed only to be awakened by cries. Often she had sighed through nights of broken sleep. *No more babies!*

Now she felt the load of another child, a secret her barbel strings had been loosening around since early summer. Every morning she eased out of bed, her hands on her hips, her back aching.

When fog rolled in banking the cove Elizabeth felt as if her face were pressed against the sea. Other times battering winds stormed over the stagehead. There was no shelter as they licked the cold water and blew it in Elizabeth's face while she reached inside the limp fish. Her fingers stiffened with cold as she dragged entrails from the split bodies lying on a bloodied table. She dropped the gory mess and it formed a damp heaviness around her feet. Again and again she slid the insides of cod out, the cold surge snaking through her veins.

Her strength petered often as she and Alvina bore a barrow bearing cod from the stage up the steep path, often after water had trenched it, making the path rough, uneven, and rocky as they trudged to the fish flakes. Children running alongside the barrow of heavy, waterlogged fish sometimes dragged on the handles. Elizabeth was wearing out from work and from the damage work could do.

One palled summer day, she strained to lift Clayton over the playpen set in a corner of the stage. After feeding him she bent to set him back down. She let out a sharp cry at the tearing inside her. It subsided and she thought how hard the work would be on Jacob if she was laid up now. *Not before summer's end, please God. Not yet!*

She went back to the fishing table, gasped as pain like a splitting knife turned in her insides and dragged her hands away from the white, leg-like belly of fish she was gutting. She turned from the table and dragged her cumbrous body through the stage. She almost crawled up the steep path with its rain trenches, pebbles rolling and scattering under her rubber boots, her feet bearing down in anguish. Her fingers, as brown as the skins of potatoes she dug from the side of a hill each fall, strained to touch and unlatch the gate and then to reach the storm door to her house. She dragged her body through the kitchen, then the hall, and crawled up the canvas-covered stairs whispering, "Stay, baby, stay, only your heartbeat is strong. You've months to go."

Her children rushed after her staring in fright at the blood her body was splashing on the steps. They flattened their shivering bodies against angels and flowers imprinted on the stairs wall as Alvina rushed by leaving her barbel reeking of fish blood and guts on the newel post.

Knowing their mother was wounded, but not knowing by whom or what, the children sensed a black presence in the house. Dropping their voices deep inside them they listened at the door to sounds muffled by creaking boards beneath the heavy feet of their aunt, who hurried down the stairs, then up to silence.

"Be quiet, all of you," Alvina admonished them.

Elsie stared at her. No one was making a sound.

There was never ranting and roaring out of Elizabeth. She always delivered her babies quietly. Her eyes were closed now, her hands on the hard mound of her belly as she bore the harsh pain expelling the baby before her time. The baby lay folded like an unopened flower. Stunned, Alvina slipped the tiny alabaster body, veiled in a thin vellum sac, from her hand into a white blanket.

The stage work was left to George as Jacob hurried up to the house. He sat down heavily on the settle and bowed his head. "Save Elizabeth," he prayed. Then out of his fear came soft, unknown words tumbling off his tongue, anguished sounds only God could understand.

Finally, Alvina called Jacob upstairs and parted a blanket to show him the tiny, unblemished body.

Elizabeth opened her eyes and in a thready voice asked, "Where's my baby?"

The faces above her, pale and drawn, eyes dull and sorrowful, spoke without words, their silence too harsh an answer. She heard it, felt it slice through her heart. Her cries to see her baby made no sound.

Time passed with Elizabeth's body resting in its white shroud.

Jacob had opened the bedroom window and a fresh breeze stirred the curtains. Disembodied voices of cove people calling from one stagehead to another drifted on the wind. Elizabeth felt far away from all of them.

Tears dried on the faces of the children as they stood hushed outside their mother's room. Then one day Jacob called them inside and Elizabeth opened her face into a smile at little faces looking in at her. She reached her hands, their washboard nails worn to the bow of her fingers, toward the rushing, soft warm flesh of her children. They let out tinkling laughs as she held them tight against the dark wave of her unpinned hair, wet with the salty flow of her tears.

After the children reluctantly started down the stairs Jacob sat on their bed and reached his hand to stroke Elizabeth's hair. He choked on his words. "I did this!"

He did! There were nights he had come to her and she had answered to his need when she hadn't been inclined.

Alvina had once leaned on a fence rail and whispered, "St. Paul said to offer due benevolence to your husband. How can a man who lived centuries ago take the power from a woman to say no to her husband?"

Elizabeth smiled. "He can only if you let him."

She had let Jacob and, in expressing his need, he had left a pain that would never leave. Her impulse was to slap his face but when he lifted his head as if it had been bowed in shame, an overwhelming tenderness filled her. It was the human condition: men rewarding themselves after a discomforting day on the water in an unsteady boat, drenched to the skin, often cold and hungry. Settling into bed against the steady warmth of a woman's body was what they thought of on their way to shore, never that a child they helped make could be pulled from the bloodied grave of a woman's body.

Smarting from the loss of her baby girl, Elizabeth later stood by the fence, hanging sopping clothes to dry on her clotheslines, complaining to Alvina, "I've been in child much of the time I've been with Jacob, bearin' children and recoverin' while carin' for them and carryin' a barrow of fish, bendin' in half to spread the fish, risin' up for a good breath and to see something other than layers of fish. A woman is never off work till she's off her feet—and not then if there's a man beside her."

"It's the way of the world," Alvina answered.

It wouldn't be the same from now on, she decided. She wouldn't be as free to turn her body into a coffin, blood tears weeping from the very place Jacob and she had found comfort in each other.

She didn't have to. Jacob kept his place folding himself with his back to her. If he stirred in need she didn't know about it. Jacob dared not reach to hug her.

"I don't want to be this way," she whispered against Jacob's back one winter night when the wind howled against the bedroom window, its lonely voice running around the house, "but losing children not only wears on my body but on my mind and heart."

Jacob turned to the night table and opened a drawer. He struck a match and lit the lamp on the bedside table. Then he took the Bible and opened it. Finally he found what he wanted. He began to read I Cor. 7:3. "Let the husband render unto the wife due benevolence: and likewise also the wife unto the husband." He skipped to verse five. "Defraud ye not one the other, except it be with consent for a time. . . ." He grinned at Elizabeth. "The like of that! God is interested in our bedtime shenanigans. He believes in time out."

"Dout the lamp," she said turning her back. Her heart skipped with hope. Jacob understood!

63

Elizabeth sent her father a Bible study with a note saying that in his twilight years he needed to know where he was going in the hereafter.

"He needs something. You can't trust him not to be a prankster," Caroline told Joe. She had seen the book lying on William's table with Elizabeth's note suggesting that if her father's eyes were too clouded for reading he could ask Joe to read it to him.

Caroline didn't have the heart to tell Elizabeth about the things William had done. Monday last, women along the lane had pinned their undergarments under other articles on the clothesline. Later that day, Ned Porter said to his neighbour, "The women's puttin' on a show for us—wonder what it could mean."

The other man's jaw dropped and he rushed to tell his wife knowing she'd be mortified. She scravelled to gather navy and orange bloomers sprawled on blueberry bushes along the side of the road threatening to kill whoever did it. Down the road another neighbour found her calico drawers stood up on a stick.

News went around that William Maley was the likely culprit. After all, they knew he had stolen a pot of soup during the potato harvest. The soup had been cooked for the six hungry men hired to gather the crop at Jessie Porter's farm.

By noon the men's clothes were grubby, their steps heavy as if their tiredness had sunk to their feet, adding to the heaviness of clotted clay around their boots. Their eyes lit up in faces holding sweat and dirt as Jessie came outside to call them to dinner. The scent of baked bread crackling under melting butter and simmering chicken soup made the work in the fields worthwhile.

Jessie went back inside, her baby in her arms. She laid him in his playpen and hurried into the kitchen. She ran back out calling in a panicky voice, "My pot of soup is gone! For the love of God, what'll I do? The pot didn't walk off by itself. Who the devil took it?"

She rushed back inside disheartened. "I'll have to make a pot of doughboys in a quick and run partridgeberry sauce over them."

William sauntered down the lane and poked his head in the doorway. "I know just where your soup might be," he said. "I hear your chickens cluckin'. They're after smellin' soup and thinkin' the aroma is familiar."

Jessie rushed to the henhouse. There with the lid on and rocks keeping it tight was the soup. William followed her, letting out an abrupt laugh. "I just left it to cool."

Jessie grabbed up the pot and hurried to the house sputtering.

"Don't be talkin'!" she told Caroline later. "The man's gone off his head since poor Mary Jane and Jamie passed away. Mary Jane wouldn't hold with what he's doin'."

"No she wouldn't, then," Caroline said. "He's been gettin' a touch of dotage since he lost Jamie."

Joe defended his brother. "A harmless thing it is, he acting the rascal. He's got a funny streak."

"He's got a funny bone and it's in his head," Caroline countered.

One day Fred Porter and other boys came to raid William's apple tree. They had assumed he wasn't home. The door was latched with a stick against it. Fred climbed the tree by a bedroom window upstairs. All of a sudden there was a roar. William had poked his head out the window and fired his gun. Fred fell to the ground as fast as the apple he was stealing. The other boys started running down the road with William calling, "Get outta here else you won't know nothin' till you wakes up in the mornin' to find yerselves dead."

A neighbour who figured what had happened intensified the boys' fright by exclaiming, "Look at all that blood!" One boy almost fainted before he realized that William had shot off a bit of gunpowder. Other boys came to his house with money. William stroked his whiskers and asked, "What do you want, me lads?" Then he filled their arms with apples for five coppers or a five-cent piece.

When Elizabeth came to see her father she stood in the doorway, her hand lifted to her forehead. "There you is, not a clean plate in sight and you eating out of your frying pan. I don't want your grandchildren to remember you as the crusty old man who didn't take care of himself. You're not givin' this place as much as a cat's lick. I'll send Elsie over for a spell."

He lifted his head looking bewildered. “I tell yer now, ’tis not all gravy livin’ in this house.”

Elsie went to stay with him for a time mixing a bun of dough to bake or fry as toutons and making him a pot of soup. As soon as she left he went back to his old ways of never washing a frying pan from one meal to the next. He made kettle tea: boiled water with milk, sugar, and tea leaves, all in the kettle and strained into his cup. He soaked hard bread in it.

“I’ve been given a fool’s pardon for being a rascal, Mary Jane,” he said, looking toward a chair as if she were sitting there.

He could hear her voice: “It’s the ghost of the *Southern Cross* with the loss of our boy that’s sent your mind a-kilter.”

He nodded. “That’s it, then.”

64

“I’ve been tryin’ to think the Bible way, ‘Perfect love casteth out fear,’” Elizabeth told Jacob as they lay in bed facing each other. “I want to be a wife to you.”

He gave her a self-conscious look. “That’s easy for me but I don’t want you fearin’ another child and with so much work while doing it.”

Her eyes grew distant. “It’s a wonder me toes aren’t worn out against me shins. It’s been uphill and downhill in this place, downhill to the fish stage and uphill to the fish flakes. From there downhill and uphill to the house. I help set seeds and drill trenches in the uphill gardens and bring in the crop many times with the weight of a baby pullin’ on me insides.”

“Don’t I know it,” Jacob said. “When you grow up in a place like I did your body grows with it. I was selfish to bring you here for me, selfish to believe you’d grow accustomed to the place.”

“I came for me,” she answered. “I wouldn’t want to be anywhere else. It’s my weariness talkin’.”

Jacob pulled her to him and she laid her head against his chest, a warm resting place. She smoothed hair away from his forehead and smiled as tension drained from his face.

* * * * *

Flora Sophie was born on the ninth day of April 1926, six months after a large, white-haired goat knocked Elizabeth down breaking her collarbone.

"It's better to have it over so I'll be ready for the flakes in June," she told Alvina as she lay against her pillow nursing the newborn, a bright-eyed, dainty child.

"Another child to worry over," she added. "The cliffs and all. A misstep in a draft of wind and a child can go over. The sea got no mercy. It's eager to swallow a body, baptize it for death."

"Shush!" Alvina said. "No one's gone over for ever so long."

Elizabeth felt a chill along her spine. She looked down at her baby safe in her arms and up at her sister-in-law and asked, "When *did* someone go over the cliff?"

Alvina's face showed her reluctance to answer. "It was long before George was born. I knows only that a little Lear boy fell over the cliff. It so happened that a gust of wind swept right under the boy and he floated down as if an angel's wing had slipped under him. He drifted like a leaf down to the sea right beside a fishing vessel. He was picked up none the worse."

Jacob and George had grown up, comfortable with cliffs facing the vast, empty space between them and the sky, and the surge of the sea below. The dark ledges and cracks shadowed a danger the brothers courted standing on the edges or lying on their stomachs and yanking shelves of shale out of the cliffs. They dropped splintered pieces down over the edges and cocked their ears for the explosion of rock against rock and the crash into the sea.

Elizabeth's children, scampering about, busy in play, never realized her constant fears of some mishap as they made their rounds playing under fish flakes on the cliffs. They heaped up piles of tree needles fallen from the branches spread overhead or they dug holes for a game of marbles. Sometimes the older children beat a barrel hoop with a stick to see how far they could get down the hill under a flake before it wobbled out of control and fell to the ground or over the cliffs. They often chased each other close to the edge despite Elizabeth's warnings.

Fishermen and their wives clearing away fish on pleasant summer days smiled when they heard the sounds of children's shouts and laughter. They listened to the singsong voices of little girls bouncing a ball: “Bouncy, bouncy bally. I broke the head of my dolly. Mother came out and gave a shout and turned my petticoat inside out.”

The lazy drift of the pure, sweet voices of happy children was a sign that all was right in the world.

Elsie had the care of Clayton, her blond and fair-skinned brother. “Keep him in the shade of the flake. Mind him so his skin don’t peel like a boiled apple,” Elizabeth cautioned as she made her way to the fishing stage on a hot afternoon. While her hands worked as fast as they could to help clear away fish her ears stayed tuned to the sounds of the children under the flake.

Despite Elizabeth’s fears, most children of the cove knew instinctively that if they didn’t watch their step, they risked tumbling over jagged rocks to the waters below.

That is every child but Sophie, still too young to join the other children. By the time she was two she was running down the lane trying to get through the gate.

The cove children were warned to stay off the flakes when their parents were down in the stage. A child crossing the flakes could easily trip up in the nets and often did and near the edge. Despite the caution, sometimes by late afternoon the children were hungry enough to sneak up on the flakes and whitenap: skin the navy napes off the spread salt fish. This practice made them thirsty and they wandered up to the nearest house and inside the porch and helped themselves to a drink from a bucket of water. One of the children on their way from Elizabeth’s house, in a hurry to get back to playing, left the gate unlatched.

Elizabeth and Alvina were chatting on their way up from the stage when they caught sight of Sophie sitting on the cliff happily swinging her legs into the air above the churning sea.

Elizabeth’s heart stood still just as it had the day she’d been mixing bread crumbs with savoury in a white enamel bowl to make dressing for a chicken when Elsie came running. “We can’t find James,” she panted.

He’s gone over the cliff! was her first thought.

The cove people left their work on the flakes and in their stages and searched for hours before they found him. He had gone into the shed beside the house and climbed down a ladder to the cellar to hide in a game of lalleck. Away from the heat of a sweltering day he had lain on a pile of old netting and fallen asleep.

This time there was real danger. Elizabeth's legs, weak with fright, could scarcely carry her as she hastened out over the road, seconds like minutes, her focus on her baby, the whole world shut out. She stepped as softly as she could toward her child, her heart beating wildly. She prayed that there wouldn't come a sound to cause the child to move or shift slightly and go over the cliff. There wasn't a stir of wind, not a sound from anything or anyone. Then Elizabeth noticed, from the corner of her eye, children starting down the hill.

If they ran toward Sophie she might turn quickly and fall to her death. Elizabeth put her fingers to her lips and they stopped, stark still, their faces frozen. Finally Elizabeth's trembling hand reached out and grabbed the back of her child's dress.

Sophie turned startled and Elizabeth reached both hands to pull her daughter to safety. Sensing her mother's tension the little girl began to wail.

Elizabeth soothed her. "Don't cry," she said even as she broke down crying so hard Sophie's dress was soaked. The thing she feared had almost come upon her.

"Sophie's guardian angel was with her," the preacher said in church the next Sunday.

Every parent said amen, each one realizing how lucky they were that their children had not fallen over the cove's cliffs.

Children aren't meant to live on cliffs, Maggie wrote back after she received a letter from Elizabeth. *A careless run and they can trip and go over and if the teeth of cliffs don't gash them open the sea is waiting, all eager to swallow a body.*

Elizabeth knew she was thinking of Jamie swallowed by the sea. Every time she saw a ship far-off crossing the bay she imagined it was the ghost of the *Southern Cross* rising from its grave.

65

"I'm coming soon," William told Mary Jane as if she were sitting across from him. He felt his life dimming like a candle pooling in the bottom of its holder, its wick burning to that last flicker. He wasn't sure where he was going but he liked to think that God knew and the devil didn't. He hoped he'd see Mary Jane and Jamie. He'd once told Mary Jane, "The journey from here to where, no one knows. Whatever it is, it don't hurt to be dead. Otherwise you'd hear a lot of complainin' from the people underground."

She had raised an eyebrow and given him an amused look.

Jacob and Elizabeth brought James, named for his uncle Jamie, to visit his grandfather. They found William shrunken and stooped, his round, healthy-looking face bearded and whiskered under a head holding a fringe of white hair around a bald crown. He was sitting in a navy guernsey on a long bench out by the door. A shoelace reeved the neck and was knotted tight.

William put his hand to his head, leaned toward James, and joked, "The arse is worn out of me hair from standing on me head." The whiskers under his nose twitched as he moved closer to the boy's face and warned, "Come here, me lad, so's I can sniff *dee* up me nostrils." He would say that to a lot of youngsters and they would always run away for fear he had a way of doing just that.

Elizabeth had told James all about his grandfather. He wasn't afraid. He kept his ground and gave William a steady look.

William drew back impressed with the young boy. "You don't have the likeness of my Jamie, now a ghost inside the chambers of me old heart, but you've got his boldness. Do yourself good and stay off the water. The sea's mouth is always open and waitin'. Jamie learned the hard way, he did, and now the ghost of the *Southern Cross* is come to haunt me every day of me life."

William stared out to sea and Elizabeth hurried to distract him.

Months later Caroline looked at Joe concerned. "I dropped in on William. He's sluggish and gone all phlegmy, coughing a lot, and by the looks of the place without a day's work in his mind. 'Sure,' I said, 'The way you're hackin' and snifflin' you'll blow your brains out in your handkerchief. What's the good of you then!' He looked up with no mind to answer me."

Johnny huddled close to the stove. "It's only what we expected," he said quietly. "He faces the sea from his chair by the door and imagines a ship slidin' under the waters with Jamie gettin' smothered to death. Years of grief is wearin' him away."

Joe said, "We *knows* where Lavinia is; he knows nothin' about Jamie."

Caroline clutched her apron. "I know enough of what William is feelin' from losing Lavinia. I'd have a mind to give up if there wasn't two men lookin' for care."

When James came downstairs one January morning he shied from his mother's look.

Elizabeth set his bowl of porridge in front of him. "Stir yourself and get your spoon in hand," she urged. "There's a new fall of snow you'll want to be tumblin' in."

"Ma." James's tone of voice made her swirl around.

"What is it?" she asked the eight-year-old. "You look as if you've seen a ghost."

He looked up at her, then. His voice trembled. "I dreamed that Pappa Maley died and was laid out on a new matchboard door, a white sheet over him." His bottom lip trembled. "Over all of him."

"Don't be talking your dreams," she admonished him. "Eat."

Her throat constricted. This would be no time for her father to go. The sea was rough with lops and spray. When the sea calmed she'd send word for him to spend the rest of the winter with her. He could come by train but she knew he wouldn't. He didn't hold with the likes of an iron horse rantin' and tearin' down the tracks on land once set in seed.

That week Les Porter from Foxtrap came into the cove and Elizabeth asked him to see her father and urge him to get on the next boat coming that way. A letter came back in Caroline's handwriting, written like William said it: "*I can't come over now, the marsh is frozen too hard fer me to dig up me money.*" Caroline had added, "*He's not well a'tall and his house is in slings.*"

Days later Elizabeth went across to Pick Eyes with a can of pudding for an elderly woman who was off her feet with influenza. A young boy came to tell her she was wanted at home. She hurried up over Jacob Porter's hill and down over Cliff Path as fast as she could. The window shades were drawn and when she went into the house she felt the darkness. "Someone died, someone close to me. Who?" she whispered lurching to one side. She grabbed the kitchen blind and it snapped away from her hands back up the window clattering against its roller.

"You could have broken the spring," Alvina said from where she was sitting on the settle.

Jacob was sitting beside her, pale and heavy-eyed. "Your father's gone, Liz."

Her voice was steady. "I'll have to go bury him."

"You can't be going over there this time of the year," Jacob said, "and the weather rough." When he saw her face begin to crumble he relented.

Elizabeth and Jacob arrived in Foxtrap the day after William died.

Caroline called them inside her home and made a pot of tea to go along with a bowl of Baccalieu bird soup. Elizabeth sat at the table pale with shock while Caroline told her about the events leading up to the discovery of her father.

It had been a bitter cold day and Caroline had looked toward William's house looking for a sign of smoke in his chimney. No smoke on a cold January morning was the sign of a calamity of one sort or another. She had turned to Joe stretched out on the daybed by the fire. "There's not a sign of smoke rising from your brother's chimney," she said. "Get on over and check on the rascal."

Joe found William's house cold and his brother nowhere to be seen. Disturbed by a heavy quietness, as if the breath had gone out of the place, he climbed the stairs. William was still in bed. Joe was gruff with him. "A cat wouldn't save her kittens in this icebox. It's about time you got on your legs and down to light a fire. The mornin' is half gone." He went closer and saw that his brother was white as marble. He touched his hand and found it hard and cold. He rushed down the stairs and hurried to tell Caroline that William was gone.

Elizabeth remembered her visit the summer before. William had been complaining. "Damn leg falls asleep!"

"Don't damn your leg," she had told him. "It's a part of you doin' its best."

He grunted and she asked, "What comfort do you give it?"

He shook his leg and answered, "I leave it idle while I sleep."

Jacob opened the creaking door and they went inside the place, a cold, empty shell. He stopped in the porch to gather an armful of kindling. Water in the bucket had frozen into a solid disk, opaque like the moon.

Joe came behind him. He shook his head. "William's been dead but for the washin' a long time. His will give out and then his body succumbed to sickness."

Only when Elizabeth saw her father laid out on a new storm matchboard door, a white sheet over him just as James had seen him in a dream, did she believe he was really gone. She and Jacob didn't use his bed. They slept on packed shavings in the house while her father was waking. She had dismantled the bed in her brother's room and the one left in hers and had taken them to Hibb's Cove the summer after Jamie disappeared. Later she had regretted leaving her father with two empty rooms to wander through. "You can come, too, with your bed," she had told him. He shook his head slowly as if it was as heavy as the warming rock in his bed. "And leave me house without people. It would never forgive me."

"You *will* leave it," she had answered.

Now it would stand like a cracked jar, yellow grass growing up through it.

She looked through the upstairs window to the dark, skeletal limbs of an apple tree. It would come back to life in the spring, but her father was gone and she his only child left to carry on. Along the eaves conkerbells glittered in strong sunlight. She smiled remembering her father's story when she was a child.

"Where do conkerbells come from?" she had asked.

He had pulled her unto his knee, his arm around her, keeping her snug against his chest as he answered, "From the ghosts in the attic. A family of ghosts lives there durin' the winter months and when they gets too warm from the wood fire below they put their fingers out under the eaves intendin' to reach the snow and cool off. Their fingers freeze into crinkly ice candles and the ghosts can't pull them back in. The thirsty sun licks the candles until they shrink and break, fallin' into the snow below."

Elizabeth's face showed disappointment until her father said that the ghosts grow new fingers each year. "It's how you know they're still there."

Elizabeth smiled at the memory. She lifted the window and put her hand out to touch a conkerbell. Licked by a blazing sun, it let go and dropped to the ground. Elizabeth listened as it tinkled against other conkerbells already fallen. Children running below the window picked the longest ice candles from the snow and chased each other sticking them out like swords.

She closed the window and turned back to Jamie's painting of *Titanic* on the wall. She blew away dust gathered across the plain wooden frame and lifted it off the nail. She held it in her arms unable to keep her composure. She bent over the painting, her cry hoarse and anguished.

There was the sound of footsteps. Caroline stood on the landing facing her.

Elizabeth sobbed. "There's been so much dying."

Caroline rushed to pat her shoulder. Then she took her hand and led her downstairs to the daybed, where they sat together in silence for a long time, hardly moving until, finally, Caroline offered, "I'll make a cup of tea."

"I wish I had as much as you," Caroline said as they sat at the table, sadness darkening the lines in her face. "Lavinia is gone with me chance for grandchildren."

"I'm sorry," Elizabeth said laying her hand on her aunt's.

Caroline gave her a wistful smile. "I have her memory. I think on that."

The two sat mimpsing tea and staring ahead.

The October after William's death, Elizabeth and Jacob sailed to Foxtrap to pick a barrel of apples from Mary Jane's tree.

Faded uncut grass lay like sheaves of wheat across the ground as if blown there by a mighty wind. Among it spruce and fir trees stood straight and tall, a tremor in their aged branches. A soft soughing wind breathed life into a faded scarecrow like an old man bowing to the elements above fallow ground.

"William hove himself away," Joe said coming down the path. "He was never the same after losin' Jamie. He took no pleasure in his work and then he went idle."

Apples lay fallen and wasting in straw grass trodden on by boys stealing the apples with no regard for the tree's limbs. Some hung like arms broken at the elbows. Elizabeth picked her way to the ravaged tree. Just as if it was yesterday she could see her father's face flushing in anger. He'd been on to boys stealing apples for years.

"Now, Pappa," she'd said, "what's your use for all the apples? Sure, you've only got one mouth beside ours."

"Yes, but the sons of guns flings them about the roads. Mary Jane would have made tarts and bottled apple sauce."

Elizabeth brought a bowl of apples inside, sliced them, and fried them in melted butter and brown sugar. She thought of Jamie and her as children lying under the table munching apples, first turning the stalk and running through the alphabet as far as they could go before the stalk broke revealing the first letter to possible names of the person they would marry. Their laughs resounded like a bell and their mother often stopped her work and smiled at them.

Her thoughts were interrupted as Caroline came with a bowl of cream for her fried apples. After the men were fed and went outside the women lingered for a visit.

Caroline followed Elizabeth's intent look out the road. She touched her arm. "You're thinking about Maggie, are you? You had likely expected her to your father's funeral."

"I thought she may have heard about my father's death," Elizabeth said.

Caroline shook her head. "I sent her a note. There was no reply. She's likely busy with a load of children."

"That's it," Elizabeth said wistfully.

When Elizabeth had written Maggie telling her about her conversion to the mission she had received a cool reply.

> *Dear Elizabeth,*
>
> *I heard tell of the Missioners and I don't need them to tell me I should be saved. If there's a Rapture I've got as much a chance of being raptured as anyone else. The minister here is more relaxed about how to get to heaven. He says that people*

must work out their own salvation. I'm going to stick with the Church of England.

Your friend always, Maggie

Elizabeth and Jacob held each other in sleep during their nights in the house. Every time a branch brushed against the window, like the fingers of a ghost, she thought of the night Jamie had flung the Labrador box against her Uncle Joe's house in the only way he could.

She stood outside the empty house alone, after Jacob had gone to the boat. A clear, amused voice sounded through her mind. "Don't take life too seriously. You'll never get out of it alive." Her father's voice.

"Maybe I will," she answered. "I believe in The Rapture."

66

Maggie had received news from Caroline that William had died, but when she told Ben, her face stricken, he had lifted the note from her hands and read the time of the funeral. Then he said sharply, "Stay away from the place and let the past lie. It's taken up too much of your mind already."

Maggie didn't reply. Every time she looked on the ocean she still imagined the *Southern Cross* sailing through the distant mist carrying Jamie and the other sealers.

That night Maggie reached her hand to Ben's back, ran her fingers along it, and laid her palm against his muscular body radiating warmth. "I'd die without you," she whispered.

He stirred slightly as if her words had caught on a dream he was having.

Something had disturbed her, an uneasy feeling waking her and keeping her awake until the night wore thin. Knowing Ben wanted an early rise she slipped out of bed to start the fire.

Ben was soon hauling on coveralls to the wails of their infant. He scowled and muttered, "A real crosspatch, that one is."

"He's on for teethin', Ben, likely like you when you was his age."

"You're right, for sure, always you is, and I the ignorant one not given to thinkin'." He grinned. "But I'm learnin' how to soften me notions because of you after these dozen years taking note of your ways."

He left the house and went to the barn to feed the horse and cow. He came back in, squinting as he lifted the damper on the stove and reached into the fire with a pair of tongs. He hoisted a coal to his pipe and drew in. He dropped the coal back and nodded to Maggie. "Storm the kettle, would yer! I need a hasty mug-up. It's a fine, clear day in the woods."

She saw a tiredness in his unshaven face. Sun-cut webs spread out from his dusty brown eyes. She didn't think she'd ever dream about Jamie again. This was a decent man who had loved her wholly, reaching past Jamie inside her heart. He hadn't complained the time he'd seen a photograph of Jamie in her Bible when they were first married. William had given her the photo a few days after the *Southern Cross* was lost. After she'd been married to Ben for a while she sent the photograph to Elizabeth with a note she told herself was true . . . *"Jamie will always be your brother but, in fairness to Ben, I can't carry him in my heart, only in my thoughts."*

Many mornings she had sat in silence beside Ben having an early breakfast, the fire crackling in the stove. She had wanted to promise him more than she gave, wanted to give him more than she had promised him in marriage, but she felt disloyal to Jamie's memory. *I married Ben to have a home and family. Why did he marry me?*

He was always gentle and tender when he came to her at night. If she told him she was tired he would say in a chipper voice, "Okay, me ducky. Another time." He'd hold her, his arm cupped around her, his body spooned against hers as if that was enough, and fall asleep as peaceful as a baby.

If he stirred to her some mornings she didn't look into his eyes. She kept hers closed. He took his pleasure from her secret place and he never asked to know the mystery of it. If his hands strayed above her waist to her breasts she didn't show the pleasure she felt or the guilt. Her breasts were to feed her children. Nothing else. She tried not to acknowledge the accidental pleasure she felt when he took his time and her body shuddered and settled. He always hugged her afterwards as if she had given him a gift. She never acknowledged what he had done for her.

Sometimes his hand went to his chest as if he felt a twinge. His face would turn pale and she'd ask him the cause. He'd shake his head as if to throw off her concern and go on out the door. She never thought for a minute his life was in danger.

Cyril, their oldest son, was eleven when his father went in the woods one day to cut wood for the kitchen stove. She nodded goodbye as she lifted a skein of wool away from her stomach hardening with her ninth child.

She glanced up at the calender on the wall—the last of January and not a speck of snow on the ground. She watched Ben harness the horse and hitch the cart, watched him take the reins and look back at the window as if he was hoping to see her there. She was standing back beside the stove seeing him, he not seeing her. Later she wished she had stood on the doorstep waving goodbye. The children were about tugging on her apron and her mind was soon on them.

The horse and cart came out alone. Searchers found Ben dead in the woods at forty-one.

The sight of Ben frozen reminded her of photographs she'd seen of dead sealers from the *Newfoundland*. Grief came, swift as an axe, splitting her heart. A heart not even mended was now broken a second time.

A neighbour laid his hand on her shoulder. "It's such a shockin' thing. He had only one junk of wood left to lift to the cart when some malady took him and he fell. We have to cut off his boots. They're frozen on his feet."

"Don't hurt him." Her voice lurched up from a tight throat, her tongue stiff and clumsy.

She hadn't really known Ben. She had not travelled his naked body with her eyes and her hands. Now she wouldn't let the neighbours take charge of his body for the washing and laying out. She washed him all over and then her lips wandered down over his body, past his private place, seeing it for the first time. It was so much smaller than she had thought from the feel of it. She went on down to the balls of his ankles. She drew back, her lips cold—tasting death. No matter what she did she could not bring his life back. She could not reach the distance it had travelled away from her. She hurried to find him clean clothes. She dragged them over his stiff body, her eyes heavy with shock.

At least she had Ben's body. Jamie had disappeared into the sea. Where? Only God knew and He didn't see fit to tell. Now her husband lay dead in her sight and would lie underground out of her sight and she wasn't sure which was worse. To look on the face of death, feel the helplessness. . . . Her eyelashes fluttered against her white face.

William once told her, "It's best to leave the ocean alone. The land is safer and more gentle. It'll wear your muscles but it won't kill you."

Ben had worked the land and his family had lived off it. He had spent just a little time on the sea. Still, death was near all along hovering as much over the land as the sea.

Maggie sat by the stove, a soft light shifting with the crackling flames in the grate. After the fire died she dragged herself up the stairs, past the sleeping children, and lay in bed listening to winter winds at her bedroom window, their shrill voices like mean-spirited creatures taunting her.

At the wake Bessie Rideout whispered, "You poor woman. You haven't had much luck with men. It should ease your heart to know Ben'll be cradled in the earth, not like Jamie tossed about by the sea."

Maggie pulled away keeping her face passive.

"You had him for a good while," Jessie Young said.

"Long enough to give me a lifetime of work with eight children and another comin'," she retorted.

Reverend Petten's words came like an empty platitude. "Sorrow is kith and kin to all of us. We'll not make it to the end without encountering it." He looked at Maggie under a black veil. "Swallow death's bitterness, my dear woman. Let God sustain you and your children bring sweetness to your future."

Her look was distant. "Jamie was my future, then Ben . . . my children . . . a burden." Her voice drifted into a heavy silence.

The minister looked away. Then he laid his hand on her shoulder. "Our future belongs to God."

Her words strained against his. "Then why does He allow us to hope and plan for a future knowin' what He does?"

The minister shook his head. "If I could answer that I'd be as wise as God. We can't say He's cruel and dismiss Him because He's not according to our perception. Nature exists and it is both cruel and kind, a reflection of God's mercy and His wrath. Look around you." He spread his hands. "See God's blessings."

Maggie's children lined a seat. *Precious children.* She gave them a faint smile and they smiled back. Though Ben's heart could not carry him through a long life he'd journey on in their children.

She stood at the grave trying to keep her balance as the children pressed against her gripping her hands. She listened to the thumps of heavy clay plonking down on the coffin and felt absolutely nothing. She was like a brook frozen in the dead of winter, everything beneath moving along.

Job's comforters were around her. "It's not natural, you not showin' emotion. Sure, Maisie down the road put her fist through a window when her man was killed in the mines."

After the burial she sat by her window and listened to the rhythm of logs thumping the ground as neighbours unloaded the wood Ben had cut. She imagined it was Ben packing wood against the shed. He would finish his work and come into the house smelling of new wood, its aromatic clean scent mingling with sweat.

One neighbour told her that woodsmen had reported hearing the sounds of chopping at the place Ben died. A token!

The neighbours went on their way and there was silence. It seemed that the house had been sawed open wide to let in northern winds. With Jamie she had lived in a promise; with Ben she had lived the reality. Just as she had mourned what she had missed with Jamie she now mourned what she had lost with Ben. He had given her something Jamie hadn't: children to be both a blessing and a burden.

She stayed by the window, the finality of his death cutting through her, hope and expectation gone.

She did not write to Elizabeth with her news. She had no will to seek comfort in a visit. At first Elizabeth had been a reminder of someone she had loved. Now she was a reminder of someone she had lost. The distance between them had widened.

Josiah was born three months after his father died. Labour was long and difficult and Maggie's cries bitter with each push. She gave birth to a child she wasn't sure she could keep. She wrapped her arms around the baby. He cried as if discomforted by her strong grip. The hardness in her softened and she slackened her hold. *I promise to be gentle.*

It was the second year after Ben died and in the dead of winter that Maggie made a dreaded decision. There was only a little flour, some potatoes, and the gun with only one shot. She got used to feeling hungry. The children were thin. Men in the community helped out as much as they could, but there were many families to keep and little to do it with. Young and old dropped from influenza. It and lack of nourishment made a deadly combination. To have a little weight on the bones was to be in wealth. A rat had gotten into her potatoes stowed in the cellar. She spied it by the outhouse one day. It skittered inside and scurried down the toilet. She ran after it, her teeth clenched. "If one of us is goin' to eat it'll be me; you won't be comin' after any more of my food." She aimed the gun down the hole and fired. She lifted the gun in triumph.

She'd just gotten back to the house when she saw Neil Butler from the next lane pass her window. She heard the farmer's step outside her door. He called, "Maggie, you in there? What's the young fellar doin'? Is he old enough to prong dry manure?"

Maggie hurried out. "Cyril is big enough."

The boy spent three days working for a dollar a day. Then he spent his time searching along the roads for pieces of coal lost from a full wagon and bringing it home to keep the fire going.

Maggie sold eggs, sewed clothes for other people, and took in their wash but it wasn't enough. The children needed more than they were getting.

An old saying plodded through Maggie's mind: *March will search. April will try. May will tell who'll live or die.*

Harris took with a cold on his chest that she nursed with ointment Clara Jones, a neighbour, had given her. "I can tell he's very sick," Clara said.

For one moment she felt a spark of optimism. *If he died there'd be one less child to worry about going hungry.* Then she realized what she'd thought. *Forgive me, God! Forgive me. I know what I need to do to save the children.*

Late spring she pushed away her misgivings and did something she never thought she'd be desperate enough to do.

"Keep the woodbox full and the stove afire," she told Cyril. "Wilhelmina, you do the drudgery around the house. I'll be back later today or early on the morrow."

She shook her head when Wilhelmina demanded to know where she was going. The girl could tell by her mother's stony look that it was best not to press for answers.

She scrubbed the children and gave them clean underclothes. She dressed Laura in a plain blue dress and Gladys in a similar one she'd sewn from one of Wilhelmina's best dresses. Harris wore a shirt and suit of clothes Maggie had made over from Ben's shirt and suit. All the time she was dressing the children they kept asking, "Mamma, where's we off to?"

"A jaunt to St. John's," she said in as light a tone as she could muster.

They knew by the tightness of her face that there was something more. She comforted herself. *They'll be fed and when I'm able I'll get them back.* Her own voice sounded through her head: *It's not like leavin' jewellery at a pawn shop. I'll get them back but what will they be like? What will have happened to them?*

She pulled a grey hat down on her head and pushed a long, pearl-headed pin through it under her hair. She tied a light scarf around her throat and pulled on summer gloves. *Right now I want them alive. I can't ask for more.*

It was a dusty day with the sun bright and warm. Maggie drew the children outside, thinking, *When you go to bed, hunger gnawin' at your belly like a rat and you wake up with worry gnawin' at you because you have little food to feed your children, it's not a good day no matter how sunny it is.*

Neil Butler brought his draft horse hitched to a buggy. The children climbed up and settled on the back seat. Maggie sat on the bench beside the driver. Neil jerked the reins and the horse started up the bumpy road with a gallop. The children turned in unison to look back at their home. They didn't cry but they dropped their heads and leaned into each other.

Neil hardly spoke on the way. He passed cows and sheep and wild horses here and there along the road. The buggy rattled over potholes, its wheels grating over rocks. The driver pulled up in front of the Church of England orphanage and slackened the horse's reins. The horse came to a halt and Neil jumped down. He tied the reins to a hitching post. Each of the children clutched their bag of meagre possessions in silence as they looked around the strange place full of people going along the many roads branching from each other. A noisy place.

Maggie pushed a lump past her throat and looked into the children's upturned faces. Their glum look tore her heart. "You'll be staying in an orphanage until I find the means to bring you home."

Gladys cried, "Pappa went to heaven and left us. Now you're gonna leave us in St. John's."

Laura let her bag fall. She fingered the shrivelled skin of an apple her mother had put in her pocket, her lips quivering, her eyes watering.

"Be brave!" Maggie said pulling the children to her. The youngest child dragged on her hand as they got closer to the orphanage. They started up the wide wooden steps to the double doors of a large grey building. Maggie lifted the brass knocker and let it down hard. The children began to sob. Maggie took her handkerchief from her sleeve and wiped their faces keeping her own face as steady as she could. There came the sound of heavy steps and a small side door that Maggie hadn't noticed was pulled open. Its hinges let out a squawk.

She looked up at the tall administrator standing in front of her. MISS BABCOCK was written on a nameplate pinned to her collar.

"I hate to take charity," Maggie said.

"It won't be charity," the woman replied, her long, thin face tightening as she faced the children. "At Job Memorial House your daughters will work for their keep—and hard. The boy will be transferred to Shannon Munn Memorial Home."

Maggie and the children followed Miss Babcock inside.

The woman walked toward a large desk. She sat down and pushed an admittance paper across the top for Maggie to fill out.

Maggie unfastened her hands from the children's and hurried toward the desk. She stooped and filled out the paper signing away her children. She passed the sheet back to the woman and then she took a piece of paper from her pocket. She held it out to Miss Babcock. "I've included a note on the children's habits, dislikes, and other things."

The woman took it with a scant look and without commenting looked past Maggie to Harris.

She nodded at him and he moved in front of his mother.

"And what is your appellation?" she asked in a lofty tone that made him cringe.

"Uh? I don't know," he answered. He turned to his mother.

Maggie looked past him to the woman behind the desk. "If you wants his name it's Harris."

The woman regarded her for a moment. Then she turned back to the boy. "You've lost your appendage, have you, boy?"

"What is that?" he asked, his eyes widening.

"That noisy part of you that is attached to a bigger part of you, your tongue, it is."

Laura spoke up. "His tongue is sometimes more important than any other part of him. He can be a chatterbox."

"Well, he'll soon lose some of his tongue. There's a home for wayward boys down the street."

Harris stared at her as if he was wondering what it would be like to lose part of his tongue. He turned back and grabbed Maggie around the waist. When she bent down and whispered that the woman meant he wouldn't be allowed to talk as much his face relaxed.

After scanning the admittance paper the woman pushed back her chair and stood up, her dull, grey eyes narrowing at the sight of the boy holding on to his mother. Maggie gently lifted his hands away.

"You'll stay here for a little while," she told the children. "Be good."

They nodded solemnly.

Miss Babcock dismissed Maggie with a nod, her voice brisk. "That will be all." She turned to the children. "Come along so we can see to your ablution."

The children looked up with a puzzled expression, then back to their mother, but her back was already turned and her hand was on the door handle. They didn't see her turn back, tears falling silently.

She left the orphanage and made her way down the steps. The horse, waiting impatiently, let out a snort, its rider barely looking at her as she climbed up to the ragged seat of the buggy. She had wanted to chide the administrator for using words the children couldn't understand but she feared the children would suffer the backlash.

I gave them up to save their lives, she told herself on the way back home. *I was sent away from home and I lived. Now my children will live the best they can until I get them back.*

* * * * *

Sometimes when the ache for her children overwhelmed Maggie she would bring them to her mind in things they said. She'd smile remembering her children's questions. Gladys was the most inquisitive. "Mamma, why do sunbeams make rainbows?" And when the moon was a quarter: "Mamma, where did the rest of the moon go?"

"You've got more questions than I can find answers for," she'd say some nights as she tucked her in.

She wondered if there would be anyone to take Gladys's questions. Would anyone show the children the affection they needed growing up without their mother? Her heart lurched. She'd given her children to a woman whose heart was cold as a winter moon.

"You need a husband," a man called as he made his way up the path, thumbs hooked in his trousers. "I'm Nicholas Conway from Manuels and I heard you're lookin'."

Maggie stared at his ruddy, round face, a spray of freckles down his nose.

The man went on. "Say yes to bein' me wife and I'll give you and your children a good home. I've likely got a longer life than you seeing I'm a good bit younger."

She ached to answer yes. She'd get her children back. Her hands went to her sides.

"No!" she said, her voice like a nail puncturing any hope he was holding.

"No!" He looked at her as if he thought a woman in need would jump at his offer. He could tell that her answer was final by the stubborn set of her mouth. He turned away before she did and lumbered down the path like a man too stunned to know where he was going.

She couldn't tell him why she wouldn't marry a man who had the means to keep her and her children comfortable. But when the women at the Quilting Bee begin discussing the young fisherman, a fatherless widower who had come calling with what they believed was a sensible offer, she felt provoked. She pushed her chair back, grinding it against the pine floor, and stood up saying, "What if I married the man, had another child, and died in childbirth? My young children would be without their mother. What if I married the man and he died while I was having his child? I'd be left with another child. My life is as it is. I'll not court trouble."

The women shook their heads. Jessie Young sliered at her and said, in a singsong voice, "Don't trouble trouble till trouble troubles you. Don't kiss a fellar till a fellar kisses you."

Maggie didn't answer.

After she married Ben she hadn't felt settled. It was as if there was a shadow on the sun, a black cloud in a blue sky and some amorphous presence readying itself to creep up behind her. And it had! It sneaked in when there was no one around to save Ben. A man could die on land not far from his home as swiftly as he could die at sea away from his family.

Caring for the children left at home and hopes that her children in the orphanage would soon be home was what kept her going.

The children came home the next summer in a box cart drawn by a ragged horse and shabby driver. Abe Porter had brought a load of eggs and fresh meat to St. John's and sold them to the shops. He'd gathered the children from the orphanage. They climbed into his bloodied cart in clean clothes. By the time they arrived home they were ragged-looking, their face and lips dusty, their clothes stained. They climbed down with shy looks, more tired than happy. Maggie didn't reach to hug them. Instead she filled the porch tub with water and scrubbed the children with soap until the scent of the orphanage was washed away.

During the weeks the children were home they kept aloof. They had life experiences Maggie knew nothing about, experiences they alluded to but were reluctant to divulge. They seemed self-conscious, afraid of being attached. When they had to leave the only sign that they didn't want to go was the way they held their bags tight against them and pulled their lower lips under their teeth, their eyes narrowing. They waved goodbye without a smile.

Maggie bore down hard on her words as if to imprint them on her children's minds as she called, "This is your home and soon you'll be home for good."

They didn't come home for good. They got their learning at the orphanage, and when they left it was to go in service to families needing domestic help. They never forgot the Grace: "Thank the Lord for what we have. If we had more we would be glad but since the times they are so bad thank the Lord for what we have."

What they didn't have was their mother and their sisters and brothers born in the same house—children their mother had kept.

67

Golden Stanley was born on the thirty-first of March 1931. The midwife took in his robust look and smiled at his lusty cries. "There'll be nothing to keeping him alive," she said in her direct way.

Until now Elizabeth had remembered this day of the year as a day to mourn. Now it was also a day to celebrate the birth of a son.

The wind was blowing a gale. Elizabeth slipped out of bed to feed the baby just as day was breaking. She could see through the curtains a puff of white cloud hovering in the cold, faint blue sky. She pulled back the curtains and gasped. Ice had come! It covered the face of the bay invading the cove and walloping the shore. Its jagged teeth had taken the grey legs out from under the stagehead. The stage platform was gone. The squished stage room hung like a forlorn, grey head. Elizabeth woke Jacob.

"That happens now and then," he said. "Spring tides with gales and ice threaten our stages." He hurried to meet George coming down the hill.

Oil casts rolled across the ice spilling rendered cod livers like golden oil. It froze into a crusty yellow. The brilliant light of the sun reflecting off the ice stung Jacob and George's eyes making them water as they scrambled over the ice bed to grab their empty casts before the ice moved out to sea as suddenly as it had come. They gathered the damaged legs of the stagehead and hauled them ashore. Children who had run down to the ice with sticks were running from pan to pan as far out as Offer Island, a large rock above water about a hundred yards from the beach. Pans loosened as if a dragon had spit out a mouthful of broken teeth now floating apart into the open sea.

Elizabeth, thinking about Jamie running from pan to pan risking his life, flung open the door. "Get in here," she called to the boys, her voice loud and harsh startling young James. He turned quickly, almost losing his balance.

"Now!"

By afternoon the ice had floated out the bay. It left a lone berg wedged between two rocks, a reminder of what ice could do.

Misfortune followed the summer. The fishing season had too many water hauls. Fall came and one day Jacob strode up from the stage, laid his cap on the doorknob of the porch door, and hove himself on the settle.

Elizabeth read the lines in his face, heard the heaviness in his breath as he lifted his head. He looked at her. Finally he said, "All the work with only water in our nets and winter soon to set upon us like a wild creature. There's hardly enough for a family. I'll spend a winter in the Sydney mines. There's more money to be made there than in the brown bowels of Bell Island. It will be hard on you but next year—" He drew his lips tight.

"You must go, then," she urged. "I don't want worry takin' you in the heart. Then you'll be no good to work at anything. There'll be fish next year. Only for a winter you'll be gone."

He glanced at the dress she was making for Jane and asked, "How many miles did you go on your sewing machine today?"

"Not half as many as I need to. I'll have to turn Elsie's blue coat and leggings for Jane. Blue fades something awful."

Elizabeth left her work and went to the kitchen stove. She lifted salt cod and new potatoes bursting out of their thin skins and laid them on a plate. Butter melted over them while Jacob sat at the table, his head bowed.

In prayer or despair? Elizabeth wondered.

"The mines are rough and dangerous," Elizabeth had overheard Jacob tell George after one of his buddies was injured in the Bell Island mines. "You could soak your skin with blood down in the mines and the boss wouldn't care."

To lessen the danger for Jacob Elizabeth bought him a Welsh miner's lamp, its light soft. According to the peddler who sold it the handsome brass lamp had flash-arresting baffling. It promised to reduce the chance of explosions in the coal dust–laden air of mines.

It was a long winter without Jacob. Elizabeth pictured him digging black rocks in the darkness of Sydney mines all the while thinking of coal ablaze in the kitchen stove of their Hibb's Cove home lighting up his family's faces.

When Jacob had spare time he wrote Elizabeth. She ran down the lane answering Elsie's voice calling her: "Ma, we've got a letter!"

Her heart leaped in tenderness at seeing her name in Jacob's strong handwriting.

> *. . . It's a lonely and wearisome spot, Liz, down in the mine far from you and the children. I think of your comfort and how I'd be gone to heaven if I could lie beside you in our bed at night and after the day rises watch you out in the summer air walking up the path, your skirts fluttering around your bare brown legs like a host of butterflies. I wish for days of dazzling sunshine sizzling on the sea emptying itself behind evening hills. And the children. I hear their laughter in my head. Tell Jane and Elsie and James and Clayton not to fight each other. Get them to help with the work and mind Doris and Sophie. I'll find a shop and bring home some sweets. I wait for the time I'll wake to the morning sun glowing against our bedroom window and filling up the room, little Golden cooing in his crib and clapping his hands. It will come. Until then I remain your ever true husband, Jake.*

The children gathered around Elizabeth to listen to her read their father's letter. They giggled at the mention of themselves wanting to see where they were in the letter. In one letter Jacob told the children to count the waves in the ocean if they wanted to know how much he loved them.

Jane crinkled her nose. "No one can count the waves."

"And no one can count how much your father loves you," Elizabeth replied.

From then on Elizabeth read Jacob's letters to the children, sometimes over and over. She had no trouble getting them ready for bed on a Saturday night once she promised to read their father's letter at least twice. She lifted a porcelain jug from a row lining her pantry shelf and dipped water from a boiler on the stove. She poured it into the wooden tub in the back porch for the children's baths. The small ones took a turn sailing one of Jamie's little boats he'd carved a long time ago, sloshing water over the porch floor. They came out of their baths rosy and fresh, ready to sleep through the night. Elizabeth wrapped heated smooth rocks and brought them to each bed. She settled the children around her, some on the bed, others on the floor and began to read. They listened, their eyes shining with the wonder of being able to hear their father's words even though he wasn't there. Through his letters they learned what he was thinking, how he was feeling, how much he missed the cove, and how much he loved them and their mother. It was down in print never to be washed away, unlike words he might say when he was home, words gone like a spent day.

After the children were in bed Elizabeth sat by the dwindling fire tatting a blanket on which to sew her family's names. Sometimes tiredness swept her away; she woke in the silence of a night half-spent and climbed the stairs to slip into bed alone.

When Jacob came home he walked in the door, his clothes soiled and his face unshaven.

"Your father's home," Elizabeth called. The children were in the back porch kneeling beside the wooden tub sailing Jamie's little boats. One child followed another in running to greet him. They moved back in a huddle, his look and scent different, his face grown over and scruffy, his blue eyes tired.

Elizabeth remembered when he'd worked in the Bell Island mines, the smell of iron ore on him as if its ochre dust had penetrated his pores. Now she smelled coal dust, saw its black traces under his fingernails.

The little boats were taken away and the wooden tub was put to Jacob's use. His hairy hands swirled water as fiercely as an easterly wind churning the sea in an Atlantic storm. Fob formed like spindrift around his ears. He lathered and shaved his stubbled face and cleaned under his nails with a paring knife. The coal dust grainting his pores would take weeks to work itself out.

Out in the front porch Elizabeth reached her knobbed hands to take down her washboard hanging beside yellow lace curtains. She laddered it against the washtub and dug into a Sunlight box, its dampened contents clumped by the sun's warm spread on the windowpane. She squeezed a berg into white dust, sprinkling it into the belly of her tub, and dropped her husband's clothes. She trounced the clothes and soapy water leaped in a swift swirl, its ivory curls soon beaten into a dark chocolate froth. She kneaded the clothes over the washboard. Then she slivered lye soap and rubbed at stubborn spots, her heart singing. Jacob was home. That's what mattered.

He'd brought an orange for each child and two for Elizabeth. A tangy scent filled the air as the children lifted their oranges from soft tissue paper. They rubbed the paper all over their faces, the zest of the fruit lingering on their skin long after the orange was eaten. Elizabeth saved an orange for Alvina.

"I've left Sydney mines for good," Jacob told Elizabeth. "Fish or no fish, we'll manage."

He didn't tell her that he had been advised by the company doctor to leave after he'd had several blackouts. The years he had spent in the iron ore mines, beginning when he was fifteen, the hauling of fishing nets, and then the coal mines, had taken their toll, straining his heart. Some men worked underground; others worked on the sea. Jacob had taken chances with both places and risked making Elizabeth a widow. At night Elizabeth drew Jacob close, her body as hungry as his. Spent, they lay in the darkness, their quickened heartbeats subsiding as they held each other and drifted into sleep, Elizabeth's fears of becoming a miner's widow ended.

After Jacob came home, they sat under a string of Christmas cards, including one from Maggie, Emily, and Olivia, only their names. No news. Elizabeth and Maggie now had a disjointed connection, their lives not only separated by a geographical distance but filled with their own families and their own religion. Neither woman had written for a while.

I should write, Elizabeth thought looking up at Maggie's Christmas card.

* * * * *

Jacob worked late into the night, in the days before Christmas, building a dollhouse, its front decorated like a castle. Two dolls he had bought in Sydney now sat together like sisters inside the dollhouse. When the dollhouse was opened on Christmas morning the two dolls had moved so close one head was leaning on the other doll's shoulder. Elizabeth smiled. "Like Elsie and Jane when they're tired."

"Or when Elsie is telling me a secret she doesn't want Doris and Sophie to know," Jane said.

Doris and Sophie each opened their Christmas box to find their first bought dresses: blue satin with pearl buttons. Golden tore the paper off a stuffed bear while James and Clayton found sleds sitting on the porch steps. "With steering gear to save you from the cliffs," their father said.

Jacob gave Elizabeth a bottle of perfume with a corked stopper and a jar of hand lotion. The skin on her hands drew tight after every washday and cracked in the cold air as she pegged articles to the clothesline during winter months. Jacob could do with lotion himself. After the layover on Sunday during the fishing season his hands were always stiff on Monday.

68

"You'll have to go on the stage and flakes this summer," Elizabeth told Elsie. "There's nothing else to be done. I can't risk losing this baby. I'll have enough to do with the household, the garden, and minding Golden."

Elsie raised her head from breakfast dishes she was washing. She nodded thinking it wouldn't be forever. She'd be gone from the place once she finished another year of school, gone away from the brackish smell of salt fish and fish flakes. She knew what her mother would say: The place you leave is the place you want to come home to.

One September day Alvina stood in the doorway of Elizabeth's kitchen, beads of sweat pooled in the spoon of her neck. She lifted the drooping peak of her bonnet and blew out a breath. "You could kill yourself trying to live in this place."

"Don't I know it," Elizabeth answered, settling her dough to rise, the fire kept in on this sweltering day. She smoothed her hand over her apron pocket bulging with peppermint knobs she kept for the children when they were indoors on a dirty day or on other days when she wanted them occupied. They each nursed their knob while she enjoyed the quiet.

Now she felt a tightness and let out a gasp. It was as good a time as any to give out the peppermints.

Alvina knew the sign of labour that passed over Elizabeth's face. She got her up to bed and soon her body was emptied of another child, Beulah Gwendlyn, born September 15, 1933. It was a joyful birth with hardly a push before the child let out a string of cries.

Alvina washed the squalling mite and wrapped her. Elizabeth pulled up her knees and leaned the swaddled baby, now quiet, against them. She wanted to remember the golden light of her hair, her squinted dark eyes, wrinkled skin fuzzy like a peach. She wanted to watch her skin unfold into smooth baby flesh and her eyes squeeze tight with a wail, hands with tiny fingers splayed one minute, fisted the next. She wanted to remember the baby's hand opening, reaching for hers.

Jacob had hurried up from the stage. He shaved and freshened his skin. Then he bounded up the stairs to see Elizabeth. There was a glow about her that he hadn't seen before.

My last baby! She knew it as sure as the day. Her journey through childbirth had ended with a baby girl. She looked at Jacob, then back to the baby as if to bind them together. A sob ripped through her. "How long will I have both of you?" The sound startled the baby and she let out a mewl.

Elizabeth's change was so sudden and unexpected that Jacob rushed to her side.

The midwife had come to check Elizabeth and the baby. She went to wash some of Elizabeth's bedclothes. She came back and saw Jacob trying to comfort his wife.

"It's the birth," the midwife explained. "She's forty-three and she's suffering the imbalance of emotion a birth can bring to someone her age. Give her time."

Elizabeth came back to herself, secure in having another healthy baby.

Beulah grew to be a cheerful child and a willing helper. And her hair! It was long, thick, and golden under a bright sun.

"Her mother's very heart, that child is," Jacob said, not knowing then how agony and ecstasy can knot and the knot untie leaving only agony.

Beulah and Golden were the only children at home. Beulah was off to school every day to learn her lessons while Golden had gone in the fishing boat.

Older children had left home and were married. When Elsie had gone to see her grandda years before she had taken notice of Fred Porter, one of the lads who had raided William's apple tree. Fred had no trouble marrying her and settling on the Maley homestead.

One evening as Jacob tidied up for Sunday Elizabeth gave his greying hair a critical look. "You're getting sprinkled," she said.

"And you, too," he answered.

"It's all the youngsters," they said in unison and laughed.

Elizabeth crooked her baby finger. "We said that together. Now we have to make a wish."

Jacob reached his finger and linked it with hers. "My wish is that we grow old together." A shadow crossed his face and he drew in a heavy breath.

Elizabeth pretended not to notice. *Who knows who God will take first!*

Jacob's face had grown slack, his girth widened under his bibbed overalls, suspenders stretched. That night he scuffed through the hall to the side room and took a small volume of poems from the shelf. He sat down on the settle by the kitchen stove and began to read a poem by Alfred, Lord Tennyson. His voice rose:

"Twilight and evening bell
And after that the dark,
And may there be no sadness of farewell
When I embark.

For tho' from out our bourne of Time and Place;
The flood may bear me far,
I hope to see my pilot face to face,
When I have crossed the bar."

He closed the book and smiled at Elizabeth. "If one goes first we will not part; each one will live in the other's heart."

"You've been readin' too much poetry, Jacob. It's spilling off your tongue in your own words."

Elizabeth had watched him in his prime, in stained coveralls and a lumberman's shirt covering a sinewy body as he sweated to harvest the sea and the land. No one knew all the words that kept building inside his head, all the words he tried to hold on to. In the garden under the sounds of the shovel beneath his calloused hands and on the sea, wet fishing twine running along his palms criss-crossing them with trenched lines that told the story of a fisherman's life, words were often swept into the wind. Those words now were not ones she wanted to hear. She pushed them aside and gave him an intent look. "There's no more children for us. Let's enjoy each other as fully as we can."

"So we will," he answered.

The next day Elizabeth walked down the path through the stage to the stagehead where James and Clayton were piling barrels. "Your father's not going fishing anymore. His legs isn't all that steady. If he fell overboard there'd be no way to haul him back in the boat, his frame so well filled out in his after years."

"We'll get his fish for the winter," James said.

"So do. And he'll help me with the gardens and give you your winter's crop."

Jacob, after writing letters to the government, got appointed as the paymaster on the Road Board. When the men working on the road came to his house for their pay they stayed around for a cuffer: telling ghost stories. Some people claimed to have seen the ghost of the *Southern Cross* on stormy nights. Others said that some relatives of the sealers had seen them walking on the waves, arms outstretched.

After Beulah and Golden listened to the stories they huddled together, afraid to go as far as the porch for a drink from the water bucket.

Elizabeth followed them upstairs to their beds and hushed them with a song. Soon they drifted past their fears.

On a Sunday the next spring Jacob didn't go to church. On Monday he got up from where he was sitting, a book about World War II in his hand. He looked through the window at a line of clothes Alvina had hung out. Elizabeth didn't answer when he mused, "One day clothes will be dried in a machine inside the house."

She didn't see him go to sit on the long bench between the table and the wall or notice his head fall to one side, his body leaning against the wall.

Beulah had just come home from school. "Pappa!" she exclaimed.

At the sound of her daughter's distress Elizabeth turned from the stove, where she was stirring a pot of soup. She lifted her apron to clear her steamed glasses. Jacob's mouth was open like the loose neck of a sock.

"Run as fast as you can and find your Uncle George," she told Beulah, who backed away as if unable to tear her eyes from the sight of her father speechless, his eyes wide open.

Elizabeth made their bed ready and George and James carried Jacob upstairs. He lay in bed like a useless junk. When he was lifted to a sitting position his unfocused eyes opened and when he was laid back on his pillow they closed.

That night Elizabeth lay beside him reaching her warm hand across his chest. She splayed her fingers over his heart. Under her fingertips she felt its unsteady thump. Her own heart lurched. *How long will you be with me?* She lifted her hand to his face, felt the rugged skin. Wind and sun had marked it well. She took his hand, criss-crossed with lines cut by trawl twine, his lifeline clearly defined. It would be easy for a fortune teller to read Jacob's hands and tell his past. *What of his future!*

By the end of three weeks Jacob's flesh had lost its blood supply on one side. The skin on his thighs looked scalded. One day, when Alvina was helping Elizabeth change him, the flesh came off and Elizabeth let out a wounded cry. Alvina pulled her away from seeing Jacob's once strong flanks in such a cruel shape. His strong legs in weathered breeches had held him steady while his boat, facing vexing winds, ploughed through swallowing seas. Now he was almost lifeless.

What is he thinkin'? Elizabeth wondered as she sat beside him. *Is he rememberin' the sea wild and wily? Is he thinkin' of me or is he taken with comin' face to face with God?* She hoped his mind wasn't blank, memory lost, taken as if by a great wave and knocked into a sea of forgetfulness. She stood and leaned to place her lips on his lips, soft and pale, drained of the passion that brought his body to life and helped bring their children into being.

"He's going, Elizabeth," Alvina warned.

Jacob's eyelids quivered and whispers of breath left his lips; then there was silence, the deepest silence of all. Elizabeth turned so suddenly she tripped against a sea chest by the wall. Alvina caught her hand. She shook it free and ran downstairs, her eyes dry and bright, lips apart in anguish.

She shouted, "Jake," his name echoing in her ears until her lungs ached. She collapsed on the settle staying there until her senses quietened. Then she climbed the stairs to sit by the bed holding Jacob's hand until it cooled. He was gone and death was a cold wind breathing down her neck.

Alvina came into the room and Elizabeth stood up. She gave her beloved Jacob over to Alvina to wash while she went downstairs. She took herself in hand and laid the flatiron on the stove. When it was heated she lowered it to Jacob's white shirt, the last one he would wear. She ironed it front and back as carefully as if he were wearing it for prayers, ironed it over and over. She brought it to Alvina.

Jacob lay in his coffin, as cold as winter clay, a man emptied of himself—his spirit gone. Instead of kissing him goodbye Elizabeth looked up and whispered, "Gone but not forever. I have the hope as sure as each sunrise that beyond the horizon we'll be together."

When it was time for the funeral she lifted a delicate, dark hairnet over her fingers like a cat's cradle, careful not to hook it on a fingernail. She reached her other hand under it and spread it over her head and down under hair rolled tight against her neck. She pressed a black felt hat with its slight lip on her head, its net shading her eyes. Beulah, her own blue eyes swimming in tears, held hatpins bunched in her hand like white balloons on metal strings. She passed them to her mother one at a time. Elizabeth pushed them into the sides of her hat to hold it against March winds. A pin pierced her scalp and she let out a sharp cry.

She stared at her face in the bureau mirror. She had been too busy to notice how far she had come from that wide-eyed slim girl Jacob had married. She looked at her hands and its brown spots. *I'm spoiling like an old apple.*

Growing old had not been real but now she saw herself as others must see her, as she saw people her age. It was as if the years from then, before she was married, to now had been swallowed whole.

"It's no distance from where you're at to where I is. One long dream and you'll be here." Her father's voice echoed from the past. It hadn't meant anything until now.

She leaned closer to the mirror. *I'm still in there, still young in spirit.* She lifted her chin and left the bedroom where Jacob had taken his last breath, in a bed that would hold only her from now on.

She looked through the upstairs hall window to the cold face of March. Snow still lay on the hills, soiled like sheets blown from a clothesline, dragged across the soggy brown earth and held down by large grey rocks. March was a cruel month. It took her brother, her cousins, her half-sister, and now it had taken her husband. She came downstairs and tucked her black-gloved hand in James's arm. They followed the white-runged, coal-black carriage holding Jacob's coffin stayed by fastening hooks. Above the coffin lay a wreath of paper flowers Beulah had made.

The minister's words at the end of his sermon lingered in Elizabeth's mind. "Our brother didn't go underground with his body. He was done with it." He paused and read from the Bible. "My flesh and my heart faileth: but God is the strength of my heart. . . ."

The spoked wheels whiled away Jacob's last day above the earth as the funeral procession made its way up over a hill and along a path to the white-fenced graveyard already awakening with the scent of heather and berry bushes. At the grave a cold wind beat into Elizabeth's face. She stared into the rectangular hole holding Jacob's coffin. *I can't imagine life without you.* She brushed away a tear. *No! That's the biggest lie I ever told. I can imagine life without you, without the scrape of the door latch liftin' under your hand, your footsteps on the floor, your place in our bed. The hole where your body is can't be as deep as the one I'm fallin' into.*

She felt Beulah's hand on her arm drawing her away. "I'm here, Mamma. I'll always be here," she said.

Elizabeth smiled believing her.

As Elizabeth and her family walked back down the cove Richard Newell, sitting on the rock wall, banged his pipe against a slate, sparks flying. "Jake's head's not aching now," he said, too low for Elizabeth to hear.

Elizabeth went on and he sat talking to his Newfoundland dog sitting beside him: "When Jacob's woman first come she was a slight thing to be climbing steep slopes holding the handles of a barrow of wet fish and while carrying youngsters in the kitte. I thought Jacob'd be wishing his cake dough. But they got on." He patted the dog and she wagged her tail.

At home, after the funeral, Alvina kissed Elizabeth's cheek and slid an arm around her shoulder. She sighed, "Oh my, Liz, what will you do now?"

"I'll sleep with a heated rock at me feet as I did before I had Jacob," she answered, determined to hold steady for the children's sake.

It wasn't that easy. Sleep came like an angel to take her away to a place of rest, only to bring her back to mornings when she woke stunned at the silence, Jacob's place beside her cold. She reached across the empty space as if to palm Jacob's back as she had often done, to feel his strong warm flesh gone now like an amputation. As days opened without him her need became a thirst, a hunger to lie with him in their bed, her cheek against his beating heart. He had gone not for a day in the boat or for months in a coal mine but forever. She wished she had loved him more instead of hurrying to a task.

She parted the curtains and stared out at the boat on collar looking as lonely as a horse without a rider. She might have known he was going, the way his heart failed him as he walked up the path these last months, the way he shuffled through the hall in his slippers.

Later, when the path to the graveyard dried and a headstone was in place she visited Jacob's grave. Her voice was soft: "Your body lies in the darkness of the earth but your life'll spring in new beginnin's. Our offspring will ride the sea you loved and be smacked by its salty kiss." She leaned in to touch the headstone. "We were happy to the end—your end. Mine will take longer."

At home she took a notebook from the bookcase and read something Jacob had written in heavy strokes under the title. "Our Family Tree: The tree embodies our growth, strength, continuity. From it is carved the cradle that holds our newborn children, the shelter that houses our family, the boat from where our livelihood is harvested, the box that holds us when we die, and when our generation passes the tree records our history in books created out of it."

"Ah, Jacob. Maybe someone will write our history. What a story that will make. Our lives will get to be lived twice."

All through the summer months after Jacob's death Elizabeth took down a china cup and saucer for her tea, a wedding gift she favoured. Bright blue flowers decorated the gold-rimmed, milky-white cup and sauce. She loved how the handle crooked as if it were the white arm of a woman waiting for a lover to link his arm in hers. She slipped her finger into the handle and lifted the cup to her lips. Steam rose like a warm breath, the tea a comforting kiss. She sat sipping her tea, a smile playing on her lips. She recalled how Jacob could make their children feel good about themselves. When Clayton was a boy he had asked his mother, "Ma, is I a common boy?"

Her brow had furrowed. "Why would you ask that?"

"Because," he said, "yesterday the teacher's wife was out on her doorstep calling, 'Reggieee. Come home. It's suppertime.' We were all together in the dark and she couldn't quite make out Reg at first. When she did she said, 'Oh, Reggie, I thought you were one of the common boys.'

"Am I common?" he asked.

Jacob, sitting on the settle reading *Reader's Digest*, lifted his head. He answered in a nettled voice. "There's two kinds of education, son. One a person gets from books. The other one is got by doing. Ask Reggie's father how to tell tomorrow's weather by observing the sky. Ask him how to build a boat, sed a trawl hook, make a coffin, or sandals for his son's feet. What makes a person common and what makes another person think he is above the common person is attitude. If you feel less than other people you won't make more of yourself. Even a king's got to lower himself to sit on a common throne—like everyone else."

Jacob had looked up and smiled, as if he could see an outhouse with a king sitting on its seat.

Elizabeth laid down her cup, satisfied that though life was short memory was long. The children would remember Jacob as a wise father.

The second summer after her father died Beulah got baptized in the Ship Cove pond. People lined the banks and the roads as converts went through the waters while Missioners sang, an accordion playing, "Where He leads me I will follow. . . ."

A few weeks later, on a warm summer day, Beulah and Clarice, her best friend, were walking down around Ship Cove pond. They were now proud young Canadians, Newfoundland having joined the Canadian federation only a few months before.

The southerly wind glancing off the pond suddenly changed to an upwind turning the waves around. Beulah felt a chill when the easterly wind struck her chest. A day after, she wasn't feeling well. She moped about, sewed a little, read a book. She came out on the doorstep to look up at her mother and aunt spreading fish on the flakes. She had no energy to help them. Golden taunted her: "Mind you don't come out and catch your death."

He flicked her at every turn and mocked her. The more Elizabeth scolded him the fiercer he got. When he came in from the fishing stage to scoop a dipper of cold water from the bucket he goaded her: "Get off the settle and go out on the fish flakes."

Days passed and Beulah lay around, no better. When she took to her bed Golden passed her door and called, "Get some muscles in your spit. You're just puttin' on."

Elizabeth lifted her daughter's damp, hot body, her hand under the slim neck, blonde hair dangling. She put water to her lips thinking, *Tomorrow she'll be better from this flu. She'll smile and make a smack at Golden for teasin' her about lyin' around.*

The next day Elizabeth nodded when Golden, his voice thick with guilt, said, "She'll need to have the doctor, Ma." He had masked a fear gathering inside him, a quiet fear emanating from his mother. Death had come to claim his father. Who was to say it wouldn't be back?

Fishermen at The Tell commiserated about the latest sickness.

"You'd think Elizabeth would've had Dr. Pritchett before now," Richard Newell said.

Dr. Pritchett, a tall man in a black hat, had come to the cove frequently to pull children's tonsils. George had become acquainted with him during little Nellie's illness. When he learned that Dr. Pritchett was going around taking out children's tonsils he had offered his table for him to perform surgery on his young patients.

Silas Bishop flicked ash from his pipe. "I minds the time the doctor come as large as life, a big black satchel in his hand, a black hat to match, to take out the tonsils of the cove children. Ever so many lost their tonsils that time, when all they needed was a bit of kerosene boiled with molasses." He laughed and nodded toward a two-storey house. "I remember one young maid being flung over her father's shoulder and she dressed in only her boots and nightgown kicking and screaming. When her father put her down in George's porch Newman, George's boy, whispered, 'The doctor's goin' cut dee t'roat.' Well, didn't she bolt! The poor maid barrelled out the door and up over the cliffs and the night dark as tarry pitch."

Sandy Porter said, "The doctor yanked out our Dotty's tonsils. Afterwards she complained that she couldn't hear well. Who would have thought it! The doctor tampered with her throat and her ears took offence."

"I didn't know that a man like George, who believes in divine healing, would allow Dr. Pritchett into his house to do the likes of that to a child," Silas said.

"'Tis all done," said Richard. "That's fer sure, and sometimes for no good reason."

Dr. Pritchett came to see Beulah twice. On his second visit he lifted her leg and she winced. His voice was grave as he gave instructions for her to be sent by ambulance to the General Hospital in St. John's.

"Sure, that's practically unheard of," Alvina told Aunt Pace. "It can't bode well."

"Elizabeth's prayers should have had the maid better by now,"

Aunt Pace said. "Jesus raised Jairus's young maid and she was more than sick. She was dead. I'll join the mission meself if Beulah gets well."

The night before Beulah was taken to the hospital she smiled and spoke to the laymen who came to pray for her. She thanked them for their prayers and said good night in a strong voice.

Those who didn't believe in mixing faith with human doctoring suggested to Elizabeth that Beulah should be left alone to wait for divine healing. "If God could make us He can cure us—or take us if it's His will," one said piously.

Elizabeth, trying to keep the anger from her voice, answered in an even tone. "You need'n think I'm waterin' down me faith by sendin' Beulah to the hospital. Luke, one of Jesus's disciples, was a physician."

Willis Lear gave her a perturbed look. "That was before he followed Jesus. After that Jesus did the doctoring."

After the laymen left, Alvina squeezed Elizabeth's arm. "Pay no heed to other people's words. I'm sure God won't turn down a little help. George didn't mind a'tall that people gossiped about him lettin' the doctor operate in our house."

Under a flake, that reached from one shed across the road at the foot of Porter Hill to a shed by the beach, fishermen sat on logs used to roll a newly built boat down to the beach, where it was pushed into the water. The flake shaded the men peering out under bibbed caps as they waited for news. They knew that over the hill, across Cliff Path, a beautiful young girl lay deathly ill. The men cast uneasy looks that way. A silent prayer rose to the heavens as they sat quietly while the ambulance passed taking Beulah away.

Monday afternoon, Elsie and Fred drove to the General Hospital in St. John's to see Beulah after nurses had settled her in a hospital bed. Elizabeth stayed in Foxtrap.

"First along, Ma thought she had the summer flu," Elsie told the doctor.

He shook his head and asked a few questions. Then he wrote in his file. Before leaving he left orders with the nurses for Beulah's medication.

Elsie told her sister, "I'll read you a story from our Sunday School paper, *The Gleaner*."

Beulah smiled, her voice faint. "Can you begin at the end and stop there? I'm tired."

"You got the Maley sense of humour, that you do," Elsie replied.

Elizabeth was startled when she heard the diagnosis: spinal meningitis.

The news reached families in Hibb's Cove creating a polarization of opinions.

"She should have been left in God's hands," some people said.

"She needs to be in the doctor's care," others said.

There were thoughts they wouldn't voice, not then. Later.

Elsie tiptoed into her sister's room on Friday daring to hope for improvement after doctors drained fluid off her spine. She came home telling Elizabeth that doctors were taking good care of Beulah.

On Saturday Beulah hardly spoke. That afternoon she reached into the air, her tired blue eyes opening wide, and exclaimed, "What beautiful flowers!" She let out a gentle breath and was gone.

Beulah lay in her coffin in Elizabeth's drawing room. She wore a white dress that Elsie had picked out. Fresh white daisies decorated a mane of golden tresses flowing down her bosom almost to her folded hands. It was only as Elizabeth looked on the still face of her daughter that she felt her limbs let go. James held her up.

Now, little more than two years after Jacob's death, Elizabeth walked through the mission graveyard above the sea. She passed little picket fences around small graves, white cradles inside with glass covers over dried flowers on the grass-blanketed earth that covered her babies. She moved past the painful scene telling herself, *My babies left only their bodies; they're in heaven.*

She walked to her husband's grave to put their youngest child beside him. Her rigid stance and stony look belied her feelings. There was no comfort in other people's words, no softening of her despair as Alvina and others hugged her. Their words fell like weeds crisped by a hot sun.

Elizabeth was deaf to a hymn wafting in the heavy air: "Will your anchor hold in the storms of life when the wild winds blow. . . ." She was adrift under a blind eye on a dark sea, her faith like a boat in a storm whose anchor had let go.

She touched Jacob's headstone. It was true what he had read in *Reader's Digest*: "Living is like licking honey from a thorn."

She came home and climbed the stairs feeling as if the house holding her had been blown away by a vicious wind and she was left huddled, her head against her knees, trying to hold on, trying not to be picked up and blown out to sea.

69

Elizabeth went to the bookcase and took out Jacob's grandfather's Bible. She held it between trembling fingers. Printed in 1813, it looked like a brick that had come out of a wall, its brown cover rough and blistered and its uneven brittle pages yellowed, their edges like something scorched. When she opened the Bible, pages against the spine showed gaps. String threaded through the sheets had frayed in places and broken away from the binding. She had taken a snippet of Beulah's blonde hair, braided it, and tied it with a blue satin ribbon. Now she slipped it between the pages of the book of Job.

Elizabeth looked upwards, her words bitter. "You got the rest of her. I'm keepin' this bit of her hair."

She touched a tiny, crisp four-leaf clover and wondered what kind of luck the person who placed it there had been looking for and what kind of luck had been found. Touching stained pages she pondered on the tears that had fallen on the old book. What sorrows had caused them! She laid the Bible aside and went to sit in her rocking chair, a chair that had been a rest for her arms while she held her babies. She remembered her time downstairs with Beulah while everyone else was asleep upstairs. Her baby's bright eyes had sparkled like gems in the flickering firelight of the stove grate, her long-lashed eyelids growing heavy with sleep, her breathing gentle. Now Beulah was a flower whose petals had closed around its heart for the night. She had to believe that it would open on a new day in a new world where roses never faded.

She recalled Jacob reading from Sirach in the common Bible he'd bought from a peddler: "Like a drop of water from the sea and a grain of sand, so are a few years in the day of eternity."

"Why am I here?" The words seemed to float out of her one day.

Alvina heard them and hurried to answer. "You came here to be with Jacob."

"No, why am I here on this earth?"

Alvina turned her face away. She was unable to answer. Beulah's death had unstitched the wound cut into her when Nellie died. She opened the door and went out. She walked up the path to her house, her feet heavy. George came into the house. He faced her drawn look with blunt words. "There's talk."

She looked at him puzzled. "Talk? About what?"

"About what really happened to Beulah. People's sayin' she took sick from havin' been baptized in water."

Alvina looked at him over her glasses. "And what about Edith Mercer in Bareneed? Sure, she had meningitis and she never went near the water."

"Your mother's down in her mind," Alvina told Elsie, in a letter, as she watched her sister-in-law standing on the barren windswept cliff and looking across the sea, the pathway to her childhood home.

Cove people's criss-crossing voices reverberated through Elizabeth's head, chiding, accusing, building a storm inside her: ". . . lack of faith to take her to the doctor. . . . She should have left Beulah to divine providence . . . letting that child go in the water and be dipped. For sure it killed her."

Accusing voices repeated like a flat stone skipping over water breaking its surface while Elizabeth sat at the table holding a letter stating that Beulah had passed the exams in her last year of high school. She laid down the letter and sat at the table, her fists holding up her chin.

For the first time she felt lifeless and gutted like a fish housed in the darkness of the fishing stage.

In a dream that night a woman from an ancient time walked toward her. "I'm Job's wife," she said.

Elizabeth nodded. "I know."

"You do?"

"I can tell by your angry look that you were ignored in your suffering."

Job's wife looked relieved. "I don't hold with mothers losing children so fathers can pass a test whose outcome God already knows and Satan got no business knowing. Job scratched his sores, worsening them, and I ready with salve to relieve his itching. For all that he's the upright one. Well, he didn't look too upright sitting on the ground and I left alone to mourn the loss of our children, grief so searing I felt skinned from my toes to my skull."

The woman's hand went to her breast. "There, I've said it."

"You have a right to speak what's in your heart," Elizabeth said.

Job's wife sighed. "Still, before I can accuse God of taking what was His all along," she said, "I must thank Him for the family He gave me, if only for a time."

Elizabeth woke in the darkness of the night. Her lips formed the words *and I must thank Him for giving Beulah to me for sixteen years.*

Jacob's voice, echoing Job's words, swept through her as if her husband were still alive: *His candle shined up on my head . . . by his light I walked through darkness.*

part seven

70

From her upstairs window Elizabeth looked out into the bay and across the ocean to the Southern Shore. Jacob's love had brought her to Hibb's Cove. Beulah's death would release her from it and its foreboding cliffs, their cragged faces lifted over the deathly cold waters of the Atlantic. She'd go back home to her father's gentle land—her land.

She faced herself in the mirror. She had come to this place not knowing what to expect, not thinking that after ever so many years her face would be lined, her eyes fading behind wired glasses, and her body spent like those of grandmothers up over the hill—like Sarah Ann's. But the young girl had not gone so far down a back lane that she couldn't reach and pull her back. She was her again, every time she looked at Jacob and her in their photograph. *I'm still a young girl inside, not this aged grandmother who's not strong enough to bear whatever comes against her.*

She dropped to her knees letting her head and arms rest on the featherbed. There was comfort in letting go of her body's heaviness. She tried to cast her burden on God.

Elsie came to visit her mother. "Come away from yourself," she urged. "You can't get back what you've lost. Let it be as it is. Otherwise, your mind'll be a whirlpool of what-ifs every mornin' when you stir from sleep."

She accepted Elsie's urging to come home and stay with her. They went by train and Fred came in his truck to get them from the station.

He didn't say much on the way home and, when they arrived, Elsie took her mother's arm and led her along the path holding tight as they went inside. "You'll have a hot cup of tea now and tomorrow we'll see what the doctor says."

She sat down on the settle and gave her daughter a straight look. "I've been quakin' inside and now I'm gone to pieces. The whole lot of us is like a crowd on a beach watchin' the sun come up and go down, watchin' tides ebb and flow, death takin' one of us away from another day and we never knowin' who'll be next. I'd be grateful if it'd take me now."

"Now, now," Elsie said. "The doctor'll get rid of this talk and remind you there's still joy to be had and pleasure to be spent."

Elizabeth had lost her girlish laughter, boxed, it seemed, inside her daughter's coffin. The bright-eyed clear look she had carried for so long was gone. Sorrow had been strained through a voice that once could ring as clear as a bell. Her eyes were misty as she sat drinking a cup of hot tea and staring at the tea cloth on the table that her mother had made. She ran her finger over an embroidered forget-me-not.

Elsie gave her mother a bedroom facing the old homestead and orchard. It had occupied a smaller space than she remembered. Her hand trembled as it closed over the back of a wicker chair. She leaned to take a look at the place where her father's house once stood. It was as if the house had never been, except for its shadowy imprint left on the pressed yellow grass beneath it.

"The house had to come down," Fred said.

Until then she hadn't thought of that ever happening. The house was the box that held her childhood and the images of her and her family. Now there was only an empty space, as if her father and mother and brother had never existed—as if her time there was only a dream. She had not been there to notice the wood eaten out by weather and age. The shelves with their few dishes had lain under dust. Death itself had stolen in through the air, its breath foul and potent taking Mary Jane and William. The ground William had turned with laboured breath and slackened muscles was nature's to do with as she willed. Grass and weeds crept up along the path. Among them evening primroses and boy's love nodded in a breath of wind. Tiger lilies leaned straggly—spent. A bumblebee droned among them. Morning glory vines that had trailed the picket fence now crept inside the opening in a window frame of a leaning old shack soon to crumble from a strong wind.

The landscape along the lane had changed. Familiar fences had disappeared. Her Aunt Caroline and Uncles Joe and Johnny had died. Their empty house was now boarded up. The faces of people Elizabeth had known as a girl were old; there were unfamiliar young faces. The young people knew nothing about the girl she was and the older people might not recognize the woman she'd become. She felt displaced.

Whenever a tree branch scraped against Fred and Elsie's house like the fingers of a ghost Elizabeth thought about how, on the night the *Southern Cross* disappeared, Jamie sent back the Labrador box.

Away from Hibb's Cove she dreamed she was tumbling over dark cliffs. She woke just before she reached the turbulent sea. A cliff was not a safe place on which to live. Neither was her mind a safe place for her thoughts. Her heart felt ready to break and drop her into the depth of nothingness.

Sometimes she wished it would.

The doctor gave Elizabeth a keen look and spoke to Elsie as if Elizabeth were deaf and dumb.

As if I'm not even here.

"What's her history?"

"Going back?"

"Yes, as far as you know."

"She had no real sisters, just two half-sisters and a half-brother. She lost her only brother, Jamie, on the *Southern Cross*. No doubt you heard of its sinking."

He nodded. "Indeed. Yes. A terrible calamity. And after that?"

"Then she lost a child."

Elizabeth looked up and Elsie hastened to add, "Twin boys, one stillborn, the other three days old, and later she lost an unborn daughter."

"And that was difficult?" he asked. Then, taking in Elizabeth's set face, he said, "I shouldn't have said that. Go on."

Elsie said, "She lost her husband almost suddenly and less than two years later Beulah, her sixteen-year-old, died in a short time of spinal meningitis. So much suddenness. . . . Other than that nothing much happened." She leaned forward. "Still, it seems she's spent all her optimism, Doctor, used it all up on one sorrow or another."

Elizabeth's look drifted. "I had to live with a graveyard in me backyard, its headstones leaning toward the kitchen window. No wonder death got into me house."

There was a moment of silence while the doctor scrutinized Elizabeth. "You know," he said gently, "a place is only where your body resides; your body is where you live. You have to do whatever it takes to keep it happy."

He bent toward his papers and began to write a prescription. "I'll give her medication to settle her nerves." He passed the prescription to Elsie. "Be patient. It could take a couple of weeks."

Elizabeth's eyes sparked. "And then I suppose I'll be dancing on me husband's grave."

"Well, Ma," Elsie said, "the way you're going, if you don't take charge you'll be in his grave."

"Is it so wrong to love your daughter so much that when she perishes you don't want to live?" Alvina had asked Elizabeth after Nellie died.

Now it was Elizabeth's turn to ask that question. She asked it silently.

Elizabeth came back to Elsie's home with a bottle of pills in all colours like decorations named hundreds and thousands used to decorate a cake. "How many grains of happiness can one bottle hold?" she said sarcastically.

"Now, Ma, it's not like that."

"No, it's not. Happiness is not in a bottle."

She scrutinized a copy of her and Jacob in a photo on a shelf in Elsie's parlour. She ran her gnarled hand over it. "When you're young you take a good picture. When you're old your face is shrivelled like the rind of an apple fallen to the ground, left to rot among yellow leaves."

"Don't think that a'tall, Ma," Elsie said. "Your face is a road map reflecting all the places you've been, in your body and in your heart. Yours isn't so bad. I ran into your old friend Maggie a while ago. She's thin as a skiver. She asked about you and said she was sorry you hadn't kept in touch."

Elizabeth nodded. Maggie was a faint memory and she herself like a frozen rag hung above a clothesline, not feeling anything and not caring about anyone or anything.

One morning she dragged herself off the sofa telling herself, *You have to survive your feelings. You have to survive your circumstances. You have to survive. You have to. You have you.*

She pulled on a sweater over her flowered dress and walked down the path to the beach where the stagehead once stood. She saw the children as if it were today. Jamie, Noah, Zachary, Maggie, Laura, Olivia, Emily—the beach children. Early in June one year they discovered a nest holding five tiny white eggs behind a barrel in a corner of the stage. A mother bird flew up startling them as they raced through the stage. Every day they watched for the eggs to break open under the beaks of babies wanting to get out. Then one day there they were, like a miracle, five babies nestled against each other, necks stretched, beaks open. Every morning the children raced down to the stage stopping all together as they came close, fingers against their lips. They listened for the clear whistle of the chickadee and then the flutter of wings and the tiny *chip-chip* of baby chickadees as the mother brought food, one dangling, tiny, green grub at a time. Her head darted from side to side and, sensing no danger, she darted inside. The father chickadee took his turn. One morning the children raced each other to the beach and to the stage. They stopped in their tracks. The familiar sound had disappeared. A lone chickadee perched on the nest. It flew away and its noise was a constant repetition: *Chick a dee-dee-dee.* The children drew closer to the nest, their faces peering down. The birds were gone. High in the sky they noticed a bald eagle. They looked at each other. The sound of silence was louder than the sea rush, louder than a mother bird's call to one of her babies. The sound of silence was deeper than any sound they had ever heard.

"Why did this happen?" Elizabeth had asked her father.

"Nature has a generous heart but a brutal hand," he said. "You'll understand later."

She understood now. Her arms had often grown heavy and unbearably tired as she carried a sleeping child up the lane to the house but never as heavy as the load her heart carried with the loss of her husband and children, a load she could never put down.

She stood silently now, tears as salty as the sea that took her brother streaming down her face.

After nights of waking to the darkness of early morning and unable to get back to sleep one morning she murmured, "I'm tired, so tired." The words *God caused a deep sleep to fall on Adam* echoed through her mind.

"Do the same for me, God," she prayed, "but don't take a rib."

Sleep drifted over her like a fog. She woke, amazed that night had passed and brilliant sunlight filled her room. She remembered her words, funny in the light of day, and a giggle bubbled through her throat. Her laughter rang out like a warm stream caught under ice, now breaking free.

She looked up. "I'm not alone, after all."

It was then that a tiny seed of faith stirred. It pushed its leaves up through her stony heart and flowered.

71

Yesteryears became a dream for Maggie. She sat in her rocking chair watching her daughter-in-law knead a pan of dough. She punched, stretched, and folded it before covering it and placing the pan on the table, the same as Maggie used to do.

"I live here. Sure, you know it's my house," she told the young bride.

"I suppose," the woman said in a mocking voice. She shrugged as if there was no more to be said about it.

Maggie had raised sons and other women got the use of them. Her youngest son had brought his woman to take over her house and have children just when she had come to peace and quiet. She got pushed into a rocking chair with a bawling baby she could hardly hold for tiredness, her bones seizing up. The daughter-in-law didn't even suppose she had dreams of how she'd like to spend a day. Women shouldn't give up their place easily. Why should they? Turning into a crotchety old woman was the least Maggie could do. The loss of her place in her own home was not an easy loss. A daughter-in-law thought this was her house and wanted things done her way. *Well, let her sweat and toil and build her own place and leave me to mine. She thinks all I'm doin' is waitin' to die. Well, I like waitin'.*

A stranger came to visit her. The slender woman, with green eyes like her own, leaned down and in a calm voice said, "I'm wondering why you sent your children to an orphanage."

Maggie gave the woman a puzzled look. Then her throat felt caught like a fish in the square of a net dragged through icy waters. She found enough breath to answer: "To save their lives." She grabbed hold of the stranger's hand and pulled her closer. She smiled hopefully. "You're my girl."

The woman spoke slowly, as if she were stepping carefully to avoid puddles that might splash and soil a white dress. "It's been a long time since I thought that," the daughter answered, letting her hand lie limp in her mother's. "I'm Gladys."

A tear slipped down Maggie's cheek. "The loss of my children is a thorn I still carry."

There was a pause and then her daughter said quietly, "I never thought of you suffering through your children's absence. Children think only of how it feels to be given up. I was too angry with you for sending me to a place where I was treated in a bad way."

"Tell me," Maggie said, her voice shaky.

Gladys shook her head. "It's not something to be talked about. You have a granddaughter out of my trouble."

"I didn't know what was expected of a mother. I grew up without one," Maggie said. "I wanted you and the other children to be properly fed and cared for."

Her look drifted. "The day I left you at the orphanage I wanted to lift each of your hands and press a kiss into your palms and tell you to hold on to it until I saw you ag'in. I hesitated and then when I lifted my hand to blow you a kiss your backs were turned. I stopped, knowin' it would be like scattering flower seed into a wind blowin' the other away." Her words clotted in her throat, then broke free in a hoarse whisper. "I didn't deserve to give you my love, not when I was givin' you away."

"You didn't give all of us away."

"Choices were not made easily," she answered.

Gladys gave Maggie a defiant look and straightened up. "I grew up thinking that someone who loved me would not have given me away. Goodbye, Mother," she said.

She left without a backward glance, the door slamming shut behind her.

Maggie could still feel her daughter's warm hand in hers. She brought her hands together as if to hold the touch and warmth of a hand she hadn't held for a long time. *At least she called me Mother. She'll be back.*

Elizabeth had been in Foxtrap with Elsie, Fred, and their two children a few years when Maggie came to see her. They hugged and Maggie gave Elizabeth a steady look. "You've changed a little. We both have."

They talked for a while, Elizabeth saying, "You had a generous heart. It made room for two men. Both of us have faced losses."

"We have been strong and stubborn," Maggie said. "When I was a young girl I wouldn't have believed I could live through so much heartache."

Elizabeth smiled. "For a time I didn't think I would. After a while grief stepped to one side. I had a lift in spirit when I held the grandchildren on me knees. Nelson, Elsie's boy, is Jamie on the spot! Still, now and ag'in, grief comes like a bully to yank on my heart and pull me back until I almost lose me balance. I try to enjoy little things: a cup of tea and cranberry loaf, a visit from a grandchild, a ride in Fred's truck to the St. John's rummage sales. God allowed me to keep seven children. I was blessed to have had so much to lose."

Maggie said, "You've done a lot of surviving. We've done a lot of surviving."

Elizabeth smiled. "And it's not over yet."

Maggie put her hand to her head and Elizabeth touched her friend's hand and asked, "Is yer ill, Maggie?"

Maggie managed a weak smile. "Sometimes me mind's not very handy to me. I told the doctor there's something wrong with me head. It feels logy and one of my legs loses its strength. He waved away my concerns. 'Old age, my dear ma'am. Old age.'

"'That's funny,' I said. 'The other leg is the same age and there's nothing wrong with it.' Then he suggested I go into an old-age home. I told him that I know people who's half dead. When they go into an old people's home the other half dies."

Maggie's throaty laugh mingled with Elizabeth's girlish laugh—an echo from a long time ago.

72

Elizabeth went back to the cove. Larger fishing boats were being built and women were still doing their own work and helping their husbands do theirs on the stagehead, in the stage and on the flakes. Women had always risked their lives giving birth, growing a family, and men had always risked their lives to net fish, sustaining the family. It was the way of the world.

She remembered when Jacob had been the first man in the cove to wire their house for electricity. At first, a bare light hung from their kitchen ceiling, lighting the whole room with the pull of a chain. It looked like the sun had been brought inside in a glass. Like magic! Now every house had electric lights. An electric light shone from a pole above Cliff Path. At night it cast a ghostly glow on the water, shadowing cliffs and beaches and collared boats. It shadowed Elizabeth's house.

Alvina and George's imminent deaths shadowed their house on the hill. Elizabeth listened to the sounds of the sea breathing through the darkness as she walked up the hill. Her in-laws lay dying, one curled against the other in the deep trench of their featherbed.

Day after day Elizabeth watched them sink low, eaten out by cancer until they were tiny, like children hiding under quilts from a malevolent presence. There would be no more leaning over Elizabeth's fence for sister-in-law chats, no more hearty interchanges between George and other cove fishermen. They were done of that. When a chicken crowed instead of a rooster one morning everyone knew it was time.

That night George murmured to Alvina, "You'll be gone in the mornin'."

By daybreak she had passed away. She was laid out and dressed and when mourners viewed her in the coffin they exclaimed, "How fresh and young she looks! The best we've ever seen her." Alvina would have been pleased.

By the time mourners returned from her funeral George was gone.

"They might have made the one job of it," someone said.

"I never expected to die," Alvina had murmured when she was pining away. "I always thought The Rapture would take me. That was a wonderful thing to hope for. I believed it with me whole heart. Sister Garrigus believed it, too. Yet she died."

"It's not meant for us to understand," Elizabeth had said. "Hold to the hope of eternal life."

After George's funeral Elizabeth sat on the wood locker under the kitchen window facing the house on the hill. She smiled. It hadn't been all bad. There was play in work women do for those they love. She climbed the stairs and sat looking through the window. She watched little boats move toward the cove under the glass eyes of windows sheened in evening light. The night drifted in and still she stayed.

She gathered her memory quilt from a chair beside her and slipped it over her knees. The pieces in a quilt were like crumbs strewn in the winding path of memory lane warding off fairies of forgetfulness. In the heart of the quilt was a square of Victor's white flannel gown and on the other side, heart to heart, was a square of white bunting for his twin unnamed. For the unborn daughter, she had placed a piece of cloth imprinted with pink forget-me-nots. She had placed several squares from Beulah's dress: a field of pink gilly flowers in one square, a solid white square beside it, and then a patch of daisies. Other inside squares were pieces from her living children's petticoats, dresses, aprons, shirts, and ties. She saved the corner squares for a piece of clothing from Jacob, Jamie, and her mother and father. Her other quilts would lie in the closets and on the beds of her children and grandchildren as they grew in the continuity of change and loss.

Elizabeth was tall and full-fashioned and dignified in her old age, as if she had sailed through life on the most agreeable seas. "A full skiff of a woman," Jacob would say. She walked erect moving as stately as a ship coming into a calm harbour. Long, lean fingers, cut from the same pottery as her mother's, lifted to pin strands of loose hair tight against her head with clips that sometimes lost their hold and pinged to the floor. Strands of white hair strayed from her hairnet. Her feet seemed large, now that her body was smaller, turning away from each other as if one was going one way and the other another to avoid that straight path toward death.

When she sat at the table she never leaned toward her food. She always lifted it to her. John, her grandson, said, "If Gran didn't have an elbow she'd starve."

Sometimes she sat in her rocking chair and looked at her hands and arms. The veins under her paper-thin skin looked like dusty-blue wool strands, her knuckles as hard as doorknobs after a lifetime scrubbing clothes on glass-roped washboards. Her skin had stretched and wrinkled making papery patterns like a calm pond over which a soft wind had stolen, crinkling its waters. She brought out the snapshot of Jacob and her in their prime. How lovely their skin was! How firm, their eyes bright and unclouded, full of love and expectation under defined brows, lips plump, unlined. Jacob had a full head of hair and hers was silky and heavy. Her mind was not what it used to be either. Sometimes when she went to say someone's name it drifted away like smoke and came back hours later. "I've got it!" she'd say, amazed that a name she wasn't even thinking of had pushed its way past other thoughts and asserted itself.

Death had sent Elizabeth many warnings that she wasn't here forever. It was going to get even more personal. *Not yet, please God. There are grandchildren I'm waiting to see and every day there's a bit of gossip to chew on with a visit from the church ladies.*

The bright young faces of her grandchildren came close and she got the scent of new life, felt the energy coursing through their bodies, quickening her own life for a moment. Their limbs were supple and lively, unlike Elizabeth's. Hers were dry as sticks and unbending but she'd had her day, a long day. She remembered the energy that gave her tired body a spark while she worked to keep her children nourished. Now she was like a day with its evening shadows falling. The world looked dimmer, details smeared. Only a few grains were left in the hourglass. She'd not want to tip it back up and start again.

Her minister's words from a Sunday's sermon echoed: "There's an end to human life for all of us; how it comes and when it comes remains a mystery. The ending to this physical story is the beginning of a spiritual one."

73

Back in Foxtrap Elizabeth answered her grandchildren's letters . . . *you can have one of my patchwork quilts. Indeed you can. People today don't take time to make quilts. They buys a blanket for five dollars to give as a wedding gift. No thought is put into it. A homemade quilt is like homemade bread. Everyone wants to have it without having to make it. That's the way of today's world. love gran*

She thought of her grandchildren wrapping themselves in her quilts without visualizing the steps taken in piecing the clothing into it, a shirt worn by her late husband, his warmth and scent remembered, the dresses she had worn over a pregnant belly, the baby clothes. . . . They would not realize the labour it took.

She licked the envelopes, closed them, and laid them on the chair under her bum to make sure they sealed. She got up leaving the letters.

Elsie scolded her: "My, look what you've done, forgotten your letters."

Your turn is coming, she wanted to say but she didn't. No need to remind her of something she'd find out soon enough.

Nelson took Elizabeth to visit Maggie now at an old-age home. Maggie, her thinning hair in a bun, nodded as she pushed her swollen feet through the hall to the sound of voices. She mumbled from the effects of a slight stroke. "I'm waitin' for the birds to come and give their song to old ears."

Elizabeth asked in an unsteady voice, "Do you still think of Jamie?"

Memories came like layers of water over the deep mountains under the ocean. As soon as one memory came and before Maggie could hold on to it another washed over it, waves of memory layering each other, dark and deep as dreams darting against the edges of her consciousness through a dark night. She lifted eyes, bright and watery, her voice trembly. "He's a dream I once had."

"Someone is here to see you," Elizabeth said.

Nelson, Elsie's son, came into the room and Maggie turned. She straightened her housecoat around her thin shoulders and put out her hand. She caught hold of the young fellow's hand and her voice came strong. "It's Jamie off the water. We'll be married now."

"That's not him a'tall. That's Elsie's boy. That's who owns him," the caregiver told her.

Elizabeth nodded. "For sure, he's got the smoky grey eyes of his uncle. Anyone knows that Jamie won't be dead as long as Nelson's alive."

Maggie's face clouded and she stared, uncertain. Nelson took her hand and goosebumps ran down her spine. A great sense of relief filled her. *It's him, for sure.* She smiled.

The caregiver took her arm. "Come and lie down now."

"Indeed," she said. Her eyes lit up like a young girl's. She went toward her room glancing back as she went. *He did come back.*

"She's been wandering off in her mind lately," the caregiver told Elizabeth. "Snatches of memories from a long time ago take hold of her. Emily Penny came to see her last week. You likely remember her. She's from your time."

Elizabeth smiled. "She was one of the children on the beach when I was a child."

The caregiver nodded. "That one did well for herself, married the merchant she worked for after his wife destroyed herself. She raised a foundling as her own, a child stolen by peddler Swartz. You remember him, most likely. He was always on the go selling sundries. He confessed on his deathbed, lightened his soul before he passed on to favour or condemnation, whatever the Master saw fit to show him."

"I knew him faintly," Elizabeth said. "I was half-grown the first time he descended on the place selling lotions and soaps and whatnot."

"'Tis everything done and not all good," said the caregiver.

"And everything that seems all bad is not always bad," Elizabeth answered. "The mother perished outside her grandmother's house with the child surviving beside her. If the peddler hadn't found her she would have died."

The caregiver shrugged. "God would have sent someone to save her."

Elizabeth smiled. "He did. He sent the peddler."

"And something else." The caregiver folded her arms as if relishing her news. "Emily brought a grandchild with her, Laura, born to Lily late in life. Emily said she loves to play on the beach."

The hint of a smile crossed Elizabeth's lips. "So she would."

Elizabeth went on down the hall to see Olivia, who had come to the same home a few weeks before. She stopped still in the doorway and stared at the man standing by Olivia's bed. His eyes were solemn, his voice sad and flat. "I expect you don't know me."

Olivia's eyelids lifted like pearly shells over milky, unseeing eyes. She was still regal and beautiful, hair falling to the side in a thick braid over her shoulder. An enigmatic look crossed her face surrounded by pure white hair. Her hand went to her heart as if to quieten its quickening, and then to her belly, emptied long ago of the child who had taken her away from Zachary. Her love for Zachary had brought her home only to face the terrible news that he was gone. She had imagined going to Boston, finding her baby, and bringing him home to Zachary's mother, a tiny woman who had a kind face under a little woollen cap. She'd hug Olivia and tell her to come in. There was an extra bedroom upstairs for her and the baby.

"Only once," she'd tell his mother blushing. "We were in love."

"That's all it takes," she'd answer and say how much the baby reminded her of Zachary. She'd be happy thinking she had something of her son. After a time Olivia would imagine the baby was Zachary's and not a child from rape.

Elizabeth knew she should not be eavesdropping. Still, she waited for Olivia's answer.

Olivia lifted herself up on an elbow and turned toward her son. Her voice was husky as if age was pressing against her, its foot on her windpipe. "I expect I do," she whispered. "I named you Abel, so you would always feel able to do anything you put your mind to. I've waited for you to find me." Her head dropped and she began to weep. "You were lost to me and I thought it was forever."

The man's drawn face had a white cast; his eyes looked vulnerable, as if he were standing on a diving board, unsure if he should yield his body to the nothingness of air and fall into the enveloping fluid of a pool. He looked at her as if sensing that his body held a secret he couldn't decipher—her secret. "Tell me about my father," he said.

Olivia stilled a gasp. *What if he knew his step-grandfather was his father? Some secrets are like one's future, the less we know the better.* She looked him in the eye and chose her words carefully. "I was in love with a sealer. He left for St. John's to claim a berth on a sealing vessel that didn't return. The *Southern Cross*. . . ." Her voice trailed off, but the hopeful look in his eyes made her add, "Zachary Butler was a fine fellow."

Olivia's arms ached to touch her son, to hold him. She had given him away and now she had no right to him. And then her son, the stranger, gathered her frail body to his strong one and she felt his strength and warmth and his forgiveness. It flowed through her, satisfied a hunger that had never left since her baby's birth. Abel, her son, held her until she fell asleep. When she woke the next morning she wondered, at first, if it had been a dream. She smiled. *A dream, indeed! One that came true.*

Ashamed of herself for eavesdropping Elizabeth hurried away. *So that's why Olivia went to Boston.*

"You have a son and he came to visit you," Elizabeth said on her next visit.

Olivia reached and pulled Elizabeth down. Then she whispered in her ear, "Zachary wasn't his father. I'll tell you the truth and know you'll keep it. It was me stepfather."

"You poor dear," Elizabeth said. "I always wondered why you left Zachary."

"I was carrying a good reason. After my child was born Great-Aunt Lila promised to look out to his welfare. I didn't want to give up my son; I did a bad thing for a good reason."

Elizabeth remembered Olivia's stepfather. Olivia's son was his spitting image.

Olivia's eyes grew misty. "I gave away my son believing I had no means to keep him and because he would remind me of my stepfather. Great-Aunt Lila and Great-Uncle Ernie died in a motor car crash soon after I came home. I never found out the whereabouts of my son. He found me. Now he tells me I have grandchildren and I will meet them. Here I was thinking I was all alone."

"Something good came out of bad," Elizabeth said.

"Someone good." Olivia gave her a satisfied smile.

* * * * *

74

Not one of the grandchildren had asked Elizabeth about her life and she didn't tell them anything. To them she was just a blank book with a faded cover. One day they'd want to reach out with questions and she wouldn't be there.

Then out of the blue a granddaughter surprised her with questions. She gave Jamie's painting an intent look and asked, "What ship is that on your wall?"

"*Titanic.* Jamie, your great-uncle, painted it."

"Who was he?"

"My brother."

"I didn't know you had a brother. I never saw him."

"Along with Jamie I had a half-brother and two half-sisters," Elizabeth told her.

The little girl screwed up her face. "How can you have half a brother and two halves of sisters?"

Elizabeth explained about Mary Jane's two families. Then she told her granddaughter her great-uncle's story, adding, "The world is full of tragedy, child. We suffer a tiny part of it. When it comes we have to be strong." She rose and went close to the painting. She lifted a steady hand to its surface. Its sky was dark and heavy, the ocean dwarfed by the huge ship.

Her granddaughter touched her sleeve and she looked down to the little girl scrutinizing her face. "You're old so you must have a long story to tell."

Elizabeth's eyes twinkled. "If only you knew," she said.

The little girl persisted. "Would it be a book with a hundred pages?"

"If each day were a page, let me see." Her long fingers moved into the air, her face holding a distant and concentrated look. "Many thousands," she answered, her voice tired and fragile. She no longer had the breath needed to tell her story.

"How old are you?" she asked her granddaughter remembering how light she once was on feet that carried her without effort. Now the weight of her years had settled in her bones and in her feet and she became aware of every movement, every step.

The child looked up into her face. “Gran. I'm new, only five.” Her eyes were clear like speckled grey pebbles the sea washes over leaving them shiny bright. They widened, full of the wonder of her age as five tiny white fingers shot up. “Look, Gran!”

“Your days are before you like the young bears,” Elizabeth said repeating her mother's words to her and Jamie so long ago.

That night she folded herself away in bed resting while her mind carried on. Every life is a book death closes, but the memory of that life remains in the lives left behind. There'd be reminders of Jacob and her in a crinkle around the eyes of grandchildren, in the way they turned their heads, lifted a spoon to their lips—in a smile. She and Jacob had woven a lively patch in their life's tapestry. Under closed lids her eyes moved as if seeing moments and scenes she was remembering. She picked through memories like she'd pick through berries on the hills discarding to the wind those unfit to keep. She pictured Jacob dressing in his Sunday clothes, putting on his black felt hat, straightening his tie, and taking his Bible. She saw him going down the lane turning first toward the henhouse, where he reached to take two fresh eggs from a nest of warm straw. He wrapped them in his handkerchiefs, one in each pocket. She followed him as he stopped at the house by the foot of the pond to bring an egg to each of his grandchildren for their breakfast. It must have been difficult for him to rise over the hills, he not well as he scuffed along to get to the mission a good ways away.

Jacob was some man. He never allowed their children to think they were inferior to other children. Now that the boys were grown they'd built many boats, one for Frank Moores, a man who became Premier Moores. He said they're among the finest boat builders in Newfoundland. Nothing common there. The Pettens, Jacob's cousins, were not too shabby, either.

Beulah took her mother's hand and led her to a beautiful garden. Its gates held a wall of sparkling jewels. Beside a mountain, trees and flowers grew, none drooping or fading. Butterflies alighted on them. The tunes of birds flittering through the air, drifted on a fresh, warm breeze. Elizabeth saw in the distance a beach where children played.

They tossed and caught precious stones laughing all the while, their eyes like speckled rocks under sun-kissed water.

"Come!" Beulah coaxed.

"No!" Her voice came clear and firm. "Not yet, though I'm ever so tired."

"You have influenza," the doctor said after he listened to her chest, "and a troublesome heart. It's skipping a beat." He put his stethoscope in his black bag. "I'll give you a needle."

The doctor finished, zippered his bag, and left.

That night Elizabeth shifted up on an elbow and looked through the window. She gazed on a field of stars and thought of Jamie and the constellation that had inspired the christening of a vessel by that name. Her look became distant as if holding the ghost of the *Southern Cross.*

It wasn't so bad living one's life to eighty, the years reeving out like the yarn from a ball of wool. One needed to look for small pleasures: the sight of clothes on a line flapping in the wind. Changing a bed and slipping sheets from a clothesline that got the scent of a spring breeze brings such contentment. The last of life was like the sunset's glow dipping into a pool of rainwater so dazzling its reflection poured in through the window, painted the walls and floors, leaving the sun's thumbprint on a doorknob. And the ending was a beginning. She'd let her mind reach out to tomorrow and imagine slipping out of her old skin and into a new one, leaving memories behind like a closed pendant for someone else to open. Memories as rich as chocolate on the tongue; others bitter as an olive.

Elizabeth was dying. No one knew it, not even her daughter. Time was like a cup of tea she'd sipped. Tomorrow the cup would be bone dry.

It was early one morning when Elsie stirred to her mother's voice. She got out of bed, the floor creaking under her heavy step as she walked across the landing to her mother's room. Elizabeth's lips were moving and Elsie stopped to listen as her mother spoke the names of each of her children. "Dressed in white, they is," she murmured, her eyes closed. "Jacob is here. He looks as young as when we first met."

"You were dreaming, Mother. Go back to sleep," Elsie said and hurried to her own bed.

Her children were beckoning her. She felt their radiance and warmth. "Dear old, faithful heart," she murmured against her warm pillow. "You have skipped and leaped like a calf at good news and you have lurched at a knock on my door, thumped in my throat like horses' hooves as I went to answer it and heard tragic tidings." She paused and took a shallow breath. "You have kept on without rest while I have rested in sleep through the years. I am satisfied to let you rest, and thankful. . . ."

Elizabeth felt a slight tremor like a woman feels the first time a child inside her makes its presence known. *A new life is being born—mine.* She didn't feel a bit afraid. She'd been curious long enough. Now the thought of meeting God Himself and listening to His heavenly choir as He welcomed her home brought relief. She closed her eyes giving God her last breath.

Three knocks, one after the other, came on a door downstairs. When Elsie opened it no one was there. She tried to ignore the token. Still, she ran upstairs to her mother's room hoping to get her ready for breakfast. She touched her mother's cold face and drew back. "When I told you to go back to sleep I didn't mean forever," she whispered pressing a kiss on her mother's cheek. "You had a good life," she added, her voice holding steady, "and I had a good mother."

Downstairs, Elsie listened to the whisper of rain and then its beat on the rain barrel outside. It came like keys tapping THE END to her mother's story.

75

Days burned themselves down to the quick and night clouds rose like a trail of smoke as Maggie rocked time away, the past so real sometimes the present didn't exist. Her legs were reluctant to start the day though her mind had been going full tilt since daylight. And for what? Nothing around her was hers. Heaven, that other place, so real to Elizabeth, was like a distant dream to Maggie. The hymn said there was no sorrow there. A good thing! There was too much of it here.

She shocked herself when she looked into a mirror. Her once fresh face was now gaunt and wrinkled. *I eat but my body must waste my food.* She felt her body's waste against her flesh and she wept. *They think of me as useless, letting food in one end and waste out the other.*

She recalled Jamie's words: "Some day I'll set you in paint." She wished he had while she was young so that young ones who looked at her now could have seen that she was once like them, hands and face smooth and firm. They'd be old like her: longevity's promise. She had grown too far from Jamie, too old to think of loving a young man. But then she'd let her mind wander back, let herself grow young, and she'd be running to the beach watching just in case a boat came from St. John's bringing the men home. Sometimes she'd turn to eye the dusty road, watch for movement around the turn, the image of galloping horses and laughing men, clothes plastered in oil and gory under a hot sun. Her mind had become a ghost roaming through her head. Other times it was as if her mind had a leak. She put something in it and it was gone and she couldn't get it back. Jamie drifted like a cloud across her mind. She'd feel sad and not remember why. She didn't realize she was speaking aloud. "There's times I'm slippin' into the darkness, too, Jamie. I hope the Lord'll light my goin'."

The caregiver's voice pushed against her ears. "Wandering off again, are we?"

"Who's we?" she asked looking around.

A child stood on the beach facing her, innocent eyes bright and clear as the ocean. She moved over sea-licked stones shining in the moonlight. She beckoned Maggie to follow. She tried but her feet wouldn't move. The child floated out over the ocean bed where Jamie had gone. She had left her footprints and Maggie pulled free and stepped into them. They fitted exactly. Her body felt brittle and unbending as she lifted a foot and reached to brush sand off the bottom.

"Don't do that," an irritated voice called.

Maggie answered, "I'm wiping the sand off."

The voice continued: "You haven't been anywhere. Now go to sleep."

She nodded and closed her eyes. Her grey head dropped. The old rocking chair made a faint creak. Then there was silence.

Some days she was lucid. "As bright as ever the sun was," Cyril, her son, told a neighbour.

She was content to sit by the window, a shawl draped around her drooping shoulders. The slack hoods of her papery eyelids lifted and she gazed on the sea. There was a stillness in her face. None of the turbulence of her life showed. "I think I see my father's boat comin' home," she said, "and the *Southern Cross*. Jamie and me father is comin' to take me with them."

The caregiver's voice rolled past Maggie's ears like marbles across stone: "She's gone off in her dotage."

Her memory was like a bottle in a vast ocean. It travelled far bobbing out of sight. Winds and tides brought it back. She saw children scampering along the beach, Elizabeth, Jamie, Laura, Olivia . . . faces unmarred by trouble, energy enough to fly with the wind, off and away like a kite. A storm whipped the sea; the sea settled. The children grabbed up white spindrift and tossed it at each other laughing hard enough and long enough to make their cheekbones ache.

No one must see her push open the door and wander out. She made faltering steps in clay newly spread over ruts in the path. The prints blurred as she scuffed down the hill to the beach. She stopped to draw in a deep, painful breath. It was too far to the logan rock. She swayed, the tail of her dress trembling in a breeze as she stooped to pick up a flat stone. Diamonds of sunlight twinkled on the water as she lifted her arm, its flesh loose and spotted. She flung the rock and it skittered across the water as blithely as she had skipped over the beach years before. Water stretched in over her feet and swam through holes bored into seashells by the tides, seashells holding the radiant colours of sunsets. Her heart remembered all the beauty she'd seen; her mind regretted all the beauty she'd missed. The warm, salty, effervescent breeze carrying the ocean's breath washed over her skin, a refreshing scrub.

She looked in the direction of the ocean, where she last saw her father. She glanced back at the rickety, aged house standing in shambles and cocked an ear as if she was expecting to hear her stepmother call—as if to ready herself to run up the path to avoid a beating. Then she relaxed. Those times had long passed. Her face lifted to the sight of an aircraft. The first time she had seen an airplane it had flashed like a pair of scissors and she had wondered if it would cut a hole in the sky and she would see into heaven. How silly was that! She now knew that the sky was deeper than she could imagine and heaven was a place only her soul could reach.

She turned back, tottered, and fell, folding down. She lay silent in the comfort of warm sand, a smooth stone under her cheek. As the tide rose waves rolled over her like a blanket. She murmured, "Jamie, I'm comin'."

It was only a dream she was having in her own bed; it ended with her final breath.

Epilogue

ACROSS THE BAY, IN THE SMALL OUTPORT OF HIBB'S COVE, A LITTLE GIRL lifted expectant eyes to gaze across blue waters, just as her grandmother Kennedy had done so many years before. She fancied she saw a black ship that resembled the Southern Cross *her grandmother had told her about. She raised her hand like a visor over her brow to better observe the large, black ship low in the water, the dark forms of sealers on its deck reaching hands for help, countenances pitiful. The barque tossed and rolled, its bow lifting and falling. It finally vanished beneath the waves. Only a mirage, her mother had cautioned her times before when she had seen the ghost of the* Southern Cross *that took Jamie, her great-uncle.*

She stayed watching circles of light floating on the water shifting in lively flashes like quicksilver. She stooped and sat back on her heels, her nimble fingers digging among beach rocks. She almost lost her balance from the weight of smooth glass and stones of varied shapes and sizes in her dress pockets. She lifted a flat slate and skittered it across the water. It skimmed along like a black bird widening circles of light, fracturing them, one splash after another.

Something far out on the high seas caught her attention. At first it was just a speck on the water; then it grew large as a bird sitting on the heaving seas under the glow of an evening sun. She knew who was coming and she held the sight of the moving object waiting for it to take a familiar form.

The evening sun strode back shadowing the hills on its way west.

Beulahland, *a sixty-five-foot boat, named after her aunt and the place where she had gone, took shape, low in the gunnels. Her father stood on the deck waving.*

She turned to look up the path to her home. Soon her mother would stand in the open doorway calling that it was suppertime. She sniffed the aroma of pea soup flavoured by new carrots and generous pieces of salt beef. There'd be doughboys floating like clouds on the creamy golden soup and a thick slice of steaming buttered bread on a plate beside it. She swallowed hard anticipating the meal.

She turned back to the beach to the sound of glass nudging pebbles. She ran to pick up a scrubbed blue bottle, a cork in its neck. Inside were scrolled papers and a pencil, its lead broken.

Her story was just beginning.

After Words

Ghost of the Southern Cross was inspired by the life of my grandparents Elizabeth Emma Maley and Jacob Taylor Kennedy (photo below, right) and the love story of James, Elizabeth's brother (photo below, left), and his intended bride, Maggie Taylor (pseudonym). James was lost on the *Southern Cross* leaving a grieving sweetheart.

A photo (next page) shows me modelling my grandmother Kennedy's wedding dress. Another photo shows Great-Uncle James Maley's painting of *Titanic*, a painting always displayed on Grandmother Kennedy's wall.

Resource material on Alice Garrigus came from my parents, who knew her well. Burton K. Janes has written extensively on this phenomenal woman. I also quoted from the King James Version of the Bible, the Common Bible, and Robert H. Schuller: "Anyone can count the seeds in an apple; only God can count the apples in a seed." Helpful information regarding the seal hunt came from *Death on the Ice* by Cassie Brown, the *Daily News*, the *Daily Mail*, the *Evening*

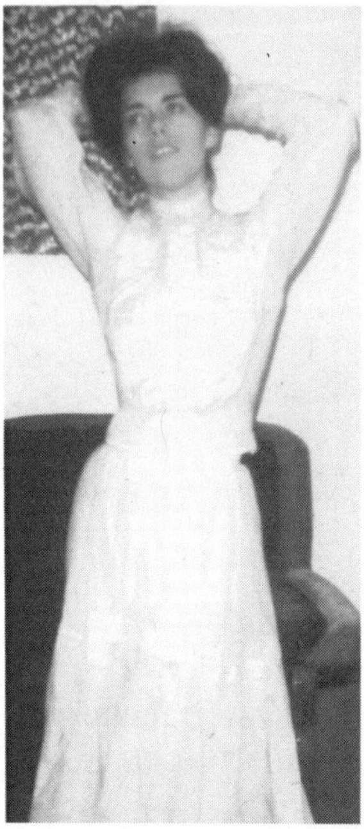

Herald, the *Evening Telegram*, the Centre for Newfoundland Studies Ship Files, *Times, Tides, and Tales Volume 2, Issue 2*; http://shipwrecks.nf.ca/news/news.shtml; *Mail and Advocate*; Rogers, T. B., "The *Southern Cross*: A Case Study in the Ballad as History (1982), *The Canadian Journal for Traditional Music*; The 1914 Sealing Disaster: Newfoundland and Labrador Heritage, "Report to Commerce of Engineering into the sealing Disaster of 1914," SH 363 N43 1915; Rogers, T. B., "The Last Voyage of the *Southern Cross*"; *Newfoundland Quarterly*, 76:3 (1980), "*Southern Cross*"; Frank Galgay and Michael McCarthy, *Shipwrecks of Newfoundland and Labrador*: "The disappearance of the *Southern Cross*" by Frank Galgay; Andrieux, J. P. 910 452 An2NR and 910453 An2 NR, *Marine Disasters of Newfoundland*; Ryan, Shannon, *The Ice Hunters: A History of Newfoundland Sealing to 1914*; Alex J. Parsons JP the *Newfoundland Quarterly* (summer) 1914.

Thanks to James Maley Kennedy for the photo of the *Titanic* painting (below).

Thanks to the ever-supporting Flanker Press staff and to Paul Butler, my meticulous editor, who made kind observations about my novel: "This is a very enjoyable, sweeping tapestry of interweaving narratives with lots of lovely writing." Also, thanks to editor Annamarie Beckel, who had her own visions for my novel.

I can be reached at

Email: nellie_strowbridge@yahoo.com
Website: http://nelliestrowbridge.com

Book Club Discussion

1. Ethel Clarke, the child of Captain Clarke of the SS *Southern Cross*, heard her uncle make a startling statement: "Whoever is out on the water in this weather will never be heard from ag'in." Discuss how children may have been drawn into the tragedies that faced their families on a regular basis.

2. How might a mother, while handling her own grief, have helped a child come to terms with her father's death during the early 1900s compared to now? Discuss ways the handling of grief by a community differs from past generations.

3. Are we typical of William, who admitted to himself that he was good at telling someone else how to mend a broken heart while his would never be mended?

4. Do you think it typical for women to shut men out of their grieving zone, believing they don't understand?

5. A single act by one person can affect the lives of one or many people at a later time. Caleb Taylor's act resulted in Elizabeth securing a job on Bell Island, where she met Jacob. Discuss how a single act by a stranger or acquaintance changed your life.

6. Elizabeth left a job to get married and move away from her family. Is there any comparison between the life of a working woman today and Elizabeth's life?

7. Elizabeth's married lifestyle was typical for her time, but extraordinary to her great-grandchildren's generation. Discuss.

8. Mary Jane told Elizabeth: "Never give a man more than you're willing to lose." Would you consider this to be sound advice?

9. Elizabeth told herself that it was the human condition: men rewarding themselves after a discomforting day on the water. How would a modern-day woman respond?

10. Discuss the implications of childbirth on Elizabeth and Jacob's relationship.

11. How would you deal with the question William asked Maggie about letting another woman get on the lifeboats in her place if she were on *Titanic*?

12. Was Jamie right in risking his future with Maggie by going on the sealing voyage?

13. Do you think there was pressure on strong young men to prove themselves by going to the ice in the 1900s?

14. How would you compare the economic necessity then and now?

15. Discuss the possibility that sealers who survived their terrible ordeal of being left on the ice, fighting a war with the elements, would have suffered post-traumatic stress, much like soldiers of war. In what ways would it be different?

16. Maggie found it difficult to move past an impossible dream. Was that fair to Ben? Should he have been able to understand?

17. How was Elizabeth's life similar to Maggie's? How was it different? How did this shape their relationship?

18. Etta Whalen told the women at the Quilting Bee: "We cut pieces of clothing belonging to each other and sew them together to make a beautiful quilt, yet we use our tongues to cut and tear each other apart." Discuss.

19. Was it fair for Maggie to blame Jamie for his own misfortune?

20. What symbolism do you see in Maggie's broken china cup? In Elizabeth's cup of tea?

21. Does this novel help the reader better understand the phenomenon of glossolalia—speaking in an unknown tongue for which there may or may not be an earthly interpretation; and the phenomenon of xenolalia—a language the speaker doesn't know but people of another nationality may recognize and understand.

22. The gift of unknown tongues frees one from the constraints of language, allowing the heart to speak to God, who understands all sound. Do you see its value in helping one communicate with God, or do you dismiss it as a religious oddity?

23. Would you find it surprising that John Wesley's Methodists spoke in tongues?

24. How do you see the Pentecostal faith as having evolved since it began in Newfoundland under Alice Belle Garrigus at a time when attire, jewellery, and hairstyle played more of a role in its moral values?

25. Discuss the implications of leaving a medical condition to divine healing—then and now.

26. What do you think of the practice of a doctor removing children's tonsils in people's homes in the mid-1900s? Have you heard of that practice?

27. Do you see a form of symbolism in the hope of The Rapture? How does it change one's perspective on death? How do you approach the truth of your own mortality?

28. We live a polarized existence. We experience the juxtaposition of birth and death, darkness and light, joy and sorrow, doubt and faith, love and hate, evil and good. Do you believe, then, that the polarization of heaven and hell has legitimacy?

29. What do you think makes a person common? Did Jacob give his son a good answer?

30. Discuss whether the following is good advice: "No matter what you lose, and who you lose, you have yourself, and keeping that self whole is a promise you make to God, whose breath you hold."

31. Do you think Maggie's daughter forgave her for leaving her in an orphanage? Do you see any significance in her calling Maggie Mother, rather than Mamma?

32. The children on the beach and the children on cliffs faced known dangers. Discuss ways we are more alert to insidious and covert dangers our children face today.

33. Mary Jane's grandfather told her, "It's a long road, gettin' from where you is to where I is. A lot of things can happen. A lot of things do happen." Discuss.

34. William told his daughter, "It's no distance from where you're at to where I is. One long dream and you'll be here." Were they both right?

35. What symbolism do you see in the blue bottle with the broken pencil lead? Can you imagine what was in the bottle?

Nellie P. Strowbridge is one of Newfoundland and Labrador's most beloved, prolific, and respected authors. She is the winner of provincial and national awards and has been published nationally and internationally. Her work is capsuled in the National Archives as Newfoundland's winner in Canada's Stamp of Approval Award for a letter written to Canada 2117.

Strowbridge, a former columnist and editorial writer, an essayist and an award-winning poet, is a seventeen-time winner in the Newfoundland and Labrador Arts Awards. She has been Writer in the Library, a mentor to young writers, an adjudicator in the Provincial Arts and Letters Awards, an assessor on the Newfoundland and Labrador Grants Committee, and a judge on the Newfoundland and Labrador Alliance Book Awards. She has held school workshops in Canada and Ireland and also hosted a Seminar/Gabfest for International Women's Day in Cobh, Ireland, where she was writer-in-residence. The Canadian Embassy in Dublin also sponsored a reading and reception. She has also read from her work during a bus tour in Scotland.

Nellie is a member of The Writers' Alliance of Newfoundland and Labrador, The Writers' Union of Canada, The League of Canadian Poets (Newfoundland and Nova Scotia Representative 2009), and Page One.

Previous books: *Widdershins: Stories of a Fisherman's Daughter*; *Doors Held Ajar* (tri-author with Isabel Brown and Peggy Krachun); *Shadows of the Heart*; *Dancing on Ochre* Sands (shortlisted for the Newfoundland and Labrador E. J. Pratt Award, 2005, and Relit Long List); *Far from Home: Dr. Grenfell's Little Orphan* (a bestseller, shortlisted for the Newfoundland and Labrador Heritage and History Award, 2006); *The Gift of Christmas* (reviewed by the *Aurora* as a Newfoundland and Labrador classic); *The Newfoundland Tongue* (a bestseller); *Catherine Snow* (a bestseller); and *Maiden from the Sea*, a favourite of many readers.

also by nellie p. strowbridge

Finalist for the 2006 Heritage and History Award

Clarissa, eleven, has been orphaned by a disease that has kept her far from home for as long as she can remember. Despite the many inmates in Dr. Grenfell's Children's Home on Newfoundland's northern tip, she lives a lonely life. She longs to be able to do something as simple as pushing her feet into boots in a blink and skipping down the road holding hands with Cora, her best friend.

Will Clarissa get to go home? If so, what will she discover about her past that will help her understand why she spent her childhood at the orphanage? There are times when she is not sure if she wants to go home. What if she doesn't like anyone there? Worse—what if no one likes her?

The story begins in 1924 at St. Anthony, with flashbacks to earlier times. One bright memory is folded in a blue handkerchief, which is given to her by a kind nurse and carried to the end like a security blanket.

also by nellie p. strowbridge

Maiden from the Sea is a breathtaking journey into the life and troubled mindscape of a servant girl from seventeenth-century France. While travelling to destinations unknown, Genevieve Laurier is tossed from the deck of an itinerant vessel and becomes stranded on an island in the middle of the stormy Atlantic. Frightened, she struggles to survive on the dark and mysterious coastline, her only company the two Irish fishermen who rescued her from the deep, a Beothuk warrior who provides her with food and clothing against his tribe's wishes, and the women who inhabit her dreams.

Genevieve finds comfort in the arms of Nasook, the Beothuk warrior . . . but when she gives birth to his child, the law of man gives chase. Genevieve must take her family and escape these abusive shores—and her increasingly disturbing dreams. But just as she makes her last desperate attempt to elude her pursuers, Genevieve Laurier's past, present, and future collide in a single revelatory moment that could spell tragedy for her and all that she holds dear.

also by nellie p. strowbridge

You think you've heard everything about Newfoundland and Labrador, but . . .

Have you had a meal of padre?

Have you ever seen a shalandi?

Have you heard of basket soup?

Would you find the term dry dough offensive?

You've tried figgy duff, but have you eaten cod sounds?

Work your tongue through conversational one-liners and much more! This book is a tribute to Newfoundland's unique culture and way of life. It explores the province's history and folklore, placing a particular emphasis on traditional language, speech, expressions, and dialect. Read, and experience Newfoundland's Old English and Irish roots as they come to the fore!